39204000020003

LORD BYRON'S

Prophecy

LORD BYRON'S
Prophecy

Sean Eads

LETHE PRESS
MAPLE SHADE, NEW JERSEY

Published in 2015 by Lethe Press, Inc.
118 Heritage Avenue ✦ Maple Shade, NJ 08052-3018 USA
www.lethepressbooks.com ✦ lethepress@aol.com
ISBN: 978-1-59021-553-1 / 1-59021-553-2

This novel is a work of fiction. Names, characters, places, and incidents are
products of the author's imagination or are used fictitiously.

Set in Jenson, Berkeley Oldstyle, and Mutlu.
Interior design: Alex Jeffers.
Cover design: Matthew Bright.

LIBRARY OF CONGRESS CATALOGING-IN-PUBLICATION DATA
TK

Dear friends are inextinguishable suns.
This book is for Darren and Jack Buford, who shine the brightest.

I had a dream, which was not all a dream.
   — George Gordon, Lord Byron, "Darkness"

PROLOGUE

Lord Byron shivers, gives a sullen glance up at the wan, clouded disc and wonders for the thousandth time what bedevils the sun.

And himself. There must be a connection between his weariness and this cold summer. It is late May but the season feels like October. Each day the sun and his body are leeched of heat and potency. He writhes against inexplicable lethargy the way a lizard agitates itself on a cooling rock. Where is his energy? He is only twenty-eight. Aren't all possibilities before him? His divorce finalized, he is free of England and will never return. All Europe and the East await him. But what good are they when he has left so much of himself behind? He thinks of his infant daughter. Ada. Such a little name, but when Byron first held her he thought even three letters much too large. Ada is six months old now: this he cannot picture. He's had no glimpse of the child past her fourth week. Shall fatherhood be for him no more than a biological condition?

Siting on a lawn chair outside his rented Swiss villa, Byron lowers his gaze to the shoreline of Lake Leman, magnificent and stretching far away. Pen and paper rest in his lap; for the past hour he's made furtive attempts to write, quitting in minutes. So tedious, this love of mine, he thinks. A cold imagination is like a cold woman: he must somehow make his own heat. So he's gathered scraps of kindling thoughts for a new poem, and though they remain wet, Byron feels the possibility of fire. What shall eventually blaze forth? A third canto for *Childe Harold*, perhaps? There are times when the idea seems less a pyre and more a raptor too quick for capture, perched some-place in his mind until the spark of creativity will let it nest on paper—and fly throughout the world.

He picks up his pen and tries to write again, but the chill air has chapped his skin, and his clothes seem soaked in cold morning dew. He writhes, cramping; the tendons in his right foot are shriveling up, tightening. A special orthopedic boot does much to hide the deformity when he is just sitting, but even then he tends to keep his left foot outstretched and conspicuous, the right drawn close. Today the pain is such that the right leg too is out, the foot flexing in small circles. The creak of leather and the crack of ligaments and joints intermingle. Several rotations do little to deaden the throbbing. Suddenly the pain flares, forces him to bend down and jam his fingers into the boot, massaging frantically. He cries out—

"Damnation! Why is it so blasted cold?"

His shout captures the attention of his nearby company, it seems: Mary, nursing her infant boy; the awful, cozening Claire, Mary's half-sister, sitting beside her; Byron's personal physician, Polidori, standing over them, twenty-one years old, attempting to impress the ladies with talk of autopsies; Fletcher, his constant servant, pulling at weeds; and the promising if obscure poet, lover of Mary (and perhaps of Claire)—but where is Shelley?

Off someplace staring dreamily into flames, Byron thinks. A fire would be nice right now.

Propping his right leg out, Byron dismisses their looks through gritted teeth and settles back to write. A few unsatisfactory lines are managed, but the words are wrong, the process sluggish. His most productive writing sessions have always felt more like bleeding, a combination of fluidity, pain and light-headedness. Readers are sharks; they like poems best when they detect some blood in the words. The lines set down here have no blood, just hock and soda water. He balls up the page and tosses it to his right before staring down his body at his most personal antagonist, the atrophied—some say, *Satanic*—flesh. We're the sum of our appearance and nothing more, Byron thinks. Sighing, he glances up toward the Lake, seeking Shelley's stark and wraithlike countenance along the shoreline. He instead finds Claire, gazing at him with a wistful smile. Byron's penis shrivels into a smaller approximation of his clubfoot.

"Fletcher—bring me wine!"

Claire giggles and says, "I have wine here, milord. Shall I bring it to you?"

Byron hardly smiles. "Only if you consider yourself my servant rather than my guest."

Goading her is a mistake and he knows it. Claire gives Mary a coy look as she takes the bottle and rises. All Byron can see of Mary is the back of her head; she is cradling her infant but her gaze seems directed down the shoreline. No doubt she also seeks Shelley. Perhaps Claire's brazenness embarrasses her, or perhaps she envies it and cannot bear to watch. Byron looks at Claire's chubby face and wonders why he ever caressed and kissed those cheeks and made promises as he penetrated her. This happened months ago in London. She's stalked him across the Channel and throughout Europe in the ensuing weeks. He thought he had escaped her, but now suddenly here she is in the company of Mary and Shelley. Did either of them know that he and Claire have, politely put, *met before?* Shelley, twenty-three, is an aspiring younger poet who wrote to Byron two weeks ago requesting an audience. Byron now suspects Claire pressured this correspondence, using any means possible to return her to Byron's company. *Conniving bitch.* Weighed against the surprising delight of meeting Shelley, however, her presence is acceptable.

She approaches him now, taking slow steps that are so absurd in their seductiveness Byron must stifle laughter. She walks placing one foot directly in front of another, as if on a narrow beam, the jug of wine held out in both hands in the posture of some supplicating priestess. Byron glances past her at Polidori, noticing how the physician's hands clench.

"By the time you reach me, child, I shall no longer be thirsty. Fletcher would have the glass filled twice by now."

Fletcher, still on his knees from pulling weeds, watches in a sort of paralysis, unsure whether or not to fulfill his master's order.

Claire reaches Byron and kneels as she presents the bottle. She whispers, to the ground at first and then at his face, her large eyes gleaming, "Whatever else can be said about me, milord, I shall always consider myself to be first and foremost your devoted—servant."

Even the weak sunlight finds strength when it weaves through her hair. Byron smiles against his wishes. *Ah, Temptation: all the water in Lake Leman could not baptize Thee from my heart.*

He looks at her, speculating how long she can keep her pose. The bottle's heaviness makes her limbs tremble. He gazes out onto the vast lake, its waters stretched further than he can follow. Five boats with crisp white sails head east. Fletcher has noted that ships come closer whenever word spreads that Lord Byron is lounging outside. Along the coastline a few locals walk, sometimes craning their heads back to look at him. He knows he's being spied upon. In the village all the talk is *L.B. was seen doing this. L.B. was witnessed doing that.* Byron has not heard directly about his presumed antics. He gets the details from Shelley, who is amused to hear the villagers code their gossip in such a fashion. The pronunciation of Byron's initials has even resulted in a little nickname that Mary in particular enjoys—*Albe*.

Claire gives a subtle moan of pain that draws Byron's attention. Her fatigued arm muscles near failure. He relents, takes the bottle and tips back a mouthful. Pleasing warmth spreads through his stomach. He drinks again. Licking his lips, he says, "Thank you, child. Return to your sister."

Claire looks toward Mary but does not leave. "Isn't William a fine little thing in Mary's arms? Wouldn't you want such a fine little thing for yourself?"

"I already have one, and you tread on dangerous ground."

Claire reaches to stroke his right foot. Byron jerks it back and almost kicks her.

"Please don't send me away. I would much rather linger beside you, milord."

"I know you would. That is why I want you far from me."

Something about English women makes them take kindly to insults from nobility. A French girl would cry at his remark and run away. An Italian would stab him herself or find a lover to do it for her. But Claire, perfectly English, responds with a shy nod and backs off with a peculiar smile, as if rebukes are a form of flirting.

Byron, keeping the bottle, drinks a third time, slow and deep. The infusion sends his head lolling back. He laughs, relaxing, stretching his legs out again. The wine puts a humming in his blood. His pen and paper fall off his lap and he does not care. The idea in his head, whatever it is, will not be captured today. He shuts his eyes.

There's Gordon crossing the quad, thinks Fane. Found him at last. He hears metal under stress and looks down at his cane; the aluminum shaft sometimes makes a curious groan when he leans too hard on it, despite his sparrow's weight. He notices his fingers, splotched red and white from squeezing the handle. And the four black hairs on his right hand, the only dark hairs left on his whole gray body. Fane strokes them with his left index finger, marveling at them as if discovering green shoots in sterile soil. Then he swallows hard and peers again across the campus. Students crisscross his vision. Where's Gordon now? Too many distractions today: twenty papers to grade; Oxley's class to audit. He pictures Oxley, her hair fiery red and burnished by the sunlight. He feels nothing.

Hobbling now across the Westervelt quad, scanning always again for Gordon. The young man should be easy enough to find at his height, Westervelt's basketball player supreme. *There.* So striking in his green sleeveless muscle shirt, supple arms glorious in the sunlight, his flanks trim and lean. His torso is tan and traced, Fane knows, with subtle golden hairs revealed only by sunlight. The two privileges of dawn: the bird's waking song and that glint of subtle hair on this youth. The legs are also bare perfection in their basketball shorts, corded from training and dark with hair.

What alchemy turns a thin boy into god?

The professor hurries, forgetting to use the cane, simply carrying it for eight labored steps until the pain in his withered right leg triggers explosive blotches across his vision. Fane breaks off his pursuit, hand pressed to his diaphragm, coaxing breath. Sweat seeps in pale splotches across the blue Oxford shirt worn beneath a tweed jacket. He watches Gordon walking and sees many girls taking appreciative second looks—while a few boys play off a first. Everywhere shifty-eyed sexuality and lust, like yellow pollen on the skin. *To see him pass conveys as much as the best poem.* Fane smiles, whispering the verse. A lone student walking close hears, looks at himself and at Fane, returns a puzzled glance and speeds past. "It's Whitman, young man," Fane says after him. The student doesn't turn, and the professor takes a last deep inhale as he spares a respectful glance at the grass.

He struggles forth again, holding his breath now as he encounters a sudden mass sampling of oncoming Student Body. Sixty of them at least, boy and girl *scholars* with venom sacks for backpacks. Fane moves into the middle of them and clears through to the other side like a splinter's subcutaneous passage. Gordon—good God, where is he? Fane turns a full circle. His quarry is gone, he is nowhere, and this is like darkness. I am womanish, thinks Fane, banging the walkway once with his cane. Women will follow beauty—many men will too, but women accept beauty's inequalities while men folly and foul it with democratic notions, as did the Good Gray Poet. *Whitman the Gray, our American Gandalf.* Fane knows well there can be no equality between the ugly and the beautiful—any more than a deformed leg can honor music by dance.

There he is.

Fane moves left, struggling to execute a broad parabolic deceit across the quad that will bring him, with all seeming randomness, in front of Gordon. He presses himself, bearing down so hard the cane makes noises again. He sees the young man's face clearly now; this is going to work. Then Fane encounters a second group of fifteen students who blindside him. He fights this human current even as it bears him back with waves of disrespect, eddies of contempt—

75-130-b.1—

Fane stops struggling. The syllables seem *visible* on so many lips that Fane actually hears the citation chorus in his mind. He goes rigid and the students just pass around him as if he were a tree stump that had always been in their way. He closes his eyes as his sallow cheeks burn. *They know.* They all know his great impropriety—his *crime*. They too have memorized the citation in the college's Code of Conduct, right down to the sub-paragraph.

He opens his teary eyes to find yet another group of students bearing down on him. The campus seems to have made a pact to isolate him from Gordon. He knows he must meet this new group with valor and courage he does not have. Still he pushes off with his cane and navigates their numbers. They are not as forgiving as the last students. They pay him no deference; they do not even seem to notice him standing right in their way. Fane merges against them, imagining himself a gondolier pushing up a rapid stream. He used to be a shark bullying through schools of tuna. ("75-130-b.1," he plainly hears a student sneer at him). But these are his toothless days.

Pushing on, braving through, Fane at last finds Gordon some sixty yards ahead, near the bench dedicated to Dr. Thomas Harper, forty years dead. Fane's professorship is endowed in Harper's name. Harper was said to have gotten his most controversial ideas sitting on that bench, *Under der Linden* as it were, as supposedly a great lime tree (long since succumbed to root rot) once grew near the bench to shade both scholar and dilettante. And the reward for his work? An endowed department seat and an engraved (tarnished) brass nameplate put on a bench so terribly undesirable in the summer now, relentlessly exposed to the sunlight. Truly literature is for asses. Those generations of students who no doubt carved their initials in the adjacent tree probably expected posterity as lasting, if not for the tree's death. Poor soft, brutalized (bruited) lime tree.

Fane shivers as the sweat cools on his skin. He wipes his forehead, feeling the mole there. He's had it since birth, has long grown used to it, but somehow it seems larger today. A reaction to the weather perhaps, for the day feels cold for California, even in November. But he alone seems chilly. Everyone else looks dressed for summer. Bad circulation, Fane thinks. Old heart, old blood. He starts again, takes two steps, and halts. He's about twenty feet from

Gordon now but Gordon is no longer alone. A woman—of course. College campuses harbor them like refugees. Fane squints and judges. Yes, they make a gorgeous couple; any eugenicist would approve the pairing. The woman has striking red hair. Coming closer, Fane realizes he knows her: young associate professor Amber Oxley, she of today's classroom audit—*Introduction to American Literature* at one o'clock. Is Gordon one of her students? How else could she know him? Of course, how could she *not* know him regardless, he who electrifies the gym by his mere presence?

Fane grimaces to see their obvious familiarity. He does not want to interrupt their pleasure but his business with the boy is critical. *And what is my business—confession?* Fane swallows, hobbling toward them, looking at his feet as his lips make odd flexes. He prepares to smile the way athletes limber up by jogging in place. Professor Fane has two smiles, characterized by duration. All tenured professors have mastery of the short smile and employ it in much the same way a boxer jabs. His long smile comes out only in a relaxed state. It does not come out often.

"Gordon," Oxley is saying, almost arguing, "I miss him too, but you're going to have to come to terms with it."

Gordon flinches away from her touch, bringing a storm of anxiety and pain into Oxley's expression. She looks about like someone checking to see if the coast is clear. Fane finds himself ducking from her sweeping gaze, but Oxley doesn't seem to see anything. Then Fane knows it's just a psychological conceit on her part to let her do what happens next: she stands up on her tiptoes to kiss Gordon's lips.

The professor swoons as if the sidewalk just buckled. Planting his cane to steady himself, he launches forward. "75-130-b.1," he says under his breath as sweat soaks him. His own guilt wars with the rage he feels that Oxley would likewise betray her professional position with a student. He's heard the rumors about Gordon, about how he goes through girls the way avid readers go through paperbacks. So is Oxley his latest text? To judge by the generous touches he now gives her, it seems he's decided she's best read in Braille. He imagines Gordon's hands feeling her body, reading passions in gooseflesh that he himself has authored. When it comes to pretty coeds, all the campus boys have literate fingers.

"That helps," Gordon says as she breaks off the kiss.

Fane's eyebrows lift. He steps forward, limping, deciding to use Oxley's presence to his advantage. He is, after all, Oxley's mentor—her coach, one might say, since Gordon would comprehend that metaphor the best. He now stands just four feet to their left, but neither seem aware of him. He stares at Gordon's smile and thinks how very similar it is to George's. This could not be a mistake of nature or a quirk of orthodontics. Gordon's smile is casual and perfect, the perfection having cost Fane thousands of dollars in braces and retainers to fix his son's teeth.

He taps the ground once with the cane to announce his presence and suddenly they're both gaping at him as he closes the last few feet between them.

"Ah, Professor Oxley, I've been seeking—"

Another boy, also built (they all are), shoots past Fane and shoves Gordon right in his chest. The impact drives Gordon down to his right knee. Fane stops. What in the hell has just happened? Gordon lifts his head to show an expression both hateful and vicious. This makes Fane cringe, thinking maybe the look is directed *at him*. Then Gordon springs up, turns and punches the second boy in his face. Oxley screams, grabbing at Gordon's arms as he advances. The world is aflame with noise, and Gordon's voice burns the hottest: "Stay back, Amber. I'm going to kill him. This is for Shiloh."

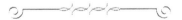

"Oh, Percy! You've returned!"

Mary's delighted voice wakes him. He sees her hurrying along the water's edge with her baby. Byron looks ahead, finds Shelley coming toward her without nearly as much enthusiasm. They've known each other only a few days, but Byron already understands how deeply Shelley fears the water. In this regard their natures could not oppose each other more, for Byron considers water to be his natural habitat. He sits straighter and squints at Shelley's face, so small in the distance. *Is he scowling again? Yes, I believe he is!* The discovery amuses Byron. Pale and dark-haired, Shelley scowls too intensely and too often. He speaks loudly of his atheism, yet he has the disapproving morals of the staunchest Catholic. Is it because of Claire? Or perhaps due to the baby in Mary's arms? Byron understands through his own sources that the child, William, is not Shelley's first. He knows little more beside that, but it is enough for sympathy. They are both fathers absent their children.

Byron rises, putting much of his weight on his left foot, and pivots west, toward England. *Whatever else, Ada, know this: every word I write from now on partakes of you. Every poem, every play I dedicate to you. Let every stanza be a goodnight kiss sent across time from your loving father.*

The rush of sentiment, fueled by wine, brings him close to tears and puts a burn on both cheeks. He wipes the wetness away and takes deliberate steps toward Shelley. Polidori and Claire stand in deference he does not acknowledge in passing. Shelley and Mary are looking at their infant, Shelley's eyes almost as beautiful and black as a Turk's. He seems only just out of boyhood, tall, slender and slight. Friendship with such men has always seemed easier for Byron, quicker to ignite. He cannot explain the reason why even to himself.

Byron raises his hand as they notice his approach. He smiles at Mary, whose eyes always widen whenever she sees him. Unlike Claire, she has self-control, a sense of propriety and decorum. She returns his polite smile and cups the back of William's head as she retreats to leave the men alone.

"So, Shelley, did you enjoy your stroll?"

"Yes," he says with no affirmation in his tone.

Shelley looks at the water and Byron notices a change in his demeanor. It is almost like the young atheist is reconsidering God.

"Is something the matter, Shelley?"

"No," he says after a moment.

"We cannot drown on the beach, you know."

"True. But being on the beach is a step closer to the possibility."

Byron bows his head at this jest and listens to the water lapping the shoreline. The sound is neither relaxing nor soothing up close. Indeed he senses urgency, like a heartbeat disguised in the wave breaks, low but insistent. A moment later he's certain that it is indeed a heart. But as he cocks his head to listen harder the sound passes.

Before they can speak further, Polidori comes up, uninvited.

"Attend to the ladies for us, doctor," Byron says. "We poets are too occupied at the moment to perform our manly duties."

The doctor often feels like an anchor tied about Byron's clubfoot. *Pollydolly* is as a little boy clutching and riding on an adult's leg as the adult walks between rooms. His complexion is swarthy with a round face dominated by thick, coal black eyebrows. He can be brilliant when not enraged and is therefore seldom brilliant. Byron hopes Shelley is just as annoyed by Polidori's company, even though Shelley's democratic mindset tends to welcome rather than refuse. Byron knows he'll have to do all the work of driving Pollydolly away.

"Tell me, doctor: do you agree that all sexual relations are an attempt to become someone else?"

"*My lord?*"

"I wish to posit that in sex men and women desire to exchange places. The man pours himself—I mean more than fluid, understand—into the woman; the woman in turns hopes to be filled—again, beyond fluid—by the man."

"I have not considered it before."

"Everyone may become Tiresias in the bedroom, though the only prophecy they receive is a warning to flee the bed at once."

Shelley shows keen consideration of the notion, treating it with obvious seriousness. Once more Byron must stifle a laugh. He is making this nonsense up as he goes.

"Well, Polidori?"

"Well *what*...my lord?"

"Do you agree with my supposition?"

"Far be it from me to disagree with anything you say."

Byron smiles. "Then you'll follow my argument and acknowledge that only by Onanism is one truly oneself."

Shelley smiles. "I begin to grasp your idea, Byron."

"If you grasp my idea then you shall keep your hands to yourself, Shelley."

"You talk wickedness, Byron," Polidori says. "The purpose of sex is not to experience becoming another person in whole. It is a mutual offering, half and half, which produces a third. This is God's first requirement of us."

Byron halts. Shelley and Polidori go on several steps before noting his absence. (Shelley in particular is a fast walker, especially for a daydreaming poet). When they turn, Byron takes three dramatic paces toward them. His right foot betrays him on the last and makes him tilt and jerk, as if he just caught himself from tripping.

"What do you know of being a father, Polidori?"

"Are you asking my opinion as a doctor?"

Byron rushes forward without a stumble and seizes Polidori by his coat. There's no chill in him now as he shakes the doctor twice.

"I *have* a daughter. Here I am in Switzerland and there she is in England with *her mother*, and you presume to tell me this is also part of God's order? Well, *hang God*, Polidori!"

Shelley applauds. "Well said!" There's always a fire in Shelley's dark eyes whenever someone speaks of God in terms of defiance, disdain or rage.

Byron releases Polidori knowing well how fast the doctor would strike him if he dared. But even a hothead isn't blithe to assault a peer of the realm.

As this mutual understanding passes between them, Byron smirks. Then he removes his own coat.

"What are you doing, Byron?"

He throws off his overcoat and unbuttons his shirt.

"I've decided to go swimming."

"Are you mad? The water will be freezing!"

"Cold enough to quell even your various jealousies, doctor?"

"Cold enough to stop your *heart*—my lord."

Byron removes his shirt, pleased how both men's gazes fly to his bare torso. As a child unable to exercise, his stomach was often bloated with food, even eclipsing his penis when he looked down. He's always known his stomach and not his penis is the part of him more likely to betray his discipline. Food, not sex, is his basest pleasure and he has inherited a tendency toward corpulence; his personality makes everything an appetite, tripling the sway actual hunger has over him. His adopted solution, starvation, has served him since he was seventeen. Eleven years later, his stomach remains famished impeccably lean, his pale skin tight around toned, desirable muscles.

He lowers his breeches. Once they crumple about his ankles, providing cover, Byron removes his shoes. His clubfoot reminds him of some sea creature's flipper.

To the water!

He spares one glance back to make sure both disapprove and then he steps out of the clothes and dashes into the lake. Thankfully it is only a few steps, for already his right foot struggles. When the water reaches his ankles he dives, despite the shallows, and scrapes and bruises his ribcage. For a moment he can only float, every part of him stunned. *Pollydolly was right.* An icy agony forces the admission. The water lashes his body with a frigid whip as he starts to swim, sputtering for air, his gums and teeth stabbed by pain. Lake Leman feels like the inspiration for Dante, a lake of pain and loneliness that locks the joints, palsies every muscle and withers the lungs into cracked leather bags. *What is wrong with the sun?* He throws his hands up and shrieks; his respiration steams along the water like dragon's breath. The urgent sound, the thudding, the *heartbeat* has returned. Is it his own? How can it be? His pulse has stopped.

Byron sinks. He may or may not be awake: the distinction never meant much to him, reality being equally unreliable on either side of the eyelid. He confronts encompassing darkness. Where—where is the waster's surface?

He looks up by instinct. There's no trace of light in any direction. Byron rolls over, cheeks bulging with precious, dwindling oxygen. There's a bolt of light coming at him. He kicks his feet without progress. As the light nears, Byron discovers a face. The visage seems unholy—terrible and sad eyes, lidless, eyes from a world where no one blinks. Its gender is indiscernible; there's hideous old age to it, screaming out its abandoned desire; there's hideous youth, crying out its desire's urgency. The eyes are black irises, and in the middle of each one burns a flame. There's a blemish on its forehead that seems to Byron like the start of a third eye. The face darts around and past him without a noise. Byron now perceives this cruel black void is not water at all.

It is the Universe.

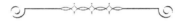

"Don't do it, Gordon! Come on, let's go!"

Oxley is trying to pull him back but she looks like a little girl grappling with a lion. Fane limps to the left as Gordon lunges again and drives the second boy onto the concrete. In the fury and chaos they lose all semblance of humanity. The fight looks like crustaceans battling, hands swinging and swiping, bodies entwining in rolling positions of dominance. Or so it must seem to everyone else, based on various horrified reactions. But Fane knows better. This is masculine frolic and he smiles, for surely his son and a friend are roughhousing. *We two boys forever clinging.*

"What in the fuck is going on?"

"Holy shit, that's Evans and John-Mark beating the hell out of each other!"

Fane glances up at the sound of rapid, heavy footfalls. So many students have come running. Oxley's still crying and Fane pivots toward her as she fumbles through her purse for a cell phone. She glances up as she starts dialing, and their gazes meet.

"Dr. Fane, why are you grinning? They're going to kill each other! Somebody help stop this!"

Fane looks around. What does she mean? Who is going to kill each other—these rugged youths, hale and hearty? Nonsense!

The fight intensifies. There must be sixty students gathered and the grim spectacle isn't yet two minutes old. Fane leans on his cane as the world wobbles and the sunlight changes into something pale and washed out. He rubs his eyes with his free hand, and when he looks up again he knows what he's seeing. It's George. He's come to avenge him after all these years. Certain of this, Fane bends forward with one fist pumping. "Pound him for me, George," he says, his voice scarcely audible to himself over the din. He strains for more detail. Is George fighting Thompson or Dooley? He hopes it's Dooley; Dooley torments him the most; Dooley is the one who held Fane down and rubbed his cheek into the concrete until it bled. And George just watched it happened. But not now. George is finally sticking up for him.

Someone in front of him says: "Gordon is going to kill John-Mark."

Both boys cry out in hurt and rage. They're both basketball players with big hands. Big hands make big fists. *John-Mark.* Fane struggles to remember the association: one of Gordon's teammates, one of Gordon's friends. The boys fighting are Gordon and not George, John-Mark and not Dooley. Fane's grip weakens on his cane.

Oxley shouts: "There's so many of you! Stop the fight!"

The crowd keeps swelling in concentric rings of curiosity. Pure accretion has moved Fane and Oxley from the fringe to almost dead center. Fane blinks as the sunlight seems to strobe. He looks up to find a forest of raised arms waving around him as everyone tries to angle their phone cameras for the best glimpse of the fight. Fane and Oxley are knocked into each other as the people jostle. One push destabilizes him so terribly that his right leg twists until the sinews almost snap. Explosive agony distorts his mind. The sun eclipses. Oxley's hair turns from red to black. The pain keeps boiling inside him until he releases the pressure in several spasms of hysterical shrieks, as a volcano might scream in jets of lava. Fane's agony overwhelms every sense but smell. His nostrils liven to scents of body sweat and fresh flung earth, foot odors, coffee breath, and stale splashes of perfume and cologne and fabric softener in the fibers of shirts. This is all too much: reality is too real. No, he is a character in a play and this character is having delusions of being a literature profession in the 21st century. But what character and what play?

Gordon staggers to his feet. His shirt is torn away, revealing a fine chest slicked with sweat and blood. Fane reaches toward him just as Gordon's torso coils with power. At his feet—at all of their feet—comes a corresponding crack and those people nearest him, those with the clearest view, look at each other as if they've just seen an execution.

Fane witnesses this even as his racing mind lights upon an answer to his question.

Of course, of course. This is *Romeo and Juliet.* He must be the Prince!

Lifting his cane and waving it over his head, he shouts, "Rebellious subjects, enemies to peace!"

He brandishes the cane, ready to bring it down on the student in front of him. But then a slim hand catches his wrist. It's Oxley—crying.

"Dr. Fane, what are you *doing?*"

Fane doesn't know. Why is he holding his cane like this? A crutch, a crutch, he thinks, blinking. He lowers it to eye level, no longer believing he's a character in a play. That he could entertain seriously such a delusion even for a second jolts him. He's getting worse. He's fading in and out, has to tell Gordon everything before it's too late.

The fight is over. People back off with puzzled expressions: *What am I doing here? Why did I stand and watch?* Fane knows their questions by heart. Meanwhile Gordon has blood running from his nose and two cuts on his forehead. His right hand pinches the torn waistband of his shorts. His torso and legs seem painted with camouflage, smeared with grass stains and dirt. Fane wills his gaze to the body on the ground, Gordon's conquered enemy. *John-Mark. His name is John-Mark, it is not Dooley or Thompson.* The young man's prior attractiveness is gone. His hair is shampooed with blood and grime; his left ear resembles Van Gogh's. There are bloody teeth in the grass and on the concrete. Fane stares at those teeth, realizing now what that little torque of Gordon's body and the corresponding *crack* meant. He kicked John-Mark square in the mouth. Fane shudders to imagine the boy's pain.

George was never so violent.

Now Fane hears Gordon's ragged breathing and wheezing, and the noise of sirens. The professor starts toward him only to stop when Gordon whispers, "Amber?" and looks around with pleading eyes. Fane turns to Oxley.

"On a first name basis, are we?"

"*Amber,*" Gordon says, his tone now plaintive, the two syllables pronounced as if a speech impediment exists. Fane watches him shove a finger into his mouth and probe.

Gordon's two front teeth are gone.

Fane claps his left hand over his own mouth and trembles. All that work, all that money, for his son's smile to be ruined in minutes.

Fane turns back to Oxley, wanting an explanation. The young professor appears to be bursting with anxiety and tension. When Gordon calls for her a third time, whatever trepidation and fear she has evaporates. She runs to him. She doesn't make it. Students get in her way. She offers them her scorn and Fane smiles with a surge of respect for her. She is learning how very bovine and stupid most students are. But his respect is short-lived. It's now clear to him she is guilty of violating 75-130-b.1, and this reminds him that *he* is guilty of it too. His crime is worse, but dark shame must cover them both like a cowl.

The police arrive accompanied by campus security and paramedics. Gordon starts sobbing as two officers force him to his knees. One of the paramedics tries to examine him.

"Tell me he's okay," Gordon says, every word frustrated. "I didn't mean to."

"That's bullshit. He totally started it," someone says. "John-Mark just walked up to him and then Gordon Evans started wailing on him. I was watching it and was like what the fuck?"

Professor Fane watches Gordon's arrest. As soon as his hands are positioned and cuffed behind his back, his ripped shorts fall to his ankles. Some students gasp at this, others laugh, and most bring their phone cameras to bear again. One of the officers yells at them. The second bends, picks up Gordon's shorts, bunches the waistband together at the back and places it into Gordon's grip. Then they take him away. Fane makes a hobbling attempt to keep up, his gaze focused on the boy's bruised body. At last their gazes meet. Gordon's mouth opens and closes. He shakes his head, whimpers, and then begs the police to drive him away. And so the encounter seems to be ending the way Fane supposes it was destined to all along, with Gordon ignoring him, ashamed Fane might try to talk to him in public.

He looks back at the situation on the ground. The paramedics are still working on John-Mark. "75-130-b.1," one says.

"75-130-b.1," the other answers.

No. No, they can't know too. Fane cups his hand to his ear to make sure.

"75-130-b.1," a female student says, passing him on the right.

Fane pushes off with his cane. His withered right leg seems to drag along rather than participate.

There's a small burst of clapping. John-Mark now sits up under his own power and flashes a smile of broken teeth. "75-130-b.1, Dr. Fane."

Fane clamps his lips down over a scream. He dare not vent his horror here.

John-Mark continues: "You've broken 75-130-b.1, Dr. Fane. When cardinal rules are broken, chaos ensues."

One of the campus security officers grabs Fane by the shoulders and forces him to look at the sky. "Do you know what chaos is coming, Dr. Fane? Nothing less than the end of the world."

Byron stands now in a world on fire. There is not one flame or two but hundreds—thousands. He stands unscathed and unfeeling in a city that is obviously London. He feels the familiarity even as every building burns. People run in all directions, their shoes scattering ash. Some are on fire themselves. Is it the Great Fire of 1666? Is that Pepys there, the little figure running through the ash with a book tucked under one arm? No, it cannot be—for Byron sees that man stop and pitch his book into the flames.

What monstrous inversions this world contains! Men and women rush about with water buckets that are stuffed with paper and trash, quick fuel for any flame. Though almost blinded by the glow of the fires, he feels none of the inferno's blaze, but the Londoners around him are not so fortunate. Their bodies are black and brown and bronzed and blistered. The heat boils the sweat off their bodies before it wets the skin. And Byron sees hundreds of them in every direction: some kneel before a personal fire as if in worship; some work stripping the clothes from the dead, which they take and burn; others, less patient, throw clothed corpses onto the nearest pyre. Byron staggers on, so small against the man-forged volcanoes. The Tower of London is a magnificent torch against the pitch-black sky; columns of lesser fire rise with added fuel, striving to its heights, as if the people of London, heeding the book of Genesis, have decided to reconstitute the Tower of Babel in flame. Pillars of fire reign everywhere but herald no exodus.

As Byron continues in a daze, he finds a group of five little children dutifully feeding their toys into the base of a burning building. The smallest girl burns her hand and screams (though Byron hears nothing) and pulls her hand to her chest. Ada, he thinks, and starts toward her. Before he reaches her, however, she runs off, and two adults, a man and a woman, rush onto the scene with an infant. Byron calls to the girl, finds she will not heed, and contents himself to study the newcomers. They've stopped before a dwindling fire. By its light they look at each other, then at the baby.

Neither kisses the child before they feed it to the flames.

My God, that man is Shelley! The woman is Mary! The child is—

Byron hears his own scream. He hears nothing else.

"For the love of God, I cannot stand to see this! Spare me! End my life but show me no more!"

Ash falls about him like snow as he drops to his knees. Byron sobs and stares straight up, weeping from the depths of his being. Penetrating past the orange dome of firelight, he gazes on a sky without stars or moon, and somehow he knows it is midday. It is noon and the sky is black. What the devil is wrong with the sun?

"Byron? My lord, can you hear us?"

His eyes won't open yet. The voice is muted like his ears are clogged.

"I believe he's safe. I should hope so, if only because where shall I go without him?"

Pollydolly—joking at his expense.

Byron's eyes open to see Polidori's face descending over his own. For a moment it's too much like the face in the water, and he fights to avoid being drawn back to that hellish world. But he's too weak. Polidori has his will and locks his mouth over Byron's, blows his stale, bourgeois breath into Byron's aristocratic lungs. Byron's eyes gape. All he can see is Polidori's hair, black like the merciless night sky in his vision. A dandruff flake falls like ash into Byron's eye, moistens and dissolves there. "*Mmmmph,*" Byron says into the doctor's mouth, forcing Polidori back. He sits up gasping.

Shelley stands behind and to the right of Polidori, clutching Mary. Claire stands nearer. She is holding his trousers and shoes in a bundle against her breasts. My foot, he thinks, my foot is exposed to all of them—

He tries to draw his right foot under his left leg. All he achieves is a small moan as his head lolls from left to right. Claire is not looking at his legs at all. Byron realizes he is entirely naked and Claire's fascination is elsewhere. The bitter chill does his manhood no favors. Claire, however, has been prior impressed.

Polidori smiles. The expression is so smug Byron feels only shame. Himself—saved from the Abyss—by *Pollydolly.*

The doctor turns to Shelley and asks for tobacco in order to fashion an emergency smoke enema, announcing that smoke must be blown at a steady pace up Byron's arse in order to assure a complete resuscitation.

"You see," he says to Claire. "I told you I would not let Lord Byron expire. Nearly sixty years ago, one of my forebears helped create the Society for Recovery of Drowned Persons—I am therefore fully qualified to meet his Lordship's present situation."

"His Lordship's present situation requires a blanket and dry clothes, not a bloody pipe!" Shelley says.

"Yes, yes." Polidori waves at a passing local.

Byron cannot speak. He cannot yell for Fletcher. Polidori, however, notices the attempt and promptly opens Byron's mouth, inserting two of his thick fingers. The effrontery! Byron attempts to bite. Oh, for stronger jaw muscles! The fingers probe his throat, gagging Byron. At the sound, Polidori retracts his fingers just ahead of a stream of water and mucus. Byron coughs twice, clutching his throat. Polidori inhales, locks his lips over Byron's mouth and delivers his final remedy. To be filled forcibly by another man's breath is at once the most mortifying and literally enlivening experiences of Byron's life. As if Polidori's air courses through his body seeking any empty space to fill, Byron's penis swells.

Claire clasps her hands together and says, "He truly lives! Thank you, doctor!"

Claire's supplication to Pollydolly is bad enough. Shelley too seems convinced of the doctor's excellence and showers him with praise. As Byron sits up, a weight falls upon his shoulders. Fletcher has draped a heavy blanket across his back. Without being told, he takes his master's shoes from Claire and returns to worry the blanket, rubbing the fabric along Byron's skin in gentle, dedicated strokes. Byron just stares out at the water, wondering about the face he saw below its depths, wondering about the world on fire.

He remains staring twenty minutes later, perched in his lawn chair and left in the toasty confines of the blanket. He is not warmed. Claire and Mary are standing a ways off, listening to Polidori detail the latest techniques to return the dead to life. Byron does not break his stare until he realizes that Shelley is standing near, looking at him. Great tension plays out in Shelley's hands, which act like the grappling mouths of two snakes.

Shelley says, "What was it like?"

"What was what like?"

"Death."

"I assure you I did not die, Shelley. Don't be swayed by dear Dr. Pollydolly's boasting. He's an inveterate liar and an utter fraud. I only took him on as my personal physician to keep him from harming some other poor fool. Why, he genuinely treats every ailment I complain about, when anyone with good sense should know it is merely hypochondria. What true doctor mistakes imagined symptoms for the real thing?"

Byron grins and stretches out his legs, careful to keep the right foot—white and blunted—draped. His penis relaxes in trapped body heat and rests against his right thigh, large and unseen. The loose blanket reminds him of the clothes he wore among the Turks ten years ago and of other luxuries and freedoms he experienced there. And will again, he thinks. The fashions of England are so stifling by comparison. But he is finished there. *If England goes, can its clothes be far behind?*

Byron looks up to judge Shelley's reaction. He frowns. Shelley is also staring out at the water with narrow eyes, his lips deep red because the flesh of his face is winter white.

"Did you see something in the water, Byron?"

"Fish, perhaps."

Polidori laughs at something and extends both hands. The ladies laugh, each taking one, and the three of them start walking along the shore. Shelley watches them a minute before returning to Byron.

"You are...a *powerful* poet. I thought perhaps, faced with death, you might have glimpsed...something."

Byron smiles after a moment's thought. "Are you asking me if I saw God, Shelley?"

Shelley looks down at him. "Great bodies of water always seem to harbor terror. Mark how the waves and eddies move...dark...then glistening. There is gloom and splendor that seem to flow straight into my mind."

Byron rises in response and gathers the massive blanket about him.

"Walk with me."

"Where?"

"Nearer the water. If we're to talk about Lake Leman, I want it to overhear."

Shelley laughs without mirth. "I prefer to stay out of the range of eavesdropping."

Byron adjusts the blanket and puts a bare arm around Shelley's shoulder. "*Walk* with me, if we be friends. I am barefoot. I cannot go far without effort and pain."

"Your shoes are here. Shall I help you?"

"I won't need the shoes," Byron says, allowing a small smile. "You'll see why if you walk with me."

Shelley pauses a moment. The joy Byron feels when Shelley nods surprises him with its intensity. The sensation reminds him of his most passionate schoolboy friendships; all they require now are mutual nicknames to complete the association. He is already *Albe*. What shall Shelley be?

PART 1:

SHILOH

CHAPTER ONE

They'd both woken up with girls in their beds. Gordon looked across at his roommate John-Mark, the slender forearm crossing his broad white back. The rest of the arm was pinned under John-Mark's side, and Gordon couldn't see anything else of the girl, but he didn't need to. He and John-Mark were both six-foot five. The girl was maybe five-two and real petite. His own girl...wasn't so good. He'd wanted John-Mark's chick and he felt damn sure he *was with her* when they left the party. They'd come back to the dorm room, and that's when the switch happened, in the dark while they were all getting drunk and naked. Somehow that bastard had swapped girls on him.

John-Mark, you clever prick, he thought. Use me to lure the cute one in, do a little sleight-of-hottie when the lights are out, and stick me with the beast. John-Mark had the nice warm bottle of milk and he had the cow. Gordon felt a stirring near his stomach and shifted his gaze down to find two chubby fingers brushing through his treasure trail. Her touch was fleshy and moist. The fingertips had the stickiness of a Cinnabon employee. Jesus. Was she awake? Was she staring at the back of his head even now? What the hell would he do if she wanted him to fuck her?

Again.

He rolled right barely half an inch, enough room to let him strain to see the floor. Clothes were piled on top of each other much like the bodies they'd covered. Now the girl's leg came like a sulking thing against his, her foot rubbing along his muscular calf. Gordon cringed, certain she had to be awake. I'm being *enjoyed*, he thought, locking his muscles to stifle a shudder. Any response from him would just encourage her.

He focused on searching the floor for his cell phone. He couldn't remember when he'd last checked his messages. Sometime around eleven last night?

Amber *had* to have texted by now—if she had any interest in him. She *was* interested, right? She'd laughed at some of his jokes in class. He'd caught her blushing a time or two when their eye contact went on a little too long. Those were *signals*, man. He'd thought last night their stars would align, but she didn't show at the Lambda Chi party. He'd been pissed off, but John-Mark had just said, "Fuck her, bro. There's ten chicks here who'll suck your dick right now." He loved John-Mark's clarity. Yeah, Gordon thought, fuck Amber if she can't even text me back. Then he zeroed in on the hottie and her dumpy friend. Fuck Amber. Christ. Did he really think, "Fuck Amber"? Gordon almost shivered, hoping for forgiveness. He'd shown an accidental lapse in faith akin to Linus. He felt like praying to the Great Pumpkin for forgiveness and understanding. *Mr. Pumpkin, that was anger and alcohol and fear thinking for me.* His feelings right now proved he was in love with Amber. Why else would he feel like he'd cheated on a woman he'd never dated?

This wasn't the first time Gordon Evans had wanted to undo a screw, but it was the most intensely he'd ever regretted an orgasm. He wanted to teleport into the shower, scrub all the odors off his skin and then go see if Amber was at Starbucks. She'd met him there on Thursday after his fourth or fifth invitation. One more refusal and he'd have given up on her—or so he told himself. He couldn't imagine really giving up; he was too competitive for that, which was maybe part of his problem. Amber probably pegged him as a jock hoping to get his knob waxed by his prof in order to sail through another boring class. That had become all too clear to him when they talked on Thursday. She showed interest but little trust, and he wasn't sure why. She wasn't his English professor anymore—that was in his freshman fall year, and it was April of his sophomore year now. He'd put that much time between them just to approach her. He wasn't an English major and would never take another class from her. Wasn't that proof his interest was genuine? Christ, he thought, she probably knows about Dad. That could explain everything. That was probably it.

In the other bed, John-Mark turned over in a large thrashing spasm that somehow didn't wake his girl—*my girl, you fucker*—as he came to lie facing forward. Gordon looked for any sign his roomie was awake. His face, even relaxed, bore a trace of smug satisfaction—the same look that made defenders in the paint foul him extra hard.

Gordon cringed and squeezed his eyes shut as the girl at his back began to cop more aggressive feels. She traced the muscles of his back and shoulders, even poked her fingers under his right arm to stroke and tease the hair of his armpit. Bitch is fucking savoring me, he thought. He shivered as she goosed him—but not because of her touch. No way. The room was cold, that's all. John-Mark always turned the room temperature down when he bedded a girl, said it encouraged her to snuggle tighter.

The girl was feeling his ass now, caressing both cheeks. Goddamn but her hands were moist and sticky. This was like being molested by dough. She gave an almost inaudible, quavering sigh. Gordon opened his eyes and his cheeks puffed as he suppressed a giggle. Like John-Mark and every other guy he knew, Gordon could pretty much fart at will. He thought about summoning a blast. That'd kill the mood. The feel of her body suggested her cooch was damn near parallel with his asshole. He could give her a little free blow dry if she was wet. He was about to do it when he heard a soft word, almost prayerful—"Perfection."

She whispered it to herself so quietly there should have been little else to discern, but Gordon found tears and gratitude in her voice. He flushed. He couldn't remember the girl's face, certainly not her name, but he realized— without being vain about it—that he was probably the best she'd ever had by a long shot. Why did he have to think such mean things about her? Maybe this moment of quiet touching would be something she'd remember all her life, something she'd fantasize about over and over again. He swallowed, his throat tight and dry. Maybe he was being vain after all. But he didn't *feel* vain as he endured her pawing. He felt oddly—generous.

I'll close my eyes and pretend its Amber. It's good karma. All I'll do is think of Amber and when I get my phone there'll be a message from—

She touched him in a new spot and everything inside him froze up—his thoughts, his lungs, even his heart seemed to pause. Gordon's eyes darted wildly left to right. She'd stroked the back of his right thigh, just tracing the skin and hair with the tip of her finger, almost no pressure at all, but... The sudden sickening revulsion he felt confounded him. It was followed by a rage he'd never felt before, terrifying in its absoluteness, as if it had been there a long time waiting for release. He jerked away from her, scrambling from the bed, shouting, "*Stop it!*" into her dopey face. John-Mark woke with his chest obviously pounding away, a slew of nonsense syllables from his lips as his arms flailed. Remarkably the girl beside him still didn't stir.

"I'm really sorry, Gordon, I didn't mean anything," the fat girl said. Everything about her, voice and body, shook. She coiled up, looked like she expected a beating.

Gordon just stared at her, seeing...all sorts of things. The images passed in a moment. He was standing naked in the middle of the room. His head pounded.

"Gordie, man, you okay?"

He didn't acknowledge John-Mark. He looked at his feet, bent for his clothes. He had his pants on before he realized he'd forgotten the underwear. Fuck the underwear. He reached in the right pocket and found his phone.

"Please, I'm *really* sorry." The girl had sat up now drawing the sheet against her breasts. She was sobbing, and Gordon couldn't stand the sound. "I didn't mean anything. It's just that you're so incredibly hot and beautiful, Gordon, like, better than anyone in the world, and I've been in love with you since the first time I saw you play—"

Gordon could hardly breathe. He held one hand out toward her. "It's okay, it's okay," he whispered.

Now John-Mark stood up. "She do something to you, man?" He looked at her. "What the hell did you do?"

"Nothing! I—I was just massaging him. I thought he'd like that—"

Gordon shoved his t-shirt down over his head—a gray tee with cracked and peeling maroon lettering that said *Westervelt Warriors*.

"Look, someone just tell me what's going on. Gordie?"

Gordon started toward the door.

"Talk to me, dude!"

He glanced back at John-Mark, who stood naked, one hand rubbing at his sleepy face, the other scratching into his pubic hair. Gordon looked down at the unconscious girl. Her body was amazing, and even with his desire for Amber, he couldn't help thinking about the stolen opportunity. "Better check to see she isn't dead," he said, and shut the door behind him. Heading down the hall, he heard the fat girl's muted voice saying, "Carla?" with great concern.

Moments later, he was pushing through a side exit, and stood gulping fresh air. He'd forgotten how suffocating and stale sex odors could be. He pulled his t-shirt up to his nose and sniffed, hoping it smelled clean. It did not. *He* did not. He brought his right arm up to his nose and inhaled along the length of his forearm. Trace scents of the girl's perfumed body lingered on him. Beer breath reeked in his mouth.

Gordon started walking, afraid to linger near the dorm in case the girls and John-Mark came looking for him. He found it hard to move. What the hell was wrong with him? His flesh tickled like her fingers were still making their proprietary pinches and caresses. He took more deep inhales, glanced to see if anyone was about, and stopped. Reached between his legs to pat himself down, reassuring his body that it was safe. Christ, he half-expected to find some horrible tumor through the thin denim. He no longer blamed the girl. Remembering her words, he just felt sorry for her, wished he'd somehow endured the groping. But it was like her fingertips had found and activated a button buried under his skin. Something was different.

This is about Amber, he thought. He was having a panic attack. That had to explain it. She hadn't contacted him at all since Thursday. Wasn't that in itself a statement? Wasn't that defeat? He shook his head. She *had* to like him. *Had* to.

He took off running at a full sprint. This was both fight and flight. He pushed himself across the campus, trying to work up a sweat to wash away the fat girl's ghost, her odors, her touches; the very memory of her existence. But it was a burdened run. As fit as he was, his body rebelled this morning. It wasn't even eight yet, and he'd gone to bed at two. He still felt a little drunk and his dehydrated muscles threatened to cramp. His bowels were loose and queasy. Worse, he heard a liquid sound in his gut as he ran that reminded him of shaking a half-full milk jug. His lungs seemed full of cigarette fumes even though he never smoked. The campus itself had a smoky haze to it, a rare fog that filtered the weak early sunlight and cast the concrete and the buildings, the grass itself, in a sepia hue that made the world appear decayed. His own skin looked jaundiced.

He stopped in the quad and came panting to a bench no one ever used. It was too exposed in every way. If you sat there in the sunlight you cooked. Its positioning was wrong and was maybe too low to the ground. At Gordon's height he couldn't be sure—so many things felt too low to him. You couldn't sit on the bench without feeling like you didn't belong on the campus at all, without feeling you were some kind of homeless person who'd come to beg change from gullible students. In his two years at Westervelt, Gordon had never seen anyone employ the bench for anything except as a prop to tie their shoelaces.

But he dropped down on it now, hunching forward as he ran his fingers through his messy hair. Brown hair that curled when it got long, since his junior year in high school he'd started buzzing it at the start of the basketball season in November, letting it grow through March. Now it was April and it needed a trim, felt thick and greasy. He fell back on the bench in despair and leaned his head over the backrest. The campus was silent, and all he could think was that if he'd been homeless and slept on this bench, he'd probably smell and feel exactly how he did now.

What was he even doing here? The question was expansive, beyond the moment. He'd been a townie all his life; he'd grown up on Westervelt's campus, just about, hauled since childbirth between the offices of his mom, a biology professor, and his father, *Doctor Reader* (this nickname given only half in jest from Mom's side of the family, all scientists contemptuous of those who called themselves doctors without ever having to stick a hand in a corpse). There were times when enrolling in Westervelt felt like the largest mistake of his life, even if it was a great school and he had a full basketball scholarship. *Other* colleges had offered him the same.

Yet here I am, he thought. Why?

He thought of his father. They seldom saw each other either off campus or on. A few people here and there knew their connection, but no one in the general student body. The back of Gordon's jersey said *Evans*—his mother's maiden name and now his legal last. *Doc Reader* gave only a small protest when Gordon made the change. He couldn't argue much when Gordon told him the change was to honor Mom. His father seemed to believe Gordon would change his name back to Fane once he also died—to likewise honor *him*. Gordon's mind went blank whenever he had to think about that.

Thinking about his mother, however, brightened his outlook for a fleeting moment, and the sunlight no longer seemed like a pall over everything. She'd always called him a golden boy despite his dark hair; she'd always made him feel like he would inherit a future of pure light. Indeed his mom was always associated with light in his mind, making her sudden eclipse even more jarring. She'd died of a heart attack, six years ago, in 2004. This confused Gordon at first. His mother was in terrific shape, and at thirteen he had never even heard of women having heart attacks. Fat old men had heart problems, not petite ladies. Months later, when his grief was blunted, confusion became selfish worry. Were her heart problems genetic? As a kid he'd always been thankful to look far more like his mom than his withered father. But what if his heart was like hers as well? He'd touch his chest and wonder if his actual inheritance was an inevitable early darkness.

Gordon was compelled to touch his chest now. His pulse was strong and even. It took strenuous exertion to set it racing. *Or just one look at Amber.* He smiled. Why was he so goofy when it came to love? Guys like John-Mark were always the same, alone or on the court or on a date, but Gordon became a romantic dork around girls he wanted. He liked entering a state of mind he thought of as being *stupid in love.* And he was damn near negative-IQ *stupid in love* with Amber.

His cell phone alerted him to a new text message. *Amber!* Gordon dug into his pants pockets, fumbling. *Yeah, that heart's racing now.* He grinned, shaking his head. The grin faded when he saw it was just John-Mark. The message read—*She ain't dead, yo!*

"Jesus Christ," Gordon said, stopping to look back in the direction of the dorm. Why in hell was he going to Starbucks to meet a woman who wasn't even going to be there? Amber didn't want his company. If they did meet right now she'd probably be disgusted by the competing foul odors coming off his body. *I'm whipped worse than ever,* he thought, not laughing this time as he gazed at Westervelt's proud, ornate red brick buildings. He'd reached the edge where campus and town blurred into each other. All the businesses here—delis, used bookstores, vintage clothing shops—catered to the students. The Starbucks was still five blocks away. Was there really any point in proceeding? He figured John-Mark had gotten rid of the girls by now. He could go back for that shower, then sleep and worry about Amber with a clear head. He was fucking stupid to just bolt like he lost his mind. He wondered what John-Mark thought. John-Mark had probably just gone back to bed. Or hell, maybe the girls were *still* there and he was enjoying their full attention. He was, as he often boasted, a man who liked his blowjobs.

Gordon turned back toward the Starbucks and sighed. Amber's love of the place was obvious. She'd always entered class with a fresh cup of coffee in hand. That's why he kept asking her to meet him there. He wasn't a coffee drinker himself, but he would take on her addictions if it gave them something in common. When she'd finally yielded to his request last week, Gordon had no idea what to order and just got what she got. He'd been stunned by how awful coffee tasted. His disgust must have shown on his face.

"You really hate coffee, don't you?" she said.

"Not alcoholic enough." He thought right away this was a bad answer, a hopelessly juvenile answer, but Amber laughed—and Gordon truly loved her laugh. She was older than him by about nine years and her age and position just seemed to demand responses a little more suave and offbeat, something really gay and flippant like, "The coffee's unbearable but anyway I come for the scones." Fuck the coffee: she was the one stimulant he craved. He'd looked to see if she realized that. He thought she did, because she blushed and glanced away. Gordon had become nervous then. He guessed in her head Amber was trying to decide whether he was date material or freak show fodder.

He looked at his phone. No message.

She had decided on freak.

He walked toward Starbucks at an ambling pace, feeling lonesome enough to sit at the table they'd shared and reminisce. Never dated her and I'm already on a fucking breakup tour, he thought, grimacing. He'd done something similar only once, when his relationship with his high school girlfriend, Stacy, just somehow ended. They never even discussed it. She'd gone away for college, he'd stayed here, and their relationship died in-between. Once Gordon realized, once he understood she'd dumped him, he got obsessed with remembering details of their time together. He revisited meaningful places, and since he and Stacy had dated almost two years the tour covered three quarters of the town. With Amber all he had was a table in a coffee shop. Gordon sighed and sensed his self-esteem deflating, flying from him like a razzing balloon.

As he walked on he noticed the transition between Westervelt's Arcadian designs and the town's deterioration. It started with the sidewalks. Cracks and chips began to appear in the concrete where none existed in the crisscrossing campus walkways. The college buildings were all old but regal. No royalty showed elsewhere in the town's architecture. Many of these neighborhoods were fifty years older than Westervelt, the college having originated as an education co-op to serve the community. Time had flipped this relationship with an almost John-Markian dexterity, and one morning everyone woke up to find that the town was now an addition to the college, a mere convenience and tool for its hundreds of employees.

Gordon knew there was strong resentment in town for Westervelt and its faculty, who were decidedly not locals. True locals who traced their ancestry back to the town's founding a hundred and thirty years ago held few jobs of importance within the system. Even fewer of their children got a chance to enroll. The school's original charter required the acceptance of all town students, but somehow this little school founded by blue-collar workers to better their children had turned into a western Harvard that resented them. Gordon knew his popularity came from the fact he was seen as a native son, a shining star born among them—he was their first All-State basketball player. When he accepted Westervelt's offer, many locals saw it as the haughty school humbling itself before the greatness of one of their own. They still packed the campus gym to root him on. Who could turn their back on such worship?

Gordon reached Starbucks and glanced through the window in passing. The business wasn't brisk this early on a weekend—five customers, none of them Amber. He didn't know what to feel and forced himself to walk past. *It's not going to happen,* he thought. *She just doesn't see anything interesting in me.* His hands squeezed into fists like they had in the days after his mom died. If he had a basketball, he'd pound the dribble like he always did when he got mad on the court. Without it, Gordon just felt like punching something. He stopped and stared at the brick building on his left. *Hit it.* In his head, he saw the brick shattering. He'd never hit something before. He'd never even been in a fight. How would it feel to punch a brick wall? He reached out and felt its rough texture. He imagined the skin of his knuckles splitting open; he imagined mangled cartilage and an agony strong enough to make him forget all about Amber.

Gordon made a fist and cocked his right hand back almost to his shoulder.

He heard a dog whining.

A young Labrador came around the side of the building, sniffing the corner and even licking it, as if the brick were flavored with meat. Gordon lowered his hand and looked. The dog's ribs showed, and he felt a pang of sadness, shock even. His upbringing had exposed him to four or five stray animals at most, and none had looked as famished as this dog. He couldn't believe it belonged to anyone in town.

Gordon took two steps toward the dog. Its gaze was fixed on him even as it kept licking the brick. Gordon heard its tongue busy against the brick and laughed. Was this dog retarded? He hunkered down, held out his hands and tapped the sidewalk with his fingertips. "C'mere, boy," he said.

The dog stopped licking, its stare still fixed. *Wow, those are intense eyes,* Gordon thought. *Game day eyes.* His admiration changed when he heard a low growl. The deep sound vibrated along the cement. Pulling his hands back, Gordon started to stand. The dog lunged half a foot and froze in a crouch, mouth open, every muscle flexed. Gordon stumbled and landed on his back, craning his head around, searching for help. The street was deserted. He could yell—someone might come out of Starbucks to save him. God, his reputation would be shot after today. Sex with a fatty and then some old lady beats a mad dog off of him with her purse. The cleansing sweat he'd tried so hard to produce less than half an hour ago came easy now. His upper lip was heavy with a wet moustache. Mad—rabid, he thought. As a little kid, with his mom, he'd watched every dog movie ever made, and suddenly all Gordon remembered was seeing *Old Yeller*.

He was on his back only a few seconds. As he tried to scramble, the dog pounced onto his chest. For one horrific moment Gordon stared at its bared teeth. Then, before he could shout, before he could make any move, the dog's tongue swiped across his face, a warm and gently loving tongue that cleaned the sweat off him in five quick, long laps. Gordon remained frozen, his eyes almost crossed as he studied the mass of golden fur. Beginning to breathe again, his nose took in an odor so foul that he sputtered and pushed the animal off him by reflex.

This startled the dog, which sprang back a couple of feet and crouched again. It didn't growl though. Gordon got to his feet, staring at the dog as he wiped slobber off his cheeks. "You fucking stink but I guess you're not rabid," he said. He looked up and down the street, expecting someone to have shown up by now. He saw no one in any direction.

The poor thing couldn't be more than a year old, Gordon figured. He sniffed again at the stench coming off the dog's fur, the odor of a well-traveled orphan. Their brief contact was enough to infect his own clothes, adding another layer of disgusting scent to his body. Gordon found himself retching and coughing, his eyes watering.

The dog sauntered up to him and rubbed up against his pants legs. Gordon cringed.

Looks like I've got myself a friend, he thought.

The dog followed alongside at a frenetic trot compared to Gordon's long, athletic strides. Gordon's childhood home was only four miles from his dorm, and he'd already covered half that distance when he encountered the dog. He could think of nowhere else to go to clean the animal. Would Amber like a dog? Was she a dog person? With so many things unknown about her, taste in pets seemed almost like discovering whether she wanted to have children.

He grinned, despite feeling the cell phone in his pocket and knowing Amber hadn't called. There was just something about this dog, like it had a halo of good luck around its head. He'd get with Amber if he kept this dog. He took out his phone as he walked and tapped in her number. Amber's number wasn't in his contacts list yet, but it was in his head. Adding her to his contacts would be presumptuous—it would be *pushing it*, and like any athlete, Gordon had certain superstitions he followed on and off the court to avoid jinxes. He looked at the dog, had a thought that made him laugh, and began a text message to her: *Do you like the color yellow?*

He stopped a moment, considering. The Labrador continued past him several yards before realizing it was alone. The dog stopped, pivoted and bounded back to him, tail wagging. Gordon laughed again and raised the phone, preparing to snap a picture. He stopped himself. The dog *looked* okay—a little dingy—but he got the idea that its odor would somehow travel with the image. Best to get it cleaned up first. The dog barked, prancing in place. Its body shook with excitement.

"I got a great idea," Gordon said. He took the picture anyway. "That'll be the *before* shot. Let's get you ready for the *during* and *after.*"

He jogged the next mile. The dog clearly loved to run but it pained Gordon to watch, considering how its ribcage showed. He stopped when he reached the beginning of his old neighborhood and walked the next half block. Two girls, perhaps fourteen, were coming his way. They giggled into each other's faces and blushed when they saw him. Gordon smiled at them.

"We like your puppy," they said, bending toward it.

"You sure about that? Get a good whiff."

"Eew," they said. Their postures became stiff and straight, their legs close together, a mother's dream.

Gordon laughed, "Gotta get this boy to the bathtub."

They went on their way, their giggles renewing behind his back. They thought they were whispering, no doubt, but these were the whispers of excited teen girls. Gordon grinned as he walked, listening to them dare each other. Finally one of them accepted, when they were about thirty feet apart. The girl shouted, "I'd like to give *you* a bath!" He turned and waved but the girls didn't see. They were clutching each other in titillation and mortification. "*I can't believe you did that!*" They giggled louder and hurried off out of sight.

He brought his forearm up to wipe sweat off his face, caught another whiff of the almost archaeological layers of odor on his skin and clothes, and remembered being touched by those relentless fingers. A shivering spasm jolted through his back. I need a brain scrub, he thought.

Gordon and the dog crossed the street and headed down a side road. He saw his parents' house, the sixth one on the left with a brown roof that was at least twenty years old. The houses, with cloned exteriors of red and yellow brick, hadn't changed much from his earliest memories. Most residents were Westervelt professors like his dad, though they seemed to have little to do with him since his wife's death. Gordon remembered his mom hosting parties, winning laughs by referring to the neighborhood as *tenure tract* houses. Being in academia, maybe they just didn't care about appearances. Only changes in siding color and the occasional newer roof or planted flowerbed gave Gordon any indication that time had passed. Despite living so close, he seldom visited. He could not explain it to himself, but whenever he even stood in the front yard, as he did now, he had to remind himself that his mother was dead.

Sometimes he returned when he knew his father had class. He'd leave a note for his dad and call it good for another month. Today, at least, he didn't have to worry about his father; Doc Reader had been in Chicago all week for a Modern Language Association conference. Gordon climbed onto the porch and put his key in the lock. Just as he opened the door, he noticed the dog was not beside him. He found it licking the concrete steps, just as it had licked the building back in town.

"What the hell?" Gordon said. He pushed the door all the way open and slapped his leg twice to summon the dog. Then paused. What sort of mess was he starting? He'd never owned a dog before and here he was about to wash it in their only bathtub. Would all the hair and filth clog the drain? Maybe I should just hose him off in the backyard, Gordon thought. He looked down at the dog, malnourished and pathetic. It deserved a hell of a lot more than a garden hose. Decided, Gordon slapped at his leg again and whistled for the dog's attention. It went on tasting the porch step. He sighed and scooped the dog up in both arms, gagging as the odor slammed his nostrils, then rushed through the door, kicked it shut behind him and marched down the hall.

The house's one bathroom overcompensated by being triple the size it needed to be, with a corner shower stall separate from the majestic centerpiece, a 67-inch slipper clawfoot soaking tub. Made of hand-hammered copper, this had been his mother's treasure. His father disdained the tub, the depths a navigation hazard with his bum leg. But he'd never removed it. Gordon used to wonder why. Maybe the decision went back to the same academic's apathy that kept most of the neighborhood houses so unchanged. Maybe there was some other reason, part sentiment, part fearful hope. His father was a very poetic man after all. Maybe he thought Mom's soul lingered in the tub or something. It would be fitting, considering how ghostly he could be in his own way, seeming to haunt whatever space he occupied—the kitchen, his office, his car. Gordon had seen a few pictures from his father's childhood, and even then his presence seemed to turn every frame into an experiment in spirit photography.

Gordon dropped the dog in and whipped his own shirt off, nauseated by the odor. He rolled it up and shot it across the room. *Two points.* The dog began to panic and growl. Its nails tapped out the dog's terrors on the copper as it circled and scraped. Gordon seized the dog by its scruff and pushed down hard on its hindquarters. The dog whined and went submissive, whimpering. I used too much force, Gordon thought, and immediately felt like an asshole, but the concern passed as the deep tub gathered the dog's scent and assaulted him with it. "*Jesus*, you stink," he said, eyes watering.

He ran water at a very low pressure, just above a trickle to start, aware that any sudden jet would rile the dog. The animal sniffed as the water reached it, and its tongue began to lap. It rose and sprang back once as the water reached its paws, looking like a creature trapped on a sinking ship. A prolonged whine seemed to come from the center of its head. The dog gave a look that Gordon translated as betrayal.

"We're friends," he said. "Look." He dabbed his fingertips into the water and made a streak across his chest. "It's not acid, pal." He dipped his hand again and cupped water against its fur. The dog stood rigid, legs locked. No amount of pushing was going to make it sit. Gordon continued bringing the water against its fur. Beads of moisture dripped off its coat as if each hair had been waterproofed. The water seemed to reactivate older, buried scents. Gordon gagged, turning away. Christ, this was like giving a manicure to a landfill.

He began to realize how ill-prepared he was for the task at hand. Dogs needed dog shampoo, didn't they? The only shampoo his father had ever used was an economy-sized green vat of Prell—his mother used to call it one step up from a pet product—so Gordon went to the corner shower to look for that. He couldn't find a bar of soap, never mind the shampoo. He rummaged through every cabinet door and counter drawer, hurried by the dog's renewed whining, and found in the third drawer a pile of his mother's old soaps and perfumes.

For a moment he forgot the dog's cries and stared. He held the perfumes up one by one—the little clear vials full of bright, colored fluids that made each glass seem like a gemstone against the light. He'd done something similar as a little boy, he remembered, back when a lot more of these bottles were sprawled in a storage basket next to the sink. He remembered taking three of the bottles outside and peering through them at the sun. Gordon swallowed. She'd always had a different scent depending on what color she chose to start the day. When he was very, very little, having only a vague sense of what his mother did and how travel worked, he thought she spent her days in exotic locations around the world, returning home at supper with their trace odors still on her skin. But she always smelled the same to him at night, fresh from applying the same lotion before coming to tuck him in.

The dog gave a long, low, pathetic howl, followed by a sharp bark.

Gordon blinked, startled. "Sorry, bud," he said over his shoulder. He rummaged through the drawer some more and found the smallest bottle of shampoo. It will work, he told himself, though he found himself unable to move. He had to argue with himself about necessity. He needed shampoo; it was an emergency situation; using these on a dog did not disgrace her memory. When he thought he was losing the battle with his conscience, Gordon became nasty to himself. His mother was buried in the ground. A drawer with her stuff shoved in it unused was just another type of grave.

He took the one bottle that had already been opened and turned back to the tub. In practical terms, he knew he was doing the right thing, but the frankness of the winning argument still felt brutal. His stomach churned as he opened the cap and squeezed the shampoo into his palm. At once the freed scent crossed a gulf of years, was recognizable immediately as *Mom*. Gordon trembled. It was as if her very soul had been bottled and kept like a genie.

He began to cry as he rubbed the shampoo into the dog's fur. He cried *and* laughed—his mother surely would have laughed as well at the idea of a mangy dog smelling so perfumed, so luxurious. She'd have laughed, he thought, and then smacked me for putting the dog in her tub. Which also made him grin. Suddenly she seemed alive and whole in his mind, sitting on the corner of the tub, shaking her head at him in amusement. He found himself looking over at the corner and thinking to her. *I swear to God I'll scrub it clean for two hours. It'll be sterile, I promise.* When mom didn't answer back he remembered the darkness of her death. For the next few minutes he sobbed without smiling as he worked the suds into the pliant dog's scalp. His tears came down in a flow as heavy as the odd weight that had settled in his chest, part and parcel of the stillness that characterized the house after she died.

The crying did not last long. He would always be susceptible to small breaks in his internal dam, but he'd learned to fortify fast. At last he could blink away the final tear and just work on the dog in silence. He rinsed and repeated twice, going slow, not thinking. Eventually the dog tired of the routine and let Gordon know he'd over-bathed it. The animal began to pace and shake, frisky, no longer content to let this strange chemical be rubbed into its fur.

"Stand still a second, bud," he said. He took out his phone and took the second picture. "We'll call that one *During*," he said, looking at the image with satisfaction. The dog looked particularly comic in the little frame of his phone, so skinny and with eyes that suggested it felt miserable to be clean.

He let the tub drain, not thinking about how slow the water became after a fast start. He lifted the dog out and onto the floor and wrapped it in a big towel. The dog shivered and Gordon worked with vigor to dry and comfort it, bending low so that his chest touched the dog's back as he massaged the towel along its body. His thoughts had shifted to Amber and how much he wanted to send the photos to her. She'd have to respond to them. Little else had worked to get her attention, but the dog pictures were his ticket. He went to drying it even faster. A powerful ghost scent of his mom came off the dog on every pass of the towel. This too made him hurry. The yellow fur began to dry and expand, giving the dog more body. It no longer seemed completely anorexic. As Gordon moved down to work the dog's hindquarters, it craned its head back and gave him a look that seemed to convey complete trust.

Gordon smiled. "Buddy, you may smell like a girl now but you smell like a damn classy one." The clean fur had the softest, warmest quality to it, almost like tufts of cotton. He folded the towel, stood up and aimed his phone again. The dog opened its mouth and seemed to grin. "Yeah, we're talking about a motherfucking star now," Gordon said. He took the photo. *After*. It was not the greatest photo. Something plaintive about the dog's eyes could easily re-title the photo as *Hunger*. Gordon was feeling famished as well. "Let's go eat," he said. But first he punched in Amber's number and sent her the pictures.

As he bent to pick up his shirt, he looked back at the water's progress. It was still draining but a heavy blond beard of fur lined the copper surface. Cleaning it was going to be a bitch. He'd do it later. He left, and the dog followed, bounding about his ankles like a bouncing ball of light. In the kitchen, Gordon opened the refrigerator door, not expecting to find much. The refrigerator was always empty when he stopped by, his gaunt dad more of a snacker. Gordon could even thank his father's gross dietary habits for his own fine physique. When he turned ten, he grew so afraid of looking like his dad he'd started eating healthy and working out. As a result there was only the remotest trace of his withered father in his features—similar noses and, prior to his braces, similar teeth.

He stared into the refrigerator, aware something was very wrong but not instantly certain what jarred him. The interior bulb had extinguished, leaving the four shelves nested in a dull gray background. The top shelf had a carton of eggs, the second a box of baking soda, the third an open package of bacon strips, their tips discolored and hardening from exposure. These weren't the root of his troubled feelings though. He looked at the door compartments. A package of cheese sat lodged where butter sticks belonged. He detected an odd shape through the tinted cheese drawer and flipped it open. He blinked, finding a bar of Irish Spring. Below that, in the slot where milk cartons belonged, sat a huge green bottle of Prell.

"What the hell?" Gordon said, shaking his head as he removed the soap and shampoo. He laughed at first, thinking of his scatterbrained dad, divorced from reality in in his academic obsessions. Then he just felt unnerved and saddened, as if a cement truck's worth of guilt was hardening like concrete about his whole body. What did he know about his dad's life now? Was he lonely? Did he care about living? How connected was he to anything if he refrigerated his shampoo and soap?

The dog rose up and planted its paws on his thigh. Gordon jumped and pushed it down. He rubbed the spot before giving the dog's ears a brisk, conciliatory scratch. What could the dog eat? The bacon was probably okay, likewise the cheese. He withdrew both, peeled off five bacon slices and placed them on the floor. The dog devoured this offering in seconds and spent two minutes licking the trace taste off the linoleum. This made Gordon laugh. "Tastes a little better than brick, right?"

Next he gave the dog three slices of cheese. While the dog gobbled these up, he pillaged the cabinets for more options. The closest he could come to dog food was a can of baked beans. He popped the tab, spooned out a few bites for himself and dumped the rest into a bowl he placed on the floor. The dog scrambled over, tail wagging so hard its hindquarters shook. Gordon straightened and stretched, pleased to watch it eat. At last, a family dog, he thought. Too bad about the family.

He took out his phone and looked at it. When would Amber reply? He glanced at the dog, admiring its single-minded hunger. Gordon placed a lot of faith in narrow focus and persistence. It had given him success on the court and he was convinced it would help him win Amber. *What if we had a family together?* He smiled at the thought and felt the silly flutters in his stomach. He was *stupid in love.*

It was only ten-thirty. Amber could still be asleep, especially if she'd gone out with her own friends. He couldn't picture her sleeping late, though; he imagined her as someone who had it all going on by six. Gordon was like that himself most of the time. Right now last night's alcohol still felt sewn into his muscles like heavy weights. The problem with hanging around John-Mark was he liked to do shots and Gordon preferred beer. Last night, John-Mark had half the team throwing back a concoction of Jagermeister, Jack Daniels and Tabasco sauce. He called it a *3-Point Shot.* Gordon figured he'd racked up about fifteen points in an hour. Never again, he thought. *3-Point Shots* got you suckered into bed with a chick whose hands were sticky like a cinnamon bun.

Now something awful occurred to him. What if Amber had shown up at the party and talked to him and he didn't even remember it? Could that be possible? What if he'd acted like a fucking idiot to her face because he was blown out of his mind?

The dog looked up as if sensing his quantum leap in anxiety. Shaking, sick to his stomach with dread and certainty, Gordon bent to take the bowl and rubbed the dog's head. *There's no way that happened,* he thought. *He'd remember talking to her.* But now the idea was lodged in his brain and he felt more certain than ever that he'd been a dickhead and blown his future with her.

He turned the water to hot and scrubbed the dish with a brush. His paranoia mounted and felt like a truth that had been buried in him for years. He was destined to fail. Gordon had never experienced negativity so certain, so absolute. His gaze fixed on the water spiraling about the black drain under a small cloud of steam. Something about that dark mouth seized him. He leaned over and gagged. The soapy bowl slipped from his fingers and shattered as his body dry-heaved. The dog barked but there was nothing Gordon could do. On the sixth or seventh heave he coughed up a large mouthful of sour stomach acid and liquor, spat it into the sink. "Oh God," he said, eyes wet from strained tears. He bent his head into the sink, jerked the faucet to cold and sucked water from the jet. The dog continued to bark and pace. Gordon heard its paws clacking over the rush of water.

Turning the faucet off, he lifted his drenched face to look between the broken ceramic pieces and the drain. He'd been thinking of killing himself. Gordon trembled with the realization he could harbor such hopelessness. It was just as he'd felt in the early days of his mom's death—a weariness and confusion that gutted him. Life was pointless, a drain. The sun rose and set—so what?

Gordon inhaled long and deep. Could he kill himself? The question seemed absurd, even if Amber refused him forever. So why was he thinking about it? Annoyed, he told himself he didn't know he *had* been thinking about it. He'd knowingly considered suicide only once in his life. His mom had been dead three weeks and the pressure of the loss was not subsiding. He'd entered the bathroom intending to slit his wrist. He had no idea how to do that, so he'd taken the most serrated blade in the drawer—his mother's bread knife. That very knife was before him on the counter right now in a cutlery block. He pulled it out and looked at it, shaking his head at the absurdity. As a kid, he'd put the knife to his wrist and just stared for a few minutes before returning it and going upstairs to sleep. He slept all the time back then, both day and night. Gordon felt tired just remembering that part of his past. Then he realized he really *was* tired. A lot of shit had happened already this morning, and he was only going on about four hours of sleep.

He was staring off in space, thinking, when the dog circled around him and stuck its nose into the back of his thigh. "*Goddamnit!*" He jumped, turned in a flash and kicked the dog before he even knew what he'd done. The dog howled, whimpered and shot under the table where it crouched low to the ground and stared at him.

"Oh, man," Gordon said, dropping at once to all fours. "I'm really sorry. I don't know what's up with me today."

He put his right hand out and tapped on the floor. The dog wouldn't budge. Their gazes locked. Trust was gone from its eyes.

I've really fucked up, he thought.

Gordon frowned and stood. He gave a final glance at the broken bowl pieces but was simply too tired to pick them all up. He wanted to sleep. The idea of napping in his old bed wasn't appealing, but it beat a long trip back to his dorm and having to deal with John-Mark. There was also the problem of the dog. Gordon rubbed his forehead and climbed the steps. At the top step, he pulled out his phone and *made sure* he'd sent Amber the three photographs. If he'd really gotten trashed last night and couldn't remember making an ass out of himself to her, the photos could repair the damage. They'd show his real nature—his *sweetness*. God, he hoped.

In his thoughts, he heard John-Mark say, *Either way, she isn't worth killing yourself over, dude.*

No doubt, he said back. *I got my shit under control—dude.*

Gordon opened his bedroom door without crossing over. He stayed in the doorway peering in. The room hadn't been touched or changed in any way since his high school graduation. It was the room of an adolescent jock, the walls filled with press clippings of sports stars arranged in silly, fading collages. The quotes and pictures of Kobe Bryant and LeBron James and Shaq and other athletes who'd inspired him were inexplicable totems to him now. *I've changed,* he thought against a swell of doubt. Had he? A half hour ago he'd sobbed over his mom as if she died a week ago. He grimaced at the power of memory. He, not the dog, was on a leash.

He must have changed. He couldn't imagine waking to these clippings and feeling warm, inspired, the way some people woke to sunlight on their face. But he remembered how he'd done exactly that, especially in his senior year when his life seemed to be in full rebound. He was leading his team to the state championship game and had everyone obsessed with him. His girlfriend Stacy had cut out every newspaper and magazine article she came across pertaining to him and the team. She fashioned these into a collage of her own, pressing them between sheets of contact paper until they became a laminated tapestry that stretched four feet across one wall. He used to lie in bed staring at it, thinking of the next great thing he'd do, the next game he'd win. Anything to generate another article she'd clip out and add to the collection. *She loves me,* he'd told himself. *She's the One.*

Girls had thrown themselves at Gordon since he was sixteen, when his skinny body finally responded to years of frustrated training. Sixteen was also the age the braces came off his spectacularly crooked teeth—*The Fane family crowns,* as his mom called them. But he intrigued girls prior to that, his mother's death turning him into a dark and tragic figure. If it hadn't been for depression and his sudden lack of interest in anything besides basketball, Gordon would have likely lost his virginity long before he got his driver's license (the occasion that caused him to change his last name). Instead his first handjob, his first blowjob and his first fuck all happened with Stacy on the very bed before him now. His father always taught Tuesday and Thursday evening classes, and in the spring of Gordon's junior year he and Stacy had spent those hours going at each other, sometimes even spooning for long stretches in the copper soaking tub, right up to the point where they were *bound* to get caught.

Gordon went rigid. Hadn't they been caught? He had an odd, nauseating memory of standing in the bathroom naked and wet with Stacy, only to find his father staring at them from the doorway. The memory was almost entirely about his father's face—its expression of desperation. Gordon shivered now. *That never happened*, he thought. *There's no way we ever got caught.* But as with his sudden certainty that he'd talked to Amber last night and was too drunk to remember, Gordon could not convince himself the memory was not all a dream.

He stepped inside and touched Stacy's collage, running his fingers along a vivid timeline, November 2006 to March 2007. Where was she now? He could find out fast enough. Ninety-nine percent of the students in his high school graduating class were his friends on Facebook—but not her. Sometimes her profile showed up on his page as a friend suggestion. He imagined his must do the same on hers. Neither acted on the prompt. Maybe neither of them understood why their relationship ended. They'd fucked long and hard on the night before she left for Pitt. Was it breakup sex for her? He'd asked that and a hundred other questions in the intervening months when it had become clear she'd cut him off, responding neither to email, text nor call. How could she be so devoted and then find him meaningless? The two of them had been in love—he knew it. If it was not love then love did not exist. Had she meant to dump him as soon as college freed her from her parents and the town? Or were her parents in on it too? The last time he saw Stacy's father, in the December of his freshman college year, their conversation was entirely about basketball. There wasn't even a trace of acknowledgement that Gordon once dated his daughter. He thought about telling Stacy's dad how often he'd fucked her, just as a memory refresher. Gordon only just managed to check himself. *It was over.*

He dug his fingernails into a corner of the collage and pried. He went slow at first, intending to accelerate into a dramatic rip. Instead he went even slower, peeling it from the wall as he might remove a bandaid too attached to a wound. The noise of the scotch tape tearing was slight and the whole process made him lethargic rather than energized. He was too tired to be angry, too sleepy to care. When the last piece of tape came off he let the entire collage drop to the floor. He'd intended to wad it up into a ball and stomp on it.

Gordon yawned and sat down on his old mattress, surrendering. The bed was actually unmade from the last time he slept in it—over Christmas, almost four months ago. Between that fact and the old clippings everywhere, the room had a museum feel to it, as if it preserved his final moments. Gordon remembered how agitated his father had become when he got up to leave on Christmas Eve—it had seemed pointless to stay the night with his dorm room so close. His father's reaction, a flustered anger that showed more in the expression and color of his face than in words, made him feel like an ass. Was a night shared under his father's roof such an imposition? He instantly felt like an ungrateful little bitch, guilty as hell for letting his dad think he didn't give a shit about him.

He hadn't realized it there and then, but on Christmas morning it clicked that his dad had wanted to tell him something, had been working his way up to it when Gordon announced he was leaving. After the brief display of emotion, despite Gordon's submission, his father had frozen up in a reflexive way, then hurried—for him—to open a bottle of wine, pouring them both a glass. It was the first alcohol Gordon had ever drunk with his father, and he automatically tried to fake virginity with a screwed up expression and a ridiculous, "So *this* is what alcohol tastes like?" like he was fourteen. His dad seemed oblivious, just quoting some verse about "the Grape." Then he poured his son another glass, more than Gordon even wanted. He drank it anyway. If he *had* to spend the night, at least the wine was getting him very sleepy.

Now Gordon yawned again, as sleepy as if he'd just drank the wine all over again. He stretched out on his back and held his phone up. He retrieved his contact list and swiped his thumb along the screen. Face of friends cascaded up. He smiled. He remembered so many good times with them. But as the list continued, Gordon's smile went away. Who were all these people? His memory of faces and names started to fog and darken. He had just over two hundred numbers stored. He rubbed at his weary eyes. Two hundred contacts and about three actual friends. The screen went dark from inactivity and left him gazing at his reflection.

Amber's not going to call, he thought, and it has nothing to do with last night. It's fate. She's a professor, I'm a student and she doesn't give a fuck about me or pictures of my fucking dog. The same dog I just fucking kicked!

Gordon sat up with one final, explosive burst of energy and threw the phone at the wall. He didn't bother to look to see if it was broke or not. Head falling back onto the pillow, he thought, Start over. Leave this goddamn school, never play ball again, get fat and see if girls will still want to cop a feel—

He'd never felt drowsy with rage before —but he was, almost deliriously so. He yawned a third time and flopped onto his stomach, one pillow clutched under his chest. He fell into a deep sleep in minutes and dreamed.

Like a horse with blinders, Gordon's vision was narrowed by enveloping darkness to a single source of light ahead of him—it looked like an archway with a man standing in the middle of it, tall but stooped. As Gordon neared, he saw that the man's clothes were tattered and faded, his skin almost bloodless. Two much smaller figures—little boys—darted in and out of the light as if by magic, waddling toward the man's feet, where they piled scraps of wood and kindling, the man shouting and motioning with his hand as they did so, apparently beckoning the children to hurry. Gordon stopped. The voice wasn't familiar but he recognized the hand gesture at once. He'd seen John-Mark move his arm in that big scooping wave during countless games when they were down in the score and the rest of team wasn't falling back fast enough.

The man turned and looked right at Gordon.

He stepped back as he saw the man's face better now. It was definitely John-Mark, but different—aged, worn thin and bled dry. His face showed a few scars and his hairline had receded. What was left of his hair showed no color or vitality. Silver, it did not even glint in the light, looked more like dirty snow, and while elements of his face suggested this John-Mark couldn't be more than forty, the whole looked nearer to sixty.

The boys kept running in and out, in and out, adding to the pile which grew at supernatural speed, making John-Mark appear frozen in place as its peak reached his kneecap, then his waist, then his shoulders. There were things on it the boys could not possibly have placed there on their own—massive truck tires, furniture, broken electronics and...bodies. Gordon stared as the structure continued to rise, its summit at least twenty feet high now and lost in darkness. He felt a childish awe and remembered when his fourth grade class went to see The Nutcracker. He'd been amazed when the Christmas tree, so bright and glittering, started to grow and become huge. This towering debris seemed like that tree's ugly, degraded twin. He now felt very small, and from the surrounding dark he sensed hundreds of people gathering near the pile, like sidelined actors waiting to put in an appearance on the stage.

Now the boys returned with empty hands, stumbling into each other in their exhaustion. Gordon had thought them to be about seven and five, but up close they looked like mutations or Progeria sufferers, pallid and frail, with heads that seemed to have clung for years to those first wisps of baby hair. They gazed at Gordon as if seeing a creature they'd been told was a myth.

"Is that the man who hurt you, Daddy?"

"Yes," John-Mark said, and Gordon gaped at the answer.

"Hurt you? How did I hurt you?"

John-Mark touched the scars on his face.

The younger child said, "Are we going to burn him, too?"

Gordon looked between John-Mark and the boy, hardly able to process what he'd just heard. John-Mark raised his left hand, and for the first time Gordon saw he held something—a small canister blowtorch. He raised it, pressed a button that ignited a two-inch flame, and said, "Yes. We are."

Gordon ran, hoping the dark would hide him. The light followed. He'd never acted, but he had the unnerving sense of being on a stage with a spotlight aimed at him from the ceiling. He felt like a mouse exposed to a thousand hidden predators. He stopped and turned, from left to right, gaze swinging wild, erratic. Was that a shout to his left? Was someone coming? He raised two fists and struck a boxer's stance. Gordon had never fought anything in his life, wasn't sure he even knew how to throw a punch really. He swallowed and panted, waiting.

The flame of John-Mark's blowtorch cut through the dark to his right. Gordon cried out, spinning toward it. The blue fire shot toward his face and then John-Mark appeared, lunging with the canister held out before him. Gordon fell over. As he started to rise, the two little boys leaped out of the dark too, and landed on his legs. Even as they attacked him, Gordon felt paralyzed. Christ, how could he fight them? He couldn't hurt kids—he couldn't hurt anyone. John-Mark's expression said otherwise. Gordon trembled as the blowtorch came closer to his face. It burned with soft noise, almost delicate, like a mother's whisper. John-Mark pushed the flame forward to claim Gordon's eyes.

He didn't succeed. Bounding out of the dark, growling and barking with such frenzy that the ground shook, came a dog. It went straight for John-Mark's wrist and clamped down, making him scream and drop the torch. The boys left Gordon's legs and beat at the dog. For one instant it released John-Mark and turned, baring its fangs at them and snarling. The boys fled. Gordon called out to them as they passed, begging them to stop. But even as he did, he felt urgent caresses all along his body. He writhed, patting at himself. He couldn't get up.

Hundreds of wriggling fingers came out of the ground now, all around him, underneath him. Gordon screamed. The fingers, rooted at the base knuckle in the soil, stroked his body all over, felt his bare arms, tugged at the hem of his shirt, writhed along the outside and inseam of his legs and thighs. Gordon moaned, enduring their touch, terrified of his subjugation. It was worse, more grotesque, that they were just fingers rather than the whole hand. As they worked his shirt up now and tickled his bare ribs, he howled and grabbed at them, jerking each one left and right with as much force has he had. Sometimes a dull snapping sound rewarded him and he knew he'd broken the finger. But two more replaced each damaged one, and soon he was on his back and exhausted, helpless to endure the madness of their consumptive fondling.

The dog growled low and almost straight into his right ear.

"Shiloh? Shiloh, help me!"

The dog's name just came to him, as if his mind recalled it across a gulf of years. It seemed an amalgam of every dog he'd ever known—dogs from movies, friends' dogs, the dog he'd found and adopted long ago. *That dog*—he couldn't remember it. His memories of that time, that life, seemed to be fading. *Amber.* Gordon gritted his teeth as he tried to keep her face in mind, her light blue eyes and radiant red hair. The fingers moved faster and multiplied. They tugged at his pants. They slipped between his toes and into his ears. The friction of their touch rubbed his skin raw. He was being erased and unwritten.

The dog crouched low and began to bite the fingers, chewing through the knuckles and ripping them apart. Gordon managed to roll onto his belly and reached forward, clawing himself clear. A screaming came from the ground. With his last strength, Gordon pulled himself up and looked back. The dog's head shook as it bit and severed, bit and severed. With white and broken fingers on the ground, the scene looked like the weeding of a strange and horrible garden.

"Gordon! Gordon! Gordon!"

Dad?

"Gordon, wake up, there's a dangerous dog in the house!"

The cry startled him awake. He sat up to find his father standing against the wall where Stacy's collage had been. The dog pressed in closer, giving a low, menacing growl. Gordon blinked against a heavy daze. *Dad? Home?* He touched his forehead. He'd been dreaming. A nightmare. The memory of it was gone.

"Gordon! Be very still. We must call the police!"

"No, Dad, it's all right—"

His father went to the ground shrieking as the dog lunged at the ankle of his bad leg. Gordon darted up to pull the dog off but froze at a new noise. From the far side of the room where his thrown cell phone had landed came the unmistakable burst of its ringtone—a triumphant swell from the theme to *Hoosiers*.

Amber!

The dog sprinted down the sidewalk like it knew the way to Amber's duplex. Gordon kept whistling it back, grinning every time the dog returned to sit a second with its head cocked, as if to say, "You needed something, bro?" before bounding off again. Gordon loved the enthusiasm. This boy just wanted to *go*, everything else be damned. Gordon knew all about it. He felt that way whenever he got on the court, whenever he had the ball in his hand, whenever he knew what he wanted and saw his chance to get it. Like an opening in the lane he could drive through and dunk. He and this dog were going to be best friends. This dog was going to be at his side always. It had already shown loyalty, in a way, by attacking his father. Gordon still couldn't figure that out. There was a lot from the last forty minutes he didn't even want to puzzle over. Falling asleep and having some kind of nightmare; waking to find his dad in his room when he should have been in Chicago; the dog going nuts on his dad's pants leg. And then his cell phone ringing like a dead thing come to life, filled with all his hopes in Amber's digits flashing on the screen.

Too strange, too weird.

Gordon had stuck around for twenty minutes or so trying to explain the dog. But Doc Reader was shaken and wouldn't listen to reason, kept insisting he'd been mauled. He'd started waving his cane and struck the wall, demanding Gordon hold the dog so he could beat it. Gordon had never seen his father like that. The rage and fright mangled his words, making him incoherent. When Gordon retreated, grabbing the dog in his arms and holding him against his chest, Dad came after them. They'd shouted at each other through the house so much that when Gordon got out the front door, the world seemed mute in comparison.

He'd got about thirty yards down the street before his father came limping into the yard, a new violence to his voice. Shit, Gordon thought, stopping with his eyes shut. *The bathroom.*

His dad screamed, "You washed that damn animal in your mother's tub? Your mother *bathed* in that tub! It's disgusting now, matted with fur! It's dried on the copper! The tub will have to be shaved!"

Gordon did not turn to confirm it, but he just knew his father was waving an empty bottle of his mother's shampoo. The image sparked a surprising hurt. As a kid, he'd assumed his parents loved each other, the way he assumed all Moms and Dads love each other. Suspicions that this wasn't so started when he was around thirteen, but by the time he was fourteen, his mom was dead and his dad had sanctified her, cherishing her in death. Gordon had clung to his father's emotions at first; he wanted to believe his father did love her and felt the same hurt. It had been years since he got over the need for this illusion. But the idea of his father waving that shampoo bottle eclipsed time and made Gordon fourteen again.

He carried the dog for two blocks, not releasing him until he knew his father wouldn't follow. Then he bent over, winded more from anxiety than exertion. He hadn't been able to answer the phone when Amber called. He hadn't *dared*, with so much commotion on his end. But what if answering then and there had been his one chance? Amber hadn't left a message. What if not answering the phone let her change her mind? What if his lane had suddenly been closed, and instead of going up for a dunk, he'd just fouled out?

But she picked up when he called back. She answered on the second ring, and he stood there on the sidewalk, talking to her as the dog went over to lick the curb. She sounded enthusiastic. The dog pictures were *so* cute (Gordon flashed the dog a thumb's up) and she was sorry for not getting back to him sooner. She had things to work out. Gordon tensed. What things? Oh, she answered, things that *still* weren't resolved. So she needed to see him. Could they meet right now? You bet your ass, Gordon thought, bending down to shake the dog by the scruff of its neck in a burst of pleasure.

So, Starbucks?

She'd laughed and given him an apartment address.

She was inviting him *over*.

He had a huge smile on his face as he pocketed the phone and met his buddy's stare. "Fuck yeah, dog!"

It barked and took off. It'd been leading the way ever since.

Gordon could have sprinted to Amber's place and been there in thirty minutes. But he didn't want to show up in a sweat, and she didn't want to meet in thirty minutes anyway. So he had an hour of walking ahead of him, his slow pace seeming to drive the dog crazy. He understood. He wanted to be the dog. In his heart, he was running full bore toward the woman he wanted.

But there was something to be said for the walk. The haze that covered everything earlier was gone. The world's brightness seemed turned up a notch, and he enjoyed staying in it. He felt he'd stepped out of some long darkness that lingered at the edge of his memory. He whistled the dog back to him again.

As it turned, suddenly, he experienced a dread so inexplicable that he had to stop. For a moment, he thought something was wrong with him, medically, like he was having a heart attack. He bent over and saw his shadow, a crisp darkness stretching behind him. And if he followed it, he thought, that shadow would lead to a wall of night that had been sneaking up on him the entire time.

As the dog arrived and started sniffing the top of his sneakers, Gordon told himself his worry was for the animal. Where was he going to keep it? Maybe he and John-Mark could hide it in the dorm room, but that arrangement wouldn't work for long. Home was out of the question. No way he'd give it to some shelter. That left one pie-in-the-sky, desperate alternative: Amber would take it. Maybe he'd been banking on that solution the entire time. He saw it all playing out to his liking with a certainty not unlike the way he felt sometimes before pulling up for a jump shot—a sensation that his imagination controlled reality and guaranteed the outcome. She *had* to take him.

Take us, he thought. From now on, this dog and I are a package deal. He smiled without much conviction. What if she didn't want either of them?

But she did. We'll get married, he thought.

The notion was suddenly just there in his mind like a prophecy he believed. Gordon was so surprised by it he reacted physically, jerking his head back. He turned around, as if trying to find someone who'd whispered in his ear. The sky seemed less bright. He looked down, feeling a tug on his pants leg. The dog had clamped down on the cuff of his jeans and now gave two more crisp tugs. Back in the direction they'd left.

If I go to her place now, he thought, we'll get married eventually. And then—one day—something bad will happen to her. To both of us.

He had no idea where these ideas came from. But fear squeezed his nuts.

He should run back to the dorm and never contact Amber again. Not if he really loved her.

The dog whined. He squatted until he was eye level with it. "What the fuck is wrong with me, huh? I'm flaking out over here. Set me straight, buddy."

The dog licked his face. Gordon grinned.

"Almost as good as John-Mark telling me I'm being a douche."

He cupped the dog's head between his hands and made it nod. "Yes," Gordon said, giving the dog a voice, "you *are* being a douche."

Resolved, he rose and started toward Amber's again. But the dread wasn't gone. He hadn't faked it out. He hadn't fooled himself. Every step closer to Amber was a step closer to a bleak fate. Goddamnit, what the fuck? This weirdness had to be fear of rejection. That was all he could think. He'd been crushing on this woman for so long, he couldn't imagine his future if she turned him down.

Is that what he'd been dreaming about when his father's shouts woke him? His future?

He stopped again and stared at his feet, thinking. He seldom recalled dreams. The ones he did remember were always peopled with strangers. Which had always tripped him out a little. Who dreamed of total strangers? The girls he'd known in high school were really into dream interpretation and always wanted to hear about his. They always assumed he dreamed about his mom. But he never had.

I was dreaming about Amber and a dog and...John-Mark, he thought. Was that right? What a strange combination. The details escaped him. But it *had* been a nightmare.

The dog barked.

"Yeah, I know. Give me a second, pal. Just trying to find my balls."

He checked the time on his cell phone. *Shit.* Now he really did need to hurry if he wasn't going to be late. When it was game time, he could always make his mind go blank. And damnit, this was *serious* game time.

He ran the rest of the way, reaching Amber's duplex in ten minutes. One minute to spare. The dog went on, overshooting the address by a hundred yards. Gordon whistled twice, and it bolted back to him with the same dopey, shortbus enthusiasm. In the seconds he waited on the dog, Gordon's doubt returned, like something physical riding his back, spurring him like a jockey to keep going. He knew it was absurd, but he couldn't help thinking that the dog racing past the duplex was a message. He shook his head. He was damned tired and had been running on empty since early morning. That was all. He'd be fine when he got to bed. And if that bed happened to be Amber's...

Time to soldier on.

The dog padded up and pawed the building door. "That's the spirit," Gordon said, grinning. No sign anywhere forbidding animals, he noted. He opened the door and they entered the foyer.

The dog sniffed around. It began to lick the wall and Gordon rolled his eyes. It was really time to name the dog. Amber would ask and it'd be dumb if he had to think up something on the spot. The dog needed something unique—but simple, a name that identified the dog immediately as a *bro*. Maxwell, maybe? Rascal? Buster? *All lame.* If he ever did have kids, he wouldn't be running the names department.

We do have a kid together. His name is—is—

Gordon squeezed his eyes shut. The thought didn't even feel like it originated in his mind. It felt like an outside thing, a post-hypnotic suggestion or something. What the hell was wrong with him? He swayed a little, had to put his hand against the wall. He became aware of sounds from the four apartment rooms. TV shows and music. At least one baby crying.

We have a son named—

Get your head out of your ass and stay on point.

The dog's name is—is—

Hannibal? Beethoven? Krueger? Krueger—he kind of liked that. But no: he wasn't about to introduce Amber to a dog named *Krueger*. That was like Freddie Krueger and Amber would think he was a goddamn freak naming his dog after a monster.

The dog started barking. The foyer thundered with the sound.

Before Gordon could muzzle it with his hand, the third door opened. Amber peaked out, saw them and gave a large smile. Gordon smiled back.

"Hey, you!"

The dog's tail went wild, wagging for both boys as Amber came out to meet them. She was tall at five-ten and goddamn, but her red hair looked great against the green of her tight t-shirt. It made him think of an emerald on fire. And her soft skin seemed even creamier against the darkness of her black Adidas soccer shorts. Gordon put his hands in his pockets and swallowed, starting to swell. There were no more thoughts of destiny beyond the next minute.

Amber bent down and roughed the dog's fur. The dog, no dummy, rolled onto its back and let her have his stomach. As she tickled him, she said in a teasing voice, "Oh, you just can't get enough, can you? Oh no you can't, oh no you can't." *No, I can't.* John-Mark would have approved the more carnal fantasy he entertained. Gordon imagined her ticking him like that in bed, maybe with his wrists handcuffed to the posts. The dog's rabid panting could just as easily have been Gordon's own.

She stood up from the dog, which immediately sprang up for more attention and looked between them. "Hey," she said.

"Hi!"

"Those pictures were *so* adorable. And he smells so pretty!"

A different anxiety asserted itself in Gordon's mind. Maybe enough of his mom's shampoo had gotten on his skin during the bathing to masque the morning's many scents. She didn't seem to react to anything wafting off him. She motioned for him to follow her and they went into her apartment.

Prom.Issed.Land.

"Want something to drink?"

"Water would be great."

"I guess you don't drink much in the way of sugary drinks, right? Always training?"

"Not always," he said. He didn't know how he wanted that to sound. Coy? Mysterious? Matter-of-fact? How could two words make him feel like a total douche?

"I take it last night was one of those exceptions," she said, coming into the room with a full glass. The soft friction of her thighs rubbing the Adidas together as she walked brought his attention back to her legs. He tried not to stare. Her calves were great. He imagined how they'd feel around the small of his back.

"You're looking a little rough, Mr. Evans," she said with a smile as she handed him the glass.

He made a stammering response before just laughing and nodding. He drank all the water in three audible gulps. The *Mister Evans* line had surprised him. It was the formal, professional way she addressed all her students in class. Hearing it now in her living room confused and worried him. It still sounded sexy as hell.

She took the glass, returned to the kitchen and refilled it. When she came back this time, however, he was horrified by what he saw. He found, almost superimposed on her youthful body, a bald and fragile creature that seemed to be freezing. Gordon stepped back with a sharp gasp

"Is something wrong?"

Gordon blinked. He was looking at Amber again, beautiful and intriguing, almost explosive in her good health.

I marry her, he thought, but she gets sick and the world dies. We have a child and his name is—

"Where's your bathroom?" he said, talking fast but very low. "I think I downed that water too fast—I'm really sorry."

"Sure! Here, it's this way."

She walked with him around the corner to a short hallway. She held his elbow the entire way, guiding him. The bathroom door was open at the end. He saw the toilet and pushed her away.

"Oh!" Amber said, but in the next moment he had the door shut and was bending over the bowl, waiting.

The dog barked.

A bead of sweat rolled from his forehead down to the tip of his nose. He watched it fall and dimple the still toilet water. He swallowed. His stomach churned but he didn't feel nauseated. *Terror* was a better fit.

The dog barked again. Gordon gritted his teeth and shook his head.

Goddamnit, Shiloh, just shut the hell up!

He moved to the sink and ran water full blast from the faucet. He splashed his face again and again, paying no attention to the splatter as he cupped his hands and ran water through his hair. With his head bent, he could smell his shirt better—and rediscovered the foul dog stink. Shit. He forgot everything else and splashed water onto his chest, until the shirt was soaked in a splotch from his pectorals to his belly button. Then he took a squirt of hand soap and rubbed it into the fabric. The soap didn't foam, but stood out like a discoloring oil slick. Gordon ran more water and scrubbed it in.

What in the hell was he doing? He stared at the mess he'd become in the mirror. Why the fuck had he become so weird since leaving his dad's house? This wasn't *stupid in love*, it was borderline schizo. How the hell was he supposed to explain this mess to her? Amber was standing right outside. He knew it even before she tapped on the door. "Gordon, are you okay?"

He looked frantically from the door to his soaked reflection in the mirror.

Hey, Amber, your faucet just exploded on me. Weird. I got it fixed, though. Don't thank me.

Amber, I'm sorry. It's been a really emotional day and I just had to get in a good, hard cry. Isn't that what you want in a guy?

Yeah, it's a sweating problem.

Amber, I'm a retard and I collected my drool for you.

"I'm fine," he said, tapping his last reserve of calm. "Just—just an athletic thing, that's all. When you train a lot you should always sip water. I just forgot."

His voice seemed improbably steady to him. Maybe it was as convincing to her. When she answered, she at least sounded more relaxed.

"So, like I was saying, I'm sorry I wasn't able to reply to your messages right away. I was just thinking about a lot of stuff."

"Yeah? Me too."

"What about?"

Gordon tugged his shirt away from his chest and stared at the wet blotch. He could never stall her long enough to get dry, but he found that wasn't the only reason he wanted to stay in the bathroom. He touched the door, thinking of her on the other side, near but separated. It wasn't how he'd imagined any conversation between them. But it was—nice. He loved her voice. He felt less intimidated just responding to it. Not seeing her made him feel like he could be daring, as if everything they said was for practice, a dry run. He felt like he could improvise. Caressing the door with his fingertips, Gordon smiled and said, "The two of us."

She laughed. "It seems to me like you'd already given that a lot of thought. Am I right?"

He nodded, pausing. Remembering she couldn't see him and might think it an awkward silence, he said, "Yeah."

"It's just that I had to play a little catch-up," she said.

The dog barked again and Gordon heard its nails on the wood.

"Shiloh, quit that!"

"Shiloh! What a great name for a dog."

Gordon smiled. The name seemed to come from the depths of memory. He couldn't place it right away. Then, in the next moment, he did: it was the title character of one of the dog movies he'd watched as a kid. God, maybe it was the first he one he *ever* saw. He explained it to Amber. "I was like three years old. I watched it with my mom."

Now Amber laughed. "I *remember* that movie! I think I was eleven. My parents took me to see it, too. I told them it was so beneath me. But I begged for a dog after that."

"I knew we had something in common," Gordon said. He put his forehead to the door, stared at the knob and at the ground.

"I happen to like basketball too, Mr. All-American. I've even been known to show up for a few games and cheer."

How he knew!

He felt the door shudder once, as if she'd leaned against it. Then he heard a sound that got lower and lower. He followed it, realizing she had put her back against the door and had slid down it until she was sitting. He adopted the same pose.

"I think Shiloh's a good name for this dog," she said, "Very literary. Did you know it was Byron's nickname for Shelley?"

He didn't know who either of those people were and thought it'd be cute if he admitted it. As soon as he heard her response, though, he knew he'd fucked up.

"I guess you slept through the poetry part of my class?"

"I—"

He pulled back and gaped, wondering why he'd been so stupid. Of course. She was a literature professor; he was going to be expected to know stuff like this, or at least seem interested. He fought through his memory for knowledge of Byron or Shelley. The only Byron he could think of was Byron Scott. This wasn't fair. He hadn't missed any of her classes, and he hadn't slept through them either. If he didn't remember what she taught, it was because he was way more into his teacher than the subject. That shouldn't have been an insult to her. Hell, she was the reason he liked any poetry at all. He loved her enthusiasm for literature. He loved the fact that she knew little facts, like the nickname one poet gave to his buddy. Otherwise his thoughts on literature could be summed up by what some previous student had once written in the margins of his tenth grade literature textbook: *Whose woods these are, I think I know. Who gives a shit, this poem blows.*

He swallowed, wanting to explain to her. Before he could speak, Amber said, "Gordon, there's a lot we have to talk about. I think I know what you want. I think I know what I want."

He almost mashed his face against the door. "What do you want?"

"I'm attracted to you, okay?" Her voice quavered. "I'm admitting that. But any woman on campus who isn't a lesbian must be a little attracted to you."

He smiled but still felt nervous, like he wasn't sure about his reprieve. "Then you're special."

"Why's that?"

"Because you're the one I'm attracted to. The only one."

Was it too much? He swallowed and waited, his face flushed. Damn this door! It made it so easy, just talking to her voice—to her mind. He wasn't a Catholic but he understood the power of the confessional booth now.

"Even though we're no longer in a teacher-student relationship," she said, "the university still frowns on it. I checked the code of conduct. It's rule 75-130-something. Westervelt forbids all teacher-student romances."

His chest hitched as he held his breath. She *was* going to reject him. No, he thought. It wasn't going to end like this, before it even began. He made a fist and hit the floor.

"What do I have to do? I'll go to Coach. Maybe he can help."

She laughed.

"Don't laugh at me. I'm serious!"

"I'm not laughing at you, Gordon. It's okay."

"Look, I won't take another English class again. Not after that—"

Her tone turned playful. "After *what?* My awful class?"

"I didn't mean that! I just meant it's not my thing. I mean, it's sort of my thing, but only when I hear it from you—when I listen to you talk about it. It's like you've got the touch with it or something."

"Care to drop the indefinite pronoun and tell me what *it* is supposed to mean?"

"Poetry, I guess. I don't know. All those poems and stories we had to read. I liked listening to you read out loud. I liked it best when you'd go line by line and show us how a word could be interpreted."

"You never really contributed in class, Gordon."

He banged the back of his skull softly on the door. "I was too busy listening."

There was silence from her side, though the dog made a contented sound. He imagined her petting it as she reflected on his answer.

After a minute, she said, "You know what I'd like to do, Gordon?"

He shook his head.

"Gordon?"

"Sorry," he said, straightening, grimacing. "What would you like to do, Amber?"

"Look at you."

She started to laugh. He did too. He looked at his shirt with its big gray blob of water and liquid soap. He heard her getting up. He also heard the soft padding of Shiloh on the carpet. He got up as well and turned the knob, opened the door and stood there for her review.

Amber looked straight at his chest, her expression carefully neutral.

"My shirt was a little stinky."

She smiled. "I'm just glad to quit playing Pyramus and Thisbe."

Clueless, he looked at the dog, whose expression seemed to say—*Just nod and go with it, guy.* Gordon did.

She came forward and kissed him, standing on her tiptoes as she grabbed his shoulder. Gordon experienced a moment of terrifying darkness. Then he realized he'd just closed his eyes.

"I fully admit I've been wanting to do that for some time. Maybe since the moment I saw you."

"Then you don't care about the code of conduct?"

"I most certainly *do* care about it."

Gordon frowned. Amber kissed him again.

"You know, when I was a freshman in high school, I had the biggest crush on my Algebra 2 teacher. Scott Moretti. He was the youngest teacher in the school and he was the assistant basketball coach. He'd played for that school and I thought he looked like he could still suit up. I guess it began my fascination for tall men."

They both smiled. Gordon said, "I guess the situation is a little reversed now, isn't it?"

"Guess so. But I need to be careful. We both do. There's going to be some trust issues between us until we get more settled. For instances, I don't think it would be good to show up at any party as your girlfriend."

"No one would care!"

"Oh, I bet your buddies wouldn't care at all, except for high-fiving you behind my back for getting a professor into bed."

He flushed, thinking of John-Mark. "Most of those guys aren't really like that, Amber."

"See," she said. "We haven't even started dating and there's conflict."

"I'll solve it. I won't go to any parties. I'll stay here with you. You, me, and Shiloh will just hang out. We'll watch TV. On Friday nights we'll play Scrabble."

She smiled and kissed him a third time.

"If we do, Mr. Evans, rest assured I'll kick your ass."

CHAPTER TWO

"**N**o," Fane whispers, managing to break free of the security guard. He spins back to John-Mark.

"The sun is setting forever, Dr. Fane," says the second paramedic. John-Mark nods.

None of this is real, he thinks. It's the hallucinations again. Think your way through them and you'll be sane again.

"Your own darkness is consuming the sun, Dr. Fane. There's nothing you can do about it now."

He turns away, helpless, and shrieks—right into the face of Dr. Oxley, who takes his arm and pulls him across the quad.

"Dr. Fane, I'm sorry. I can't teach my class today. I've got to cancel your audit."

Audit? Class? Now he remembers. Of course. He squares his thin shoulders, bears down on the cane and starts walking.

"You can't cancel. You've got responsibilities. As do I."

She grabs him again, then pulls back. Her hands tremble. "*Please,* Professor."

"Maintaining your class schedule is a mark of order. The students need order. Otherwise there's chaos."

"We just witnessed chaos, Dr. Fane! I want to help those students."

Fane lifts the tip of his cane and waves at her, a giant admonishing finger. "*Both,* Ms. Oxley, or just one?"

She swallows. Her voice drops a notch lower. "What are you saying?"

He waits until a group of students pass, leaving them alone. "75-130-b.1. We all know what you've done. Say goodbye to the sun."

Goodbye to my son.

"What?" he says, looking around. A wave of dizziness staggers him and he plants the cane back on the ground to lean on it.

"Dr. Fane? Are you—"

He jerks away from her touch. What was he about to say to her? Oh, yes.

"If I'm not mistaken from what I just saw, you've violated a certain rule in Westervelt's code of conduct—75-130-b.1. Do you know what it says?"

He squints to scrutinize her reaction.

She draws back, pale. Even her hair seems to lose its color.

Fane smiles. "I see you *do* know what it means. I'll have to decide how to proceed next. You have some talent. But what is talent against indiscretion? No, Dr. Oxley, I suggest you plan on teaching your class. I will be there one way or another."

He leaves her, the cane squeaking as he cuts across the quad in labored, dragging steps. He reaches the Humanities' administrative building at the east end of campus in twenty minutes, twice the amount of time most people require. Like many old colleges, Westervelt's grand buildings weren't built with the disabled in mind. He has only to conquer a shallow rise of seven steps to reach the door but in his present state it feels like summiting a mountain peak. He leans on the handrail, breathing heavily, remembering the last time his leg hurt this intensely. The first time George took him to the cave.

The memory makes him gulp even more air.

He might have stayed at the bottom step longer, but the door opens and there's Dr. Monroe heading down. Monroe, fifteen years younger than Fane, is the current chair of the English department. He descends with his head bowed, typical of his determination to appear lost in thoughts that aren't there. He almost runs into Fane at the last step.

"Adam! Didn't see you there."

"Hello, Matt."

"Beautiful day, isn't it?"

Fane looks at the sky—typical California blue with wispy white clouds no child's imagination could sculpt.

"How's the leg today?"

"*Fine.*"

Monroe smiles. "I guess it doesn't predict rain, does it?"

"It certainly does not."

Fane hobbles onto the first and then second step.

"Have a good day, Adam."

Fane raises his left hand without looking back. He reaches the fourth step. "Oh, and Adam—"

Fane turns.

"75-130-b.1," Dr. Monroe says.

Fane drops his cane, clutches the railing and puts weight onto his right leg until pain surges through his brain like an electric shock. It has the clarifying effect he hoped it might. Matt Monroe isn't there. Was he there at all? Is Fane hallucinating entire people now as well as their words?

He grabs his cane, limps up to the door and enters. The faculty chairs all have their offices on the first floor. Monroe's door is open and Fane dares not glance in, fearing he'll discover Matt at his desk. He hears the office secretary stuffing papers into the faculty mailboxes and sneaks past, carrying the cane to avoid any telltale tap that might draw her attention, though it becomes a necessity again after a few yards. Sighing, he continues down the central hallway and enters the elevator. He exits on the fifth floor, steps into a hallway that always seems much darker than the rest of the building, as if lit by ceiling bulbs of lower quality. His own office is at the end of this corridor, the last of six doors.

He stops, having to touch his forehead as a burst of sound runs through his mind. A memory of the fight. That was what, half an hour ago? Or did it happen at all? Where is Gordon? I've got to tell him, he thinks. I've got to confess.

He looks up. Where is he? He was in the quad, searching for Gordon. He *left* this place to go looking for him.

Fane starts again. He'll be better once he's inside his office. It's the one place where everything still makes sense.

Reaching his door, he pauses to consider the one across from it. All of the doors are brown panels, but this one stands out in stark contrast to the rest, wallpapered in a growing cloud of media clippings that includes both colorful glossy magazine stock and bland newsprint. This lively mural tortures the eye with images and paragraphs that are meant to be, Fane supposes, some visual cousin to *found poetry*. Here an exotic photo, there an absurd quip removed from its context, all exactingly pruned and shaped according to a mysterious standard of whimsy, until it all forms a sort of splatter of meaning on the door, as if Jackson Pollack was resurrected to continue his work in magazine clip collage.

This cancer has been growing since Fane first noticed a solitary blurb taped to the door at some point in the summer. The office having been vacant since last year, he assumed a student stuck it there for a student's idiotic reason. Fane tore it off and had considered the matter closed, when three days later five more clippings appeared. As he was bending to read them, the door opened, and Fane instead found himself studying a woman's breasts. "Do you like them?" she said, and Fane straightened and swallowed. The woman smiled. "Forgive my teasing. I just thought you of all people would appreciate such randomness, Dr. Fane." She pulled the door forward and pointed out the clippings as if they were not self-evident. He flashed his quick, short smile. She was a new hire for the department, Dr. Myra Margolis, and in fact Fane did *not* appreciate such randomness.

Since then he's had to endure its accretion every day though. There are even afternoons when he feels somehow connected to the collage, that its randomness is a purposeful reflection of his mind. Hadn't his downward spiral been slow and manageable back when the door was unadorned? Is Margolis a type of witchdoctor? Has she created a *voodoo door?*

And to think his own dedicated work had inspired Margolis and so many like her into glorified acts of garbage collecting!

The chaotic arrangement of this collage that now covers almost half the surface overwhelms Fane's vision and causes him to swoon against his own door. There's so much color, yet he finds only impending darkness in the patterns, like a final burst of brilliance before a star dies. Is there something subliminal here? Has Margolis secreted untimely obituaries and fragments of catastrophe into the otherwise vibrant presentation? Is there some glint of prophecy buried in the banal?

Trembling, Fane unlocks his door and shoulders through, almost falling. The office is only seventy square feet. He deserves larger, but has never asked for more, perhaps because the narrower confines feel safer. The walls define the whole of the world into something manageable. The world? No, this is the universe—or his secure piece of it, at any rate. Here no one will say, "75-130-b.1," as everyone has been doing for weeks now. He tells himself again and again that his crime cannot be known, these aural hallucinations only the product of his guilty mind.

Like a heartbeat from the floorboard. Or elsewhere.

Fane pales.

He scans the room for familiar comforts. Green metal shelves mounted on the east and west walls overflow with a bounty of used books. Some people keep old, yellowed paperbacks as a badge of honor, evidence of their thrift and concern for substance over presentation. Fane, however, has made his career from them. He *found* his career in them, in a real sense. The pages of every book on these shelves are sewn with marginalia and underscores and exclamation marks and highlights from previous owners. The books come from everywhere—bookstores and estate sales and, most famously, the waiting room of the town hospital. That was what changed his career in fact—the book he grabbed from under a pile of magazines in that waiting room, while fretting over Gordon's impending birth.

The book—*Heart of Darkness*—was not an entirely improbable find in the waiting room of a hospital that served so many college kids. Some Westervelt student, blinking at it for an assignment as he sweated out the results of an STD test, probably forgot it there after receiving the good or bad news. Fane, enduring the second hour of his wife's labor, wondering how he could possibly become a father, and entertaining the *tiniest* black hope that disaster might spare him the fate, thumbed through the book in a daze. Every page featured heavy and perplexing handwritten annotations. Each paragraph was commented upon in tiny, urgent handwriting. He grunted at the discovery. Many of his colleagues believed a book unwritten in was a book unread. He had always preferred to keep his books unmarked. Initially impressed at the sheer effort the previous reader had taken to understand the novel, Fane soon realized the margin notes were wholly nonsense. In fact, studying further, he could not conceive of a consistently worse misinterpretation of a literary text.

This made him think—even as a nurse came out and said, "Congratulations, Mr. Fane, come and see your baby boy!"—there might be something in analyzing all those notes people jot off to the left or right of a text, often with the solemn certainty of a *Penetrating Insight*. He took his wife home from the hospital two days later, saw her safely ensconced in bed, and then systematically visited all the local used bookstores to toil through their musty paperbacks. His first book on the topic, *Marginal Thoughts*, became an academic sensation, a hybrid work of popular culture, reader-response criticism, and psychology. People sent him copies of books from their school days, asking him to analyze the quality of their own notes. He became a champion of the common man in ways he'd never wanted. Suddenly every fool who ever jotted something off to the side of a paragraph—the ramblings of some reading group trollop or confused teenager—thought of themselves as literary critics.

Adam Fane the Thought Collector. He can hear George saying this so clearly he looks over his shoulder. He's not there, of course. And if he was it'd be an illusion. Get control of yourself, thinks Fane. You're the master of your mind. Ignore what you know can't be.

He frowns. George *could* be. George was, is, and shall be.

Fane goes to the room's only window, which overlooks one of the faculty parking lots. Taller adjacent buildings clip the sunlight and leave the room muted and dim. He has not turned on the lights and the floor tiles seem ashen, the walls and ceiling bleached. A stack of student papers on his desk has no color except for black print and his own comments in red ink, fresh welts on whipped backs. A glistening black rock a little larger than his fist holds the papers down.

"75-130-b.1!"

The shout echoes down the hallway followed by snickering like machine gun fire. Enraged, Fane lunges toward the door without using the cane. A fresh stab of pain reels him back.

How do they know? How can they possibly know?

He'd like to bash in someone's head. His desk has to substitute. The cane strikes across the surface, sending the black rock to the floor and scattering student papers into the air. Not content, he swings at one of the bookshelves on the wall. Even wielded in his frail arms, the cane hits hard enough to send half the books to the floor. Fane attacks again, his body's torque searing in his leg, and the bottom shelf breaks free of its brackets, dumps everything across his desk and floor.

The cane clangs on the ground as Fane grips the desk with both hands. Leaning forward, he spies the black rock and sobs. Rounding the desk, he manages to stretch, stoop and take it into his right hand. Even now, as in adolescence, the rock's heft is almost too much for him. It's far heavier than its weight and its blackness is perfect and deep. "George," he says.

It's like a piece of night in his hand. He stares into its darkness for what seems like hours, and when he looks up the darkness surrounds him. The office is gone.

"No," Fane mumbles.

You are master of your mind, he thinks. Make the hallucination go away. You're not standing in a black void. There's a floor under your feet. Find your cane.

This flash of reason is like a flame extinguished fast by the fact that the desk is gone. Shaking, he nevertheless bends his knees and makes a sweeping motion for the cane. He can't find it. He can't even sense a floor exists. Whatever this darkness is, it has a different quality than his previous hallucinations. The only sense of his own physical existence is the rock in his right hand. He squeezes it, glad for its solidity and resistance. The rock is real and he is real and this isn't the dream again.

The dream has plagued Fane's sleep the last three months: he is in a pitch-black place, and suddenly a white, almost Satanic face rushes at him; he has his cane and defends himself with it. He never gets a good look at the face's features, but he always wakes knowing it was George. George is trying to tell him something.

No face appears before him now though.

I'm in my office, he thinks. If I just start walking I'll find a wall. Then I can find the door and exit to the hallway.

Fane tries, but the dimensions have changed and the totality of the blackness overwhelms him. If he had his cane, he'd use it more like a blind man than a cripple. After a few hesitant steps, he does get some sense of the floor: the tile is gone, replaced by a rocky, uneven footing.

I'm in our cave, he thinks.

"George," he says, speaking just above a whisper. "George, it's Adam. I've come back to—to help you."

Fane hears himself breathing, just like he did the first time George brought him here. He remembers thinking that despite the darkness it would be impossible to hide from someone here unless you could hold your breath for a long time. The cave's acoustics amplified even the subtlest of sounds. He cocks his head and listens for evidence of George.

A crackling noise comes off the floor ahead. Fane squints and crouches. It sounds like burning kindling. A campfire? But how can that be? He and George never made a fire.

Then Fane knows he's no longer in the cave. Stop the hallucination, he thinks. Stop the delusion. You are in your office. The world is the same as it always was. But if this is Earth, it is a strange and unacceptable Earth.

Before him materialize suggestions of desolate figures. Fane retreats, trying one final stab at reason. His office walls *have* to surround him. The door and desk and his cane *have* to be near. But from where he imagines the door might be comes a sudden cascade of sparks, and a dim halo of light appears. Within it, he sees four wretched humans, three men and a woman, crouching half-naked about a circle of rock and debris.

"Hello?"

They do not acknowledge him. A cursory glance suggests they suffer from radiation poisoning, though Fane somehow just knows this is not the case. Something *else* is wrong with their world, something that defies belief; their very existence defies natural law. Endless darkness and a hopeless imperative to survive have altered them into sallow, sunken creatures with only dank, decaying strands of colorless hair on their heads. The woman is bald. Their ragged clothes betray hints of a former culture—moldering advertising logos, tattered marketing brands, faded sports team insignias. Stamped on these lifeless things. Fane watches them trying to nurture the fire, knowing they will not last long without it. The cold pantomime provides a grim fascination.

The woman gathers her bony knees to her concave chest and weeps. The man to her right quits working on the fire and holds her. The two remaining men look at them with scorn, cast baleful glances into the black sky, and work harder on the fire.

Now the man stops consoling the woman and pulls away, clumps of colorless hair falling from his ashen pate like piles of soot. He turns toward Fane, his mouth moving. No words are audible but Fane is certain the man says, "Are you satisfied now?" Damaged and aged far before its time, the man's face has an air of familiarity, but at first Fane cannot place it at all. Then realization jolts him.

"Gordon," he whispers.

He reaches out his hand only to have his fingers pass through his son's body. Before he can even register astonishment, Fane receives a second shock of recognition: he knows the woman, too. Even haggard, even without her radiant red hair, this is Amber Oxley. Up close, the perfection of her baldness fascinates him. It's as if she's shaved her hair, fearing someone might mistake it in the dark for fire and try to take her head. She comes up behind Gordon and snakes her left hand up to his chest, which has only the vaguest hint of the beautiful torso that once existed.

Gordon, he thinks, what's happened to you? Where are the beautiful hairs on your body? Where is the sunlight to privilege them?

Fane retreats, shaken at how the two of them stare right through him. Behind them rise the two men who kept working on the fire. Their expressions convey unmistakable malevolence.

"Oh, Gordon, turn around quick," Fane says even as they lunge, first knocking Oxley to the ground. Her mouth opens in a silent scream. Gordon tries to fight. His struggle is so pathetic compared to the battle Fane witnessed—when? An hour ago? A lifetime? They beat Gordon down until his head lolls like a thing too heavy for the stalk of his neck. Then they seize and drag him to the fire pit.

Fane stretches forth his hand again. "Stop! Stop what you're doing! That's my—that's my son!"

The ghastly men are oblivious as they bring Gordon's right arm toward the fire pit. Feeling the heat on his flesh must stir the last ounce of will in Gordon's body. He spasms. This provokes a beating until he goes limp.

The men consult each other. One blows into the fire pit, and the light there brightens. They pull Gordon's arm over it now, the flesh catching fire, burning with a queer light, blinding white as a magnesium flare, and Fane grunts and turns away as the light expands, driving back the surrounding darkness until...

He finds himself standing in his office with his left arm raised to shield his eyes.

He swallows, his throat dry and sore. He sees the broken metal shelf, the books and papers scattered everywhere. His cane on the floor. The black rock is in his right hand, and he quickly drops it onto the desk before rubbing his palm against his pants.

That hallucination was different. More... His mental thesaurus cannot find an adequate word. He settles for *substantive*.

Gordon, he thinks, what's to happen? George, where are you?

"75-130-b.1, 75-130-b.1," a voice says from the corridor outside. Fane seizes the rock and throws it at the door, hard as he can. The rock lands well short of its target.

"Go away! Leave me alone!"

They all know. They all know what I've done, he thinks. Give me the dark again!

Fane reaches for the center of his universe, the black rock on the desk. It's not there. "What? George, did you take back the present? I know you're angry with me." He turns, oblivious to the wreck his office has become, and spies the rock on the floor, staggers over to it. He stoops once, twice, a third time, and then the old heft is in his hand again. He caresses it, thinking about George touching the rock. Of course this is his universe; it is the last remaining connection to George's fingertips. Fane makes a sad and quiet intonation as his gaze rediscovers the chaos of papers and books scattered everywhere. The mess makes him think of George sprawled in cold darkness. But the rock is an unyielding wholeness. George is whole. There's that, at least. Fane places the rock in the left pocket of his tweed jacket, straining the seams to get it in, and then cups his hand over the absurd bulge as he never did over his wife's pregnant belly, long ago.

"75-130-b.1," a new voice says from the hallway.

Fane answers by pulling at his thinning gray hair.

What time is it? Oxley's class to audit at one. Gordon still to find. Gordon—

His eyes narrow with consideration. Gordon's been arrested, hasn't he? Did that happen? Did Gordon beat another student half to death and get taken away?

He falls into his chair, sweeps stray books to the floor and finds his rolodex. Trembling fingers flip through too many cards. He looks under *Fane, Gordon*. Not there. Of course. His fingers reverse. There's the entry. *Evans, Gordon*.

He calms his hand enough to put the receiver to his ear and punch in Gordon's number. The phone rings and rings.

Gordon's recorded voice answers, a frustrating development. Nevertheless Fane cherishes each syllable. This is how George would have sounded. The tone is deep but wonderfully mellow. But the message is too short: *Hey, I guess I'm out ballin'. Leave a message.* Fane hangs up and calls again and again, just to hear the two sentences. But after the fourth time, Gordon's tone suddenly changes and the message expands—

"*You think I don't know, Dad? You think I was asleep?*"

Fane gasps.

A new voice replaces Gordon's.

"*It was always okay. I know you were trying to reach me. Every man has a cave or two in his life, mate. The secret's in knowing they're all the same cavern.*"

"God," Fane says, throwing the receiver down as he sobs. Forehead on the desk, he cries until he's out of tears.

"*Mate? You there?*"

Fane raises his head and blinks at the receiver. He whimpers, shaking his head and biting his bottom lip.

"*Don't leave me hanging, mate. Don't you know this is a long distance call?*"

Swallowing, his throat a desert, he brings the receiver to his ear. "George?"

"*I found a poem for us, mate.*"

Fane closes his eyes and waits for George to begin reading. A moment later he does: "*Sun of the sleepless! Melancholy star!*"

Fane listens. Gordon, son of this sleepless man, he thinks, I am sorry.

George finishes:

> So gleams the past, the light of other days,
> Which shines, but warms not with its powerful rays;
> A night-beam Sorrow watcheth to behold,
> Distinct, but distant—clear—but, oh how cold!

"So haunting," Fane says. "Who wrote it?"

"*Byron, mate.*"

Fane wipes his eyes. "I don't like Byron the way I used to."

"*The world's coming to an end, Adam.*"

Fane nods. He leans back. At last, he says, "For me it ended a long time ago."

He hangs up. The phone rings again immediately. Fane's hand trembles above the receiver. One by one his fingers curl into his palm. No. The past comes calling every day, but it's the here and now that requires attention.

Oxley's class to audit. Gordon to see about. Where did the police take him? To jail? To the hospital?

Maybe, for today at least, he can make an alliance with Oxley based on a shared concern. Gordon's obviously no mere student to either of them. When did the relationship start? How long has it been going on? How much of Gordon's body has she explored and known and *savored*? He grunts a little louder on each question. Rising, finding his cane again, Fane hobbles toward the door. Opening it, he confronts the collage on the door across the hallway. Sneering, he reaches with his left hand and claws the whole thing off in three swipes. Wadding it all into a massive ball, he tosses it onto his office floor and locks the door behind him.

Thirty minutes until Oxley's class. He needs only fifteen. Are they in love? Who would not love Gordon? Who would not sacrifice everything for him? But what if it is George she loves? What if it is George who loves her back? His sympathy wanes. Fane reaches the elevator, enters and descends. The pain in his right leg strums up his body. Acid stabs the back of his throat. He passes Matt Monroe's office and pauses. All the lights are out and the exterior window shows a midnight world. He glances at the main door in front of him and sees California sunshine. Day in front of him; night in Matt's office. How can this be? Matt's secretary is sobbing. Fane steps closer and finds her pulling all the papers from the faculty mail slots, gathering them into a pile on the floor. She opens a supply cabinet and dumps reams of typing paper on top of the heap. Then she lights a match. The paper catches at once, and the orange glow reveals the details of her face—streaked with age. Matt's secretary is at most thirty-five years old, but this woman looks nearer to an ill used seventy.

Hallucination. Hallucination. Make them stop. Think and they'll go away.

He pushes off with his cane and bursts through the exit so fast that his momentum threatens to send him tumbling down the steps. He indeed takes them faster than he can remember ever doing before, but finishes feeling okay. He can even laugh, and pats the rock in his jacket pocket. Good luck charm. Good luck George.

He turns right and heads toward Mayer Auditorium.

He should have been more generous to her, let her excuse her class. She loves Gordon. She's upset. Why inflict her with anxious hours? Why impose his will upon her? He's curious to know if she has ignored his warnings and cancelled anyway. And if she has, he tells himself, I must not get upset.

He reaches Mayer, stopping to regard its handsome façade. The building honored a Westervelt graduate who died at Normandy. An auditorium, a bench, a new library wing, or an endowed chair: all altars to the dead, Gedenkschrifts of wood and marble and steel. George's cave. Fane lowers his gaze and heads in.

Mayer has four entrances, at the top, bottom and each side. Fane takes the top entrance, knowing the class will be huddled at the front, nearest to the stage. The theater seats three hundred and typically hosts author readings or community events, in as much as the community bothers with any light that Westervelt might shine on their mundane lives. To Fane it's silly to hold a class like Oxley's in so large a space.

Looking down, he counts seventeen heads. The students are scattered about the first five rows, a few in groups but most alone. Already his stomach sours. It's a minor point, but the theater's setup invites chaos and Oxley should make more of an attempt to order her students, reminding them they *are* in class. These students are slouching and many have their feet against the backs of the next row. As Fane walks down the right aisle, he notices that each student is communing with a little light in their hands—their damn cell phones. Fane fights the urge to poke the backs of their heads with his cane.

Where is Oxley? Is she not going to be here? Or perhaps she's learned something from him at last. Fane has always believed professors should be the last person into the room. Entrances like that set a tone of authority.

As he nears the stage, Fane hears sounds coming from the students' phones. They all seem to be watching the same video. The class is three-quarters female, and Fane notices most have their hands over their mouth. One says, "Oh my God."

Fane leans toward her, looking over her shoulder. "What is it?"

The girl startles, turns in obvious confusion, and finally just holds up the phone. The footage is chaotic, shaking, almost a collage of body parts. Suddenly Fane sees himself—or the back of himself. And there's Oxley to his left. The camera angle rises above them, aims at the sky a moment, then pivots down. Now Fane watches Gordon and John-Mark beat each other. Punch and kick. Clawing for dominance. Strangulation. Good God, Gordon's hands are on John-Mark's throat. Brutal and murderous. Fane never saw that at the time. John-Mark quits moving. The camera angle loses most of Gordon's body as he staggers to his feet. But it captures the kick. The toe of Gordon's sneaker pounds into John-Mark's mouth.

How primitive, how inconsequential his memories of being bullied are against that graphic footage. At Fowler, his tormentors were cruel, even sadistic, but not brutal. Memories of Thompson and Dooley's bullying feel like an elementary school problem compared to what's captured on the recording.

He studies other phone screens to confirm the earlier suspicion. Yes, the students *are* watching the same footage. Whoever took it must have done something—*uploaded it*, is that the term? Two girls, one fat and one thin, sitting in the third row, are on the verge of tears. The heavier girl says, "I can't believe this is happening. Gordon's like the greatest guy ever."

"He was a real asshole to you in his dorm room last spring. And kind of a freak, running out like that. Besides, John-Mark's way hotter."

"I'll never, ever forget him," the fat one says, as if Gordon's died.

Fane clears his throat. "Where is Dr. Oxley?"

The girls look up at him with expressions that cross contempt with confusion. Who is this old man and why is he talking to them? They glance at each other, and then the thin one gets a coy smile and says, "75-130-b.1."

"Oh, that's *exactly* what she's violated, no doubt about it."

He stabs the floor with his cane and moves on

"Professor Fane?"

It's a graduate student coming up behind him. He knows her face but not her name.

"Yes?"

"I'm Jill, Dr. Oxley's research assistant."

"I remember you from my Romanticism seminar last year," Fane said.

She brightens. "It was a terrific class."

"I'm in expectation of attending another terrific class today. Where is Dr. Oxley? The class is already starting late."

The graduate student bites her lower lip. "Gone. She asked me to explain."

"Gone?"

He hears his tone of voice and remembers that he must not get upset.

"She experienced an emergency this morning. She didn't feel capable to teach."

"Are you supposed to be her stand-in?"

"No, no," Jill says. "It just so happens she created this really amazing lecture that sort of gives itself, I guess you'd say."

Fane's eyebrows arch. "A self-lecturing lecture? Amazing, indeed."

They both turn at the sound of grunts from the left side-entrance. Two more students come carrying what appears to be a massive piece of plywood. It must be at least five feet long and wide and is draped with the most hideous fabric Fane has ever seen, a greenish-yellow mishmash of florid Victorian crests, sewn in threads of gilt and burnt sienna with touches of orange and beige. Between the crests are more flourishes and curlicues in a thread color he cannot determine but which provokes within him an immediate and intense dislike. Yet he cannot turn away, losing himself in the digressive patterns, which deepen the fabric the way Pollack's best works turn canvases into nebulas. Why has Oxley chosen such a tarp to hide her presentation? And what presentation could possibly require such a large platform?

Fane turns on the graduate student. "Just what the hell is this?"

"It's my lecture," Dr. Oxley says, approaching from behind.

Jill the graduate student practically runs to her. Oxley whispers something to her, and as Jill leaves, Oxley meets Fane at the bottom of the stage, some ten feet from the first row of chairs. The students have put their phones away and observe now, watching the two professors and the mystery display with equal interest.

"So you're going to deliver the self-delivering lecture after all, Dr. Oxley?"

Her expression remains neutral, but Fane detects the underlying anxiety and anger readily enough.

"With some reluctance. I'd intended to deliver today's presentation next week, but I'm afraid I'm too upset at the moment. I've spent the morning struggling to find out...information about the fight."

"About Gordon, you mean?"

Her blush answers him before her words. "Yes. Please excuse me."

She goes on stage and addresses the class, first apologizing for the delay, then making mention of today's *distinguished guest*. It's almost impossible to tell Oxley's true mood, and Fane smiles with approval.

"Last week in our discussion of 'The Yellow Wallpaper,' most of you expressed skepticism about the narrator's condition—confined to a bed for almost twenty-four hours a day with nothing to look at but some moldy old wall—"

Fane clears his throat with an alarming staccato.

"—paper," Oxley says, firing a rapid smile at him. "I happen to believe that the best literary experiences can be lived, and today—for the next forty minutes—we're going to live out the conditions of the story. Books away, pens down, cell phones off if they're not already. No talking—no whispering. No sleeping. No *blinking*. You are all to stare at this representational wallpaper for the remainder of the class."

The students murmur as Oxley leaves the stage. Fane glares at her as she approaches him. In a low voice, he says, "This is *outrageous*."

"Nevertheless, this is my lecture. Grade it as you will."

Fane now realizes the students are focused on their exchange. He looks at Oxley. Young, foolish, silly. This is stunt education, magic show frivolity. Like the collage on the office door, his own work, his own *fame*, has spawned this sort of garbage—*somehow*. He leans in close. "Even if I humor you—and I assure you, I find no humor here—this puts us in a difficult position. Should I go back to Dr. Monroe and tell him you think an inanimate object outclasses your ability to instruct students on a rather tedious short story? Hardly a note of confidence. Is that what you want?"

Her anger flashes. "I am a dedicated scholar, Dr. Fane."

"You have potential. But of the three of us, only the wallpaper and I have been in print."

The class snickers at this and he whirls on them. But what can he do? He's gone too far already. His outrage is genuine but inappropriate in front of students. Whispering an apology, he walks back several rows and sits down.

"I'm going to dim the lights now," Oxley says. "Start staring."

A minute later, the lights drop until the room is enveloped in darkness with just the wallpaper illuminated. Then Oxley does the most surprising thing and sits down beside him, and they start to whisper, neither looking at the other.

"If you'd humor me," she says, "I'd like you to do as my students and look at the wallpaper too."

He shakes his head. "I meant what I said about you having potential. That's what makes this whole stunt all the more excruciating."

"It's not a stunt. Literature can be a lived experience. Its joys, its horrors—"

"Oh, they'll be horrors when you read my evaluation. Westervelt wants its professors to be great scholars but even better teachers. What can be said about an instructor who asks her students to stare at something for an hour? Of course, what can be said for a teacher who pursues a relationship with a student?"

More than a minute passes before she answers. "It says I'm human."

Fane stares at the wallpaper. Minutes pass in deepening silence. The garish patterns pull at his attention, lulling him to drowsiness and jolting him awake at the same time. He slides down a little in his chair. It feels good to let his right leg stretch out a little.

Yes, human. Be kind to her. Is it so hard?

Fane manages to turn his head just a little until Oxley is in his peripheral vision. Even in the dark her hair seems fiery. It's so easy to comprehend Gordon's attraction.

He allows himself a murmur: "What did you find out—about the fight?"

A moment passes as if she didn't hear him. Then she says, "Both are in the hospital. There's going to be charges."

"Charges?"

Her low voice quavers. "First or second degree assault, I heard."

"Prison?"

She doesn't answer. Perhaps she doesn't know, or perhaps the truth is too large for her mouth.

Gordon will be locked away.

Staring at the wallpaper, he takes his cane and runs it along the length of his right leg. He can almost feel the bone tapering, losing its marrow. Incarceration could mean safety. He imagines Gordon behind bars, tucked away, his location always certain. He reaches into his jacket pocket and touches the black rock.

"An intriguing idea."

Now Oxley's head turns. There's some excitement in her voice as she whispers to him. "I've always wanted to do this. It took me forever to find the sample. Ever since I read the story in high school, I wanted to experience that wallpaper. Imagine being forced to stare at it for hours—*days*."

Fane sighs. Too loud, he says, "Reading the story is sufficiently mimetic. The tedious writing is prison enough."

The nearest student a few rows head stifle a laugh. Fane wonders how much of their conversation has been overhead. He resolves to say no more.

Prison enough, he thinks.

Why can't they just talk? Probably Oxley feels as grim and conflicted as he, and certainly they are imagining the same thing, a world with Gordon incarcerated. It will be so much worse for her. Surely they are sleeping together. Oxley, he thinks, how cold our nights will be when our sun is gone. He does not need to turn his head to see her through Gordon's eyes. Gordon must have fallen first for the splash of freckles on her pale face—two on her nose, six—no, five—on the cusp of her left cheek, and three across her upper lip like Orion's Belt. He imagines Gordon kissing her. They've no doubt kissed often. Did they kiss this morning? Might her lips still have some trace of Gordon to discover if he, Fane, kissed them now?

"Dr. Oxley," he whispers, leaning closer.

Her "Yes?" is followed fast by "Gah!" as she discovers his face so shockingly close.

A student says, "*Are they making out?*" loud enough for everyone to hear.

Fane and Oxley go rigid in their seats. Oxley orders the class to be quiet. She brushes back a lock of her red hair, so darkly glorious even in this muted light. Fane thinks of Gordon seeing Oxley's hair like this late at night. He imagines their bedroom, smells its fragrances, feels its temperature. The wallpaper becomes part of the room, and Fane becomes a figure watching them through its veil: Oxley, removing her bra, walks toward a naked Gordon who rests propped on pillows, hands clasped behind the back of his head. How Fane wants to join them, but he cannot escape the wallpaper. To the lovers in this conjured bedroom, he must resemble—if they notice him at all—a bleak stain on the wall suggestive of a face, with eyes that peak through those gilt crests hoping to achieve a more salacious view.

Fane must get to them. He must be with them and break free of the wallpaper. He twists his body and claws at the barrier, his will pouring forth, until he hears a fantastic tearing sound, and then he falls forward, landing on his hands and knees, there in the room. But when he rises now, Oxley and Gordon are gone, and without them, the room is like the wallpaper, another prison. He goes to the bed, sweeping his arms along the indentations made by Gordon's body, zealous for any trace heat. Then he weeps.

"No need to cry, mate."

He looks up to find George standing in front of him, aged fifteen or so, wearing his winter pea coat. The room is different. It has become the hotel room they shared in New York. He hears the muted sound of the traffic in the street below and glances over his shoulder toward the window. Oh, if only he could really relive that one crucial day—and night.

He scrambles off the bed.

"You sure made me mad," George says. "Sorry I left you here. I just had to go walking and sort things out in my head."

Fane cannot keep the tremor from his voice. "I remember."

"Do you remember what happens next? I've been in the cave so long, I'm not sure if I do."

Fane wipes tears from his eyes and nods. As George steps toward him, Fane collapses onto his knees, arms at his sides, palms supinated. He feels like praying. Praying to George, who looks down at him.

"Isn't it amazing, mate? So many people talk about how they find light in their darkest hour. But it's more often the reverse, isn't it? Your brightest moment hides an eclipse. You do something great and think it's the best day of your life. Then the sun sets and stays down a long, long time."

"That's not like you, George. You always saw the bright side."

"Until my best friend in the world showed me the dark."

Fane screams. A murmur sweeps through the room and he hears footsteps. Someone rushes to turn on the lights and Fane finds himself standing and brandishing the cane. There seem to be so many more students present than before. As heads turn toward him, the questioning, challenging stares multiply.

"Dr. Fane? Are you okay?"

He hears: *"Adam, mate, the dark is coming. I read it in the book you left for me. I've been preparing. Come see."*

"I'll see," he says. A thick wall of mucus builds in his throat, turning his words into a garble.

The students stare at him in disbelief. Vaguely he hears Oxley imploring them all to leave.

Fane sees Oxley's hand wave in front of his eyes. He blinks once, a languid, sleepy gesture, and then her hand is gone, replaced by total darkness. George is up ahead calling to him. Fane takes a step and teeters. His right leg hurts so badly.

Suddenly George's face appears right in front of him, a mix of light and shadow. Almost evil. Fane jerks back. Just as quickly, the light and the face are gone. The flashlight. Only now does he remember it. George put the flashlight under his chin and turned it on. It had scared Fane, a long time ago.

"I'm coming, George! I know where you're going!"

He gropes his way through the darkness, edging along the cave wall until he finds the gap. He begins to push himself up it. His adult body shouldn't be able to navigate the passage, but he makes it.

He climbs into a room lit by a small fire.

There was never a fire before. It never occurred to either of them about making a fire or carrying the fuel needed to start one in the cave. They just had their flashlights. But the fire is here now and so is George. The handsome fifteen-year-old boy is gone, yet unmistakably present in the bald, alienated features of the creature that crouches by the flames. As Fane approaches, George looks at him, his expression severe and sour. Contempt shows in George's cataract-encrusted eyes.

"Came to visit me at last, eh, mate?"

The fire explodes, driving him out of the room with his hands over his eyes. He falls back into the main cave and rolls onto his back. "George...George..."

His body jostles. He hears the hum of a motor. Opening his eyes, he sees a white ceiling and a man sitting beside him. The man's crisp white shirt has a sewn emblem on its short sleeves—a caduceus.

Then Fane knows he's in an ambulance.

A face hovers over him. It's not George. He's young, hardly older than Gordon. A fleck of spit strikes Fane's nose as the man questions him. Does he know where he is? Is he aware of what's happened to him? Fane nods. Whenever in doubt, just nod.

"Can you tell me your name?"

"George."

The paramedic's eyebrows knit. Fane sees him consult a clipboard. He realizes he has straps across his chest and legs. His jacket has been removed. He cranes his neck and says, "Where is it?"

"Where's what?"

"My jacket. There's a rock inside of it. I need to hold onto it."

He starts struggling against the straps. He feels his efforts making the entire ambulance shake.

"I'm not sure about your jacket, but I'll see what I can find out for you. Now, can you tell me your name again?"

"Why?"

"You said it was George. Is that your middle name? Do you go by that?"

"No." He shakes his head, fighting a haze. Have they injected him with something? "Fane. My name is Adam Fane."

"Why did you say George? Is that a brother, perhaps? Someone we should call?"

"Did I really say George? Well I suppose it is my name, much in the manner that Athena adopted the name of Pallas."

"*Excuse me?*"

Fane smiles. It's wonderful to make a confession so literal no one understands it to be a confession.

The paramedic—*Todd*, his badge reads—pats Fane's wrist and looks toward the cabin, his body swaying with the ambulance. He has a lean, muscular neck with a bobbing Adam's apple, just a little prickly from a rushed shave. Fane becomes fixated on it, wishing he could make a bold declaration. Male beauty is a perfection that should be spoken plainly, not rendered in deceits of symbolism. Let cigars always be cigars and bring forth the penis to speak for itself. As indeed Fane's has, for he feels his rare erection aching and obvious in his pants.

"*Todd*," Fane says, drawing the man's attention down to him. "How long have I been out?"

"Oh, I'd say—" and then Todd's eyes sees Fane's excitement. Something passes behind his eyes, a contempt Fane has noticed in his own eyes in the mirror. The question goes unanswered. Todd's kindness is gone. He says, "We're going to get you checked out real soon, Professor Fane. Just close your eyes. Better not to talk at all, you know?"

Fane knows. Close your eyes. Yes, he thinks, that is good advice. Sleep is coming. With any luck, George will come with it.

"Be a sport, Fane. Here, I'll belt you on your weak side. That will let me do all the heavy lifting."

Resting against the base of a tree in the forest that borders Fowler, his private school, fourteen-year-old Adam Fane stares harder into his poetry anthology on a brilliant Sunday afternoon so at odds with his bitterness. Is George going to be sweet to him again and act like he never saw Thompson and Dooley knee him in the back and smear his face into the walkway, chanting, "Hindu, Hindu, Hindu"? That was yesterday. Fane touches the mole near the center of his forehead. That's what Dooley had been trying to attack, but Fane managed to turn his head so that his cheek bore the entire assault. There are tiny blood scabs there.

George puts both ends of the belt together and cracks it.

"Come on, Adam," he says. His voice is soft and perfect except when he's being sarcastic. "Let's do this."

The boys at Fowler call each other by their last name—a cynical, militant tradition that Fane considers exceptionally cold, even dehumanizing. At the same time, he doesn't want to be on a first name basis with the likes of Thompson and Dooley. With any of them, really, except for George. He can't bear to call George by his last name, despite the smirks it earns him in the halls and in the dorm. George always uses everyone's last name. But when they are alone together he says *Adam*.

"You can't leave me in this situation, mate. It's a three-legged race, after all."

Fane drills his gaze at a poem called "The Giaour" but has no comprehension. His face flushes hot with coy power, for here is George seeking to make amends. They both know George failed to protect him yesterday. They both also know that George's reparations must require a little more coaxing—a little more *seduction*, perhaps—than the simple effort George is making so far. He reads—

To love the softest hearts are prone,
But such can ne'er be all his own

—and waits.

George closes in until his shadow covers the page. The sun's too bright even through the leaves for any shadow to censor the words. Now he smiles up at George, unable to help himself. George is his only friend at Fowler—but such a friend! His great pal, his St. George with curly brown hair and blue eyes, a small nose and small, lobeless ears. He stands slightly above average height but his combination of features collectively scream *puppy*. Fane however has found him to be a ferocious watchdog in temperament and loyalty.

Except for yesterday.

As he gazes at George, he thinks not for the first time how the differences in their looks will one day threaten their friendship. He knows by instinct and experience that equality exists only between those of roughly equal beauty. Attractiveness is the true class system. His father, for instance, once complained he was denied a promotion because he wasn't six feet tall. When Fane imagines George as an adult, he sees a Senator or President. He has the kind of beauty reserved for someone destined to rule. And so he distrusted George's hand the first time it reached down to help him from the snow. That was in January, at the start of the winter term. Thompson and Dooley had tripped him for the hundredth time. He sprawled face first in the snow but did not move, knowing the assault wasn't done until the boys had stepped on him. As he prepared for their weight, Fane instead heard an *umph*. He looked up just as Thompson landed beside him on the ground, blood running like bright fire from his nose. Dooley went down a few seconds later, arms and legs spread wide, as if he'd decided to make an improbable snow angel. When Fane dared turn over, he found the real thing holding out his hand.

He took it—for weren't Thompson and Dooley lying there bleeding enough proof of benevolence? Until yesterday, Dooley and Thompson never again bullied Fane in George's presence. He still doesn't understand why George let them. They knocked him down, stepped on him and then *stood* on him until their weight made him cry out. When he tried to call for George he had no air. If George only knew what was happening, Thompson and Dooley would both have broken bones. But George didn't know, couldn't know, and Fane realized he was doomed to writhe beneath their feet, pinned to the ground. Then they stepped off him, and Fane hoped they were done. He lifted his head and squinted. How could this be? There was George leaning against the side of the library, hands in his pockets, coolly watching the assault. Fane coughed and sputtered, causing the bullies to laugh. They bent down and rubbed his cheek against the walkway. Fane's gaze remained locked on George the entire time, staring at him as if in a dream.

Was George angry with him? Was he reminding Fane of his place? He hardly needed a reminder. George's friendship was like manna. Before George, Fane's life had known nothing but starving days.

George gives the belt another crack, stirring Fane from reflection. "Get your head out of the book and out of your ass and let's go destroy the competition, mate!"

Fane thrills every time George says *mate*. He picked up the word in England or Australia—his family had just returned from being overseas in December, something to do with his father's work. The word cemented George's affections, and he speaks it with a certain gentleness and warmth, as if the syllable was created for his voice alone. *Mate*. The usage is not American, yet it seems to Fane more American, more democratic, than *friend*. Now when George says, "Mate," Fane's mind sings out—*We two boys forever clinging!* He has only recently discovered Whitman's work on page 270 of his poetry anthology. It is the first time a poem has ever suggested the possibility of a bright future.

"You don't want me as a partner," Fane says. "I'll slow you down. We won't win—not against Dooley and Thompson. With me anchored to you, you won't even beat Hollingsworth and Carter."

He stares at the book as he speaks. His head feels heavy with shame, cowardice, and something else that he cannot name.

Why did George let them hurt him?

Fane bends closer to the open pages. If he looks at George now, he'll scream the question loud enough to shake the leaves off the trees. But Fane knows his voice isn't much. Worse, when he's angry his tone becomes squeaky. He can't shout a petal off a daisy. And so the venomous question must stay inside him. As he realizes this, the book becomes heavy in his lap, as if all the poets' ghosts are jumping up and down to say that poisonous questions find their antidote in the asking. But that's the safety of paper talking. In the real world Fane knows asking questions does more harm than good. Certain things must be kept bottled up—a great many things, actually.

For the first time in their friendship, Fane wishes George would just go away. But George isn't leaving, and if Fane asked him to leave it would just make him more determined to stay. So Fane begins turning pages, paying no attention to the text.

"If you're trying to prove how fast you can read, Adam, I'm not interested. I want to know how fast you can run."

"Not very, I can assure you," Fane says into the book. His voice drops to a whisper.

"'I cahn ahhshure yew,'" George says. "Fane the Aristocrat. Should I ask milord's butler if he'll run in your place, since milord can't be bothered?"

"Which one of us has lived in London?"

George snickers at this comeback. Then he sighs. Fane listens. A little bit of George is visible in his peripheral vision. He hears the scuffle of George's shoes and dares to glance up to verify George is leaving. He receives a thrill when his saint instead sits down beside him, almost nuzzling bodily against him, their backs sharing the same large oak tree.

"Read me some of that business."

"*What?*"

"If you won't do what I want to do, I might as well do what you want. You want to read, so read. Just don't be selfish with it."

"I—I *couldn't*—"

"What do you mean? We all have to read out loud in class."

"But you wouldn't want to hear—"

"Oh, now we know the truth," George says, jabbing two fingers into Fane's ribs.

Fane squirms, starting to laugh. "What truth? Quit—quit—what?"

George relents. "You think I'm too stupid to understand what you're reading? Fine then."

He reaches for the book only to have Fane pull it away by reflex.

"If you won't read it out loud, I will," George says. "Just to show you how smart I am."

Fane rubs his ribcage. Then he smiles, feeling daring. "It's not your intelligence, George. It's just we both know pronunciation isn't your strong suit."

George's eyes open wide. He grins. "I'll be damned. Fane with a wisecrack!"

"You sound like you talk with your mouth full of marbles, that's all."

George shakes his head. "Fane the *Funnyman*! Who knew?"

"I bet whenever your family eats supper with you, they call it the Feast of the Enunciation."

Fane exalts in this joke until he sees George's furrowing eyebrows. Then he knows that once again he's said something that makes him seem weird. Stammering to explain, Fane only gets out a few words before George gives him a playful shove and says, "Adam Fane the Big Tickle."

Fane's poetry book lands spine up, pages spread against the dirt. He lands on his back, hooting as George wrestles him and begins playing his ribcage like some crazed pianist. Fane writhes, half-laughing, half-screaming, trying to fight back but entranced with the *nearness* of George and his open-mouthed grin.

"Pluh-please—"

"What's that? What are you saying, Adam? I can't understand you, mate."

"Can't take any—"

George tickles him harder. "Just talk slowly, Adam. You want to write it out, that's okay. I'm here for you. I'll wait."

Fane's flailing hand finds the poetry book, grabs it and swings it at George's head. The anthology's too heavy to be wielded by one arm, and George dodges it easily. He takes no offense; he even seems to think the counterattack hilarious. But Fane sees the book's arc directed by his own arm and suddenly no amount of tickling can reach him. He lets go of it, perplexed by his actions, numbed at the idea that he could have hurt George. In his imagination, he sees the book slamming into George's face and knocking out teeth. The vision is too much. He starts to cry.

This must shock George, who stops at once. His whole demeanor changes. "Adam, did I hurt you? Mate, I'm sorry."

"I'm fine." He wipes his eyes, sitting up. He's okay. George is okay. He looks at the book and vows not to touch it again. It's poisonous to him now that he tried to use it as a weapon against his best and only friend.

"You feel better now, mate? Got whatever it is all out of your system?"

He takes George's hand. *Why didn't he offer his hand yesterday? Why didn't he help?* Fane pushes the questions away. He has no right to ask them now. Not after what just happened.

Fane kicks the book with his left foot, startling George.

"Why did you do that?"

"It's a stupid book."

"No, it isn't. I like it."

He claps a hand on Fane's shoulder. Fane answers with a shy smile that freezes on his face as he notices the sweat and grime on George's throat. The desire it provokes mystifies and clarifies. Is he becoming some sort of vampire, tempted by the fine details of skin with its little golden hairs? He wants to feel George's pulse every place it beats.

George settles back against the oak tree, his legs stretched out before him. The anthology rests a few feet off his right loafer. They both wear their Fowler uniforms, minus their school jackets—khaki pants, long-sleeve blue Oxford shirts with the Fowler crest sewn over the left breast. On Sundays the boys can wear whatever they want but Fane almost always keeps to the uniform. George wears his today because the rest of his clothes are being laundered. Their present clothes need a good wash as well. He and George look like they've tumbled down a hill together, a fact he points out with some concern.

"We'll say we fell in the race."

But the race has already started. The forest makes Fowler seem a hundred miles away, but in reality it's less than two hundred yards. Fane hears his classmates shouting and cheering from the track and field area. Some are even still calling out George's name. Fane glances at George, who shows no reaction. He seems amiable and serene, completely passive except for his feet, which wag back and forth in a frenzy.

Fane bows his head. He's costing George so much fun. George wanted to be in the race in the worst way. Why is he wasting his time with pouting? He should be on the field, tied to George's calf, demonstrating his loyalty. But he feared the humiliation of having his right leg collapse under the strain. That's why he snuck into the woods. Someone had gotten the idea to recreate the chariot scene from *Ben Hur* as a three-legged race. That meant boys crashing into each other, trying to trip each other up, trying to break arms and legs. George's enthusiasm for the event shot up several notches as a result, but George seems unbreakable while Fane knows he is an easy target. After all, his right ankle is not much wider than his wrist.

"I'm sorry, George."

"Sorry about what, mate?"

"Making you miss the race. Maybe it's not too late for you to pair up with someone else."

George gets up. "I was going to break Dooley's ankles. Crash right into him—like this." George rushes against Fane like he means to throw him to the ground with his hip. But at the last moment his momentum slows, turning the impact into a gentle, playful nudge. He slings an arm around Fane's shoulder. "We'll never know how much damage we might have done. So you've got to make it up to me. *Read.*"

Fane looks at the book on the ground. Reading to George, alone? The idea dictates a new rhythm for his heart.

"Okay," he says. "Take a seat."

George picks up the anthology and hands it to him. The book feels strange to him now, but only for a moment. George is making everything okay.

"I expect to be entertained," George says, looking very pleased as he returns to sitting by the tree. He stretches out his legs.

"I'm not sure I can guarantee that. What should I read?"

"Pick anything. Chances are I won't understand it anyway."

"Yes, you will. You know you will."

George shifts his weight against the tree trunk, bringing one hand up against his chin. Fane hears a small pop as his friend adjusts some bone in his body. The Fowler boys are constantly lectured about the evils of cracking their joints. There are sermons about manners and prophecies of arthritis. But who cares what happens to you in your forties?

"I'm *waiting.*"

Fane turns the pages. There must be a thousand poems at his fingertips. How many has he read in the last year? Not many. When he finds a poem he likes he prefers to reread it over and over rather than experience a new one. Poems attract him when they make him feel hollow inside and older. Inevitably his tastes run toward poems about death and loneliness. He cannot help himself: such poems only reflect reality as he knows it. Even the happier, lighter verse he favors seems limned with a dark knowledge, a wry sense of laughing before gloom. But he does not want to read such things to George. George is the opposite of all that.

"God aw-*mighty*, Fane. The crowd's going to throw rotten fruit at the screen if this movie doesn't start soon."

Fane's page turning increases. He scans titles without quite seeing them. His initial embarrassment is over, replaced with an intense obsession to find the perfect poem. Only one comes to mind: *We two boys together clinging.* But no, he will not—he *dare* not—read those lines to George. But there must be another poem *like it.* As his search intensifies, he knows he'll never consciously find what he seeks. His fingers must dowse for it. A poem will call out to them, a poem whose lines are elevated above the rest on the page, raised like Braille. But George's impatience, a joke at first, is becoming real. What can he do?

His right index finger suddenly stops and taps. Fane smiles at George, who just scratches his head.

"It was hard to make a selection, George. I think I've read nearly every poem in this anthology, you know."

"The Apache call you Worm-Who-Dwells-In-Books."

"I wanted to find something very special."

George draws his legs up to his chest and rests his forehead on his kneecaps. He looked bored. "Just get on with it, Fane."

Fane grimaces. "I just wanted to show you how seriously I take this."

"It's all about you, I know," George says, smiling. "Are you sure your last name isn't *vain*? Maybe you just misheard it—"

"Oh, shut up." Fane ducks his head shyly to examine the poem his finger picked. He starts to read—

> *No specious splendour of this stone*
> *Endears it to my memory ever;*
> *With lustre only once it shone,*
> *And blushes modest as the giver.*

George snickers. "Oh, this is just *precious*."

Nervousness like an electric jolt makes his lower lip tremble. Not a promising start, to be sure. The poem's by Byron. Fane's read Byron before and liked him, but he's never encountered a poem like this. Has his finger betrayed him? He continues—

> *Some, who can sneer at friendship's ties,*
> *Have, for my weakness, oft reprov'd me;*
> *Yet still the simple gift I prize,*
> *For I am sure, the giver lov'd me.*
> *He offer'd it with downcast look,*
> *As if fearful that I might refuse it;*
> *I told him, when the gift I took,*
> *My only fear should be, to lose it.*

Fane casts a quick glance at George, whose expression is unreadable. Inwardly, Fane groans. Why didn't he just read one of Shakespeare's sonnets instead? *Shall I compare thee to a summer's day?* He has done so constantly in fact, since the winter afternoon when George picked him up out of the snow.

George remains quiet, causing Fane great anxiety. His blue eyes are squinting a little and his body makes a slight rocking with his knees drawn up. "Who wrote that, mate?"

"Lord Byron."

"I think I like him."

Fane goes wide-eyed. "I do too!"

"It gives me an idea. How about I give you something to seal our friendship?"

"But you don't have to do that. I..." *love you.*

The book drops to the ground.

George stands up. "What was the gift again?"

"What?"

"In the poem."

Fane bends for the anthology, brushes off dirt and finds the poem again. Rereading it, he shrugs. "I think it was a stone."

"A rock? Well, that's easy enough. Doesn't cost anything either."

George looks about, kicking at the dirt here and there. Several rocks are picked up, examined, and rejected. Fane just stands there, his pulse increasing by the moment, at first amused by George's joke but quickly eager for his choice.

"You know, I think *stone* in this sense means a diamond, George."

Casting aside another rock, George says, "Yeah, well, you give those to girlfriends, not mates." Fane blushes automatically.

George disappears behind some trees. Then he exclaims, "I found it!"

He jogs over to Fane with a rock a little larger than his hand. It looks like a handful of perfect darkness. "Look at this Adam. It's so strange."

He takes a step toward George and a stab of pain shoots up his right leg, hobbling him. George puts his arm around Fane's shoulder. "You okay, mate?"

"I think so."

He steadies himself and nods. George grins and holds up the rock. "Think we should ask Mr. Preston about it?"

"Maybe. But I think it's a piece of hard coal."

"Yeah?" George tosses the rock in the air and catches it. Then he presses it against Fane's chest. "Looks like you got your diamond after all. Hope you're willing to wait for it."

Fane cradles it against his chest. How will he get it into the dormitory without someone asking about it? How will he keep it safe? At Fowler, cherished possessions get swiped if left unprotected. Just now Fane feels the need to guard this rock with his life.

George punches him lightly on the arm. "Mates?"

"Always," Fane says. "But I've got nothing for you. Let me find a rock—"

"You can read to me—right here, every Sunday. I think I can stomach one poem a week. Maybe even two. That's better than a rock."

Fane nods. The arrangement and the gift exceed all expectations. He'd let Dooley and Thompson grind his face into the concrete a hundred Saturdays if it meant a hundred Sundays like this followed it.

"You want to walk back with me?"

Every part of him does. But experience tells him to stay put, and even George nods in unspoken agreement. "I'll stay here and find another poem for next week. Something good."

"Then I'll see you for supper, Adam." George disappears through the trees and back to Fowler, back to the other boys who even now still call out his name.

CHAPTER THREE

They walk the shoreline with Byron between Shelley and the water. Not too far ahead, but outpacing them by the second, are Polidori, Mary and Claire; they appear as figures in a painting whose artist has no sense of scale, seeming too small for the environs and the distance. Polidori's boisterous voice, which must be deafening in the ladies' ears, reaches them above a whisper. His lecture on the end of death has expanded to include a tale about a mysterious work by America's Dr. Franklin—

"These writings, believed to have been lost or suppressed by the Directory, but studied thoroughly by Napoleon, detail further experimentations with the reviving effects of lightning following the inquest against Anton Mesmer."

This conversation seems too large for what they all are, lost and ignorant fools with no subtle knowledge of anything. Soon the distance between them is so great even Polidori's voice becomes inaudible.

"Everything is receding here," Byron says. Light. Sound. Warmth. Ada.

Shelley stops. "You *did* have a vision, didn't you?"

Shelley is a man who shows everything in the color of his face. He can go from ghostly white to rose red in moments. Byron loves this. It is like reading a book whose author never lies. Right now Shelley is both electrified and afraid.

"If you're so eager to know, Shelley, perhaps you should put yourself in similar jeopardy."

Shelley blanches. Byron laughs.

"You really are religious, aren't you, dear Shelley? Or rather, you *want* to be; you desire God's existence more than anything. Do you want me to say that I saw the face of the Almighty and heard His voice calling to me? Do you want me to say that I saw Hell?"

Shelley swallows. His voice comes very faint and stuttering. "Did you see Hell?"

Close enough, Byron thinks, and almost tells everything. But at the last moment he recovers himself.

"I'm not of the visionary company, Shelley. I'm not Wordsworth or Coleridge. I am Lord Byron, an exile in Switzerland—poet of a foreign lake."

They give a mutual glance to Lake Leman again and resume their walk. Already the pain in his right foot exceeds his usual tolerance, but Byron pushes on. He'll need help very soon.

"I assure you I am an atheist, Byron."

"Atheists are far more obsessed about God than any Christian, Hebrew or Moslem. Tell me what bothers you about the lake. Do you think God walks upon its waters? Was this the original Deep?"

Now Shelley scoffs. "I certainly don't believe—"

Byron smiles. "Is the lake haunted, then? Does it contain a ghost or phantasm? Perhaps it is the Lady of the Lake's long absent Mister?"

"Pray he doesn't discover how you tarried with his wife today."

"Shelley," Byron says. Shelley won't do, he thinks. They *do* need nicknames. He asks Shelley.

"I've never had one, Byron. You?"

"Several. But we must come up with one for you. It must be appropriately biblical, to highlight your religious devotion. Give me time to meditate."

Shelley laughs.

Byron claps his right hand on Shelley's shoulder. He feels the man's muscles relax and is glad. Shelley strikes him as a permanently coiled spring—or serpent, perhaps. But Byron sees nothing of the snake in his new friend. If anything, he seems a hopelessly naïve Adam, which makes Byron wonder about his pretty little Eve in the distance. What, exactly, is Pollydolly whispering into her ear?

Shelley says, "You won't tell me what you really saw, will you?"

"One day, perhaps, when we are better friends."

"I should like that."

"Then let us begin now. Will you help me?"

"How?"

"I need a crutch if I'm to hobble any further without shoes."

Byron studies Shelley's face. There's a moment when the younger man *almost* glances down at Byron's foot. But his stare remains firm and level.

"Lean on me," Shelley says.

Byron nods in gratitude and gathers the blanket about him.

"I think the world is very fine today, Shelley, even if the sun is cold."

"I think the world is never fine."

"No? Then perhaps I don't like you as much as I thought. Or perhaps I like you more."

He leans against Shelley for support and they follow the shoreline, Shelley still queerly fixated by the water, Byron's gaze straying more often toward the sun, its mysterious impotence all the more striking when compared to the warmth of human friendship.

Amazing, he thinks, the things people leave out in the privacy of their own rooms.

It was Shiloh who inadvertently gave him the idea to snoop. They were all sitting by the fire, trying to amuse themselves, when Shelley recounted another rumor he'd heard about Byron in the village earlier that day: *LB is buying any available chickens he can find and is sacrificing them at midnight in dedication to the Satanic arts.*

"Rubbish," Byron answered. "I never practice the Satanic arts later than six in the evening."

They all laughed, and Shelley said that money was to be made in recording all of these absurd rumors. Byron knew it was true. More to the point, he doubted the fact had escaped Murray, his London publisher, who was surely desirous for any accounting of his celebrated poet's exile. What better source could he have than one of Byron's inner circle? He studied their faces. Could it be Claire? Shiloh himself? No, no, if Murray *had* entreated a spy in Byron's company, what superior choice was there than his personal physician?

The next morning, while Pollydolly was again out with the ladies, Byron entered his quarters and found a journal on the writing desk. There's a high price to pay in hunting for gossip about himself: he must endure Polidori's exceedingly mundane observations, the writing so pained and forced it cannot conceivably be recorded for his own pleasure. Yes, it must be that Murray—or someone—has put him up to it. Byron's sense of betrayal at the thought of such spying was outweighed by the absurd entertainment of the dull surveillance itself. In the ensuing forty-eight hours since the peeping, Byron has taken to describing everything he sees to himself in a parody of Polidori's banality.

Sandwiches and fresh fruits consumed near the water's edge, ten boats sailing in the distance, two gray clouds in the sky that hearken more rain. Sun in the sky but no heat on the ground. Shelley acting dire again about the Lake but L.B.'s company has no doubt done him much good. Polidori still hopeless. Mary interesting. Claire remains a bitch.

Byron stretches out in his lawn chair and looks at what remains of the food. He's touched none of it, mindful of corpulence. He has a headache: a result of his restricted diet, perhaps, or of the tedious, enduring cold weather. He suspects it is neither. The unfathomed idea in his head, the poem that still refuses the paper, is growing like an Athena. He thinks of Ada. How big has she become?

He looks further off to his right and finds Shelley near the shoreline, staring out at the water with the gaze of a hopeless prophet. His obsession with Lake Leman has started to wear thin even with Mary, who lounges with Claire on a blanket several yards to Byron's left. Sometimes they laugh to themselves over some private confidence. Byron tenses. Women secure their diaries much better than do certain doctors. And what does Claire's diary say about last night? For she came to him in the dark, rowing herself across the lake at one in the morning, to sneak into his villa and then his chamber, a woman possessed of missionary zeal—and lo! How she *evangelized* him! Kneeling at his feet, she said, "The waters are not as tumultuous as my feelings for you—and I sense you are not as cold as the waters!"

Does her diary record the icy sweat that was on his brow, the paleness of his flesh, or the terror that was overtaking him even as she opened the door? Does she know how close to a breakdown he was last night from a feeling of *such pressure* in his head? Byron touches his forehead. The pain now is nothing like last night. Claire interrupted a birth. He was about to jam his writing pen into his ear and bleed the stubborn idea onto paper when she appeared in his doorway. Fear of death and the night's solitary desperation raised his white flag to her.

Hours later he woke in a pitch black room, his clubfoot feeling swollen huge, burning beneath the bedclothes. Claire slept beside him undisturbed and he contemplated her body's outline with regret. Then she rolled over, and he found himself staring at a different face, pale and hideous. He gasped, hand over his mouth. This was the face from Lake Leman, the face that met him even as he drowned. But somehow it was aged, an older, wearier face. The black eyes simply stared at him, the irises touched by a pitiless orange glow. In them, he found the vision again, and saw houses and shops engulfed in fire, every city and cemetery aflame. Tree limb and mammal bone alike fed the egalitarian pyres.

He shrieked and swiped at Claire, hoping to knock the hideous mask off her face. She woke terrified, sobbing, scampering in the dark. But none the worse for wear now, it seems. Oh what does her diary record?

"Albe," Mary says, noticing his attentions, "have you come up with a nickname for Shelley yet? I was thinking, perhaps, of *Gazer*."

Claire presses her lips together in an impish smile and looks between the men.

In truth, Byron has already decided. His thoughts, dwelling on a world consumed by fire, landed on the name this morning. "Shiloh," he says.

"Shiloh," Mary says softly, with a laugh. "What does it mean, Albe?"

He starts to answer when he hears the heartbeat coming from the waters again. His attention and his eyesight snap to Lake Leman—and Shelley.

"The name," he says, finding it difficult to talk, "appertains...appertains to the Second Coming."

Does no one else hear this sound but I? Byron thinks.

Shelley is either transfixed or trying very hard to give the appearance. He's crossed his arms about his chest, his spine straight and rigid. The posture conveys frustration. No, Byron realizes, Shelley does *not* hear the heartbeat. He *wants* to. He *suspects* it's there. The Lake has reminded him that much is hidden, and if Byron can see when he cannot...

"The Second Coming, Albe?" says Claire.

Byron scans further down the waterline for Polidori. But Pollydolly obviously does not hear the heartbeat either. His peek into the doctor's journal has already revealed their vast differences in experiences with Lake Leman. The latest entry, from two days ago, June 3, 1816, was particularly jarring—

Coming back, the sunset, the mountains on one side, a dark mass of outline on the other, trees, houses hardly visible, just distinguishable; a white mist, resting on the hills around, formed the blue into a circular dome bespangled with stars only and lighted by the moon which gilt the lake. The dome of heaven seemed oval. At 10 landed and drank tea. Madness...

He forces himself to say, "Surely you know the reference, Claire. Madame Southcott is not long in her grave."

Pollydolly saw stars? They were in the same boat, rowing across the Lake after a visit with Shelley. Polidori did the work. Byron sat enduring a sudden vision—he thought they crossed a dark void with no stars, no moon, and no signal fire to guide them. Nor was there a white mist or moonlight or any dome of heaven. There was just a terrifying black universe and a heartbeat sounding everywhere that seemed to dictate Polidori's pace. Then, suddenly, they were at the villa's dock and Byron found the world restored.

"Madame Southcott? I do remember!" Claire says to Mary. "She said she was pregnant with the messiah—Shiloh. That's very clever of you, Albe."

Whose heart is it? What blood does it pump?

"Shelley," Mary says, "do come over here and tell us if you like the name Albe has chosen for you... Oh, he is lost in thought. Tell me, Albe, how can..."

Byron struggles to stay in the present and hear Mary's voice over the heartbeat. His mind slips toward darkness and hunger. He touches his stomach, which is burning with acid and demanding fuel.

Claire and Mary laugh at something.

"Can an atheist possibly be the messiah, Albe?"

Byron manages a smile. "What better disguise is there?"

Two boats crisscross far off in the middle of the lake. For a moment their sails seem to commingle and their differing patterns, like the sudden fusion of two clouds, make a pale face that billows with the wind. Byron jumps up, all his weight on his left foot, gaping. As he does, the boats complete their transit, the sails separate and the face is gone.

"Albe, is there something wrong?"

Byron forces himself to sit down. "No," he says.

Claire stands and takes several demure steps toward the remaining food. Byron almost winces when her hand strokes his arm in passing. Taking an apple in hand, she bends her mouth to his ear and says, "Tonight, my Lord, if the waters are calm..."

He jerks back to reproach her and sees the awful face again, fitting like a perfect mask over Claire's. The eyes burn. He kicks convulsively to escape. The chair tilts back. The world goes upside down and black.

The heatbeat is so loud in the dark.

It's my own heart, he thinks.

Has it always been?

Byron opens his eyes expecting fire. Shelley's face hovers near—so gentle, so feminine and fine, framed by falling black hair. *Shiloh.* He lifts his hand to touch the face but freezes in terror. Shelley's face is actually a fragile mask of gray ash. A frothy spit comes from Byron's mouth as he tries to speak. Flecks of it moisten the ash, binding it. As the rest of Shelley's face starts to disintegrate, Byron gets an idea.

Only wetting the ash will give it cohesion.

He reaches up and grabs Shelley by the throat, sending him stumbling back as Byron lurches to his feet. He must act fast to preserve Shelley's head. In the next instant, Byron is dragging him in a headlock almost, toward the lake, begging him to relent as Shelley twists and turns, putting a terrible strain on Byron's clubfoot in his struggle for momentum. Claire and Mary, shrieking, land several feminine slaps on Byron's back, but he winces not from their assault, rather from the frigid water penetrating his boots now. The deformed toes of his right foot curl down. Still he pushes on, reaching waist deep, shoving Shelley's face under the water, holding it there.

"*Lord Byron!*"

Polidori's scolding voice reaches some key core of Byron's consciousness. He looks around in confusion. Why is he standing in the water? He sees Shelley's thrashing and the water splashing up as from the flailing of a hundred arms.

Why is he drowning Shiloh?

Byron releases him and Shelley rises, gasping and sputtering but so terrified of the water that he clings to the very man who brought him here. His cheeks are a deep, burnished red and his hair hangs like strands of dark seaweed from his scalp. He coughs and vomits water, arms flailing as he cries out that he's drowning. Polidori wades out to them and grabs Shelley by the waist, wrestling him away from Byron.

"Pollydolly—" Byron begins.

Polidori slaps his face.

"We must get to shore and strip ourselves before we catch the ague. Though it would be a justice for you to suffer so, Byron!"

It's a slow return, and Byron rubs his face on every step. Reaching the shore, Shelley slumps to the ground with Mary holding him. He seems to be babbling. After a moment of listening, Byron realizes Shelley is laughing.

"A face! I have seen it, Byron! I have seen what you've seen at last!"

"He's insensate," Polidori says. "Help me with his clothes. Claire, get blankets."

But as Mary works at Shelley's clothing, Claire seems determined to do the same for Byron. Byron, woozy, snatches her by the wrist.

"Did you see Polidori strike me?"

Claire nods.

"Is the imprint of his hand still there?"

Her eyes develop a quick glaze of tears. Her head drops, giving Byron his answer.

"Tell me, is it red or white?"

"M'lord?"

"His *mark* upon me."

Her gaze rises to meet his. "Red."

"The mark is as red as your lips, I hope—" he says, snatching her into a kiss. He bends her back so he can look at Shelley on the ground, moaning, with Mary and Pollydolly tugging at his soaked, swaddling breeches. Mary seems to be wrestling with death itself, ferocious. Such pain on her face for love of Shiloh, such pain on Byron's cheek from Polidori's slap, and now this fierce kiss that makes his lips ache. Why? Why kiss her, why encourage this woman he cannot stand? He hears a rapid thudding sound, the noise of more than one beating heart. His, hers—*a third?*

He pulls back. Claire is holding her stomach.

He shoves her aside and turns to stare down at Shelley. As Shelley looks up at him, an intelligence passes between them. Shelley's frustrations are over. He *has* seen.

Or has he?

Shelley breaks into another burst of mad laughter.

"Oh, Shelley, what is it?"

"Mary—I saw—I saw—"

"What did you see?"

"A face in the water that showed me a deluged world. All was water, and millions of people floated upon it, starving beneath a broiling sun."

Water? This is not right. What is Shiloh talking about?

"Dr. Polidori," Mary says, fighting tears, "what is wrong with him? What is he talking about?"

Polidori finally gets Shelley's right trousers leg off. "It is a natural hallucination to have in reaction to almost drowning." He gives Byron an icy glance.

Shelley pushes himself into a sitting position. His soaked limbs tremble and he talks, even breathes, through chattering teeth. Mary holds him, petting his head, raking excess water from his hair.

"A baptism is coming for the world."

Now Shelley fights Polidori and stands without shame at being undressed. He spins around, calling for his infant son. "Mary, bring William from his nurse. We must teach the child to swim—quickly!"

He turns to Byron.

"I *have seen*, Byron! We are alike."

Byron shakes his head. You are wrong, Shiloh, he thinks. What game is this? The world will end in darkness and fire—not water.

Mary looks between them, and then shakes her own head in complete horror, casting a pleading look at Polidori who is now shedding his own clothes. The doctor's answering pose, hands on hips, would seem authoritative were he not half-naked. "We must get them inside at once. It is odd for men accustomed to England's climate, but the cooler air has sparked a temporary madness in both of them. A fire will restore sanity."

Byron laughs.

"A face!" Shelley says.

Shelley takes two steps toward the shoreline, walking almost as awkwardly as Byron. Polidori seizes him.

"*You must go inside*," the doctor says, his tone close to seething. "Mary, Claire, come here."

The women hurry to the doctor's aid. Byron finds himself looking at all of them and past them until he, like Shelley, stares at Lake Leman.

I am possessed, he thinks. Shelley, are you possessed?

He hears the heartbeat. Shelley turns to him. "Byron, did you not hear me? I have had a vision. I too."

Byron shakes his head again.

"We must go sailing," Shelley says. "Byron, don't you agree?"

Mary gapes at her husband.

"*Sailing?*"

"On the water?" Polidori says.

"That is the traditional habitat for boats, Pollydo—ri. Now go and tell Fletcher to ready the boat."

"Why must *I* go and tell Lord Byron's *servant* anything?"

Now Byron speaks. "Because you too are in my employment—like Fletcher, only a good deal less trustworthy."

"I swear, Byron, were you not ill—"

Byron storms over, bad foot and all, and shakes Polidori by his shoulders. "Is this the strength of a sick man?"

"The two of you are out of your minds."

"Then prescribe your other hand for me! Knock me insensate!"

The doctor's eyes flare—yes, flare, they are aflame—and Byron prepares for the strike. Ah, Pollydolly—so easily provoked! He feints just in time to avoid the doctor's roundhouse. A fist in place of a slap? Strong medicine, doctor; strong medicine, indeed! Byron laughs and turns. Something goes wrong. The world tumbles and barrel rolls. His damned foot, treacherous as always with his weight! Polidori lumbers toward him, pressing his advantage. Mary and Claire plead with him. This causes Byron to gnash his teeth. He won't be saved by women! Polidori's shadow falls across him. The doctor is hunching over, drawing back his fist to pummel Byron into the dirt. Byron sees it coming at his face like a comet.

Shelley intercedes, gripping the doctor by his right shoulder. Polidori loses his balances a moment, then pivots and strikes Shelley in the mouth. Mary screams, running to Shelley as he falls. Claire joins them.

Polidori bares his teeth at Byron.

"I'll kill you both—that will cure you! I challenge you to a duel!"

"*What?*" Mary says.

Polidori's theatrics increase. His fingers spread wide and he lifts his arms as if he means to become Atlas. He rants about them all—their lives of privilege and their bouts of insanity, as if they all cherish madness as an indulgence, a way to pass idle hours.

"Polidori," Byron says quietly, getting to his feet, "*enough.*"

The young doctor just smirks. "You who indulge in everything to gross extravagance have the gall to tell me *enough*? Do you know the definition of the word, Byron?"

"If not I shall write a new one to suit my purposes. Besides, what argument could you have with Shelley?"

"The same argument I have with you. The same argument any sane man has with insanity—it must be confronted and destroyed. *Guns!* We need guns." Polidori turns and yells toward the villa. "Fletcher! Bring us your master's pistols so I may kill these fools!"

Fletcher steps onto the balcony, his bewilderment obvious as he stares down at a soaking wet Byron, a trousers-less Shelley, a raving doctor and two frightened women.

"Milord?"

"Don't 'milord' me, Fletcher. Bring me guns."

"Did the doctor say guns?"

Polidori steps forward. "Guns! Byron sleeps with guns—I've seen them."

This is quite true and not even the half of it. Stilettos and daggers are also to be found near his mattress. His sleeping chambers have always been an armory. They keep things—*safer*.

"I need them there to protect me from you, Polidori, considering your bedside manner." He rubs his face where the doctor struck him.

Shelley begins to laugh, hale and hearty. His laughter is like a gentle flame that spreads among them. It catches first in Claire, then Mary. Byron turns to them and begins to laugh as well. What have they been fighting about? What darkness has dwelled among them? The explosion of anger and confusion, warming them far more than the sun, is gone—or so it seems. Polidori has not joined in the laughter. His rage has not receded. He looks about with an expression that is almost despairing, and as the group's laughter increases he forces himself to join. Poor Polldolly, Byron thinks, watching the doctor rush to catch up with their merriment, awkward and unsure. Will he record this moment in his journal? Will he attempt an analysis?

Suddenly Byron groans from a stab of pain in the center of his forehead. What is stirring in his brain? He glances at Shelley. Did he really have a vision? Byron cannot believe it. He cannot believe Lake Leman would offer two men such opposing images of the world's end—unless the vision accounts not for the world but for an individual fate. And what is the world but a collection of separate births and deaths, private miseries and a few moments of shared joy? Byron looks about at this little circle of friends joined together by mysterious laughter. The ladies go to the doctor. Mary thanks him for bringing Shelley back to land. Polidori and Shelley shake hands. No one even mentions Byron. No one asks why he hauled Shelley into the water. Byron looks toward the balcony and dismisses Fletcher with the barest nod. He turns back to the group expecting all to be well. A superficial amnesia rules them—all, that is, but Claire. Byron finds her standing apart from the group, a world unto herself, touching her lips with her left hand and her stomach with the right.

And a heartbeat sounds again from the vast lake waters.

"I'll kill myself!" Near the boat dock where they prepare to depart, Polidori is shaking a small vial in his right fist and raving. "I'm going to kill myself, Byron, if you won't let me come with you!"

Byron clucks his tongue. "Your expressed wish to shoot Shelley and myself a mere four days ago makes you a disquieting shipmate. I must decline."

"But this is Prussic acid I'm about to swallow—*conceive you?*"

"Women conceive. Men comprehend—*doctor.*"

"How dare you exclude me after all I've—"

Byron smiles. "This particular outing, Polidori, is for my guest."

"Am I not also a guest?"

"No. Do you see Fletcher or my other paid servants joining us? This is a private excursion. I wish to make amends to Shelley."

"For attempting to drown him—also a mere four days ago? So noble of you—my lord! And all the more reason I should accompany you. How can I possibly wade out to the rescue if you're miles away?"

Byron's lips press together. "There'll be no repeat of that incident, I can assure you."

Will there?

Polidori's voice drops to a seething whisper. "You're both crazed. I need to accompany you as the only sane man around."

"Shelley is quite sane."

"You say this even after *his* incident—a mere *three* days ago?"

Byron stares, wondering if Pollydolly is being insolent or delicate. Without question the doctor knows how to spare as well as spear one's feelings. Very quickly, he decides on insolence. This makes Byron less remorseful about denigrating him.

"You stand here threatening suicide and call yourself sane? My dear Polly—"

Shelley's hand falls on Byron's right shoulder from behind. His touch has the annoying weight of moral reproach but Byron is too disciplined to flinch. When Shelley's fingers squeeze, the sentiment seems to be: *enough. Relent.* There's a moment when Byron almost jerks the hand away with a desire to break its fingers for daring to come between him and a domestic. But his disposition relaxes with Shelley's grip. Shelley would not watch anyone kick a dog, even one that had threatened to bite him. Shelley is my friend, Byron thinks, and Polidori finds himself friendless. That is what brings him here to rant and wave his vial of fluid around. The simplest desire of man is for companionship with a clean face, a mutual desire without desiring—like two candles placed side-by-side whose flames burn constant on eternal wicks, mirror images that never commingle as they stand firm against a mutual darkness. The hell of loneliness is to be a solitary candle in the night.

But this is what we are, he thinks. With sudden vividness he can picture the world peopled by men and women carved from candle wax, each with a single lock of burning hair. Old age eventually brings all to expire in a pool of their own melt, their flame snuffed. But sometimes a man like Shelley comes along, a man who cannot pass an extinguished fellow without hoping he might burn a little longer. Such a man will stop, bow his head and lend his spark to the fallen. Can such an act have meaning though, when a wider ken reveals that all of these candle people live too close to the shores of a perilous dark sea, and towering black tidal waves are rushing in to extinguish all fires?

By reflex he looks past the boat and his gaze sweeps across Lake Leman. Shelley suddenly steps to his side and also looks.

"*What?*" Polidori says. The poison makes the slightest sloshing noise as he motions with the bottle. "What in *hell* are you finding out there? I see nothing but water and ships and the distant glaciers."

Byron says, slowly, "If that is all you sense, then be glad you have no imagination, Polidori."

"I have imagination!"

Shelley extends a hand. "Then why extinguish it? Here, John—give me the bottle."

Byron's attention snaps back to see it pass into Shelley's palm. With his pale face, Shelley looks like he's already taken a draught.

Byron watches with discomfiture as Shelley pockets the vial. He thinks of Shelley's *incident*. Perhaps, he thinks, it would be best if I kept the bottle. But then he considers his own incident and realizes they are both equal candidates to quaff the poison in a fit of madness. Stepping onto the boat, he wonders if perhaps Polidori should not be banned from the day's voyage. After all, the doctor is probably the only one among them merely faking insanity.

But no: he must not come. Whatever must be spoken between Byron and Shelley regarding their perceptions of Lake Leman will not happen if the doctor is with them. Today's task is for poets alone. Still, echoes of Shelley's compassion remain in him. Even Pollydolly does not deserve to be left on the dock without hope.

"We shall talk at length over a good bottle of port upon our return from Chillon, Polidori."

"But what should I do until then?"

Byron shrugs. "Sex with Claire might speed the hours along."

Polidori scowls at this as Byron steps onto the boat. Shelley, wobbly-kneed, follows and is quick to sit. As Byron unties the mooring, Polidori bends close to say, "I did not really wish to shoot either of you."

"A pity," Byron says, giving a last conciliatory smile. "The best conversations are held with those who wish you dead. I find myself holding a good conversation with almost every man I meet."

He shoves off. Their boat has a single mast and could not seat three people anyway. The cramped conditions torture his foot but he ignores the pain, happy to be captain and crew as he raises sail. When the billowing canvas captures the strong breeze and bloats, Byron feels satisfied. If the sun has disappointed them this summer, at least the wind has lost none of its potency. *The Venti have overmatched Apollo.*

They gain speed. Byron's stomach feels an even greater acceleration. As he steers, he imagines himself a traveler daring unknown seas, racing toward towers of ice and crystal, far from a daughter who will only know of him by the reports of his adventures. With such cool and wet weather to abet his imagination, Byron needs only minutes to be convinced by this fantasy. He will sail further and further away with his face turned from England. He will burn in the sky as a receding sun. He will extinguish himself in isolation but he will have blazed for Ada.

When he snaps back to the present, he notices Shelley tugging his jacket tighter about his chest with his right hand. Water spray bejewels his dark hair and lends him a sylvan appearance, like a fawn covered with morning dew. With his tucked hand and hunched shoulders, he seems like something new unfolding in the world. Byron laughs and reaches forward to rifle his fingers through Shiloh's hair. Beaded water flies off him like a dog shaking itself.

"Not as wet as when I dunked you last week," he says.

It is an invitation to speak. Byron leans forward, expecting Shelley to say—*what?* Whatever cannot be said in the company of the others. In drawing rooms by the fire or lounging near the shoreline, their circle is content to banter about philosophy and literature, life and death. The summer's cold sunlight has kept them all so huddled together there are only snippets of privacy. Byron needs this time alone with Shelley to understand what his friend sees and hears in the waters of Lake Leman. They are, he thinks, a key to comprehending his own hallucinations.

Why is Shiloh quiet? Does he not feel the same sense that, in this freezing summer, though time is sluggish, something immense is slipping fast away? He no longer believes, as he did before, that this immensity, this urge inside him is a *poem* that eludes him. It may be that, but it is also something more.

Absently he turns to look across the vast lake.

What is this despair that stalks me? Is it a living thing, with a face to leer at me from the darkness and a heartbeat to sound from the water?

"You're Cassius," Shelley says.

Byron turns his head. "What?"

"You think too much," he says, smiling.

Byron understands at once. Aye, he thinks, I am Cassius. I think too much, even starve myself into a lean and hungry look. But am I dangerous? In London they said I was mad, bad and dangerous to know. But who truly knows me?

He thinks of Ada.

His daughter will never know him.

Shelley pulls out Polidori's bottle of acid. It is pretty and blue as a jewel against his white skin. He holds it up and peers through it at Byron's face.

"Death has so many guises."

"Perhaps you mean *faces*, Shiloh. We see so many faces, don't we?"

"Or merely many masks. Bounty is a mask for emptiness, order a mask for anarchy, love a mask for loneliness. But really there is only one face, isn't there? Death."

Shelley has said all of this while continuing to peer at Byron through the glass and its deadly contents as if it were a monocle. The tumultuous water sends them both up and down, up and down as if on a seesaw.

"We can quit talking in parables, Shiloh. We can be frank now."

"Was I talking in parables? How Christ-like."

Shelley slips the bottle back into his jacket.

"Is that what you see in Lake Leman—death?"

"I don't know what I see."

Byron glances fast out at the water, as if afraid he's steering the boat into a rock. But the lake is open for miles.

"Then will you tell me what you saw the other night?"

Byron has seldom experienced a question he regretted asking, but Shelley's reaction makes him wish he had not spoken. But is the question unfair? Shelley's *incident*, as Polidori termed it, was so bizarre that Byron felt an immediate connection between it and the hallucinations that have plagued him. Three nights ago, as the entire company took turns reading ghost stories and poems by the fireplace in Byron's drawing room, Shelley began to point at Mary and scream.

"*Eyes...oh so horrible, looking out at me! Eyes!*"

Shelley's outburst happened as Byron was reciting some private and unpublished verses given to him by Coleridge. He'd glanced about to see the poem's influence on his company. In a room that seemed made darker by the fire, their faces were all half-shadowed and all turned toward Byron—except Shelley, who was staring at Mary with a gaze of growing intensity. His pale face resembled an eclipsing moon as Byron continued.

> *Her silken robe and inner vest*
> *Dropped to her feet, and full in view*
> *Behold! her bosom and half her side,*
> *Hideous, deformed, and pale of hue—*

That was when Shelley screamed.

"*Mary has eyes where her nipples should be! The eyes are looking at me!*"

In the next moment he was charging toward the fireplace as if he meant to roast himself. Polidori reacted fast, catching and spinning Shelley toward the divan, then dousing his head with water before administering his favorite prescription—a hard slap to the check.

"It is okay to tell me everything, Shiloh. Alone, we can be conferential and talk as friends and fellow poets."

"You say that! You want me to share my vision, Byron, when you have not shared yours."

They verge on the first true quarrel of their friendship. The argument's birth is delayed, however, by the sudden rise of the spires of the Castle of Chillon. Byron turns and gapes as their boat trims toward it. The mighty fortress comes into view like the world's first and last standing structure, its stone construction demonstrating an ancient precision that seems beyond the craft of man. Built right at the shore, the castle's battlements seem to rise straight from the water as a tower of coral might from the sea.

"What vision has either of us had that compares to this?"

Byron brings the boat around and they discover a dock. There they disembark and both men, exchanging a quick look, become like giddy school boys in a race. Shelley sprints ahead, challenging Byron to keep up. But Byron's clubfoot cannot manage the steps that well and he can only limp after Shiloh, who now waits for him. Together they roam through courtyards and walkways, passing under arches both great and narrow.

They are alone and not alone: the castle has several caretakers who note Byron's presence with a bow, as if they expected his arrival; but they do not speak, and Byron cannot help but think that somehow two existences are happening at the same time. The people of the past and present can see each other, he imagines. See but not hear and certainly not touch. The sensation leaves him breathless and disturbed, so that he must halt and lean against one of the hewn walls. The chill of the rock against his right cheek jolts him away and he shouts at the sun. "Why? Why are you fading? Goddamn you!" His cry carries far across the lake and Byron is stunned by his own outburst. Now all is quiet and cold.

"Byron?"

His shoulders sag. He lowers his head and says, "You want to know my vision, Shiloh? Here is what I've seen."

He confesses everything: the heartbeat, the visage that accosted him in the water when he almost drowned, the vision of the world burning. But as the details come out, he realizes he cannot say *everything*. He omits the scene of Shelley and Mary throwing their own child into the fire in order to coax out a few more minutes of light and warmth. That is too dark: too dark altogether, especially as Shelley's grip on his arm tightens by the moment and he punctuates the details of Byron's vision with "As have I" and "I, too, saw it."

Shelley's face appears wild to him as it threatens to smother Byron's view. Their noses are almost touching. His breath, tinged with chives and tea, is almost a flavor in Byron's mouth. He pushes back. He knows he must push back, because something is happening. There is fire. Out on the horizon, Lake Leman is blazing. The boats have sails of flame. On the far shore the houses are burning. From here they seem only little torches.

Byron trembles, averting his eyes. "Tell me you see it too, Shiloh."

Shelley turns. After a moment's silence, he says, "I do, Byron. I see it too."

There is a doubt, though, in Byron's mind. Something about Shelley's reluctance to speak makes him wonder. He stores it away as everything is stored and hoarded in a poet's mind.

Then he risks another look. The fire is everywhere now. The caretakers of the past are walking by them and, a few feet away, strangely dressed men kneel around a fire that's fueled by a kindling he cannot understand. It felt before as if two existences were happening simultaneously, the past and the present. Now he believes a third has joined them. These fires burn on some future Earth.

Crying out, he casts Shelley away and races off, a ludicrous act in his hobbling steps. There's a door to his right. He tries it, finds it unlocked. It opens to an immense, descending darkness. He stares a moment, fearful, but a glance back at the fiery lake decides him. Down he goes. Shiloh calls to him and then follows, and they enter an all-encompassing night.

Byron stumbles at the landing, surprised by the last step, and falls on his face. The totality of the darkness is such that he must use his fingers to guarantee that his eyes are open.

"Shiloh, where are you?"

"Here."

His voice comes from everywhere. Byron feels for the wall and pulls himself up. He knows what this place is now. Shelley surely knows too. The Castle of Chillon is famous for one man imprisoned here, Francois Bonivard, and this must be the dungeon where he was kept. There is a soft, incessant sound, not a heartbeat but more like a tapping. Listening, Byron realizes they have descended below the water line. It is the noise of Lake Leman lapping against the stone.

"Shiloh—"

"How long, Byron?"

"What?"

"How long could a man live trapped in a room without light? What would become of his mind? How long would sanity last, so subjugated?"

Shelley asks no more of him, but Byron continues the questions in his mind, his face turning up in the dark toward the world above, the world as it was in the past, as it is in the present, as it will be in the future. The gap of centuries has closed and time has collapsed upon itself. Eternal darkness. Cold void. What bestial things might a man consigned to such a place due just to gain the brief reprieve of a matchstick's flare? Byron shudders, knowing he already has the answer, in a vision of parents feeding their children to the flame.

He stands suddenly in the lit, cold world of the present. Lake Leman, not burning, is crystalline blue beneath the gray sky. The sun is out, but the sunlight feels like rain against his skin. Shelley stands beside him, one hand on his right shoulder. Byron has no memory of leaving the dungeon, but the searing ache in his foot tells him it was a rapid, harried ascent.

Shelley holds the bottle of poison in his free hand. It has a cork stopper that Shelley's tapering fingers wedge off. He raises the rim to his lips and waits for Byron's reaction.

"Are you suddenly Pollydolly?" says Byron, wearied.

Shelley's lips quiver. The bottle shakes in his hand. It seems like any motion might accidentally slosh the acid across his tongue. Despite this, Byron's muscles relax. He exhales air that seems to have been locked inside him since birth. Perhaps it is his soul escaping.

"Drink it, Shelley. I care not."

"No?"

He turns to the vastness of Lake Leman. He *does* care, but why should he, when he has seen the world burning and feels the inexorable truth of it, the predetermination of the darkness and the fire? If Shelley wants his night to come a little sooner, then so be it. The sun sets on all things, and every man's night lasts forever. The only difference in people is the length and quality of their day.

He turns at the sound of glass breaking. Shelley has hurled the vial against the stone wall, smashing it to bits. The poison leaves a dark, wet stain on the rock that the weak sunlight is in no hurry to dry.

"I have lied to you, Byron."

"How?"

Shelley laughs. "You don't feign ignorance well, Byron."

"So you truly know nothing of my visions? You haven't shared in them at all? You hear no heartbeat upon the waters. You see the sun continuing in the sky and no horror of darkness."

Shelley nods.

"And you cannot bear it. I cannot bear to see the vision, you cannot bear to *not* see it. Staring at the water as hard as you can, praying to whatever God is out there for some glimpse, and all you see is the water. All you hear is the water. And so you have lied."

"Yes, I have lied."

"Was it for friendship's sake?"

Shelley nods.

"Was it because you wish for a universe ruled by God?"

"No."

"That is good," Byron says. "For what I've seen is surely a world without the Divine. If anything, I've glimpsed nothing but Hell."

"Visions of hell will do if visions are few." Shelley's tone is petulant as he continues. "What poet can I be without vision?"

"Were you also lying when you claimed to see the eyes in Mary's—"

Shelley's expression is answer enough. A man accustomed to fits of loneliness and melancholy, the fit Byron suffers from now is unique. He had thought it both terrible and comforting to have camaraderie in the vision, to at least know the madness was not his alone. But it *is* his alone and even worse, it is not madness. The world's doom is coming and he feels responsible for it in ways he cannot pinpoint except in the sorrows of Shelley's face.

"Come, Shiloh. Let us sail. We've been prisoners of Chillon long enough."

He takes five steps past Shelley, hoping to goad him into following, and turns to see Shelley dashing toward the wall, putting his face against the rock to lap at the acid, lick it right off the stone. With a shout, Byron lunges at him, his foot close to snapping, and drives them both to the ground. They lie there stunned, arms about each other, their embrace furious, desperate and ill-met. They both cry, and when the caretakers of Chillon come, they pass by without comment. Perhaps they have seen many people in such a state. Perhaps so many people cry at Chillon that all their tears flow toward Lake Leman and increase it. Perhaps its waters consist of nothing but tears.

For how else could it be so haunted?

Byron brings the wick of a new tallow candle to the dying flame of the old. The transfer of fire seems like a handshake, and he smiles without mirth: if only the transaction of words between mind and paper could be as seamless.

He remembers the rumors of him practicing Satanic arts at midnight. It is already half past and cold rain falls against the windowpanes, lulling him toward sleep and gloom. A writer experiencing his sort of block might very well sacrifice a chicken or two. The candlelight keeps his attention and reminds him of life. The reminder is hardly celebratory though. Life, like fire, is parasitic, riding the back of any host. Life is vicious and cruel. To live is to participate in that viciousness, that cruelty. Life claws itself from night to sunrise because it purposes itself for light, but its ways are darkness. Writing is like life, as the idea born of the midnight mind claws toward daylight paper. Writing is like fire, incinerating the mind, escaping the ash heap on paper wings.

The top page of a stack of paper before him has a single line that has taken him hours to compose: *This dream of mine is not wholly a dream.*

Much is wrong about the line besides the weakness of the meter. It is flat, a bald statement rather than skillful verse. Nevertheless the words provoke him to chills and he feels on the edge of a breakthrough.

The hallucinations have been very bad the last two days. Yesterday he did not even get out of bed. He did not eat or drink, partook of nothing but the draughts Polidori poured down his throat. He was not awake nor was he asleep. He saw his bedroom, but he saw it burning. He saw Pollydolly's face hovering over him with his hair on fire. He looked at the ceiling and through it, to the black sky.

There was no sun.

For the first time he can remember, he hates being awake late at night. The outer dark has too much portent. Byron worries it will not go away in the morning.

I am alone, he thinks.

He sighs in the long, bleak hour. The summer has turned lonesome now that his time is frittered away in the dull companionship of Polidori. Even Claire would be a better companion. But she, Shelley and Mary are on a two-week tour of the glaciers beyond Lake Leman. Byron closes his eyes and pictures Shiloh's face. All he can see is the stricken expression Shelley had at Chillon when he confessed his fraud. Only now does Byron comprehend how much his loneliness deepened at that moment. Some burdens, like his separation from Ada, must be born alone, but his hallucinations are another thing. There was succor in believing Shelley experienced the same terrors. There was hope in thinking his fine, philosophical mind could explain them. There was the simple desire, above all, to be convinced of his sanity.

Being alone with Polidori has only heightened his anxieties. The doctor, with his contacts in medicine and science, has been relaying reports of strange observations about the sun—flares and dark blotches seen at the Royal Greenwich Observatory and verified by astronomers at Highbury, Leiden and Paris. Polidori explains how this dreary summer is a worldwide phenomenon. He says the witch doctors of primitive tribes believe the sun is dying like a stricken god. Fears of a sparse fall harvest dominate the talk in taverns and inns. Across Europe there are concerns about famine. In London there is concern for falling commodities.

"It is all most curious," Polidori keeps saying, in a sort of boyish glee that commixes poorly with Byron's mood. For Polidori's news convinces him that his near-death vision beneath Lake Leman was a glimpse of times to come. He cannot bear the doctor's amused tone when he has dwelt under a future sky, a sky with an extinguished sun and a departed moon; a sky that reigns above motionless seas and burning cities where families huddle near their smoldering homes, parent and child studying each other's faces in the flicker because, as ghastly as the flames make them, even that final image is some boon against the lording dark.

It is impossible. It is a dream.

But not all a dream.

It is impossible, he writes, *to have a dream,* and on the line below completes the thought: *That is not all a dream.*

Tonight he refuses to sleep. He is sick of going to bed and falling into a nightmare world where wood and babes are equal kindling. He is done with waking paralyzed and fearful. Damnit, even those words do not describe his affliction. *Pregnancy* is the nearer term. He can *feel* the idea in his head, kicking on the other side of the bone. It is alive; it has a heartbeat that sounds both from his skull and from the waters of Lake Leman. Pollydolly can dose him with every medicine known to man. Byron now realizes that only pen and paper can perform the caesarean section he requires.

The patter of rain on the window makes another play for his eyelids, and for a moment he nods off. In that instant, he is transported to a vast black sea where he floats, one man among millions. The sea bursts into flame as if made of oil, boils skin and muscle from the bone. The true horror, however, is that every other soul in the shared sea laughs, because the light of their destruction stabs at the darkness.

Byron jolts up in his chair, hand over his mouth. Did he scream? He listens to the quiet house. The last two nights he has screamed loud enough to wake everyone. Polidori has even moved his rooms closer to Byron's in anticipation.

But not tonight, Byron thinks, clutching himself and gazing at the candle-light until an afterimage burns bright behind his eyelids, a torch against his inner dark.

Tonight will be the breaking point—of bone, of rock, of time itself. He rises from the desk and touches his forehead. It hurts. He feels a vibration in his skull, as if his brain is turning. The vague idea that's possessed him since the first day he sat by the waters of Lake Leman has grown. It is not endemic to his mind; it was planted there. He has been impregnated. He used to think that could happen, when he was a boy. He thought men or women could give birth at any time. On certain nights and early mornings of his childhood, the family nurse would sneak into his room and play tricks with his person. Some tricks he enjoyed, while others left him feeling as he feels now—abused, robbed, frightened that something within him is vastly changed.

Byron groans as the pain increases. He grits his teeth against a shriek. The agony has a peculiar ebb and flow, like a pulse. No, it *is* a pulse. His fingertips, pressed to his forehead, detect it in the bone.

The hour of birth, the hour of trepanning is at hand.

He hears the heartbeat from outside, summoning him into the rain, the night. He limps across the room, toward the French doors of the balcony, fascinated by the little beads of rain on the glass, glittering in the low light like pasted pearls.

He stops at the doors. All doors are forbidden fruit. All doors open Pandora's box. That's why women are such dangerous lovers—because they have three doors. But he has never been a man to leave a door unopened, never stopped before a closed door to deliberate on whether it's been shut for a good reason. He knows that lingering now is just pretense: he *will* open the door, even if to do so causes the world's end. And somehow, at this moment, Byron senses the world's fate does hang on the twisting of a knob.

He opens the door and steps outside.

The rain assaults him, soaking his hair and robe as he stands a minute, shivering, peering out across the lake. The moon hangs low and distant over the water.

Then he realizes just what it is he sees. It is the face of a man, disembodied, hovering, staring straight at him. Black, soulless eyes confront Byron from a white, stricken face. The mouth is oval and tilted to the left in a frozen cry of anguish. It is a death mask.

He's seen it before. Subtract the toll of years, and it is the very face that swam around him as he drowned. Add a few of those years back, and it is the face he saw imposed over Claire's on the night she seduced and stayed with him. What monster is this? What demon? He cannot imagine, but he feels sorrow rather than fear. It is the mask of a man who died without hope.

Perhaps it is even his future self, though Byron thinks otherwise. Up close, he can see a curious dark spot high on the forehead, like the seed of a Cyclopean eye that never matured. No, this is someone else's face.

"My God," Byron says, two words that ghost from his mouth in the cold. Then his lungs freeze up. The face is coming toward him, its transit marked by the sound of the heartbeat. The pulse is accelerating and getting louder.

With a mute groan, Byron urges his paralyzed body to obey, bears down on his clubfoot until hot agony spurs submission. He gropes behind him, the safe side of the door suddenly a desire greater than any he has ever known. He retreats, never taking his gaze from the pursuing face.

He backs into the room, locks the French doors, and retreats further, trailing water across the floor. His left hip strikes the writing desk, almost upsets the candle as he falls into the chair. For a moment Byron is insensible to everything. Then he perceives a change in the candle's flame. It lengthens and turns a hideous blue-black, like hellfire. New pain gives his voice some substance that he uses in an agonized cry as he clutches his head.

The bone is cracking.

Gasping, he looks teary-eyed across the room at the French doors. The face hovers there, staring at him through the glass.

"Ada," says Byron. "God, Ada, this must be how you'll see me—an ancient man with anguish for features!"

Pain whips him again, forcing a genuine scream. Vaguely he wonders why Polidori has not come. Then a force seizes him, so powerful he can almost feel its physical grip on his shoulders. Thrown forward, he slams his forehead into the desk. The sharp report dizzies him and he dry heaves, saved from vomit by an empty stomach. He strikes his head again, so hard the desk threatens to buckle. The candlestick falls with its flame to his hair, and his soaked scalp snuffs the flame.

Byron's hands find the pen and paper in the dark. He looks to the French doors and locks eyes with the awful apparition that just gazes through the glass at him. As he does, his right hand blazes into action. His left holds the paper down.

I had a dream, which was not all a dream.
The bright sun was extinguish'd, and the stars
Did wander darkling in the eternal space.

Tears flow down his face. His wrist strains from exertion—his hand is outpacing his breath. *It's happening.* He is giving birth. His midwife accosts him from the balcony.

Most amazingly of all, a little boy's voice emanates from the scratch of the pen, reading the words as they are composed. The voice sounds hurt, haunted and hunted. To hear a sweet and fragile voice speak such despair shocks all of Byron's senses. It is like inhaling into a summer rose and receiving the reek of rotten meat. Like drinking wine and tasting poison. Like kissing a lover's mouth and getting bitten. Though it is a boy's voice, Byron cannot help imagining Ada saying these things, and he has a grim certainty that he will never hear his daughter's real voice.

Even dogs assail'd their masters, all save one,
And he was faithful to a corpse, and kept
The birds and beasts and famish'd men at bay

"Boatswain," Byron says in a whisper, images bursting across his vision and mixing with memory. He sees a dog standing over its dead master, snarling at men who want to burn the corpse for fuel. It looks uncannily like Boatswain, Byron's Newfoundland, the firmest friend he ever had, who died eight years ago from hydrophobia. Even now Byron can see himself kneeling beside the dog as he suffered. He risked being bit and spent hours wiping Boatswain's foaming saliva away with his own hand—the same hand that now grips the pen.

Ships sailorless lay rotting on the sea
And their masts fell down piecemeal: as they dropp'd
They slept on the abyss without a surge—

"God!"

Byron screams for the third time as his composing hand jolts with another burst of speed. The boy's voice also accelerates, becoming a sort of droning buzz. Between the wrist and elbow he feels nothing at all, which makes the explosive pain in the joints and sinews of his hand all the worse. The agony surpasses anything experienced in his clubfoot. As Byron gnashes his teeth against a fourth scream, the pen drops. He gasps in the dark, delirious, skeptical that the writing is finished. But he controls his hand again. The fingers bend arthritically, each joint swollen. He looks down and sees the pen through the darkness, its tip faintly glowing, like metal hot from a forge but cooling. Touching it against the candle by accident, the wick ignites with bright flame.

"Stop," the boy says from the fire. "Please stop him."

A command? A plea?

"Don't go," Byron says in a rush. He winces as his eager breath threatens the tiny flame. "I'll protect you. *Cherish* you."

"Daddy, don't..."

Byron clutches the pen tight to his chest. *Daddy.* That word should always be spoken in faith. The little boy's voice is faithless. Who could the father be? Who would—

He looks to the face outside the room and a different sort of revulsion and understanding seizes him. He falls backwards, overturning his chair and spilling onto the floor. He begins to crawl and stagger toward his bed. At last other sounds stir throughout the villa. Polidori, Fletcher and his other servants are waking, scrambling to his aid. They cannot help him. They cannot help the boy. Byron reaches his mattress. On the nightstand are the very same dueling pistols Polidori wanted to try with Shelley.

He reaches for them but pulls back at the last moment. His right hand, so recently possessed—can he trust it to obey his commands? He decides fast. If the hand turns the pistol against him, the betrayal will mean little. A bullet to the temple might even be a favor considering the horrors he's seen, the horrors he knows are coming. Standing, Byron pivots on his left foot with both guns pointed at the French doors.

He charges, hobbling, the barrels unwavering at the end of his outstretched arms. He reaches the French doors and puts the guns against the glass. The face shows no reaction. Byron fires. The report rocks his hands sideways as the glass shatters and wind and rain invade the room.

The face is gone. Byron staggers toward the place where it had been, only to be driven back by the pelleting rain. Gusting wind snuffs the candle and then Byron hears it rustling the paper. *No!* He lurches toward the desk, certain the wind conspires to carry his writing out to Lake Leman to drown it one syllable at a time.

The door rattles and shakes. Polidori and Fletcher pound on the other side. Their voices beg through the wood. *"For the love of God, Byron! Unlock the door!"*

Byron stumbles and pivots, chasing paper around the room. He catches a page and holds it up, angling for any sliver of light from outside. He sees enough to determine the page is blank and he wads it into a ball. Another page flies past his face and he snatches it. Again blank. Where is the written page?

Where is the prophecy?

He pauses at the thought, stunned by his certainty. What claim does he have to knowing anything? How can one reason anything in the dark? The wind gusts through the windows again and Byron hears the renewed soft minuet of airborne paper. *There.* He closes his eyes and has faith. He lunges, throwing his body along the floor.

"Byron! Byron, speak to us!"

"He is dead! I heard the gunshots!"

So they believe the Mad Lord has killed himself, do they?

"Byron," Polidori says and repeats his favorite cajoling: "For the love of God!"

But there is no God, Byron thinks. Or maybe there is: for the prophecy is in his hand and no gale will tear it free. The paper has a peculiar weight. His sweeping fingers detect the pen's heavy indentions. The pain in his forehead is gone. The idea is finished. It *is* a prophecy. But whose prophet is he? What god has used him? A single thought comes to him, a bit of verse from Wordsworth: *The Child is father of the Man.*

Exhausted, he slumps into the corner with the wind and the rain still blowing in, and clutches the prophecy against his chest just as he held his daughter in the moments following her birth.

Polidori and Fletcher break the lock and enter. There's time before the wind blows out their lamps for Byron to see the shock on their faces. It is gratifying to know that his death shocks them. But it is even more rewarding, when the wind annihilates their light, to startle them by laughing like a fiend in the joined darkness.

CHAPTER FOUR

"You think she'll go for it?"

"I wouldn't even ask. That's *R*, by the way."

"C'mon, Gordo, man—it's fucking freshman comp. She's got to know no one gives a shit. Like it matters if I get an A or a D. Why can't she just fudge a little for her boyfriend's best bud?"

Gordon dribbled the ball a little harder. He still didn't know if John-Mark was joking or not.

"Because she's a great teacher and cares about her students."

"Well she can't care too much about rules if she's dating you."

"I want her to keep dating me too. That's *R*." Gordon shot the ball to John-Mark in a chest pass. They were in Westervelt's small gym alone, shooting around after practice. John-Mark had suggested his own bitter variation of HORSE, which surprised Gordon since it seemed like middle school shit. But as they reached *W-H-O-R-* with John-Mark talking about Amber on every shot, Gordon got queasy. He was only too aware John-Mark had signed up for her freshman comp class, which could actually be taken at any time before graduating. Despising both reading and writing, John-Mark had pushed it off to the start of their junior year. He probably would have left it for his senior year, except he discovered Gordon was dating his potential teacher.

He put his hands on his hips and looked down, waiting for John-Mark's shot. Why did he have to be a dumbass and tell John-Mark what was up? John-Mark of course had passed the info on to the whole team. Knowing those guys, it was a miracle half the squad hadn't tried to sign up for the class under John-Mark's exact assumptions.

They were already a month into the fall semester. He'd assured Amber no one on the team knew they were dating and was relieved to hear John-Mark acted fine, even respectable in class. It figured he was just biding his time, waiting to suggest a little nepotism. Apparently the time was now.

John-Mark was taking forever on his shot. Gordon laced his fingers across the top of his head and watched him shoot and miss. John-Mark couldn't hit for shit outside of the paint and Gordon had put up a twenty-three footer on him. John-Mark's ugly, line-drive shot ricocheted off the front of the rim. Gordon went after it.

"Actually," he said as he got the ball, "I want her to marry me."

John-Mark smirked.

"What?" Gordon said with a laugh.

"*What?*" John-Mark mocked. "All these hot chicks our age, and you go for a teacher."

"She's not even ten years older than us."

"Hey, that's cool. I guess your cradle robs itself."

Gordon laughed again and dribbled, though the unusual edge in John-Mark's tone kept him tense. "I love her. She's passionate. She's going places. You and me will probably be garbage men or something and she'll be chair of the English department at Harvard in five years."

"Gordo, you're whipped hard. I fall asleep in her class every day. She's a pretty sad teacher."

"What's sad is a junior taking freshman comp."

"I just figured—"

"You figured since I'm dating Amber, I could just tell her to give you an A. Since you and I are such great pals, right?"

John-Mark laughed and shook his head. "Give me the ball if you aren't going to shoot it."

Gordon gave the ball an exaggerated bounce and loped toward half-court. Maybe John-Mark was just fucking with him. The simple fact was they *were* best friends despite any number of annoying quirks in John-Mark's personality. Now that he was spending most nights at Amber's instead of their dorm room, he happened to notice those quirks a little better.

He stood on the stylized *W* of the Westervelt logo and turned to the basket.

"I've got *E* for you right here."

"Yeah, bullshit."

He shot—and made it. Son of a bitch! Gordon jumped up and down, whooping it up as John-Mark shook his head and ran his tongue around the inside of his lower lip.

"Luck."

"Love. I'm inspired by love," said Gordon.

"Too bad you couldn't make that prayer you threw up against UCCD last year," John-Mark said, coming toward him.

Gordon didn't care about the taunt. He hooted again and said, "Haters gonna hate, bitch. Now either put that ball in the hoop or go back to blowing coach for playing time."

"I hate blowing coach. All I ever taste is your ass."

He gave John-Mark the ball. They were both laughing. Suddenly Gordon felt very good hanging out with John-Mark like this, and could let the tension between them over Amber slide. Maybe the weirdness that had been between them this semester was about to end. They weren't really roommates anymore except on paper. He lived with Amber now, an arrangement she'd deemed out of the question at first. That had disappointed him, but he'd accepted it, and the summer semester had melted her resistance bit by bit. An occasional overnight stay Friday or Saturday soon became a full weekend, then half a week, then Sunday to Sunday. Her teaching schedule was light and he was only taking two classes. Since the end of June, Gordon had spent less than twenty days in the dorm.

The last two years had taught him to hate campus in the summertime anyway. The departure of all his friends reminded him he was a townie. The dorms were boring with most people gone, and he had to work to find excuses not to go home more often. John-Mark always spent the summer in Los Angeles with his parents. He had a girlfriend down there and last year they did so much stuff together Gordon hadn't got a single message from him the whole summer. This year had been different. About two weeks into the break, John-Mark started calling and texting. A lot. He seemed lonely but afraid to admit it. There were invites to come down and hang out. He'd even suggested a camping trip. It seemed absurd.

Gordon had been too wrapped up in Amber to spare much thought for John-Mark. The handful of times they did talk, the conversations were so short that nothing got said. He found out John-Mark had returned two weeks before the fall semester when he stopped off at the dorm room for a shirt he'd forgotten to move over to Amber's place. Finding him there was kind of a shock. In the past, John-Mark never came back until a day or two before classes started. But there he was, stretched out on his bed, staring at the ceiling. They caught up—a little. John-Mark's depression was obvious, and eventually he told Gordon why. His parents were divorcing. His girl in Los Angeles broke up with him. To top it off, he'd gotten into a car accident—nothing major, but his neck was a little fucked up, and he needed a chiropractor to nail down the problem before practice started. His summer sounded like it had been total hell.

"You should have called me when you got in, man," Gordon had said. "I didn't know."

"Where the fuck have you been? Where's all your shit?"

His internal wrestling over whether to tell John-Mark about Amber lasted less than two minutes. He wished he could say he was caught off-guard by the situation and told John-Mark the truth because he couldn't think of a lie. That was part of it; but another part of him wanted to boast. But more than anything was the fact he felt happy, obnoxiously happy, and he wanted to tell his buddy the reason why. He figured John-Mark would be pumped for him. And he seemed to be for a few minutes. When Gordon said he planned to keep staying at Amber's, though, John-Mark quit smiling and turned away.

This reaction completely threw Gordon, who said, "What's wrong, dude?"

"Nothing."

"I...just figured you'd like having the room to yourself. You might set a record for all the tail it'd let you get."

Gordon wasn't joking. John-Mark had no trouble getting girls. Chicks loved his tall, muscular frame; they were all over him until he opened his mouth and started talking, and even that only weeded out about a quarter of the women willing to go down on him. The bottom line was John-Mark was a player, and Gordon saw moving out as giving him room to play. John-Mark wasn't thinking straight if he didn't see the advantages.

At last he'd said, "Yeah. Thanks for thinking of me, man."

They'd both let it drop after that. John-Mark hadn't even mentioned Amber again until tonight.

"Hey, Gordo," John-Mark said, dribbling the ball. Gordon blinked back to the present and looked up. John-Mark was standing on the *W* and taking aim. "Watch me nail this. You're going to be stunned." He lined up his shot and released...

"*E*," Gordon said as the ball fell a foot shy of the rim. He came over and gave John-Mark's shoulder a light, *better luck next time* pat.

"Prick."

"C'mon, man," he said, walking away. "Nice game of WHORE. Next time just change it to HO. Same outcome in five minutes and we'd be chowing down on some tacos right now. Let's go. I'll buy."

He heard the basketball slam super hard. Gordon turned around, shocked to see John-Mark looking so pissed off.

"Ho's a good name for the taco *you're* munching on."

Gordon walked back to him, tension knotting in the back of his neck. "Dude, what's up? Did I do something?"

"Fuck yeah you did."

"What?"

"You know what. All I'm asking for is a little favor."

"I can't believe you. Listen to yourself."

"I am. I hear everything I say."

"Man, go fuck yourself. It's taken Amber forever to not be completely paranoid about all this. Can you imagine how she'd feel if I was pushing her to give my friend a good grade?"

John-Mark answered with a large, goofy smile. "So don't let her think it. Just be smooth. Talk me up. Tell her how you think I'm a super good writer. If her first reaction is to give me a C, she'll remember all that you've said and doubt her judgment."

Gordon laughed. "What are you, Hannibal Lecter here? You're joking, right?"

"What do you even have in common with her, anyway? I've been trying to figure that out. I mean sure, use her to kennel Shiloh, but—"

"John-Mark, I'm seriously about to kick your ass."

John-Mark raised his hands as if he couldn't imagine how he'd caused an offense. "Don't get me wrong, Shiloh's a cool dog. And I got respect for any animal that can blow itself. Since we can't, we're stuck with dating bitches like Amber."

"Amber's not a bitch.

"Whatever, man," John-Mark said.

Gordon just stood there. What the fuck was happening? It was like their friendship had just suddenly exploded in front of him, and he still didn't know if John-Mark was serious. Not knowing what else to say, he turned to go. He heard John-Mark start to dribble the ball hard.

Without changing, Gordon left the gym and jogged back to Amber's apartment. His legs felt lifeless to him, disconnected from his torso. As he ran, he imagined John-Mark blackmailing Amber. The idea stunned him, and he felt ashamed he could even picture his best friend doing something like that over *anything*, much less something as trivial as a grade in a class he didn't give a damn about. But John-Mark was being...strange. Like getting dumped had activated some buried mean streak in him.

Oh God, he thought, why in the hell did I ever tell him I was dating her?

When he got about half a block from their place, Gordon slowed to a walk. He wished he had Shiloh with him; he seemed to think better with the dog around. Should he even tell Amber what John-Mark wanted? It seemed only fair to warn her, but he also knew she'd go sleepless if he did.

He wasn't sworn to *absolute* secrecy about his relationship, but he knew better than to advertise. Even now, Amber still acted really stiff around him in public. Her smile said *just friends*. At private parties with *her* friends, she was way more revealing, even proprietary, but if they were eating out, say, anywhere near campus, Gordon felt like he was meant to pretend they'd just finished a tutoring session instead of pounding the sheets. When all the guys on the team had gotten back in late August and wanted to party, Gordon hadn't been able to get her to come out. And he found he hated being without her, so he'd started to just stay in and watch a movie with her or whatever. She must have sensed his disappointment, though. It was one thing to fantasize about staying at home with her before they were dating. Now that they were dating, staying in on the weekends, when the entire campus was a party scene, caused Gordon to fidget.

At last Amber relented and they did go out. They went to a bar—where Gordon preened, local celebrity that he was, because he wasn't twenty-one but no one bothered to card him. He toned it down when he saw how annoyed Amber seemed. But it turned out to be anxiety more than annoyance. Some students had recognized her. As soon as that happened, she pushed Gordon away through body language, staring down at her phone and tapping text messages, as if she expected her real date to show up any minute. The whole thing was a disaster.

But the awkwardness was not always one sided. At her friends' parties, he sensed his *jockness* distinctly, and there were passing remarks that made Gordon feel like he'd been snatched from his cradle. Then it was Amber's turn to preen and show off the young stud she'd landed. It was in those moments when his uncertainties peaked, the fears that he knew he, as a guy, shouldn't have: that maybe she only liked him for his looks. Someone like John-Mark would just say, "So?" and enjoy the ride. But to Gordon these moments made the years between them feel greater than they were, a gulf that expanded to include a range of emotional issues—style, self-esteem, and intelligence.

There'd even been a few times when he suddenly thought their romance was doomed. Once, the gloom overtook him in class, another time while he shot hoops alone. A third time, less than a week ago, he'd entered the apartment before she got home and been overcome with a certainty that she wanted to break up. He'd gone into the bathroom, looked the door, sat down on the toilet and actually cried in shock. It was something he'd done more than once after his mother had died, and the pain bubbled out in uncontrollable sobs. Amber was going to be like his high school girlfriend. History was going to repeat itself.

It hadn't happened yet, though. The gloom passed quick, driven away by Amber's easy smiles, and he forgot his doubts as he forgot bad dreams.

Reaching Amber's duplex now, he walked through the door and found Shiloh jumping on him and barking.

"He's been missing daddy, I guess." Amber came out from the second bedroom, which she'd turned into an office. "I've walked him three times and he still has so much energy."

"Yeah, he does," Gordon said, grinning as he bent to let the dog lick at his sweaty face.

As it turned out Amber had some energy of her own and joined him under the water as he took a shower. She was assertive, telling him to face the wall, head under the shower jet. Gordon put his hands against the stall and moaned as she washed him, exploring and working his muscles from head to toe, her fingers and the hot water draining the tension out of him. He was almost asleep on his feet when she finished, and she laughed as he swayed while she dried him. They went straight to the bedroom. He looked at her with a drowsy gaze.

"Maybe I was missing daddy a little, too," she said.

He gave a low chuckle and lay sprawled on his back, loving how the ceiling light made her awesome red hair vibrant even when darkened by dampness. His back arched as she straddled him and took his erection, pushing him to the limit, giving him aspirations, making him want to be great for her. His fatigue seemed to enhance rather than subdue the intensity of his orgasm. It was as if she found one last hidden spark in his body and coaxed it out, leaving him spent and ready for a delicious sleep. Then she pulled the sheet over them and snuggled up against his chest with her left hand on his stomach. Gordon felt like a cold orphan boy suddenly adopted and sheltered. Overjoyed. He didn't think there could be a greater happiness than this, not in this world at least. It was in moments like these with her that he most believed there must be a benevolent God.

He woke with a jolt a few minutes before midnight. Amber had rolled away from him onto her side, but his sudden kick woke her as well. She blinked at him and smiled. The ceiling light was still on. They'd both teased each other about turning it off but neither had had the energy to get up. Gordon still didn't. He put one forearm across his eyes as Amber said, "Someone turn off the sun."

"I'll try to train Shiloh to get the light switch. Maybe he can jump up and paw it."

He heard the dog, who always slept on the floor at his side of the bed, stir a moment. Gordon sighed.

"You okay, honey? Did you have a bad dream?

He smiled. "My mom used to ask me that."

"I think pretty much every mom does. I wonder if I will too, one day."

He rolled over and they looked into each other's eyes.

"I hope so."

"Not so fast," she said with a laugh. "Let's get you graduated and me on a tenure track someplace before I plan to—God, how did your friend John-Mark put it?—have your *shortie?*"

"What?"

"Just something he actually wrote in an assignment. I had to look the word up. Does he actually talk like that when he's not in class, with all that slang?"

"Sometimes."

He was fully awake now and thinking about the end of practice. He looked at Amber and thought about being married to her, having children by her. Was John-Mark a threat to that dream? Was he more of a threat if Gordon didn't tell Amber about what John-Mark had suggested? He swallowed.

"I have to tell you something."

Amber listened, her expression neutral. Her fingers stroked his forearm as if to draw the words from him. He told her everything, about John-Mark's awful summer and the weirdness between them. He finished talking staring straight up at the light. It felt like an interrogation. When he was done, she responded to the threat with a shrug. She'd factored such a possibility into her feelings from the start. Gordon sighed, amazed at her composure. This amazement was soon gone, however, as Amber revealed her true fixation.

"He sounds really possessive to me. Like he has a crush."

"What do you mean?"

Amber propped herself up on her elbow. Her hand caressed his stomach. "You don't think he could be gay?"

Gordon blinked. Then he laughed. A lot.

"I know you haven't read Foucault or Klein or Judith Butler, Gordon, but if you had, you'd know he's showing some classic signs. It's easy to hide identity stress when you're living so close to the object of your affections. Now that you're removed—"

Gordon quit laughing but didn't lose his smile. "All you English majors are *perverts*. It's all about sex for you—I'm not necessarily complaining, mind you."

"I'm just saying it explains the aggression, and why he was calling you so much."

"He didn't call me at all last summer. This was different. He was lonely after he got dumped. *By a girl.*"

"You said he has a lot of girls."

"John-Mark's a player. He'll be okay once he gets a new chick."

"Maybe he doesn't want a chick. Maybe all the chicks are his way of compensating. Did you know Lord Byron once claimed to have slept with 250 women in one year?"

"So? Sounds like a player."

"So Byron was gay. And miserable, conflicted. He's the classic example of a closet case. Historically, lots of gay men have been notorious womanizers."

Gordon fought off a surge of frustration, an urge toward sarcasm. Was Amber messing with him? He didn't know jack shit about Lord Byron, but he was pretty sure he knew everything about John-Mark.

"So you're saying he wants *me*?" He shook his head. "We've lived together for two years. I guarantee you he never made a move."

"Like I said, he wouldn't have to, especially if he was very conflicted. You were close—that was enough."

Now Gordon screwed his face up in an expression of disgust. "Shit, you're saying he *skeeved* on me from across the room, like when I was asleep? Goddamn, Amber."

"Sexuality is a complicated thing. I'm sure you two have gotten drunk together."

"What the hell is that supposed to mean? No amount of beer in the world would make me suck John-Mark's dick."

"Who said anything about you sucking him?"

Gordon's mouth unhinged.

"You drink a lot, you pass out. He makes his move. It happens to women all the time."

"You're scary, Amber. You're saying John-Mark got his rocks off by fondling me in my sleep?"

"Anything's possible."

"No," Gordon said. "Actually, it *isn't.*"

"Imagine him kneeling over you, crying because he's so conflicted. He loves you so much but he can't express it." Her expression became almost distant and Gordon frowned. She was clearly revving up, starting to believe this fantasy that had come out of nowhere. "The desire is so strong; he just wants to *see* how you look. He raises the waistband of your boxers and peeks. But of course seeing isn't enough. It never is. He bends over and brings his lips to your stomach and gives you the softest kiss. Then, afraid he's done too much, he bolts back to his bed to see if you've reacted at all, scared you might be more conscious than you've let on. Imagine—"

Gordon sat up. "Uh, no! No, I really don't want to imagine any of this. I'm done listening to you talk about John-Mark molesting me like it's some beautiful moment. Fuck, how about I invite him over right now so you can watch him ream me?" He pushed himself off the mattress and lunged across the room for the light switch.

He settled back into the dark more confused than ever and still hearing the dreamy wonder in her voice. She'd described John-Mark groping him like she was relaying a vision. That was creepy enough, but there was something else, something *new* and disturbing in his mind and under his skin that also felt like a vision. It felt like an awakening, and he thought it must be the awakening of those insecurities that plagued him. Amber could give herself authority by spouting off names of French and German writers he didn't know. What was he doing with a woman like this, so vastly more intelligent and learned? Was it just his looks that kept him in the game? Hell, maybe she was implying that he and John-Mark were at least compatible *intellectually*. He went to sleep feeling, against his will, the sensation of lips kissing his stomach—

—and woke from a nightmare with his hands punching toward the ceiling and a heavy, pounding panic in his mind. He gasped and looked over at Amber only to find her still asleep. Very slowly, he managed to sit and glance about the dark room. What had happened? Something awful. Within a few moments he was close to crying. Some fear and helplessness suffered in the dream were still in his chest. Was he dreaming about Mom? His body tingled with a sensation like bugs had been crawling on him.

Shiloh rose and poked his cold nose into Gordon's leg. He barely suppressed a scream and rubbed the spot like he was scouring out a stain. Gordon sensed a bark coming and reached down to grip the dog's muzzle.

He looked down at his body, certain someone had been touching him. He scanned about the room, half-expecting an intruder to be lurking in the corner. Cold sweat beaded on his forehead. Go back to sleep, he thought. It was just a dream he couldn't even remember.

But he *could* remember. Lips on his stomach. Fingers caressing his legs and thighs. Disembodied fingers, floating fingers.

He squinted into the darkness, his stomach hollowed out with dread. He remembered a face. A white face, so awful in the gloom. A man's face. And a man's hands. Not John-Mark's. The face was murky to him. He remembered nothing except the whiteness of the skin, and how the eyes were like two black holes.

Gordon took several deep breaths and tried to laugh off the creepy feeling. Maybe he'd gotten abducted by aliens like every other asshole in California.

He eased out of bed and walked to the door. He was starving, having not eaten a thing since practice. He turned in the hallway to look back at Amber. The limited moonlight in the room did not fall on her but he stood there staring anyway. He liked watching her sleep. Since the first night he'd ever spent with a girl, he'd discovered how much he liked waking up before them in the morning, when he could just enjoy looking at the soft architecture of their bodies, the curves that seemed to make them rest naturally on a mattress.

Above all, he enjoyed all the ways a girl's skin could look in the early sunlight. Most of them were tanned. Amber was the palest girl he'd ever dated, and in the morning her skin was like milk that seemed suddenly and marvelously to float carnation petals. The sunlight brought out pinks and golden freckles on her arms and shoulders and breasts. She colored with the sun, came alive in a way that had a dreamy, fairytale quality to it, as if he'd just kissed Sleeping Beauty. *Stupid in love,* he'd think, smiling in contentment as he allowed his fingers to trace her body. Sometimes he'd even lean in close and blow softly along her torso, and the brightening pink of her skin made him feel like he was nurturing and protecting some small and threatened flame responsible for the sun's very existence. Then came the moment when the fire sparked, and her eyes opened, and they stared at each other, both blue-eyed and healthy and happy.

Looking at her in the dark now proved very different. He thought of Amber waking up before him, gazing on his sleeping, helpless form, and groping him. Only it wasn't Amber but someone else. He shuddered. He remembered—months ago—being touched by some gross girl he'd somehow taken to bed. He remembered the feeling of violation, so sharp and unexpected. What if Amber felt that way when he woke her up with his touch? Was he just a pervert, copping feels on sleeping women and calling it love? Did he feel guilty? Gordon turned, woozy, and slouched down the hallway toward the kitchen.

He felt sicker on every step. Reaching the living room, he had to stop and pat down his thighs and stomach, close to screaming with the sense of something crawling on him. He raked his fingernails along his skin and hair, brushing away a disturbance he knew did not exist. He could only stand still so long. Years of sports had drilled the phrase *walk it off* into his mind as a cure for everything, so he forced himself to move, even though the crawling sensation intensified right away. It felt like walking naked through a forest, breaking thousands of spider webs across his body along the way.

Gordon stopped in the kitchen and scratched again, rubbed at his flesh until his skin burned. What in hell did he dream about? He opened the refrigerator door and winced, blinded a moment by the burst of light. As he looked down, Gordon's mouth gaped as he saw white fingers, hundreds of them, gently stroking up and down his legs. They seemed to be coming out of his body, knuckled within the meat of his muscles. He screamed, lurching back as if he could escape them. Shiloh came bounding into the room and slid on the linoleum and began to bark.

"*Gordon?*"

In a panic, he stared down at his legs. The strange fingers were gone, but the feeling of their touch lingered. He slammed the refrigerator door shut and cocked his head toward the bedroom. Amber was already out of bed, standing in the living room—dark save for traces of moonlight and streetlamps that snuck in through the blind slats.

"Don't turn on the light."

"What is it? Are you okay?"

"Just got hungry. Shiloh startled me." He forced his hand away from his legs, turned back just long enough to snag a loaf of bread off the countertop, and coming into the living room with two pieces in hand, started eating. The bread was dry as hell, like ash in his mouth. Somehow he knew exactly what ash tasted like. Unfathomably.

"You sure, honey?"

"I'm fine. I just didn't eat after practice, and it was messing up my sleep. You gave me a pretty good workout too." He grinned at her despite knowing it was lost in the dark. He hadn't felt less like grinning since his mother's funeral.

"I should have made you something. I wasn't thinking."

"It's okay. I just needed a sandwich. I was planning on going straight back to bed. It's close to four. Go on back to sleep. You've got class in a few hours."

"So do you."

Gordon sighed.

Amber came nearer until her face showed in the dim light. Gordon stifled a cry. Her red hair disappeared into the surrounding darkness, so that she seemed bald. Her face was white, her forehead unnaturally high and her eyes two shadows. The face belonged to her and yet it didn't, of course it didn't, it could belong to nothing living. Was this the face from his nightmare? As if to answer, the trace of fingers on his legs jolted him again and he actually jumped. This weird behavior seemed to verify whatever doubts Amber entertained. He saw her coming to him. She touched his arm and he pulled away, stepping back from her. He was afraid, he realized, genuinely afraid of being touched by anything. He *was* being touched by invisible fingers he could do nothing about.

Amber's tone was plaintive. "Gordon, please, just tell me what's wrong."

"Look, just—leave me alone. I'm okay."

"Are you sick? I want to stay up with you if you are. I can't sleep if you can't."

"I didn't say I couldn't sleep, I just said I was hungry—"

"Why won't you look at me?"

He did. He forced his gaze. The changes in her face were impossible but un-deniable. He didn't know what he was seeing. He couldn't judge her age at all, but she *had* aged. She *was* bald. Gordon saw a broken woman, an anguished and dying woman. He'd seen her before. He knew he had, but couldn't say where or how. That was the damn misery of it. This was a dying woman, and he was certain that, somehow, he was the cause of her dying.

"I'm going to turn on the light."

"Really, don't—"

Gordon flinched when he heard the switch flip, but the room stayed dark. Instead, outside, behind the slats, the world blazed into light. He stared at the orange and yellow panels the blinds had become, and jumped back as narrow rays of sunlight struck at his feet. He gasped. What had happened? Did they have a light switch in their apartment that could turn on the sun? The room's darkness began to change to an overwhelming deep red, as if he saw everything through the haze of Amber's hair. He was still dreaming. *Had to be—*

Pain burst across his forehead as the brightness increased, an agony with the speed of a needle matched to a swollen balloon. "Turn it off," he said, his voice low, his eyes shut as he rubbed at his skull.

"What?"

Shiloh barked. Amber bent and tried to quiet the dog.

"Nothing...nothing, Amber."

Gordon swayed a moment, then closed his eyes and rubbed them hard with his knuckles. The pain and the weirdness had come over him like a tsunami, but now he felt like he'd crested the wave. He opened his eyes and squinted through the swirl of dark colors to find Amber. She looked as she should even in a dim room, young and vibrant.

But she will fade.

The voice in his head was his own, but it spoke with more authority than he could imagine for himself. The crawling sensation returned to the skin around his inner thigh. To hell with this, he thought. Something's just fuck-ing wrong with me right now. I've got to get out of here.

"I think I'm going for a run."

He knew the idea was ridiculous and probably frightened her. He hung his head.

"Running? No, you're not!"

"It's just something I have to do."

"Bullshit, Gordon!"

He raised his hands to her lips. "It's early. You want to get the police called on us?"

"The police, an ambulance, the Westervelt fire department—whatever it takes to help you."

He went past her. As soon as she tried to touch him, he flinched away and rubbed the spot on his arm. She stared at him.

"Sorry," he said.

"Gordon," Amber said, her tone reduced to begging. "*Please*. Is it something I said? Something I did?"

He backed down the hallway and into the bedroom, expecting her to follow. She didn't. He bent for his workout gear from last night, slipped into the t-shirt and shorts and shoes. The clothes were hard from dried sweat. Their odor nauseated him but he had to move fast—no time to bother with changing clothes. As he started back down the hallway, he found Amber blocking the door.

"You're not leaving."

"Move out of the way, Amber." He started to reach for her, and then pulled back. She noticed.

"Not until you tell me what's going on."

"I just need to clear my head. I do that best by running."

"You just *collapsed* five minutes ago."

"Oh come on, I didn't *collapse*."

"There could be something really wrong with you. Are you that selfish—you're going to leave me here to worry? What if you have a stroke or something?"

Gordon laughed and instantly hated himself for mocking her. With gentleness, he said, "I'll be fine. Really. I know my body—I'm okay."

"I'll jog with you. Let me get my clothes on."

"Amber—*no*."

She was crying now. He felt like the biggest asshole in the world, but he couldn't bring himself to console her. His legs were so consumed with the crawling sensation, it was all he could do not to jump up and down in front of her. He loathed the entire idea of touch, even hers. The one thing he'd desired most for over a year, the one thing he'd enjoyed and savored for an entire summer, now tormented him. He heard her sobs and all he could think was: *Run, run, run, run.*

"I'm going now," he said.

She continued to cry. He waited a moment, wondering if he'd have to summon up the courage to move her. But she stepped aside.

He opened the door.

"Please take Shiloh," she said. Her voice sounded dead.

"Okay."

"Can I have a kiss before you go?"

He looked at her face. It appeared normal, except for the stress and pain he'd caused. She was not bald, not aged. Why had he seen her like that? Was he going nuts? Even now, the vision of Amber changed was more powerful to him than the face he saw in front of him, the face of the woman he *loved*. And he sensed, seeing the puffiness of her crying eyes, that this moment was their first shared step toward that future face.

It's my fault, he thought. Everything is my fault.

Unable to cope with the idea, enraged by the very notion, he bent down and kissed her lips. He kissed past the revulsion of touch, past the sense that these were indeed Amber's lips but colder, past the certainty that he detected a bitter inflexibility about her mouth. These things were not real, could not possibly be so: he was kissing *her*, the woman he loved. He would always kiss her. The tears on Amber's cheeks wetted his face. As he reached up to touch it, her hands caressed his elbows. His spine stiffened in reaction and he broke away from her. Amber hugged herself and looked at the ground.

He stepped into the duplex hallway. The only sound was a humming fluorescent light and Shiloh's eager panting. He headed toward the stairs. Then Amber whispered, "When will you be back?"

He turned and found her leaning out of the door. She was beautiful. Once again he felt breathless and sick for giving her pain. There was never going to be a day when he wasn't in love with her. He kissed her lips and face, her neck. She beckoned him back inside, coaxing him, tugging on him. For a moment, all was light. But light was the cruelest tease, and his legs seemed to be covered in ants. He had to go. "It'll be okay," he managed to say before breaking away from her.

Then he ran.

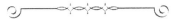

When Gordon saw the cemetery gates he wondered if he'd somehow planned this destination from the start. He'd not taken a direct route.

It was five in the morning now, an hour since he'd left Amber and about thirty minutes before dawn. He stopped at the iron fence, wrapping his fingers around the bars as he peered at the murky, scattered tombstones on the other side. Shiloh reached him a moment later and the ragged panting of man and dog were joined. They needed water. Shiloh's thin, pink tongue dangled out as if hoping for sudden rainfall.

Mom, he thought.

Gazing through these black bars made him think he was an inmate of a bizarre outdoor prison. He sighed, turning to put his back against the fence. At his mom's funeral service, he'd stared at her grave and swore to never forget any detail of it. Even now he remembered how he'd felt *making* that vow, as if a sudden wind had gusted against his face and hair to signal and seal a pact.

He'd been determined to visit her grave every day, a promise he kept by biking across town after school for many painful months. At first he would even talk to her tombstone and make it answer back, a stammering ventriloquist of grief. Sometimes a few adults visiting their own deceased overheard and stared at him. He'd see them making their shy, sad assessments, and wish just one of them would actually come over so he could tell them about her.

She'd been a hell of a mom, engaged in every aspect of his life. Movies, Cub Scouts, homework, sports, girl crushes (especially those). His father was a Doctor of Literature, but Gordon had thought of his mother as a Doctor of Everything. Dead, she must not go a day unvisited, and who would do it if not him? He sensed his father would never come, though Gordon liked to imagine him visiting in private. He liked to believe his father ate his lunch at the graveside every afternoon with a book of poetry he read from out loud. A cemetery needed its ghost.

Lifting his head now, Gordon turned back to the tombstones. How long had it been since his last visit? More than two years. The pointlessness of the journey had asserted itself in stages. At first he'd quit talking to the tombstone and just stared at it with regret. Then his silent, daily visits became shorter. Then they became weekly rather than daily.

He slapped his thigh to get Shiloh's attention and walked the fence perimeter to the gate, which was closed and chained. He scaled it without effort and Shiloh wriggled his body through a gap in the posts to join him. They walked along the concrete path under shade trees that seemed oppressive in moonlight. After a moment Gordon realized the dog had stopped padding beside him. He turned and saw Shiloh lifting his leg near a tombstone. "No!"

he said with a sharp handclap. The dog dropped its leg but refused to leave. It settled down along the tree and began to lick at the grass. The blades had precious drops of dew.

Figuring Shiloh would cause no problems, Gordon continued alone, buoyed by some vague remembrance of the tombstones asserting themselves in the diminishing dark. Many of the stones pre-dated the town's incorporation and bore the last names of just seven or eight families. The town had another, newer cemetery on its north side, as well as a mausoleum; this one was filled mostly with the town's founding families, and Gordon wasn't sure how his mom had even come to be here. There seemed to be no space for his dad to rest near her. Had one or the other planned it that way? What did it mean? He assumed she'd loved her husband, but she'd never seemed to miss him when he was away. They'd seemed attentive and interested in each other but not in love the way Gordon thought love should be.

Walking past the graves reminded Gordon of the last part of his freshman English class with Amber. She'd asked the class to analyze *Our Town*. Gordon's enthusiasm for Amber was already so great that he actually did try to read the play, but in the end boredom overwhelmed passion and he needed SparkNotes to write the C-minus paper. Still he'd been intrigued at the part in the play where the dead talk from their graves. He wondered what his mom would say.

She was the Universe.

Gordon stopped walking, looked about as if a voice had spoken from the trees. He bent over and touched his calves. The sensation of being fondled by some invisible force had ended. Maybe he'd chased it out of his system. If so, couldn't he go home now? Couldn't he run back to Amber and hope she wouldn't demand an explanation, since he couldn't provide one? Or if she did, couldn't he just look her in the eyes and say, "You are my universe," and let that somehow settle the matter?

He ran his fingers up to his thighs. The crawling sensation was immediate and he stopped, drawing a sharp intake of breath as he snatched his hands away. It was like he had something buried inside him. Could his skin be keeping a secret from his brain?

Just relax.

He walked on, mapping what he saw against memory. With the dark in retreat, the trees began to seem familiar. He was sure if he went past the third maple and cut left across the grounds, he'd find his mother's grave. He did so only to find himself mistaken. It wasn't there. He circled about, looking left and right, stepping over and around graves. Then, suddenly, the tombstone was just there, with its inscription—*Rachel Fane*—*Beloved Wife and Mother*. The name shocked him a moment; he'd come to so closely identify with his mother's maiden name that it seemed wrong she'd died under his father's.

She was happy with it. Why should I hate it?

He'd never asked himself the question so directly. Did he hate his name? It sounded ugly, like a sneer. It fit his father in ways Gordon couldn't explain even to himself. Dad wasn't a bad man, just aloof, shy, and odd in his preoccupations. He had the respect of his peers—didn't that deserve a son's admiration? Growing up, listening to his dad practice his lecture notes in his study, Gordon had thought him the smartest man in the world. He'd looked like his father too, especially as a little boy with his thin, knobby legs.

The shame and insecurity came later, around the age of twelve, when Gordon first saw his father use a cane. He'd already realized his dad wasn't exactly a good-looking guy, with that mole on his forehead. He began to fear he'd grow one too, and started taking stock of any way he might resemble his father, even wrapping a tape measure around his legs, hardly able to breathe as he looked to see if one was getting thicker than the other.

Gordon knew how different things would be if Mom had lived. He certainly would have visited home more often. He guessed he would've left the dorm to eat with his parents every night. And his jersey would say *Fane* across the back. He thought of his father alone in the house. He remembered the day he found Shiloh and took him home to bathe him; how he'd opened the refrigerator only to find it empty except for the soap and shampoo bottle stored in the side compartments. Once Mom was dead and it was just the two of them, Gordon had felt more like an adopted orphan having to explain his life to a foster father. Dad knew nothing of his school, his friends, his sports or what girls he liked. One night, about a month after Mom's death, Dad started coming into Gordon's room at night with an anthology of poems and a glass of warm milk, as if determined to read his son to sleep. It had struck Gordon as both inept and sad, the efforts of a man trying to do for his son at fourteen what should have been done when he was four. Still, Gordon had relented, each time with a thousand regrets as the readings went on for over an hour.

> *There will be time, there will be time*
> *To prepare a face to meet the faces that you meet—*

His father was a good speaker, as he'd have to be after years of lecturing, but this didn't transfer over to dramatic performance. He read the poems as if scared by them, enunciating each word with an unsure passion that attempted to convey *something* to Gordon. He had the impression they were like two people on opposite ends of a chasm, stretching their hands out toward each other. His father seemed locked inside himself as he read, never looking up from the page to see what effect the poems were having on his son, who sipped the milk with increasing boredom. He had no memory of ever staying awake through these uninvited reading sessions, but his father never got angry.

Then came a morning Gordon was too sick to go to school. It was about four months after his mother died, and when his father came to wake him, Gordon moaned and said he felt bad. At this, his father got strange even for him. His expression changed to grave concern, and he rushed to sit on the edge of the mattress. He became too attentive, feeling Gordon's forehead, the side of his face, his chest, his stomach, his arms. Being groped like that had creeped Gordon out, and he'd tried to sit up, saying he would go to school after all. "No, you're too sick!" his father yelled, pushing Gordon onto his back. Before he could move, his dad touched his forehead again, brushing back his hair, even stroking his eyebrows. That was when Gordon couldn't stand it any more and shouted, "*Wanna stick a finger up my ass and see if I'm constipated while you're at it?*"

He remembered his father just gaping at him and retreating. "I'm sorry. I never meant to—I know you aren't—I'm sorry."

He'd stumbled out of the room. Minutes later, Gordon heard the front door open and close, the car start in the driveway. His father was just going to work, no calling the school, no Tylenol, no gentle words. At that point Gordon realized the true difference between his mother and father. They both had the same desire for tenderness, but what his mother had expressed so naturally was somehow blocked in his dad. His father was like some gardener who always over-watered his plants, embracing the unstable deluge because he didn't know how to sprinkle.

After that morning, Gordon had decided he wanted to be *her* son only, and began researching how to change his last name.

The sound of Shiloh's trotting stirred Gordon from his memories. The dog's fur seemed almost orange in the dawn light, and he thought of how Amber would look with the sun streaming through the bedroom window right now.

His head bowed. Of course she wouldn't be sleeping, not with the worry he'd caused. I'm such an asshole, he thought. He bent and scratched the dog's ears, shoulders sagging in defeat. He owed her an apology and some kind of truth. He'd freaked out over a hallucination. If he put it that plainly, would she understand? Would she demand he go to a doctor? Well, if she did, then he'd go. He just had to be true to her no matter what. She was the Universe.

"Everything's clear in the daylight, isn't it, Shiloh? Too bad the sun doesn't always shine when you need it."

He gave one last, respectful glance at his mother's tombstone. There was nothing for him here but memories, and he wanted to be done with those, both the pleasant and the sad. He stepped away and snapped his fingers to get Shiloh to follow. They slipped out of the cemetery, and he walked without direction, his head down. But in their town all roads led to Westervelt, and seeing the campus, so much nearer now than either Amber's place or his father's house, he decided to crash in his old dorm with its promise of a more immediate shower and bed. Then he'd find Amber in her office and confess everything.

He didn't think about Shiloh at all until he reached his dorm building, but the dog's presence caused only a momentary problem. He walked up to the security guard, a guy in his fifties who liked to think he was best friends with all the jocks, and said he wanted to show the dog off to someone real fast. Gordon was surprised when the guard seemed reluctant. In the end he had to barter some of his celebrity, agreeing to shoot hoops with the man at the Student Center next week. Then Gordon and the dog walked down the hallway, stopped three times by girls who fell in love with Shiloh on the spot. A couple of them gave the dog a pet, then gave Gordon's arm one too, their fingers lingering. Gordon almost winced both times. The crawling feeling from last night's dream reignited again, and he only just kept himself from flinching away. The girls looked at him and one asked if he was okay. He smiled, nodding, and got away from them. He knocked on the door to his room and said, "Hey, John-Mark. You up?"

No one stirred on the other side. Frowning, as he hadn't a room key on him, he tried the knob. The door was not locked. Gordon's frown became a grin. Finally something was breaking his way. He and the dog entered.

The room was dim and it took him a moment to realize John-Mark wasn't there. Both the beds were unmade, which made Gordon chuckle. He hoped it meant John-Mark had been hosting some chicks and wasn't pissed off about being abandoned.

Shiloh pawed his leg, startling him. The dog's tongue hung long and desperate from its mouth again, the sound of panting filling the room. Gordon looked around and spotted the only viable water dish, a small Tupperware container John-Mark used to store whatever he found in his pockets at the end of the night. Gordon dumped the contents on John-Mark's bed—three quarters, two golf pencils, a flash drive, three condom packages, a button—and went down the hall to the bathroom. Shiloh attacked the water as soon as he returned to set it down, and Gordon smiled at the loud slurping, having to hold the Tupperware down with his hand to keep the dog from knocking it over in eagerness.

When finished, Shiloh immediately stretched out, and Gordon knew the dog would be asleep in moments. He rifled through his closet and dresser for the few clothes he'd never got round to moving to Amber's. Then he went to the shower and lingered under the water, almost asleep on his feet. He remembered how he'd felt in the shower last night with Amber, her hands all over him and how terrific her touch had felt. Before the dream or whatever the hell it was. He leaned forward and gently banged his forehead against the tile. No, he wouldn't go to sleep after all. He had to find Amber right away and tell her everything, even if it was crazy.

As soon as he turned the water off, he heard the sound of Shiloh barking. The showers were an entire hallway away from his room, but the barking echoed, rapid, aggressive. Shit. Gordon swiped the towel over his body and raced into his clothes, blotching them with water. He sprinted from the showers and into his hallway. A crowd of about fifteen people were gathered outside his dorm room. Inside, Shiloh sounded furious. The unmistakable voice of John-Mark screamed over it.

"Someone open that door and help him," a girl said.

"I'm not opening that door! Sounds like Cujo's in there."

Another student, aiming his cellphone camera at the door, said, "John-Mark sounds like he's getting raped, yo. *Fuck.*"

Gordon shoved people aside and said, "Let me through!"

The students cleared for him on one side. They were clearing on the other, too, and Gordon was beat to the door by the security officer.

"What the hell is going on?"

From inside, John-Mark yelled, "There's a fucking vicious dog in here. It bit me and it's blocking the door!"

Gordon and the officer looked at each other. Even more students were gathering.

"I can take care of the dog."

"If the dog bit—"

"He didn't. You know John-Mark—he's just dicking around." He leaned toward the guard. "You and me will play him two-on-one next week. How's that sound?"

The guard's eyebrows lifted. In a low voice, he said, "My brother's pretty good. He's a huge fan of yours, too. How about you and me against him and John-Mark?"

"You know it," Gordon said, forcing a smile. The security guard raised his hands and started yelling at the other students to clear out. Gordon touched the door. Shiloh's growling vibrated through the wood.

He opened the door and slipped in. Before he got the door shut, he heard a guy say, "How come Evans can have a dog in his room? That's favoritism!" He didn't hear the guard's answer. He was staring at John-Mark.

John-Mark was at his bed, almost standing on it, clutching his right hand at the wrist. Blood soaked the carpet beneath in steady drops. His pale blue t-shirt had a wet red smear on it. Gordon looked at Shiloh. The dog was standing in front of the bed, silent now but with an intense stare trained on John-Mark, the fur around its mouth red with his roommate's blood.

"Holy shit," Gordon whispered.

"What the hell is this, dude?" John-Mark's voice was strained by fear and rage.

"Hey, man, are you okay?"

"Fuck no I'm not okay."

"I—I was out jogging, and I wanted to stop by and—talk about last night. You weren't here, so I figured I'd take a shower and—"

"That goddamn dog is dangerous."

"I don't know what to say. He's never bitten... He must have been startled or something. That has to be it. Hell, the dog *knows* you, man. Why would he..."

"Just get it the fuck out of here before I kill it."

Gordon stepped forward. "How bad is the bite?"

"See all the blood, asshole? I can't bend my fingers!"

"Let's go to the doctor. C'mon, I'll take you. Maybe you just need stitches."

"I said I can't bend my fingers! I can't even feel my hand. My whole season's over."

Gordon squeezed his eyes against a stab of pain in his head. He felt dizzy, reaching back for the door just as it opened. The doorway was suddenly crammed with people watching them in eerie silence.

"He just needs a few stiches," Gordon said to them, as if appealing to a jury.

"Call the cops," John-Mark said, holding up his hand again to show his own evidence.

Gordon realized he had nothing to counter the awfulness of the scene, despite being certain John-Mark's injuries looked worse than they were. He bent down and wrapped his arms around Shiloh, hoisting him to his chest. The dog had grown since the last time he'd done this. It shocked him how heavy and large Shiloh had become.

"You think you're just going to walk out of here, dude?"

"I'm taking the dog away until you calm down."

Red-hot rage showed in John-Mark's eyes. He thrust his hand into Gordon's face. "How am I supposed to hoop it up now? I'll be benched. You've fucking killed me, man. First my English grade and now this. You happy, Gordo?"

"I'm sorry! I'll get Amber to give you a good grade. I'll convince her somehow."

"Fuck a good grade. I get a piece of her ass for this."

A mix of gasps and giggles filtered in from the hallway.

"Dude, shut the fuck up—"

He froze as John-Mark stepped down from the mattress and presented his blood hand to everyone. Shiloh growled.

"That dog's going down."

"Just be cool, okay? You surprised him, that's all—"

John-Mark swung at him with his good hand, causing Gordon to stumble and drop the dog. Shiloh lunged at John-Mark, locking onto his left ankle. Gordon shouted as people began to crowd in around him. In a moment there wasn't even room to stand. He couldn't see what was happening between John-Mark and the dog. The crowd almost seemed to be rooting for man and beast to fight. Then, over all the chaos, Gordon heard a high-pitched yelp and knew Shiloh had been injured. Gordon swung his arms and fought for room to stand.

He did not get up on his own power. New voices joined the commotion in the room, and their authority cut through it, silencing the rest. A hand pulled

Gordon to his feet. He was about to thank the person when he saw the police badge.

In short order, the crowd was dispersed, leaving Gordon alone with two officers and a paramedic bandaging John-Mark as he sat on his bed. Gordon rolled his eyes at the drama. It looked like John-Mark could move his fingers after all, and the blood had mostly stopped. He kept trying to point this out to the cops, but finally one of them told him to shut up.

"Stick to answering our questions. You brought this dog in here?"

"Yes."

"How long have you owned it?"

"Several months. Not even a year."

"Where did you get it?"

"I found it."

"It was a stray?"

"No, I just took him out of someone's back yard. What do you think?"

A look from the officer ended Gordon's sarcasm. They were asking so many questions that didn't seem important. Shiloh was obviously safe. John-Mark had startled the dog and got bit. If John-Mark would just quit acting like an ass the whole situation would be over.

He looked at the dog. Shiloh was hunkered down in the corner, on his best behavior despite the strangers in the room. Good boy, Gordon thought. Just stay calm and we'll all get through this fine.

Two more officers entered. Their badges were a little different from the others; they said *Animal Control*. After a moment of conferring with the regular police, one of them looked at him and said, "Gordon Evans?"

"That's right."

"Mr. Evans, are you confirming this animal did bite that man?"

Gordon swallowed. "He's my roommate. He knows the dog. He must have just startled it."

"Mr. Evans, how long have you had possession of this dog?"

"Christ, *they* just asked me that. Do I have to answer the same question a hundred times?"

"Is he registered?"

"Yeah. He's got all his shots. He's fine."

"You've got proof of that?"

"Well obviously I don't have his papers on me."

The officer was writing stuff down. Gordon frowned.

"Has the dog bitten anyone before?"

He thought of Shiloh and his father. It seemed like a hundred years ago.

"Mr. Evans?"

"No," Gordon said. "The dog's just really tired. We were out jogging really early this morning. He was thirsty and worn out. John-Mark knows this dog. John-Mark, tell them, man!" He swallowed against the quaver in his voice.

The paramedic was now helping John-Mark to stand. The roommates locked gazes.

"I've never seen this dog before."

"That's a goddamn lie!"

"Mr. Evans, I suggest you get a hold of yourself."

But Gordon wasn't listening. As John-Mark and the paramedic went past, he said, "You're a fucking asshole."

John-Mark stopped and looked at the officers. "Why isn't that dog locked up? What are you all doing?"

"We're handling it."

Gordon shook his head. "Locked up? You can't lock up a dog. What are you talking about?"

"The animal has to go into quarantine."

Gordon let out a disbelieving gasp. "John-Mark, are you actually pressing charges against a *dog*?"

"Whatever your roommate decides to do has nothing to do with quarantine procedures. The dog has to come with us."

John-Mark cast a smirk at Gordon and then left with the paramedic. One of the animal control officers now produced a pole with a hoop on the end.

Gordon grabbed it by reflex. "Can't we talk this over?"

"No."

The officer moved the hoop over Shiloh's muzzle. The dog remained rigid as the hoop passed over his face. But when it cinched around his neck, Shiloh sprang up and began a furious barking.

Gordon reached for the dog only to be pulled back by the policemen. His anger exploded at them. "It's hurting him! Let him go!"

"Mr. Evans, you've got a few seconds to calm down or else we'll take you away too."

"Where are you taking him?"

"Quarantine."

It was a meaningless answer to him, but he backed away. He wished Amber were here. She'd be able to talk to them. She was a professor. The police would respect her authority.

"Strong bastard," the officer holding the pole said as Shiloh fought him. He pulled on it, backing out the door as another officer cleared the hallway ahead of them. Gordon put his hands to his head and pulled at his hair. The dog was thrashing like a huge, dying fish on the end of the pole.

Gordon followed as Shiloh was dragged into the hallway. One end was blocked by the crowd of students who'd fallen back rather than dispersed. About twenty cell phones were raised to record the scene. Gordon yelled at them and then turned to follow his dog. The tug-o-war between Shiloh and the officer lasted until they got outside the dormitory itself, where the officer was free to use the pole in new ways. Shiloh resisted a moment longer, then broke to the officer's will, whimpering as he was forced in a trot toward a white van. A cage was placed on the ground and the dog marched into it. Gordon swallowed hard at this defeat and watched as the cage was lifted into the vehicle. Shiloh began to bark again.

"What happens now?" His voice was barely a whisper.

"Like I said, the dog's going into quarantine for thirty days regardless of whatever else happens."

"*Thirty* days? That's a month."

"Taught you that at Westervelt, did they?"

Gordon narrowed his eyes. It'd figure these officers were a bunch of townies raised to hate the college. He bit back a response.

They slammed the bay door, muting Shiloh's bark.

"You're not going to drug him, are you?"

"Not planning on it."

"How do I get him back after the thirty days?"

"That," the officer said, "depends on a lot of things. The dog is going to get evaluated first."

"Evaluated for what?"

"Aggression."

"I'm telling you, he's a good dog—"

The second animal control officer came with a piece of paper—a citation.

"No collar, no tags, no papers. You'll need to bring in his records to the address on the back."

"Is that where Shiloh will be?"

"Yes."

They opened their doors to get in.

"Wait a minute. So thirty days passes and you find out the dog is fine. *Then* do I get my dog?"

"I guess that depends on what happens with John-Mark," the first officer said, getting into the van. Gordon was startled to hear him use the name. "I hope neither of you get kicked off the team. I remember in your freshman year when he almost got ejected for a technical. You pulled him aside, got him straight. Hate to lose two good players over a dog."

The answer dazed him. Was this asshole talking about basketball? He just stared as the officer shut the door.

As the van pulled away, Gordon already knew he'd never see the dog alive again.

PART 2:

GEORGE

CHAPTER FIVE

He opens his eyes to an unfamiliar environment. He's on a bed that's angled in a way that makes his lower half feel like it's sliding off the mattress at a glacial pace. He looks down at his arms. There's a handcuff on his right wrist. After the initial shock, Fane realizes it's not a handcuff at all, but rather a plastic identification bracelet of some sort.

Where is he?

It must be the town hospital, the same place where Gordon was born. Fane can picture the building—across the street from the orthodontics office where Gordon's smile was perfected through three years of labor akin to soldering and welding.

Fane flinches at a sudden image: bloody teeth on the sidewalk and on the grass, the grass blades glistening red. Vicious grass, switchblade grass, as if Walt Whitman had gotten an attitude. Where is Gordon? What has happened to him?

He groans, feeling an intense throb in his left temple.

Now he hears his own panting breath mixed with the sound of machines stationed behind him. They seem to be activating all at once. Fane cranes his neck back to see them, though their connection to him is not mysterious. He has an IV in his left arm. God knows what they're feeding into him. Truth serum, perhaps. Staring down the length of his body, mostly draped under a white sheet, he sees both feet visible and naked. One looks quite normal, the other narrower and yellowed, the unnatural conclusion of an unnatural leg. He tries to kick the sheet over it and thinks, not for the first time, of Frankenstein's creation. It's a hideous thing to open your eyes and discover you seem to be a man constructed from different animals.

He swallows, alarmed by the sharp dryness of his throat, the act itself producing a low, raspy clicking sound as from a machine that hasn't operated in years. Wincing, he studies the room with growing despair and confusion. Despite various health problems, his worsening leg being chief among them, Fane has assiduously avoided hospital rooms over the years. It surprises him therefore to find this room is not as sterile as he would have supposed; what he sees—which has some of the trappings of a musty motel—makes him wish it were. Is there some psychological advantage in making a patient feel like a stranded, desperate tourist?

But why is he a patient?

A doctor enters, a man with short red hair, his body gangly, too thin for his clothes. The doctor ignores him, spends the first two minutes studying the machines and typing on a computer console. Fane's right hand reaches automatically for something that isn't there.

"Where's my cane?"

Now the doctor says, "Glad you're awake, Adam. Do you know where you are?"

"Why wouldn't I?"

"Humor me," the doctor says, his tone quite kind.

"This is the hospital near campus."

"Which campus?"

"Westervelt, of course. What happened to me? Was I in a car accident?"

"Tell me the last thing you remember."

Fane blinks. "I was…I was auditing a junior professor's class. I'm Professor Emeritus of English, you see."

"Yes, you are. While you were auditing the class, it seems you entered a dissociative state. You were completely unresponsive to your environment."

"I remember the ambulance."

"That's good. What else do you remember?"

He remembers Gordon's fight, but decides he better not mention that just yet. So he shakes his head.

"You were rather dehydrated and undernourished when you arrived, Adam. Do you eat on a regular basis?"

"I eat when I'm hungry."

The doctor nods, his expression neutral. Fane tries to read anything into it—sympathy, disapproval—and finds a blank page.

"What about your leg? Is it giving you any pain?"

"It always does."

"As a Westervelt employee you have generous access to this hospital's services. This includes physical therapy. Has your personal physician ever discussed this option with you?"

"I don't have a doctor," Fane says, "and I don't want one. There's no quicker way to get sick than to have a personal doctor."

The doctor laughs. "That sounds like a quote."

"It is a quote. From me."

"Unfortunately, people eventually get sick whether they have a doctor or not. Do you live alone, Mr. Fane?"

"*Professor* Fane, please. Yes, I do."

"No family? The only emergency contact Westervelt had on file was your wife. I understand she died some time ago."

"I also have a son."

"How old is he? Does he live nearby?"

"Gordon," Fane says. "He lives very close. He plays basketball for Westervelt."

The doctor purses his lips, pausing.

"Do you mean Gordon *Evans?*"

"Yes."

"You think he is your son?"

Fane laughs. "I don't think he's my son, I know he is. He changed his last name to honor his mother. Evans was her maiden name, you see. When I die, he'll change it back to honor me."

The doctor just stands there.

"You don't believe me? You think I'm crazy? Instead of checking my emergency contact listing, check my life insurance policy. You'll find him listed as my sole beneficiary. Now I need you to release me. Gordon was in a fight of some sort this morning."

"I am well aware of that, Professor Fane."

"How would you...?"

"The police brought him here for a time before booking him. They also brought in the other boy. He's laying unconscious in the ICU."

Fane struggles to push himself up. "But what of Gordon? How is he?"

"I wasn't the attending physician. My understanding is he wasn't too badly—"

"Teeth," Fane says. "What of his teeth?"

Bewildered, the doctor says, "They're in his mouth, I suppose."

"I spent too much money perfecting his smile to see it all ruined by a fist to the jaw."

The doctor raises his hands in a calming gesture. "Those boys are not my patients. You are. Let's talk about how you're doing."

"I should like to sit up straighter."

"The bed is adjustable."

The doctor circles to the other side and shows Fane the control buttons. As the bed moves closer to a right angle, Fane finds himself panting as if he's had to physically adjust the bed himself.

"What in hell is wrong with me? I've never felt so weak."

"You're showing signs of moderate malnutrition. Do you ever go through long stretches where you seem to forget to eat, Professor Fane?"

Now Fane detects an agenda in the doctor's question. He's asking about appetite and desire and starvation. Fane sees it right in the doctor's pale blue eyes—75-130-b.1. Subtly, he tries moving his legs, convinced invisible straps bind him. The doctors and the police and Westervelt's administration are going to punish him for transgressing. They probably have Gordon in another room, likewise bound and tormented. Punish the father through the son, he thinks.

"Why don't you prescribe a pad of post-it notes for me with messages reminding me to eat, and I'll happily be on my way."

The doctor pats Fane's shoulder. "I think we can do better than that. But get some rest right now. I'll see what information I can find about Gordon. If he's your son then he's probably been trying to get in touch with you."

"From *where?*"

"Well, I believe he's in custody now. I don't know the specifics. I'm sorry."

Fane weeps, imagining Gordon shut away. Poor, poor George.

"Professor Fane?"

"George," he says.

The doctor cocks his head, furrowing his brow. "Who's George?"

George? How does he know about George?

Then Fane sees George sitting on the floor. Of the cave. He looks between George and the doctor. All three of them are in the cave. His lower lip trembles.

"Want to read me some poetry, mate?"

Fane brings his hands over his ears. "No, no, no, no, no!"

"Professor Fane, who are you shouting at?"

"George!"

The doctor's face comes between him and George. Fane feels the man's hands steady on his shoulders. "Professor Fane, do you see someone else in this room besides the two of us?"

"You call this cave a room?"

"Cave?"

"Oh, God," Fane says, crying harder, bending forward. "Everyone I love is trapped."

"How are they trapped?"

Fane glares at the man. His lips open but he cannot speak. Gordon in a jail cell; George in the cave; his wife in a coffin; various colleagues in urns. He feels the loss of all hope like a drop in blood pressure. We begin and end, he thinks, trapped in tight spaces. George—

He shrieks from guilt. He might have gone on screaming for hours, except the top sheet falls away and he sees his legs bare all the way to the thigh. He wears only a patient's gown. Who stripped off his clothes? What did the person think, seeing his old body, his deformed right leg? These questions stop his screaming and his tears. He imagines the hospital staff making wagers on the leg, even measuring the diminishing circumference between knee and ankle. The body is not like a cave. Nothing about it is measureless to man—or beyond man's ridicule.

"Professor Fane, we're going to sedate you. It won't make you lose consciousness, but it will put you at ease."

"George."

"We'll find him for you. Is he a friend? Perhaps your brother?"

Fane hears the man's voice but not his words. He keeps staring at his legs, thinking of the lengths he's gone in his adult life to avoid looking at them. Like wearing laceless shoes and slippers that keep him from having to bend toward his feet. At night, he changes from slacks to pajama bottoms in the absolute dark; in the morning he showers looking straight ahead or at the ceiling, his hands soaping his lower half fast and blind. He dries himself the same way. A lifetime of evasions only to find his hateful, worsening deformity raging at him now. The white, hairless flesh of his right leg is like the skin of a baby animal born premature. Networks of varicose veins show so close beneath the waxy epidermis that it seems a paper cut might slit them open. I am Frankenstein's Creature, he thinks, forged from charnel house bits and slaughter room sweepings. My left leg is human and my right is a mule's bone.

His thoughts go even darker, to images of Auschwitz survivors. His is the leg of a concentration camp prisoner after the cleansing fire. Anyone looking at Gordon's legs would be enrapt by the trappings of corded muscle and sinew, dark hair, and firm, healthy skin. Such trappings are not present here, only bone and a narrow teardrop of muscle masquerading as a calf, all encased in onionskin flesh.

"Dr. Fane? Adam?"

He allows one petulant glance at the doctor and then confronts his legs again. He remembers the bravery of childhood. There'd been a time when he actually wore shorts. The permanent long pants came later, around the time George quit caring for him, around the time his left leg began responding to puberty, becoming hairy and strong—over-developing out of necessity. The right leg aged without changing.

Would it not be interesting, Fane thinks, to suppose the leg represents some eternal innocence of his, a grotesque appendage of Peter Pan crossed with Dorian Gray's portrait, ageless in a way but ancient at the same time? This leg whose whiteness is ironic, it having kept and suffered for the sins his other body parts committed?

"Cut it off."

"What do you want cut off, Adam? The pain?"

"The leg."

Adam. Mate.

A ghostly face rises now from the foot of the bed. As their gazes meet, a lip-less grin alters the face by revealing jagged, decaying teeth. Fraying brows arch above its colorless eyes. Fane coughs and sputters, one hand going to his chest. The machines behind him chorus his terror. George. This is what I've done to you, he thinks. This is what Gordon will look like after years of confinement.

The face lifts higher, and Fane realizes it has no body at all. It is just a head, and now it knocks against the ceiling like some helium balloon, but with the capacity to glare down at him.

"George—" But he can only sound out the soft consonant. George's name is now too large for Fane's mouth, too difficult for his tongue.

The face changes, becoming young and handsome, the face he's long re-membered and sought in his dreams. How George looked, sleeping in their hotel room that spring break they spent together in New York. When did

Fane see it? Sometime in the early morning—he was determined to wake up first, just to see his friend's face in the early morning light. But how soon the darkness would fall on them.

"George, if I could just do it differently. Don't judge me like this."

He thrashes, trying to leave the bed. So many people are holding him down—a throng of medical staff in his room, it seems. Then comes the sting, and he begins to sink into the bed, beyond it, into a darkness where perhaps even George cannot follow. He floats in a void, thrown out of time. But he feels, distantly, little touches all over his body, just aware enough to perceive how the doctors and nurses must be moving him, shifting him. Could Gordon perhaps have felt—

He refuses to let his mind complete the thought. But he knows Dante should have imagined a circle of hell where sinners have their own crimes committed against them.

Now he thinks of Rachel, his improbable wife. How many times did he wake in the morning to find her caressing him? His attractiveness to her mystified and saddened him, for he could barely pretend to reciprocate. How often had her fingers sparked resentment in him because they massaged him out of dreams about George? What was the old quote from Freud about all marital beds being a foursome—the couple in bed and the couple in their heads? In his dreams he relived and improved upon his youth as a time traveler might. What is the subconscious mind if not a time machine? In his sleep he could go back to his boyhood, back to George. George was with him even on his wedding night, waiting behind Fane's lids after the consummation, more vivid in his imagining than ever before. Somehow after marriage Fane's dreams expanded beyond simply reliving moments with George. He began to create new experiences so real to him that he woke convinced they'd happened. It was as if marriage had somehow opened an unlimited vault of memory deep in his subconscious. Some days he woke with tears in his eyes and he'd kiss Rachel with a gratitude he knew she misinterpreted as love for her.

He hears shouting across the void: *Are we losing him?*

Is he losing George?

F ane looks around the dense woods. Wasn't he in a hospital room? This must be a hallucination. But he knows this place: it was a hot day, in the summer of...1960 maybe, and he was angry because he thought George had left him here and—

George leaps out from behind a tree, startling him, and in that instant, the past subsumes Fane, and he is fourteen years old with no concept of a future that does not include Fowler, or his parents, or George.

George has a knapsack slung over his right shoulder. His right hand is pressed close to his thigh, thumb and index finger out to form a gun. Grinning, he sings: "From the town of Agua Fria rode a stranger one fine day."

Fane laughs and sings back: "Hardly spoke to folks around him, didn't have too much to say."

George circles him ,raising his hand and taking aim at Fane's chest.

"No one dared to ask his business, no one dared to make a slip. For the stranger there among them had—"

Their voices join: "A big iron on his hip!"

It's the third day of his summer stay with George. On their first night together, George's parents let them haul the record player from the living room to his bedroom and the boys sat on the bed with their legs drawn to their chests listening to Marty Robbins' *Gunfighter Ballads and Trail Songs.* They both especially loved "Big Iron" but what Fane loved more was watching George listen to it, his blue eyes wide and vivid as a watercolor, his entire body seeming to engage the song even though he never moved. "Now *that's* a poem, mate," he said after the first listen. He sprang up just long enough to draw the needle back to the start. They listened to "Big Iron" so many times, singing it together in a near shout, that George's father came upstairs and told them to at least move on to a different song. Fane had liked both of George's parents at once.

"You know, Adam, the way you limp along, it's sort of like you have a big iron on *your* hip. Or got shot by one. You ever think about that?"

Fane grimaces. He's forgotten he was mad at George for running ahead of him and hiding. "How am I supposed to keep up with all this weight on my back? Do you know how bad this hurts my leg?"

George seems chastened but Fane knows it's an act. George is never apologetic right away.

"Give," he says, holding out a hand. Fane doesn't understand until George tries to take his knapsack. He flinches away.

"I can handle the weight."

"Doesn't sound like it."

"Forget about that."

"The cave is still kind of far. Your leg holding up?"

"It's holding *me* up," Fane says.

George laughs.

"What?"

"Fane the Funnyman. Fane's in pain but he's still fun for a pun. 'Holding you up'—but you really mean it's slowing you down. I get it. Clever, mate."

Fane looks at the ground. Is George mocking him or being earnest?

"At least part of me is quick."

Now the boys stand in silence, each looking in different directions at the trees. Fane's leg throbs. He can't remember the last time it hurt so much. They are on the second mile of their hike through the forest behind George's house. This is not at all like the simple, civilized woods near Fowler. There are no marked paths and the difficult terrain is marked with surface roots and heavy brush that catch the toes of their shoes and turn ankles. One clumsy step during the first mile made Fane have to stop. That's when George seemed to get mad at him.

"I'll take your backpack if it'll help, Adam."

"I'm fine. I can carry my own stuff. I'm not weak."

"I never thought you were."

"Here, give me your pack. I'll carry *both*."

"Adam Fane the big tickle," George says. He wipes sweat off his brow with his forearm and laughs as he walks over to a fallen tree and sits down. "Let's eat a sandwich before we go on."

Fane slings his pack to the ground and sits down beside him. George lifts the pack by one shoulder strap and makes an exaggerated grunt. "Good God, Fane, no wonder you're so slow. It's not a big iron on your hip, it's ten bricks in your bag."

"Just one brick," he says, turning back the flap to take out the poetry anthology.

"I guess heavy thoughts are bound to have some weight. Don't read too much or you'll get fat like Dooley."

Fane actually snorts, making George rock with glee. He takes the book and holds it in his lap, one finger caressing the cover. The book's importance exceeds articulation for either of them. It has cemented their friendship in ways neither could imagine. They kept up the Sunday poetry readings until the spring term ended. George insisted on them despite having no apparent interest in most of the poems Fane chose. He liked to mock the poems even as Fane read them, but sometimes Fane found one that made George draw his knees to his chest and haunch forward, his eyes very much like they were when "Big Iron" played.

Over the term, finding poems that could elicit such a response became Fane's obsession. He'd sneak the book open on his lap during class and scan page after page until he thought he had a winner. He'd mark each poem with a slip of paper and then reread the choice over and over again during the week, wanting to speak so well, wanting to perform their brave or funny or lovelorn words with impressive skill. He could do so quite well in his head or alone, but George's physical presence had a way of shrinking Fane's mouth until even simple syllables were too large. George never complained, however, and when the session was over and they walked back to Fowler together, Fane would think to himself, it didn't matter that George didn't stop Dooley from hurting him that time. He'd made up for it. He'd made up for everything.

Fane can hardly believe he's here now, visiting George during the summer. The invitation came a month ago—a letter asking Fane to come down and spend two weeks with him. The length of time seemed impossible. Fourteen days in George's company? Their mothers spoke at length over the phone. Their fathers got involved. Wasn't two weeks too long? Surely the boys would get bored of each other's company. Fane sat at the kitchen table blushing fiercely as he heard his father talk. He and George bored by each other? What did his father know about friendship? Who the hell was he to make such a prophecy?

Their families both lived in Pennsylvania, but George's house was almost a hundred miles across the state, and it was decided Fane should travel there by train. This was the final touch, the total perfection of the arrangement. He had traveled alone by rail before, but this trip, rescuing him from a haunted and lonely summer, seemed as exotic as a journey to Tibet. It was George who told him to bring the anthology. Once the visit was certain, Fane spent hours in his room scrutinizing every page with a fresh intensity, circling exceptional poems and then doubting their worth. He read and reread, selected and reselected at a speed dictated by his pulse.

George and his parents met him at the station. Fane was struck by the changes in his friend after just a few weeks apart. George seemed taller and even more athletic. He'd gotten a haircut, almost a buzz, and looked sleek as a bullet. For a moment Fane was too overawed to speak. How could such changes happen without his knowledge? It did not seem right that time could move on without his permission. Finding these differences in George after the briefest of separations was like coming back to a statue that was already perfect and realizing that in his absence someone had conducted some new, unsupervised chiseling.

Introductions were made. As soon as he met George's parents, Fane cast his own mother and father aside. Was he not George's true brother, a twin in thought and feeling if not in appearance? The way George's parents embraced him felt more like the consummation of an adoption rather than a welcome, and since then, every hour of his visit has accelerated these feelings.

But now he and George are off adventuring alone like the last people on Earth, carefree orphans rambling through the forest to a home they've made for themselves. George told him about the cave on the first night of his stay, but Fane did not believe they would actually go to it. Yesterday was spent fishing side-by-side from morning until evening. George talked nonstop about everything as he reeled in one fish after another, while Fane stood there transfixed by the point where his line entered the water. Even the fish were not interested in him.

His leg started hurting after ninety minutes of just standing, and so he sat down on the bank of the pond. He watched George and listened to him, determined to remember every detail and syllable. George talked about girls, travel, Fowler, and the Yankees. And still George kept pulling fish from the water while Fane got no bites. Of course he threw every one back, and Fane began to wonder if perhaps the pond had only one fish in it that George knew just how to catch, so that he caught and released the same one over and over again.

Eventually George sat down beside him, and neither of them paid much attention to the fish. Fane stared at the pond, which was a quarter acre in size and featured a narrow, rickety pier on its southern tip. George said it sure was hot and Fane nodded, looking at his friend and the little bit of sweat on his face. Suddenly he knew what he wanted. It was a sin unlike any he'd ever known before because he had the time to contemplate whether or not to commit it. Temptation, he thought. So this is temptation. Well, he was tempted and he looked at the sun again, a god that did not care about the morality that obsessed Fane's mother. The sun's light fell upon the world like a pair of expanding arms bestowing the world to him. Its brilliant disc said,

Yes, here is temptation: surrendering to temptation is the essence of my worship. I have given unto you temptation to teach you how to pray.

When Fane considered that, the blasphemy came easy. He leaned in a little toward George and inhaled deep through his nose. The scents he received were very fine to him—the odor of George's blue cotton t-shirt and the fragrance of laundry soap residue baked into the fibers, reactivated by heat and sweat. This made him tremble and desire still more, and he leaned over until their shoulders touched. George, surprised, responded with a nudge and a laugh. He had caught another fish but he let the line play out and didn't bother with the reel.

"I'm glad you're here, mate. Are you glad you're here?"

"Yeah. God, yeah."

George laughed. Fane watched more line play out and wondered if George just didn't notice. His friend's lips were smiling and his bright eyes were looking at the water. That's when Fane knew it wasn't about the fishing, but about having a friend and looking at the mysteries of water and talking. Perhaps they might even swim. The idea repulsed Fane a little, given that he had only ever swum in a pool. How would it feel to be in the brown water, knowing hundreds of fish were thriving unseen around you? How would it feel in that water, bodies brushing bodies?

At seven-thirty in the evening, with the sunlight almost gone, Fane caught his first and only fish. George whooped at first and then it was hauled from the water and what they found was the smallest fish either had seen. "Dad knows a taxidermist and we'll have it mounted," George said. "He'll make it look nice and then he'll pin it to a piece of foam and you can mount it right next to your butterfly collection."

"I don't have a butterfly collection."

"Fane the big game hunter," George said.

The boys walked home after throwing the fish back. Fane got George to hold his rod straight out and sort of tucked under his arm, like a jousting knight. St. George, he thought with a smile. Suddenly George's arm slipped around his shoulder and pressed Fane close. George said they'd camp out tomorrow. They'd go to the cave tomorrow. The resulting thrill that went through Fane was greater than any energy he could conceive. It was as if a muse had descended and told him he would no longer be a reader of poetry; he would be its creator. He made up verse in his head as he listened to George talk about the cave and as he felt the heat of George's bare arm around his neck. George said no one else knew about the cave and it was important to go as often as possible before they got too big to enter. Fane did not understand and George explained how the opening was not some cartoonish black arc in the middle of a hillside, but a tight crevice at the top of some rocks that had to be squeezed through before the passageway opened into a vast cavern. Only when he grasped the complexities of the descent did Fane's mind turn from lofty poetry to mundane terror that kept him awake most of the night. What if his leg wouldn't let him manage? What if it snapped? By the morning, as George packed up the necessary equipment, Fane's panic was all encompassing.

So far, the difficult trek through the woods has only increased his anxieties. His leg aches and the bone feels even thinner, as if the journey has whittled it further. He sits on the tree eating his sandwich and fretting while George pulls a compass from his pocket. Having this device was his mother's sole concern before they started out. Fane still feels envy and fright that George has such freedom. Part of him even thinks George's mother is crazy. Yet he cannot help feeling betrayed by his own parents, that their sensible caution is in fact insensible smothering that has retarded him. No wonder George is so brave, so confident, so developed—he has parents who trust him.

Fane bites off too large a piece and swallows hard, having barely chewed it. Why is he like this? Why doesn't he have any faith in himself? Why is he so—so—

Prissy.

He looks down at his legs, which are spread shoulder-length apart. He's wearing shorts and his legs don't look *too* different from each other unless they're pressed close together.

George says, "I wish there was a cave near Fowler. We could really have fun then, mate. We could trick Dooley and Thompson down there. Then we'd steal their flashlights and run."

Fane imagines it, George and himself racing through the dark, both of them laughing as they explode from darkness into green forest light, riding the echoes of Dooley's terror-stricken sobs.

"I've got a pun for you, mate. Fowler: it's like fouler—you know, like a foul ball. Fits that school pretty good, I think."

Fane's eyes widen at this brilliance. George laughs again.

"You ready to go on?"

Fane nods, though really he'd be content if they just stayed here and made camp. They could just sit and talk. He knows it's a queer notion, like nothing any other boy at Fowler would suggest if offered the opportunity to explore a cave. He cannot stop thinking of the cave as a complicated test George has created to determine Fane's value as a friend. The cave is already as vast and dark as Fane's mind can make it. At some point he just knows his stupid leg is going to ruin the adventure, and George will have to haul him back into the light, disappointed and determined to find a mate less...fragile.

Fane gulps the last bite of his sandwich.

"You okay, mate?"

"Sure! What makes you think I'm not?"

"Just seems like you might be a little scared."

"I'm not."

"Oh. Well, I'm glad you got that rabies shot."

Fane blinks. "*What?*"

George seems alarmed. "You got the booster shot for rabies, right? There are bats in the cave, mate. I got rabies once so I'm immune, but if you—"

Fane's voice squeaks. "You didn't say anything about that! No, I haven't had a shot!"

George snickers, then doubles over with laughter. "Jeez, Adam, relax! I'm just joking."

Fane frowns at his shoes. He sees an earthworm writhing by his toe, squirming to escape. He bends closer. *That's me. That's how I looked when Thompson and Dooley stepped on me and George didn't save me.*

He toes the worm away with a kick.

"What's wrong?"

"Nothing."

"You're brooding again."

"I don't...brood."

"Like hell. It's all that poetry in your head, I figure."

"Then I'll stop reading it. I don't care."

George's arm settles over his shoulder, jolting him.

"I like it that you know poetry and that it gives you a kick. I like it that I have friends who like different things."

Friends. Of course George has more than one. Who else? How Fane hates every particle of himself right now—hates above all the swell of hurt bubbling in his heart.

"Who *else* from Fowler is coming this summer?"

George's expression is completely blank and Fane knows he's caught him off guard. His voice softer than usual, George says, "You got invited first."

"The expression is you save the best for last."

He can't look at George as he says this. He doesn't *want* to say it at all but he cannot stop himself. His head sinks even lower when George answers with a laugh. I'm a stupid fool, he thinks. No wonder he just stood by and let Dooley—

"Not with me. Best comes first, you know that. I eat my dessert before my peas. I couldn't even go a few weeks without having you down here, mate. You think I could make it to the end of the summer? Besides, it wouldn't make coming back to Fowler any good to me if I'd just seen you."

Consoling him like a child. Yet Fane loves it and this disgusts him. Too often he feels nothing about him is natural or right. But what possesses him? What makes him...whatever he is?

"I'm sorry. I don't know why I asked that."

"If it means anything, you're staying the longest. No one else gets more than a few days."

George nudges his leg.

"*Mates?*"

Another nudge, stronger than the last. Fane smiles. Here too he cannot help himself. He stands up, still unable to look directly at George. George catches on to this fast and starts weaving around in front of him, trying to maneuver his face into Fane's dodging vision. To Fane George's head is like a bobbing balloon flying in and out of sight.

"Stop it," Fane says, laughing. He reaches for his knapsack but George grabs it first.

"Okay, let's go. And if I carry your pack the rest of the way, I get your second sandwich."

"Give it here, then!"

"What?"

"Come on, give!"

"Not a chance, Fane! I'm still hungry. Heck, I think I'll go eat your sandwich right now. My mom makes them good."

George sprints off. Fane's satisfaction at watching him does not last. He feels a trace of tears around his eyes. He'd been on the verge of *crying* the entire time. In a pathetic way, he figures he should be proud. A year ago he surely would have cried outright. Perhaps he's getting better at hardening himself against his incomprehensible sensitivities.

"Hey, Adam! Come on!" George's not far off, but Fane can't see him for all the trees. He starts forward only to discover the ligaments in his right leg have tightened during their lunch break. He puts too much weight down, and the pain's so bad he gets woozy. Bent over to recover himself, he dimly realizes George has come back to investigate.

"Adam—is there really something wrong?"

Why didn't he stop Dooley? And who else did he invite? Dooley or Thompson? What if he's friends with them when Fane is not around?

Why, Fane thinks, did I imagine I was the one fish in his pond?

"Mate?"

"I'm fine. I'm fine. Just needed to work the leg a little."

They start off side-by-side. Above them the forest canopy creates a green darkness broken here and there with blotchy sunlight.

"It's really not far from here. Less than an hour at this pace. That's all you need to give me."

"I can do that."

"Good man!"

Eventually the forest thins out and the ground becomes a little more hardscrabble. The sunlight's intensity is unbelievable after the protection of the woods. Fane's eyes sting from sweat. His head aches a little. Both their shirts are soaked.

George points to an outcropping of rock about fifteen feet high. Fane squints to see it—everything's too bright, too blinding. The rock face glistens all over with mineral deposits and seems otherworldly. As his eyes adjust, he sees waves of heat coming off the rock.

George grins, lifting his shirt to wipe sweat from his forehead. "We have to climb those rocks but there's sort of a natural path to follow. We don't really have to scale anything, but it's still a little hard. Then at the top we'll see the crevice going down."

Fane grunts. What George calls *a little hard* looks to him like the promise of a broken leg. "George—"

"What?"

"I..." He notices George's gaze straying to his bad leg. "I can do this."

George smiles. "I *know* you can."

They climb, with George taking the lead. Fane soon falls behind but refuses to stop, clawing for every inch with his fingernails. His right leg feels like some useless ornament, simply hanging from his body. His heartbeat has never been so fast. His eyes have never seen such color burst across his vision, but he can see George through the explosions, several feet above him, pushing on without effort. Fane makes a fist and hits the rock, bears down on his right leg until pain courses through him like a second blood for a second heart. A *truer* heart.

The agony clarifies and focuses. It expands his mind. He imagines his ribcage opening, the ribs themselves separating, suddenly dexterous like the legs of a centipede, gripping at every little crevice with the one goal of moving his body forward. Nothing has ever challenged him so much. He remembers failures—so many failures. But here, for the first time, he finds his mind and body united in intent. The whole of his willpower has always seemed to inhabit his weak leg with its shrunken calf and troubled bone. Now it migrates up to its true seat of power, his brain, and from there it pushes him upward. He hears his ragged breath and knows he sounds like a dying thing, his fingernails splintering, his palms seared by the rock. But he has never felt more alive. The cave and its promise calls to him. It cools him. The cave is inside *him* before he's inside it, and he yearns for the soothing cool its darkness will bring as reward.

George suddenly sounds out a great whooping yell. Fane sees him standing at the summit, superb against the brilliant sky, a second sun. His triumphant voice must echo over the treetops. Perhaps his parents are standing on their porch, hearing their son from afar and nodding in approval. Fane grins, shot through with new strength. His right leg is twisted up, the muscles and ligaments a taunt rubber band about the bone. He grits his teeth and goads the sharp complaints to stop him now. He roars, gains another inch, another foothold, and stretches one hand toward George. For one delirious moment, Fane thinks he truly is *Adam*, a painted figure reaching toward his God. Their slippery hands lock together and George's strength lifts him the rest of the way.

Now, at the top, his spent legs tremble too violently to let him stand with any safety. He crouches down until he can sit, and then he laughs as he's never laughed before. George laughs too, both of them flushed and soaked with a grimy sweat. Then he points to the left and Fane sees the crevice. From here it seems hardly more than the width of his hand, and he pants, shaking his head.

"It's wide enough, trust me."

"I do trust you. With everything."

George grins, raising his arms to the sky to shout again. Turning, he says, "Are you ready?"

"I think so."

Fane gets up with George's help and goes to the crevice. It *is* wider than it appears.

"Try to keep as much of your leverage on your left leg. The angle sort of helps with that, but there'll be a few times when all your weight has to be on your right foot. You can do this."

"I know I can."

And Fane believes it. The look of pride and happiness on George's face makes him believe. He's becoming different, he senses. The same sculptor that has worked on George in their brief time apart has now set to work on him. He feels a mysterious chisel improving him. Will his parents recognize the change? Will they recognize *him*? He looks at George with fresh understanding.

George is his sculptor.

"I want to tell you something, Adam. I won't take *anyone* else to this place. No one, not ever. This is our cave. You and I may be the only people who ever explore it. Then one day we'll show it to our kids."

Fane's thoughts chase the scope of George's words. Their children, yes. Somehow.

"I want to go first," he says.

George cocks his head. "What?"

"It's important to me, George."

George squeezes his shoulder, making way. "It's important to me, too."

Fane takes the lead. George helps him position himself into the crevice with his left foot forward.

"You and me, mate, together—as long as it takes. But wait."

George opens his pack and takes out two flashlights. He gives one to Fane. "The sunlight is gone in seconds. You'll need this."

Fane turns it on. He starts down only to have George grab him one more time.

"Another thing. It's going to get narrow, Adam. We won't be able to swap places once we start. The only way to do that is to come all the way back and start over."

Fane pushes down on his right foot, feels the pain as keen and clear as ice in his body. He can bear it.

"Then I hope you're able to keep up," he says.

"Adam Fane the *conqueror*," says George, and turns a final time to howl at the blue sky.

Down they go. George was right about the passage narrowing, but it happens sooner then Fane expects. After two minutes of relative ease, he finds he has to turn his body sideways, left leg leading. His pack must be carried in his right hand, the flashlight in his left. Old fears buffet him. Old doubts threaten to turn back the work of the chisel. I can't do it! he thinks. He gulps air. Thank God George cannot see his face. The tears are there, hot and hateful. And they're only at the start.

He takes one sideways step and then another. So slow. His body trembles from the strain. "George?"

"Right with you."

Yes.

Fane's gaze goes to the wall as the flashlight's beam reveals it, mere inches from his nose. The gray stone has accents of red and brown, arranged in faint layers like tree rings. Granules of shiny minerals reflect the light. The whole thing is beautiful like the black rock George gave him is beautiful. Beauty might be everywhere. Here is a revelation: loneliness is being blind to unexpected beauty. Fane shivers, feeling profound. I'm done with not seeing, he thinks. Eyes open wide to the flashlight's beam and to the darkness ahead, he starts to laugh.

"Adam?"

He doesn't answer. As the passage narrows further, until his cheek must press lightly to the rock, the one memory that comes to mind is having his face rubbed into the concrete by Dooley. Why didn't George— But no. The question does not matter.

Besides the rock is warm and strangely smooth. Not like concrete, more like skin itself. The tight confines create a terrifying intimacy. This is how it would feel to lay chest to chest with—

He gulps air, and his tongue finds the rock, tastes it. He's not Catholic but he understands the Eucharist. Faith, desperate faith, has turned rock to flesh.

Fane purses his lips, trailing the rock with delicate kisses. How wonderful it is, but whose body is it? Whose torso has he just licked and tasted and loved? Is faith particular? Might it change rock into *specific* flesh? A delirium seizes him. He might swoon, except the narrowness of the passage holds him upright. He feels the same profundity he felt above, when he made his realization about loneliness and beauty. Now he realizes something else: the essence of courage is the willingness to taste.

He's still crying, but the tears are different now. The passage widens again just as George promised. And then his feet stand flat, and he senses himself in a vast space. He aims the flashlight and its beam shears off into darkness.

"Good job. We made it, mate."

He turns only to be blinded as he spins straight into George's flashlight. George seizes his forearm.

"You're—you're *crying*—"

The light leaves his face. He hears the thud of George's pack hitting the ground and then finds himself wrapped in a two-arm embrace.

His whisper seems thunderous. "*Why?*"

"Because you're really hurting, aren't you, mate? And it's my fault."

The embrace ends as quickly as it happened, so much so Fane wonders if it happened at all. More, he wonders if George wishes it hadn't happened. He senses they'll never speak of it again. Nevertheless George acts differently. He takes both of their packs and sweeps the ground with his light.

"Careful right here. There's like a crack or something."

"Okay."

"And here, too. Your leg okay?"

"It feels a lot better now."

"Stop just a second," says George. "I've got to find it."

"What? My leg?"

George laughs. "No. I mean the string."

His flashlight's beam sweeps the nearest wall. Fane sees the string first, looped through a spike George must have hammered into the rock. He points it out and limps over to touch it.

"Is this your guide?"

"Yeah. When I discovered the cave last summer, I almost got lost a foot away from the opening."

"You mean you came down here without even a light?"

"Sure. You have to take a chance, right?"

Fane smiles. "Yes, you do. You have to have the courage to taste."

George's flashlight pivots toward him. "What?"

"Nothing. So how much mapping have you done? How big is this place?"

He moves his beam to probe into the darkness. "I don't know. I guess I've put down about a mile of string. How's your leg doing?"

"Okay, I guess. Sort of tightening up. Maybe because it's colder."

"Do you want to leave?"

The light pivots back to catch Fane shaking his head.

"Good. I've got something to show you. Something amazing."

"This is already amazing."

"Amazing-er then. Come on."

They both hold on to the string, letting it pass through their fingers as George leads. For about a hundred yards, Fane follows George's flashlight, which makes a cheery trail on the wall, then suddenly its bright circle disappears and George stops.

"Here it is!"

"What?"

"Another passageway. Come on."

George slips into the opening and Fane follows. The new passage is the hardest of all. It requires getting onto his hands and knees and making a steep crawl. But at least it's a short climb, taking only a minute. Fane pokes his head into what seems to be a confined chamber, like the secret rooms he's heard the Egyptian pyramids have. He follows the sweep of George's flashlight beam and adds his own. Combined, the light is almost enough to illuminate the entire space, which can't be more than fifty square feet. There are four genuine walls and Fane marvels at the design, for this room was surely not created by accident.

It was made for us, he thinks. From the moment the universe started, the plan for this room existed.

George sets their packs down. "Isn't this great?"

"I can't believe it. It's like a world within a world."

George points his flashlight at Fane's face. "What else is it like?"

"I don't know."

"Come on, Fane! Don't disappoint. Dig deep into all that poetry you've read and tell me."

Fane aims his light at George and grins. George has sprawled himself out on the chamber floor with his pack like a pillow. His eyes are two blue diamonds birthed from a sea of coal.

"It's...a dragon's cave. And you're a knight that's come to kill it."

"A dragon's cave? That's good. I'm a knight? Aren't you a knight too?"

"No. I'm more a squire, I think."

George makes no answer to this, sparking Fane's anxiety. Has he said too much? Has he said the wrong thing, or something that *hinted* at wrongness?

Finally George says, "Do you think the Texas Ranger could kill a dragon with the big iron on his hip?"

Automatically, Fane says, "I think it would depend on whether the dragon—"

George laughs. "Adam Fane, the big tickle. Let's hear some poetry, mate."

"*Here?*"

"Sure. I didn't have you truck that book all this way for your health."

Fane finds his pack, opens the clasps and pulls out the anthology. Sitting down, he places it in his lap, holding the flashlight in his left hand while his right turns to carefully marked pages. Since their last reading in the forest near Fowler, Fane's marked at least twenty poems, in hopes that doing so will somehow guarantee the readings resume when they return to school in the fall. He has no doubt at all now that it will happen.

But why is he rushing? He can take his time here in a way he never could at Fowler. Even in the woods, he always feared someone might overhear or interrupt them. But here they are alone, finally and terrifically by themselves. The heart can be unburdened.

But then George's impatience lances at him in the form of his flashlight's beam. "What's taking so long, mate?"

"Sorry. I'm just searching."

"Whose poetry were you reading the last time? It was a lady."

"I think it was Emily Dickinson."

"Don't give me any more of her."

"I like her."

"Oh, that's swell. But *I'm* the audience, Fane. You know, the *patron*. So give me what I want or I'll start getting...hostile."

Fane goes through the pages he's marked, trying to steady his light. He's never read under a flashlight before. Even as a child he never snuck a book to bed with him. What fascinates him now is how the light does not illuminate all the text on the page. Some words show brilliantly while others are left to a dark margin. Reading this way, Fane almost feels he's decoding a message.

"How about just *one* Emily Dickinson poem?"

George's grunt strikes him as playful sullenness. "Fine," he says, "but you have to read it the tune of 'Yellow Rose of Texas.'"

Fane looks up. "*What?*"

"All her stuff sounds like that to me."

Fane studies his Dickinson selection, humming the song as he reads. Delighted, he grins at George. "You're right! That's amazing!"

George starts cracking up. "Well, let's hear it. Really sing it, mate. Put your lungs into it."

"I can't sing."

"You did great with 'Big Iron.' Just let it flow."

Courage is daring to taste. Taste the words and let loose.

He sings the poem to the tune:

> *Faith is a fine invention*
> *When human eyes can see*
> *But microscopes are prudent*
> *In an ee-mer-gen-cee!*

"*Brilliant,* Fane! All that twang on the last word—no one else would have thought to do that. I love it when you get into something. I love having a mate like you—Adam Fane, the Mitch Miller of the Cave!"

George hollers, making a riotous echo in the chamber. He waves the flashlight everywhere, dizzying Fane. Then he says, "I hate Mitch Miller. When I was little, all I wanted to do was listen to 'Rock Around the Clock.' Then one day, boom—all the radio plays is 'Yellow Rose of Texas.'"

"I did the same thing!" Fane can only marvel at how similar they are *in spirit,* for he too remembers weeks on end standing by the radio anticipating the Haley song. And for weeks it seemed to be all the radio played. Fane never got tired of it. Then one day the song was gone, usurped.

George put the beam under his chin, turning his face into a mask of dark and light. "I'm still bitter about it. Give me another poem to wash it away."

"Okay," Fane says, and then stops cold. *Of course.*

"What is it, Adam?"

"I'm an idiot. There's a perfect poem to read in a cave, and I didn't even think about it until just now."

George leans forward. "Let me hear it."

"Let me find it. It's in here somewhere."

He begins mussing through the pages. He knows it's somewhere in the middle. Before he finds it, George starts kicking the rocky ground and shouting, "Poem! Poem! Poem!"

Fane stands, ending George's mocking fit. His flashlight still under his chin, he gazes at Fane in an expectant hush. Fane smiles. What he's about to do will change him forever. He's read this poem so many times he doesn't *need* the book.

He throws it aside.

George's flashlight beam darts to where the book lands, finds it, and then pivots back to George's face. "Adam? What—"

Fane puts his own light under his chin. He looks at George and beyond him into the darkness—into time.

His voice starts out low, growing steadier and more assured on each syllable. A deep concentration comes over George, over himself, over everything. The chamber loses its echo, as if the rock itself wants to keep his words:

> *In Xanadu did Kubla Khan*
> *A stately pleasure-dome decree:*
> *Where Alph, the sacred river, ran*
> *Through caverns measureless to man*
> *Down to a sunless sea.*
> *So twice five miles of fertile ground*
> *With walls and towers were girdled round:*
> *And there were gardens bright with sinuous rills,*
> *Where blossomed many an incense-bearing tree;*
> *And here were forests ancient as the hills,*
> *Enfolding sunny spots of greenery.*

Fane pauses, telling himself he needs to give George room for one of his usual sarcastic comments. But none are forthcoming. George seems serious—even studious. And then Fane knows he's made a mistake in stopping, and that he stopped because his faith began to falter.

"Is it over?" says George.

Awkwardly searching for an excuse, Fane says, "It's kind of long. Do you want me to go on?"

"Yes!"

Fane clears his throat to continue, but the words are gone. He feels an old fear returning like a demon after temporary exorcism. A sense of failure, of embarrassment. He can't think of a single word of the poem now. Pointing the flashlight at the ground, he finds the anthology and takes it. He reads the rest of the poem, fiercely aware of the difference in his voice—a lack of conviction. What's wrong with him? As he finishes the last line—"*And drunk the milk of Paradise*"—he verges on tears.

Why did I stop? he thinks. Why did I doubt myself?

"Is something wrong, Adam?"

"Just picked a lousy poem. It wasn't as good as I thought it was."

"It seemed pretty good to me, especially the first part. It's a lot better than most of what you read. Or maybe I'm just hopeless. I keep waiting for you to pick one that will really tear me up inside. That's how my mom is about poetry, but she doesn't read what you read."

George's flashlight goes out, startling Fane. He aims his light at him, keeping him in its circle. "Your battery die?"

"No. Turn your light off, Adam."

"Why?"

"Just *do* it."

He does. The darkness surges at him. His thumb starts to press on the flashlight button again, only to stop when George gives another warning. Fane stands paralyzed, hearing too much. He knows George has gotten to his feet, but now the chamber seems to have a hundred other people in it. People or animals—or insects. Fane shivers. Yes, he feels them now. He slaps them off his leg. George's footsteps are in front of him, and then behind him. He's leaving me, Fane thinks. He's going to leave me in this cave. He'll take the string and I'll never find my way out.

"George—"

And then George's face just explodes in front of him, a sinister rictus as the flashlight comes on. George is almost nose-to-nose with him. Fane feels his breath on his skin, and it's almost enough to keep him from screaming. How could he not scream when George's face looks so inhuman, like a black skeleton papered over with flaking yellow skin?

Then George laughs and says, "Scared you?"

Fane trembles and sinks to the ground. "Yes," he says, trying to make his breath less ragged.

"Adam Fane, the Scaredy Cat." He pats Fane's shoulder and adds, "Got anything scary in that book? Can a poem even be scary?"

Recovering, Fane says, "The one right after what I was reading is about a vampire woman named Christabel. You want to give that one a try?"

George sits down right next to him, and pulls the anthology over until their laps share it, draping an arm over Fane's shoulder.

"Proceed, mate!" he says.

M*ate, don't go! Adam!*
George calls out to him in a plaintive voice: *Don't leave me here alone again!*

They are in the cave, reading to each other. Then something happens, as it always does, and Fane knows he's in a dream. For a few seconds he tries to maintain the fabric of the past, but it unravels and the cave's darkness is only his closed eyes.

As he lies there, Fane remembers the dream he had the night before Rachel died. George seemed anxious and weary. They were in the cave and George wanted to leave. Their flashlight batteries produced sickly beams and the dark felt threatening. George said they had stayed in the cave too long. "But it's only been an hour," Fane said, sure he was right. They followed the string trail back to its starting point and started the ascent. Then George cried out. He had grown too much. He could no longer escape. Fane, smaller, could still squeeze through.

George had held the light to his face. The weak beam barely outlined a trace of his features. He said, "Escape while you still can. I'll follow you somehow. Wait for me."

He dreamed of George only once after that. It happened three weeks following Rachel's funeral. In the dream, Fane reentered the cave determined to bring George food and water. But George was not there. Shouting for him, Fane followed the string to the smaller chamber and found it empty as well. Had George gone off into the far depths, seeking another exit? He started to cry in the supreme loneliness of the dark, and then arms wrapped around his chest from behind and he heard, "I got out, mate. I got out. I've been with you all this time."

Fane woke to find arms still embracing him. "Rachel," he started to say before remembering her death. Turning, he found Gordon in bed with him.

His son had entered the room sometime in the night and clung to him. Fane's tears at this discovery were not silent, but Gordon did not stir. The boy's heavy, trauma-induced sleep made him almost comatose, and did not break even when Fane reached over to stroke his son's cheeks and forehead. Gordon had not entered his amazing growth spurt yet, but his appearance was already pleasing. His skin was warm and perfect, lacking even the blemish of acne. His parted lips showed a glint of the metal braces. Fane swallowed and stared, looking at his son with George's echo in his mind. He seemed to see Gordon for the first time. He had always seemed like a miracle, such a handsome and attractive boy, so active and vigorous. He resembled his mother more closely but really looked like neither of them, in Fane's opinion. People had even asked if they'd adopted Gordon.

In a way, Fane began to think, his pulse quickening with a crazed possibility, perhaps they had.

Fane's fingers soothed back Gordon's curly hair, so very much like George's, and then touched the bare arms that were still wrapped around his own waist. He touched Gordon's arms at the elbows, moving them away as he gentled his son onto his back. The bottom of his t-shirt pulled up to his bellybutton and Fane's trembling fingertips swept the few hairs there. His fingers moved up, pushing the shirt along and past the ribcage until its hem revealed his nipples. Gordon's skin was fair, given to quick sunburns. George had been much the same.

Could this be possible?

As he embraced the idea, Fane shed even more tears. They fell upon the boy's chest and ran like beads of sweat down his torso to the waistband of his pajamas. Fane's right hand massaged the liquid gently into Gordon's body, down and down back toward his navel. The boy stirred but didn't wake. Still Fane's hand shot back in fear. He remembered how George had started to wake in the hotel room, and how he'd lacked the presence of mind to withdraw his hand. Fane did not repeat the mistake this time.

He sat up and swung his legs over the side of the bed and bent, cupping his hands over the aching hardness in his groin. Behind him, Gordon said in a confused, waking voice, "*Mom...*"

Now Fane is suddenly pushed back up out of the darkness, back into a body that feels, if possible, even more worn and aching than before. He senses he has dwelled in archaeological layers of dreams and memory, and time has fossilized his body. He opens his eyes to find himself in a different room, much warmer—cozier than his bedroom or study, and he remembers both more vividly than he would have believed. A man sits next to him tapping on a tablet computer. The man sighs and glances at Fane.

"You've come out of it, haven't you, Adam?"

Fane tries to talk and touches his throat, amazed by its dryness. Its rawness reminds him of how he sometimes felt at the peak of his fame, when he constantly guest lectured and gave conference presentations around the country. There's no doubt about it: he's been talking.

A lot.

The man gives him some water.

"I was...I was in a hospital room. It seems I collapsed during... I don't remember her name now. Gordon... My son was in a brawl."

The man nods, his right hand continuously tapping on the console. "Please wait a moment," he says.

"For what?"

"I'm cross-referencing what you just said. The day your son got into a fight. That was 2011, I believe."

Fane's spine stiffens at the use of past tense. "What year is it now?"

"2027."

He lifts his arms and hands to observe them. They look *decrepit*. He blinks. "You mean I'm...in my *eighties*?"

"Give yourself a few minutes. You've been doing very well recently keeping track of current time and events. The new medicine has really helped."

Fane examines the room again. It doesn't look like it belongs to the future. But how should a room in 2027 appear? He drinks more water and rubs the bridge of his nose. "George," he says, the name coming out as naturally as his breath.

"We were trying a hypnosis and drug combo treatment to help you with your memory and control problems. I was guiding you through some childhood recollections."

Fane stiffens, hands clutching the armrests. Seeing the doctor's eyes narrow, he tries to relax his posture. "What did you find out?"

"Not as much as I had hoped. This childhood friend of yours is a very powerful memory for you. It keeps breaking you from the trance. That shouldn't happen. I'd like to put you under again and continue."

Fane shakes his head.

"No? Well then, 75-130-b.1, Professor Fane. 75-130-b.1."

"*What?* What did you say?"

The man leans forward. "What do you think I said?"

"Something...it's not important."

"I see. 75-130-b.1."

"Stop saying that!"

All at once Fane starts flailing his hands and swearing. The surge of rage is primal.

The doctor rises without hurrying and just puts his fingertips against Fane's shoulder. He presses without much initial force, gradually increasing it. Fane does not understand, but all his thoughts, like a liquid, suddenly seem to calm and flow toward that point of pressure.

"Here, Adam, this might help keep you centered." The doctor places a black rock into Fane's lap. Fane clutches it to his chest.

"It was in my jacket pocket. I—I put it there just before..."

"It was a gift from George, if I understand."

"Yes. The sort of present only boys can give to each other."

The doctor nods. "I would very much like to know more about George. I think if we can focus on your memories of him, we might be able to slow your deterioration."

"I'm *old*."

"You're healthier than many men your age, in most respects. You've got time ahead of you still. If that means nothing to you, it certainly means something to your son—and grandson."

"Grandson...yes... Is his name George?"

The doctor sighs. "Let's stop the session for today. I know you're tired. I'll give you something to help you sleep better."

He's taken to another room with a bed. This place looks much more like a hospital room. The equipment gives it away. He's helped onto the mattress and feels immediately sleepy. The doctor gives him a pill anyway and he swallows it. As the doctor's face fades in and out, Fane can only wonder what the man *really* knows about George.

Oh God, what secrets has he told?

Then the darkness returns and Fane looks about with no disorientation at all, for this is the cave.

"George?"

"Right where you've been keeping me, mate."

Fane pivots just as a light flares. A campfire on the floor burns with harsh, white fire. Fane cannot recognize the monster clutching itself at the edge of the light. But when it speaks it has George's voice.

"I'm glad to see you again."

"Are you, mate? Then why did you leave me here?"

"I didn't leave you, George. I came back. But you got out. You were reborn. You're Gordon."

The white light flares, pushing all darkness from the chamber. Fane twists away, a forearm over his eyes until they can adjust. Then he sees George, naked and aged—as old as Fane himself, but somehow both far older and younger, not ageless but...*preserved*. The figure before him has lost his clothes long ago. Ashen and hairless, his parchment skin keeps a tight wrap about the bones. All of George's body reminds Fane of his right leg. As their gazes meet, George's expression changes to one of sour petulance.

"Read me a poem, mate."

"I don't have the book."

The thing that was once George laughs and reaches behind him. Fane hears a dull scraping sound and a moment later finds what seems to be a grimy, deteriorating box being shoved along the floor of the cave to him. Bending closer, he realizes it is his poetry anthology, tattered and rotting. Between the fraying covers, the pages are a decaying mush, wet and moldy. But how? There's no water down here. The cave is arid.

George gestures to his eyes. "I cried. I cried onto the pages every day. You thought I was dead. I woke up and found my flashlight but I was too weak to get out. I lost consciousness. When I woke up again, I couldn't move. My neck was stiff—so stiff the slightest movement made me scream. I called out to you. I thought my own voice would drive me mad but I had to keep calling, knowing you'd come. *Adam! Adam!* I figured someone else must have been down here. Robbers, maybe, and they attacked me. I could only hope that at least you escaped. My thirst and hunger started to make me whimper. I still didn't cry because I had hope. Adam Fane, my best friend, would save me. I lingered another day and then I did cry, because I knew all along that you were the one. You hit me in the back of the head. You did this to me. And I'd never leave the cave now. I took the light and found your poetry book. I opened and I began to read. The light was dying; I knew I didn't have much time. I read the poems out loud like prayers. I knew I had to memorize the words and keep them in me. When the light went out, I kept crying and crying."

Fane squats near the fire and hugs his knees against his chest. His right leg makes no complaint. The fire gives no heat.

"I kept lingering. Maybe the poetry kept me alive. Maybe it was something else. I changed. I became one with the dark. I could see in it: the dark became my light. I read the book, anticipating your return. I read them as perhaps you read them for me, with care. It's taken me years to find us just the right poem. See there where I marked it for you?"

Fane sees.

"Read it to me, mate."

"No. I can't, George."

"Page 350. Second column."

Stifling a sob, Fane opens the book. Chunks of pages fall from their binding and break apart on the floor. But the page George marked is invincible. Fane knows the poem. He looks up to find George staring intently at him. The warm blue seas that were his eyes have long drained away, leaving bleached coral.

Fane puts a trembling finger on the first word and reads, tracing down as he goes.

> "In the desert,
> I saw a creature, naked, bestial,
> Who, squatting upon the ground,
> Held his heart in his hands...
> And...and ate of it."

Fane's chest aches. He beseeches George for mercy only to receive an icy command—"Continue!"

> "I said, 'Is it good, friend?'
> 'It is bitter—bitter,' he answered;
> 'But...but I like it
> Because it is bitter,
> And because it is my...heart.'"

Fane casts the book at the wall where it shatters like a ball of mud. To this George gives a sickening squeal and crawls over to scoop up the pages. He begins to cram them into his mouth and chew. But he takes a particularly large piece of mush and hands it to Fane.

"Do you have the courage to taste, Adam?"

Fane takes the decaying wad of paper and brings it to his lips. Opening his mouth, he lets the nasty mass dissolve on his tongue.

Instantly he says, "*I had a dream, which was not all a dream.*"

"Take another piece, mate."

Fane does and eats.

"*The meager by the meager were devoured.*"

"How's the end of the world taste, Adam?"

CHAPTER SIX

Outside on the marble balcony overlooking Venice, Byron finally cannot hear the little girl screaming. He stares down at the traffic floating along the canals. For a moment, the scene dissolves away and the water rises and joins into one vast body. It is Lake Leman, clear and horrible in his memory even after three years. He looks up at the mirroring blue sky, his gaze seeking the sun. It has moved behind him. He cannot find it, but it is there. It will always be there.

Shaking away the vision, he turns, hobbling more than usual on his way to the writing desk in his chambers. Weight added over three years has made walking more laborious than ever. A surfeit of pounds, a deficit of hair: such is man's accounting in Fate's cruel ledger book. He slumps onto the desk chair and reaches for a pen, but a thought intercepts his purpose, redirecting the hand to his mouth. He touches one tooth, then another, applying pressure to each in turn. Some are sturdy like they were in the past; others dance a disturbing jig between his thumb and forefinger.

The sun will always be here. Man will not. That is a prophecy all can believe.

The girl's shrieks are incessant.

He now takes up the pen, thinking of a poem. The business at hand is not art. He is answering a letter he began over an hour ago and stopped after the first sentence, a rush of hateful memory forcing him away from the writing and to the balcony. For a while Byron thought he might jump over the stone railing and plunge to his death.

Mine will be no quick death, he thinks. He has engaged a slow suicide through an overabundance of food and wine and sex. A British peer should die over-sated. All should die fat and save the corpse the trouble of bloating.

Byron can hear the girl shouting, "Papa! Papa! Papa!" He swallows against the stab of stomach acid in the back of his throat.

He picks up the letter again and reads:

> *To John Murray, Venice, May 15, 1819*
> *Dear Sir,-*
> *The story of Shelley's agitation is true. I cannot tell what seized him, for*
> *he does not want for courage.*

Murray is Byron's publisher, which also makes him the pimp of his most notorious author's infamy. And an audacious pimp he is proving to be, for he has revealed himself to be in possession of Polidori's account of their stay in Geneva. Byron only vaguely remembers the time he perused Pollydolly's diary after suspecting him of recording events for future publication. As it turns out, such suspicions only scythed the top of the wheat, leaving the roots untouched. Murray has now admitted he solicited Polidori to keep the journal, even offering the doctor a sum of five hundred pounds. Hefty wages for a swarthy, freelance Boswell! But Murray has at least gotten his money's worth in way of quantity. The scope, if not the quality, of Polidori's observations as relayed by Murray amazes Byron.

Even Polidori, though, chose to make certain judicious redactions in his account of that summer. Perhaps the editing is what delayed Polidori in getting his erstwhile manuscript to Murray. He would almost like to question Pollydolly about it, but their paths have not crossed since Byron dismissed him three years ago. Evidently his final product has certain gaps and unfathomable moments that have agitated Murray into showing his hand and asking Byron himself for greater insight.

The gall of the man, to ask the spied upon for clarification of the spy's report!

Until the last month, Byron has thought his mind purged of the summer of 1816. He's had no disturbing visions of the inexplicable. Other summers have been warm and natural, and the present season is sweltering. After three years now, readers regard the poem his pen produced that strange, haunted night as a curiosity at best, at worst a waste of time. Certainly no one discerns therein a vision of the future. This irked Byron a great deal at first; if he were a prophet then he must surely be from the line of Cassandra. What did he expect though? Mass revolution? Fear and trembling, fasting and prayer? In the ensuing years, he had come to believe all he experienced, in truth, was a fit of madness, nothing more. The sun rises and sets and always will, to the end of time: to imagine otherwise is fancy; to believe otherwise is folly.

Recent events have caused him to reassess matters. The demon of Lake Leman has come to commence the world's reckoning.

"Papa!"

Perhaps it is the only word the child knows. She has many different ways of shrieking it. Her screams strike through the villa and terrorize the servants who've been left to deal with her.

Gasping from a sudden constriction in the throat, Byron hoists himself up and makes yet another hobbled dash to the balcony. He lifts his arms in praise as he sucks in the hot air. This is true summer. This is eternal sunlight. This is proof that his prophecy was delusion.

Pollydolly certainly thought it so. Truth be told, Byron dismissed the doctor out of a certainty the man was about to leave his services of his own accord, convinced of his client's incurable insanity. Pride would not allow Byron to surrender the upper hand.

"You've been infected with some madness from Shelley," Polidori said after Byron forced him to read the poem that sprang from his possessed pen that night.

"Your jealousy of the man is unbecoming, doctor."

"What's unbecoming is your state of mind—my lord. This poem has undeniable power. It is horrific. But to call it a prophecy? Laughable."

Byron had been relieved rather than enraged at Polidori's blatant skepticism. He'd wanted to succumb to skepticism himself. But he could not. Perhaps once again it was pride that made Byron obstinate.

"What I've seen will come to pass. I promise you. I have been visited by something. A demon. The phantasm of Lake Leman. I have seen an old man's death mask speak with a young boy's voice. Such darkness!"

This conversation was excised from Polidori's manuscript. Byron wonders if this is a touching gesture on the doctor's part, a way to preserve his client's dignity. More than likely it implies a parting insult: Byron's most passionate belief is too ridiculous to credence and beneath any worthy reader's notice.

Polidori has not, however, spared any detail in describing Shelley's numerous displays of insanity, and upon these Murray's queries press the hardest. In particular, he wishes to know more about the night when a hysterical Shelley claimed he saw eyes in Mary's nipples. Byron is at a loss about how to answer such an inquest. Much of Shelley's behavior during that summer does seem ridiculous to Byron now—and sad, since Shelley himself revealed his fakery at the Castle of Chillon. Byron's immediate instinct was to protect Shiloh, to discredit the account. But their friendship is not what it used to be, and a small but growing part of Byron wants to inflict pain.

Even Shiloh did not believe him.

He goes back to the desk and crumbles the ill-started reply into a ball. As he does, the girl's shrieking sobs blast through the door. Byron cringes.

When you fornicate with madness, he thinks, only insanity will be sired.

The living totem of that icy summer once more shrieks out, "Papa! Papa!" The girl screams as if she means to kill herself.

The world should be so fortunate!

He stands teetering a moment, grasping the desk's edge. Words enter his mouth like food rising up from his gorge—*Shut up, Ada!* Byron blushes and casts his gaze down to the ground as his posture stoops. The screaming girl is not Ada, his first and true daughter, his dear, unseen child back in England. The child who bedevils him is named Allegra and she is the thing that grew in Claire after their one bewitched and frigid night together in 1816. That he could for a second confuse this girl with Ada makes him hate her all the more.

Fletcher knocks on the door and bids entrance.

"I'm afraid this time the child won't rest until she sees her father, milord."

Then throw her into Lake Leman, he thinks.

"You have my answer on that," he says, "for last week, for yesterday, for today and all eternity."

"But milord, a month approaches since you accepted the child. If she cannot see her mother, then at least let her know her father—"

"Calm the child as you will, Fletcher. Feed her warm milk or dash her head against the mantel. I care not!"

Fletcher retreats so fast it is as if the thunder in Byron's voice slams the door. Byron scowls, shuddering at the violence coursing through him.

Dash a two-year-old girl's head against a fireplace? His lips curl against his teeth, both the steadfast and the loose.

The truth is he can see himself taking the sniveling little bitch and breaking her skull against the marble. How has he come to have such darkness in him? It makes his stomach into a gurgling acid pit, and for the third time in thirty minutes he returns to the balcony. This time he leans over and retches. Little comes out except a bright, silver line of spit, as gossamer as spider silk. He has been starving himself again in an attempt to fight corpulence.

His view of Venice is made hazy by watery eyes. Too much is happening at once: his life's tapestry is unraveling, and again the loosest threads belong to 1816. He remembers well the night Claire rowed herself across Lake Leman and kneeled before him. The intercourse is less clear—a blur of wine and laudanum. He remembers waking sometime in the dark and glancing over at her, only to find a different face than hers staring back. It was white and ghoulish—the same face that came to his window on the later night of prophecy. What face was it? What spirit possessed him on both nights, used him to father both the prophecy and the girl? And the boy's voice that issued from his pen—could it not have belonged to a girl instead? Yes, he is sure of it. He is very certain of one thing—

The child is evil and will cause the very darkness he has seen.

He has not dared to voice outright his opinion of this false second daughter. Who would comprehend it? Who would hear and not straight away take him to a mad house? He cannot risk being separated from this creature called Allegra, despite his revulsion and dread. He must determine what part she plays. But what part could she play? How could she—or any person—cause such a catastrophe? Such a deed is impossible, even to the irrational mind.

Nevertheless.

No one would believe him, not even Shiloh. Especially not Shiloh. Neither are the same men who commenced a friendship by the waters of Lake Leman; perhaps the men they are now cannot be friends at all. Shelley has sought to be a prophet in his own right, embracing the political, ranting against every social ill or inequality, every economic disparity. He rages against the material world in fine verse that often approaches the apocalyptic. This, Byron believes, is a direct reaction to Byron's visions. Unable to reproduce the mystic, Shelley now embraces the evident, openly scoffing at what he calls Byron's sordid fairytale of the sun's death. At best, he concedes the work has many fine images. But fine images do not feed the homeless or clothe the poor. That, Shelley says, is the poet's true purpose.

Less than a month ago, indeed, he mocked the prophecy to Byron's face with more impertinence that Pollydolly ever dared. Acting as an emissary of Claire, Shelley brought Allegra to him and marked Byron's immediate shock upon seeing the girl. The child did not stand in his presence longer than five minutes before Byron ordered Fletcher to remove her.

"Good God, Byron! Why do you act so?"

"Her face," Byron said.

"It is fine and beautiful, a perfect blend of her parents."

Byron gritted his teeth at this. Poor Shiloh could not see the familiar, ghastly visage so obviously present in the girl. Poor Shiloh could not detect the sinister.

They argued about it. Shelley suggested he take Allegra back to Claire at once. Byron refused. When Shelley demanded to know why, since he obviously would not have the girl in his sight, Byron had limped to one corner of his room and opened a chest from which he retrieved a book—a collection of poems from 1816 called *The Prisoner of Chillon*. When Shelley read the title a flush colored his pale cheeks. His gaze became chastising.

As Byron's fingers made a noisy shuffling through the pages, Shelley said, "You're going to read that damnable hallucination to me again, aren't you?"

Byron grunted and looked down to see his fingers had stopped of their own volition at the page he wanted. He read the first line, choking back an involuntary sob. The prophecy. The only thing it did not have after that remarkable night of writing was a title. Byron, hoping against hope, had decided to call it "A Dream." It was Murray who published it as "Darkness."

"I don't understand," Shelley said. "Why do you read this now? Surely this is a happy occasion. Allegra is your daughter, Byron. Why forsake concrete happiness for..."

"For what?"

"Morbid obscurity."

"The author of *Alastor* dares to accuse me of obscurity?"

Shelley smiled. "The point of your poem is entirely alien. The reader misunderstands that the darkness you describe is really a personal failure. The darkness is the heart of man, not the sun's eclipse."

"Quite wrong, Shelley."

"I think not. The problem, Byron, is that poets are not prophets. They are legislators. Unacknowledged, perhaps, but—"

"Oh, I am quite acknowledged, Shiloh."

"The poet must be political. He must engage with the real problems—"

"Perhaps you did not hear my speech years ago in the House of Lords, defending the frame-breakers?"

"I'd prefer *that* Byron to the one who talks of visions."

"You would not call it talk, Shelley, had you experienced them rather than excelled yourself at fraud."

The prolonged silence that followed had caused good, loyal, eavesdropping Fletcher to knock on the door. He opened it, peering in timidly, and said, "May I be of service to your Lordship?"

"No," Byron said. His curt tone had belied his gratitude at the intervention; the interruption did not break the anger building between himself and Shelley, but it did keep it from exploding outright. Shelley, however, seemed eager for ignition.

"The desolate fires you describe are really the guilt burning in the mind of man over his past and current inequities. These start with parents. Your poem obscures the practical with symbolism."

Byron glared at Shelley after this pronouncement. "Are you suggesting that in some fit of madness I wrote about my own failures as a father?"

"Not at all," Shelley said, his tone indicating otherwise. "The poem is expansive: we are all failures. Our parents failed us; we fail our children. Who can argue?"

"Certainly not you, if I recall correctly."

Shelley leaned closer to him. "The future is always directed by the present course of affairs. Today's unloved, neglected children will become tomorrow's stewards. It is a cycle, Byron, a devious system. A father's violations will consume his son, as a mother's will consume her daughter. What is Wordsworth's grand line?"

"Wordsworth has no grand lines."

"He has at least one. 'The child is father of the man.'"

Shelley walked away, leaving the argument hanging between them. Byron has not seen him since.

I cannot do it, he thinks. I haven't the capacity to—to kill a child.

A terrible racket from within the villa stirs Byron. He turns toward the sturdy wooden door, which like every other door here seems built for barricades and sieges. There is good reason, for he resides in the home of Count Guiccioli, a political radical and cuckold. The Count is an old man with a beautiful young wife named Teresa. Such men doom themselves to betrayal in love. It is an old and familiar story, and Byron merely plays his part. Damned by double liaisons, he may one day need a sturdy door to keep out the Count's political enemies—or the Count himself. He can foresee either happening very clearly. Sometimes he feels he's written and read too much to think of himself as anything except a character living in a story.

The world is a story, he thinks, and I have glimpsed the last page.

Byron limps forward as the commotion increases, drowning out all other sound, all thought, becoming so loud indeed, he wonders if the Count's men have begun a revolution. Surely all this chaos is not of Allegra's making. Or is this a foretaste of the havoc she'll incite in maturity? Why did he not let Shelley take this wretch back with him? What ruin has he brought upon himself?

The answer is more complicated than he'll admit. When he learned Claire had a daughter by him, his first thoughts were of Ada. His ex-wife had taken her from him. Could he not avenge himself on all women by hurting Claire, taking what she loved most? A woman had stripped him of his first daughter; now he'd strip a woman of his second.

In this sense, Allegra hardly seemed a living being to him. The idea of another daughter, a second Ada, had overwhelmed his sensibilities and focused all of his desire. If he could not raise Ada, he would raise Allegra, and she would love him. Allegra, he'd vowed, would go forth in all the love and devotion he could bestow on Ada only from afar.

Then, of course, he saw her face and knew.

Now Byron can only imagine her going forth in bloodshed and eternal night. The cries she makes are a howl of death. How is it that no one else understands? The servants, reacting to the girl's fierce temper tantrums, say, "How much like her father she is!" Already her eyes flash with a will to subjugate. Her womanhood will be terrible. Will she seduce some future warlord, some purer Napoleon, and urge a bloodbath that blots out the sun? Or will she, standing fully grown on some mountain peak, simply lift her hand toward the sun and kill it with a gesture?

I had a dream that was not all a dream, he thinks. For it has become my daughter.

A frantic knock assaults his frayed nerves. The door opens before he can speak, and one of the Count's servants enters, a handsome middle-aged woman. The sound of Allegra's straining throat triples in volume without the door as barrier.

"Your daughter, she is very spirited," says the servant in Italian. "I think she would benefit from her father's presence."

"I do not," he answers in her language.

Being an Italian woman, she obviously considers rebukes from a nobleman to be of little consequence. She tries again and Byron shouts at her.

Now the servant fumes. "Is this the English way with their children?"

"It is my way. That is all that matters."

The woman bows and retreats. Before Byron can realize this is a feint, a ruse, Allegra enters. She rushes in and stops, staring up at Byron with her small mouth gaping.

"Papa!"

Byron sees the doorway empty. The woman has tricked him, and he is alone with the girl. "Fletcher!" he shouts. "Fletcher, come to me at once!"

Allegra steps nearer. "Papa?" She says this with a giggle of delight.

"Papa, papa, papa!"

Byron steps back on each repetition.

They stare at each other. Byron sees Claire and himself in equal measure in the girl's face. He sees also the unmistakable *third* element, the demon laughing at him behind her vibrant eyes. Turn her face but an inch to the left or right, and it reveals itself wholly.

"Fletcher!"

"Papa, papa, papa," she says, rushing at him.

Byron shouts again. The girl is flying at him. She hisses; she has fangs. Byron stumbles, his clubfoot spilling him shrieking to the ground. He strikes his forehead on the marble, and the pain, so sharp, stirs memories of a prior agony. The butt of his right hand pressed to the spot, and he thinks—as Allegra throws herself upon him, crying out, "Papa! Papa! Papa!"—that Claire and he were both used. Something lurking in Lake Leman possessed their bodies to conceive this monster. I was used, he thinks, to give birth to the prophecy of darkness. Claire was used to give birth to the darkness itself—

"Enough!"

He swings his arm, connecting with the little girl, striking her, sending her screaming off him. Bleary eyed, Byron reaches for anything to help him stand. When he rises, he finds the sky darkening. A pall settles over the world. He watches the shadow fall across the city, turning the canal waters into black ink. Beyond the city, the horizon becomes murky, revealing stars that blink out of existence almost as soon as they appear. He limps all the way to the balcony. His breath comes out in white blasts. The sea, the city, the boats in the canals below cannot be seen.

"Papa," Allegra says.

Byron gasps. She is a grown woman now, her expression cold. She holds a candle in her left hand. In her right, the book, opened to the poem—to the prophecy.

"I had a dream, which was not all a dream," she reads.

"Stop it."

"The bright sun was extinguished, and the stars—"

"Silence!"

Byron lunges forward and slaps the book to the ground. Allegra continues her recitation without it. Of course she knows it. The words are the marrow of her bones. Her face becomes hideous, revealed in full. Suddenly so much blood comes from her mouth it drowns her words and splashes the floor.

"You were right, Father: the prophecy and I are twins."

Screaming, he grapples with the woman. As he seizes her, she becomes a little girl again. Her tiny legs kick and she screams as he lifts her over his head. Her small scratching fingers dig at Byron's ears, then at his eyes. For a moment he can see nothing, his vision blocked by her swirling hair, her writhing body. He lifts her higher, sees the balcony barely visible against the midnight world. He marches toward it with the girl hoisted high and horizontal, is about to throw her into the canals below, when a sight freezes him. It is an orange flicker blossoming. A building has been set ablaze. Below him, one of the canal boats also flares. The fires begin fast.

The world's great burning has begun.

"Stop!" he shouts into the darkness. "Stop! I shall restore the sun!"

He moves to cast this hellspawn down—

"Lord Byron!"

Hands seize his elbows, his wrists. His forehead pounds with pain, and he falls, feeling the weight of so many burdens lifted. The child, the demon— where is she? He finds Fletcher with the girl in his arms, trying to calm her, guarded by a handful of the Count's men. These are political agitators, Carbonari—some known to Byron, some unknown. Rough louts with bushy beards, who keep a bevy of women with them, usually wet and half-dressed like a school of mermaids just appeared from the canals. They have seen everything, which makes their astonishment more jarring to Byron's ears—

"Lord Byron has tried to kill his own daughter! He is mad!"

Even Fletcher gapes at his master in horror. Allegra turns her crying, stricken face to them all.

Do these fools not see? Do they not see the night sky in the middle of the day? He looks up. The blue sky is a luxurious fabric overhead, sewn with thin seams of white clouds. The sun is a gold broach.

"Take her away," Byron says. His voice barely musters sound.

Fletcher turns and gives Allegra to a woman—who strokes the child's hair as she hurries from the room.

"Let me summon you a doctor, milord."

Fletcher waits until Byron's silence suggests he will not answer. When he turns to leave, Byron says, "No. Summon me a priest."

Fletcher's hands come out in a beseeching gesture. Byron waves him off.

"Not for myself, Fletcher. Bring a priest and tell him I have a daughter I wish to commit to a convent and the security of nuns."

They are better equipped than I to do God's will, he thinks.

Fletcher lingers. Byron curses at him and sends him running. Alone, he studies the bright sky. The day is fine and so is the city. Life teems.

But the darkness is coming.

S hiloh is dead.

Byron's eyelids open to darkness. His fingers curl the bedclothes into his damp palms. "Shelley." His voice sounds childish to his ears, defenseless, and he shivers. He was having a dream of boyhood, of his nurse entering his room. She motions him to be quiet and then her hands curl the bedclothes to her palms before she brings them down. She looks at his clubfoot and then lifts his nightshirt to uncover his penis, telling him they look a bit alike. It was a dream, but was not all a dream. For the next few waking moments those hands remain too real, more real even than the crushing news of Shelley's drowning. Restless in the darkness, he realizes for the first time that he hates the touch of women. They all have the same devious hands.

Grunting, he swings his legs off the bed, his left hand groping the nightstand for one of the many pistols he keeps nearby out of old habit. Armed, he limps sightless toward the western wall and his memory of its wooden shutters. When he cannot find them, Byron's panic becomes inexplicable even to himself, and he raises the gun and fires. The flare of gunpowder is, for a second, like a sunburst showing every detail of the room. Then the darkness recovers, everywhere except for a single hole in front of him showing silver light. Byron smiles. He has aimed and shot true, hitting the shutters over the windowless glass. The bullet hole lets in a stream of precious moonlight.

Drawn to it, he pushes the shutters until they swing forward and his face finds the generosity of the warm Pisan air. The moon is full and he gazes up at it like a penitent. Ah, Shiloh, he thinks, how different this summer of 1822 is compared to 1816. By the waters of Lake Leman none of us could go a-roving, and now you shall go no more a-roving—though the moon be still as bright.

His expression turns petulant.

Behind him, almost materializing in the room, lithe hands touch the small of his back. Byron flinches and turns, though he knows it is Teresa, the wife of Count Guiccioli. Likely the gunfire woke her. Woke her but did not concern her, being the wife of a revolutionary: Byron approves.

"The moon when it is like this, Byron; it is…heavy."

"Full."

"It is for lovers."

Without looking at her, he says, "The full moon is nothing but the sun for the sleepless."

"You are sleepless because of your dear friend?"

Dear friend? When? In 1816? Perhaps not even then.

"In my experience, Teresa, friendships die before the friend. This conveniently shortens grief."

Byron knows he has confused her. Teresa begins another attempt in her stilted English, pauses, and then launches into a barrage of Italian. She weeps in that language. Once Byron imagined sorrow was a universal tongue, but at the age of thirty-four he now knows better. Grief is subject not only to gender but to nationality, and Byron is supposed to mourn as an Englishman. An *aristocratic* Englishman. Yet he is a poet too. Stiff upper lips are not the stuff of epicedes.

"I *am* a poet," he says to the moon, in the tone of an old man recovering fogged memories. As he stares at it, the moon takes on a face, the same death mask that confronted him on the strange and terrifying night he composed his prophecy. Byron gasps, straightening, though the sight does not terrify him as it did the first time. Now it feels like the start of an answer to years of questions.

"Who are you?" he says. "Where have you been?"

"Byron," Teresa says, her tone uncertain.

"Have you not afflicted me enough? The prophecy was a lie. This fabrication has cost me dear!"

He hears Teresa's small, retreating steps and risks a glance back to see her far back in the room, her hands clasped prayerfully at her chest. "You talk to ghosts," she says, her tone quavering.

"Ghosts? Yes. The ghost of Shelley. The ghost of Allegra."

The mention of the little girl's name causes Teresa to sob out, "Padre dolente, padre dolente!" and run from the room. Byron grabs hold of the windowsill and cranes his head back up at the moon.

"My child—my second child! I should have named her Isaac since she was born to be sacrificed by her father. What God are you, not to stay my hand? Now she is dead because of *my* madness, *my* idiocy. *Padre dolente* indeed! Thank the stars sharing the night sky with you that Ada is far removed from me. I can only hope my lunacy is equally distant and that she inherited no fiber of my mind!"

The death mask looks down on him with no expression. Returning a glare, he thinks, I will make you suffer, and leaves the window, limping back to fetch another loaded gun he can fire into the sky.

Instead, he changes course for the trunk in the corner of the room. Opening it, he shifts through stacks of papers until he finds *it*, the haunted prophecy from 1816. Clutching the manuscript, Byron limps from his room, down the hallway and out of the villa's front door, waving the pages up at the moon along the way. His crippled gait develops a savage intensity. He will throw the prophecy into the sea under this strange countenance's staring eyes.

When he reaches the beach several minutes later though, he pauses, stunned to see Shelley and Allegra walking hand in hand along the coast. Their backs are to him and they will not turn, no matter how hard he calls.

"Allegra, I am sorry. This," he says, waving the pages, "is my torment and madness. Come back to me, child."

He rushes after them, plunging his clubfoot into the forgiving sand to ameliorate the pain of his hurried stride. He has never walked faster in his life, yet he cannot catch them despite their slow, loving stroll.

God, he thinks, if I am to hallucinate them, then let me hallucinate a hundred Shilohs walking with a hundred Allegras, so I might at least speak to a single pair. Let the ghosts of the dead be abundant tonight. Come forth, Pollydolly, he thinks; join with Shiloh and Allegra and confront me as a trinity of wraiths.

"You both died so quick," he says, continuing his pursuit. "Does no one sicken and linger long enough anymore to grant forgiveness before expiring?"

For a moment it seems like they hear him. Byron gains ground. Here is Shelley, dead in a boating accident weeks ago, his body found but yesterday, washed up on a beach; there is Allegra, just three months dead following a sudden fever in the care of the very nuns Byron thought might—what? Tame her soul? Exorcise the demon Byron had seen in her, believed to be in league with the prophecy he holds in his hands?

He twists the manuscript tight as if to strangle it.

"Shiloh, you were always right. There is no prophecy. There is only symbolism, buried guilt, hurt children and failed parents. I should have listened to you. My own madness has consumed me. Turn and see my solution, Shelley! I am Kronos!"

He tears off a corner of paper and puts it into his mouth. It melts into his spit, dissolves, and is swallowed. At once Byron rips off a larger piece.

That damned freezing summer. How different life would be had he gone elsewhere six years ago. There would be no Shiloh to know, wound and lose. No Allegra to conceive, fear and consign to a lonely death. No damnable prophecy to rule his life. Prophecy? he thinks. Even now do I call it a prophecy?

"Shelley! Won't you turn to me? Do the dead keep life's regrets? Do ghosts hold to the grudges of flesh? I know you were trapped. You had your duties as Claire's...friend."

If only he had given the child back to her mother, as Shiloh urged. Why was he so determined that Allegra should be kept from Claire? Was it really his fear of the prophecy exerting its force? Now the child is dead. Who needs a vision of the world on fire? he thinks. Each of us burns the world down in front of us every day.

Byron stops, staggers his weight on his good foot, wads the whole manuscript into a ball and bites into it as he might the juiciest apple.

As he does, the two wraiths stop. Only Shelley's ghost turns.

"What else will you do to prevent the end of the world, Byron?"

"Shelley," Byron says after struggling to swallow.

"What else, Albe?"

"I have done enough."

"You have killed a child."

"I believed she was dangerous. I believed—"

"In your prophecy?"

"Yes."

The ghost of Shelley laughs. "You are a coward, Byron. You call your poem a prophecy, yet you won't say so before the public. How can one read 'Darkness' and discern prophecy from fancy? The true prophet stands on the street shouting his case. You fear to be thought mad. You fear to lose your audience. You fear, ultimately, that you yourself believe in nothing you write. Was there ever so faithless a prophet as you?"

"I doomed the child, Shelley. At least her death has freed me. I know what the prophecy is now: pointless scribbling, conceived in guilt. Shiloh, don't turn away. Here is what remains of it. Watch me consume the prophecy before it consumes me. Shelley!"

But the ghost reaches for Allegra's hand, and both shades shimmer and disappear, leaving Byron in a rage. He flashes his gaze up to the moon. The death mask is not there. It was never there. He stares, gratified the moonlight can still seem cold even in this warm summer air, and watches the bright orb accelerate in its transit across the sky. He stays rooted there as the sun rises and sets, rises and sets.

And rises.

"Byron?"

He blinks, stirring from his trance. The sun is high and sweltering overhead. The beach glistens, each particle an atom of sunlight. Where is he? Only a moment ago it was night, and he chased after the ghosts of Shelley and Allegra. But that was weeks ago.

On a different beach.

Viareggio. He is at Viareggio.

Like the doddering old man he is certain he'll never live to become, Byron turns away from the sea and finds a nearby crowd. He pivots again to see what they're looking at, as if he needs to remember Shelley's funeral pyre. Shiloh's body washed ashore at last after being lost at sea, and the authorities have not let Mary or anyone else move it for fear of disease.

Now it is to be burned.

Mary is not here. She mourns in seclusion, leaving the task of cremation to a small circle of Shelley's associates—Byron, the insipid Leigh Hunt, and a fascinating adventurer named Trelawney. It is Trelawney who calls Byron's name a second time, once more demanding his attention to the present. Byron limps toward him, though his gaze remains upon the onlookers, come to see a poet and an atheist burned. He sees children with their mothers, and thinks back to the first vision he experienced when he dove into the frigid waters of Lake Leman. He thought he saw Shiloh feeding his child to a fire. Instead children will watch him burn.

Shelley's body lies across the metal grate of a furnace designed by Trelawney for the task at hand. The grate is itself suspended above a secondary iron grid piled with wood and coal. The corpse's flesh has an unearthly indigo tint, a blue-black darkness like that of a Hindu god. Trelawny has a torch, which he begins to wave in extravagant motions as he chants ritualistic things that seem quite pagan. More appropriate for my funeral, Byron thinks, than for Shiloh's. This strange sermon delays the inevitable only a few minutes, and then Trelawny touches the torch to the pyre's fuel. Flames race across the length of the grid. Waves of clear heat follow an initial burst of smoke as the flames lengthen, tonguing through each and every opening to taste Shelley's body as some eager scavenger.

Byron covers his mouth and shakes his head. *This* is how a body burns? He dips into the reservoirs of his self-control in order not to laugh out loud. Once more Shiloh is victorious: even his death mocks the prophecy. In Byron's visions the bodies burned so fast, the fire turning even the bones to ash in minutes. Yet here Shelley's body has not even begun to smoke! How could the vision be true, when it is wrong on this key detail?

He sways, pounded by the heat of the sun and the growing intensity of the blaze. Trewlany's furnace sends a rippling sear in all directions, forcing even the keenest onlookers to a cooler retreat. There's a subtle, sickening noise as Shelley's torso breaks open, followed by a shocking hiss like air screaming from a teakettle. The furnace walls amplify the noises of liquefaction. Byron's nausea triples. He must not leave here until this business is finished. Is it not finished? The first traces of Shelley's ashes have started their ascent into a Godless sky.

Drawing a collective gasp from the crowd, including Trelawney, Byron purposely hobbles away, moving down the beach and shedding his clothes as he nears the water. He hears the murmurs of those behind him, some enchanted by this display of madness, others calling it the most obscene act of whoring, to upstage a friend's cremation. Trelawny calls out to him. Down to his breeches and his boots now, Byron simply laughs. He eases his clubfoot out of its special shoe. His trousers fall about his ankles as he reaches the shoreline. The Mediterranean makes furtive passes at his toes and then a strong surge washes over his feet. He stares at his personal yacht, *Bolivar*, anchored a few miles out. He does not remember arriving on it, but it is there and he will swim to it. He looks once to his right and left, half wishing Shelley and Polidori were beside him again on an icy cold summer's day. All lakes are the same Lake. All seas are the same Sea. The sun torments his pale, exposed shoulders. How could he ever imagine a force so powerful simply dying?

Nothing bedevils the sun, he thinks. The sun bedevils us.

He walks forward until the sea encircles his waist. Leaning forward, he lets the current lift him off his feet and launch him. The water does not mind that he is older, fatter. The water does not freeze his lungs, does not call him under to dark visions. Within moments he feels ten years younger. These limbs are the same that once got him across the Hellespont. But as he kicks and strokes harder, Byron soon fatigues. Out less than a mile, he surrenders and lets himself float. He turns, facing the receding land. The beach from this distance has a striking, haunting beauty. The sunlight's angle gives the sand a browner, more fertile hue and makes the greenery in the distance dark and somber. The only thing unchanged is the sun's intense heat. His skin has reddened considerably. There will be blisters.

Laughing, swearing, Byron floats on his back and gives the front of his torso to the scorching light. See, Shiloh, he thinks, am I not a friend in the end? Do I let you suffer alone? Each of us on our backs in our own furnace. Fare thee well.

He rolls onto his stomach. The sun's rays whip his back and shoulders, buttocks and legs. He cannot stand the pain of roasting like this, and tears come to his eyes. There is something particularly futile about crying into the sea. He stares, eyes wide open, into the lifeless blue depths.

And then, shockingly, there is a face. It rushes past him, provoking an obscene chill against the intense sun. He screams the last of his oxygen at it in five furious bubbles—"*Go back to Lake Leman!*"

The face moves past him. Byron shrieks, lifting his head from the water as he turns looking in all directions. That face again. But how can it be? What can it be?

To his right, a dolphin breaks the surface and launches into the air. Byron gapes at it, realizing this is all he saw. The prophecy is dead, the visions unreal. Life is for living.

The dolphin splashes back into the water and swims far away. Byron tries to follow but the glare on the waves overwhelms him. When he dips his gaze into the water again, the only face that meets him is the expansive, eternal sea, and when he lifts himself from the surface again, he is a poet not a prophet, a man not a god, and he is alive and he is swimming in light.

CHAPTER SEVEN

Fane lowers the poetry anthology and peeks at George, asleep in the other bed, lying on his side, with his back to Fane. The poem's words echo in Fane's head.

Do I dare
Disturb the universe?
In a minute there is time
For decisions and revisions which a minute will reverse.

What if he's awake? thinks Fane. What if he's waiting for me to come to him?

The thought excites him to the point of discomfort. His hopes are too wild, like horses dragging him toward a ravine. He rises as stealthily as he can and goes to the hotel room window. Even at one in the morning, New York is not a place of darkness, though just now Fane finds enough gloom in his thoughts to blacken all of those lights.

Courage to taste. Courage to touch. Courage to disturb the universe.

His universe is on the bed. His universe is snoring.

Fane turns, beaming. So George snores. What a wonderful discovery!

He wishes he could hear it...more closely.

He sits down on his bed across from George and regards the ticking clock. Morning's coming, and it will be busy from the sound of it. They arrived yesterday and George soon proved himself the master of the city. He'd spent two years here before his parents moved, and he led George through the streets and the subway system without need of a compass or a map. Once again Fane had felt cheated by his parents; if they'd only given him the same freedom as George got from his parents, his life would be different. He'd be confident. Maybe he'd even be leading *George* someplace, and would live life rather than read about it.

He's not sure why he even brought the book along. George didn't tell him to, and there shouldn't be time for reading; this trip is about living. Why else did he risk turning on the light? He had to see what George looked like sleeping. And if I woke him, Fane thinks—well. But instead he turned on the light and grabbed the blasted book, pretending to be absorbed in it for twenty minutes, while his gaze kept wanting to leave the page and find the *real* poetry in the room.

It's not right. I mustn't, he thinks.

He forces himself to read the book again.

The poem's by T.S. Eliot, and at this moment Fane thinks T.S. Eliot the greatest, truest poet who ever lived. He wants to live in Whitman's world of exuberant daring, but the truth is he's breathing air in Eliot's. He's come across this poem many times in the past and always skipped past it, being unable to understand any of it. But in the last few weeks that's changed. He's found an affinity for the poem's tone and mood. One particular line rings especially true—

It is impossible to say just what I mean!

Fane reads those words now and nods, his lips pressing tighter. He looks at George again, covered to the shoulders by the sheet and bedspread. An imagined arm bridges the distance between the beds; an imagined hand pulls the covers down.

Shall I dare disturb the Universe?

Fane closes the book. He does so loudly, hoping to goad George awake. He'll turn and say, "Mate?" and then, perhaps, Fane will be able to say what he means. But George's light snoring continues.

He turns off the light and manages a few hours of restive sleep before sunlight strikes him through the unshielded window. He wakes to confusion, forgetting where he is, wondering why this isn't his room at home or the Fowler dormitory. Then George turns in the other bed, finally facing Fane. It happens like a shot, paralyzing him. Why he should be paralyzed he has no idea; he's looked George in the face hundreds of times. Never like this though.

His eyes seem so little, his eyelids more delicate than flower petals. The sunlight moves over his face, and those eyelids now take on a soft pink tint that makes the blue eyes they protect even more precious. His tousled hair seems a lighter shade of brown, almost golden. But Fane scarcely has time to appreciate that detail, as George's eyebrows now capture his attention. They seem like they'd be so soft to the touch, and cool. He smiles at the absurdity. Yet he finds his right hand stretching toward George's face to feel.

He falls out of bed.

The impact of his body sounds tremendous, and he lies there a moment wondering what's happened. Has he been stricken by God? Has the earth moved? Slowly picking himself up, he finds George still asleep. He's standing almost beside George now. Isn't this the time to reach down his hand and—what? The answer so overwhelms him that he rushes over to the window. Maybe the blinding sunlight will purge his desires.

How strange it is to be in a room like this, he feels, with the sounds of the vast, waking city audible but muted here on the seventh story. Mornings are much louder in the Fowler dorms, though next fall he and George will start their junior years. Juniors and seniors are afforded private rooms. He and George will room together, won't they? Why hasn't George asked him yet?

Maybe he'll ask this summer.

George hasn't brought it up, but Fane's certain he'll invite him over again. They'll make another visit to the cave—perhaps their last, for even Fane has hit a growth spurt since last summer. It might be impossible for them to wedge through the crevice. He hopes not; he's certain George is waiting until they get into the cavern chamber again before discussing rooming together in the fall.

Then every day could be like this.

Imagine waking up every day in a private room with George, he thinks. Imagine watching his best friend sleeping. Such peace, such contentment. He turns away from the window and regards the beds. How will the beds be arranged in their room at Fowler? Parallel to each other? Perpendicular? What if they're placed in a strange pattern that means he can't see George's face? Fane touches his chest as his heartbeat accelerates.

Then he realizes George is awake and staring at him. When he speaks, his voice sounds seductively sleepy. "You okay, Adam?"

"I couldn't sleep. Too excited."

George sits up, stretching.

"We'll get an early start."

"I want to do it all."

He laughs. "Adam Fane, the master of Broadway and Boardwalk."

They wash up and get dressed. While George finishes showering, Fane takes his Fowler pea coat and lays it out on the bed. George has warned him New York might be chilly, not the usual place to go for spring break. That's only a plus in Fane's opinion, since he prefers winter clothes and considers his school coat the single garment he actually looks good wearing.

"You ready?"

"Yeah," Fane says.

George pops out of the bathroom fully dressed, but his hair still wet. "I thought you said you were ready, Fane."

Fane looks at himself. "What's wrong?"

"Come here, mate."

George pulls him back into the bathroom. The heat of the shower hangs heavy in the air, and steam fogs the mirror. George wipes the mirror clean with a washcloth and they stand side-by-side, staring into the mirror. Fane keeps his gaze locked on his own reflection.

"You've got to start combing your hair differently, Adam. It's always plastered too much to your skull. Girls don't go for the Hitler look. Here, do this." George takes a comb through his own wet bangs and slicks his hair back. It reminds Fane a bit of watching his mother sculpt icing on a cake. "See? Just like President Kennedy."

His pulse rapid, his whole being aching for change, Fane takes the comb and tries to imitate George's maneuver. The result is abominable and Fane groans.

"Don't give up yet, mate. Here."

"You're going to comb my hair for me?"

George pauses. "When you put it like that, I guess I won't."

"Good. I don't like the wet dog look."

He grins into the mirror. "Wet dog? Just wait until we hit the streets where the pretty girls are. They can pet me all day long."

Fane nods. "You're right, though. I should comb my hair differently. Maybe hide the mole."

"Why do you want to hide it?"

"It's...ugly."

"If I had that mole, I'd be pointing it out to every girl I saw. I'd tell them that's where they're supposed to kiss me. And there's a *lot* of girls in New York."

Fane looks at the countertop. George prods him and laughs.

"Don't worry, mate. I'll leave some for you."

"What sort of girls?"

George shrugs and now he does start combing Fane's hair. "Guess I never thought about it. Just girls. There's one street I remember where all the girls sit out on their stoops and talk to men as they pass by."

Fane pictures a street lined by girls and women on both side. He imagines them all dressed like waitresses eager to take an order.

"What do they say, George?"

"*Hello.*"

"Just hello?"

"Yeah. Quit turning your head. You're messing me up."

"And—and what do *we* do?"

"We say hello back. It's what boys on holiday do."

When George finishes, Fane's hair is parted on the left and combed forward a little. He actually has brought the bangs down a bit to hide the mole. Fane stares at his reflection—*their* reflection—and his eyes water. He looks...normal. Natural. He cannot explain it, but suddenly he *feels* natural. He'd like just to stand here looking at the two of them, but George claps him on the shoulder and they put on their coats and go down to the lobby. The hotel has a café attached to it.

"My parents always used this hotel for guests when company came. Our place in the city was small. I don't know how many times I've eaten breakfast here."

"Your parents are really amazing, letting you do this."

"Your parents are amazing too."

"Only because they trust *you.*"

"You sure? I think my parents only let me come because they trust you."

"It's because I'm more mature, being older."

"Adam Fane the Big Tickle."

Fane's known George's birthday almost from the moment they met, but they actually discovered their age difference on the train ride to New York. George was born in February, Fane in June. Fane just assumed George was older by four months and was shocked to discover they were not born in the same year. He's actually older than George by *eight months*. Being older than George feels unnatural. It unsettles the universe.

"I'll keep you safe from harm, George."

"Babysitting is dirty business."

"Wipe your tears away, diaper you as needed."

George screws his face up. Blushing, Fane starts apologizing only to realize George is holding back a laugh.

"How come you never show this side to anyone?"

"What side?"

"Your *funny* side, Fane. You'd own Fowler if you just let loose."

"Oh yeah," Fane says, looking at the patterns in the wood tabletop. "Dooley and his lot are so big on jokes."

"Well, if you save all the comedy for me, I'm honored."

"I feel comfortable with you."

George smiles.

A waitress comes over. George orders them a larger breakfast than Fane wants or can afford. He'd like to know how much cash George's parents gave him, because it is already clear his own parents radically shorted him. Not out of malice, but ignorance. George's parents have been places. They know what things cost, and they know how to make their son confident. Fane's confidence is as thin as his wallet, and getting thinner each time he watches George pay for this and that. Yesterday he picked up both lunch and supper. He insisted on it.

Just as he insists on paying for breakfast now, but since Fane ate so little, he feels less complicated about it.

Now they set off. Yesterday was spent walking and riding buses and subways. Now George ostentatiously hails a cab. Puzzled at first, Fane bursts into panic when a taxi actually pulls up to the curb.

"What are you doing? You're going to get us into trouble!"

George laughs, opening the door and gesturing. "Come on, Fane."

"You mean we're actually getting in?"

"You bet. Your leg will thank me later."

Fane gets in, still convinced George is playing a joke. He'll shut the door, lean through the window and tell the driver to take him back to Fowler. But George gets in too and says, "Take us to the museum."

"Which museum, kid?"

George frowns. For the first time, Fane senses a touch of nervousness about his friend. Finally he says, "The big one," and sits back with a smile as the taxi joins traffic. He slaps Fane's arm with the back of his hand. "How great is this, Fane? This town has so many museums you've got to specify."

The driver looks at them in the rearview mirror. "Boys, I'm assuming you either want the Met or MOMA. What'll it be?"

George and Fane exchange glances.

"What's MOMA?"

"The Museum of Modern Art."

"Then take us to the Met," George says. "Does my friend here look like a guy who enjoys modern art?"

Now Fane finds the taxi driver peering at him through the window. He's never felt so inspected, so judged. He blurts out, "I—I like all art. I don't care where we go. I like modern things. Tell him, George."

"My mate likes modern things," and both George and the driver laugh.

George nudges him again, getting Fane to smile. Nervous energy swells in him. Are they going to the museum to appease him? Does George know the idea of seeing a museum excites him far more than walking down a street full of girls?

The drive takes only fifteen minutes, and when they get out George pays again, and they start up the steps to the intimidating entrance. Fane pauses, looking back as the taxi pulls away. It's becoming too easy to watch George peel off dollar bills. He feels in his coat pocket for his wallet, so slim it might be empty. George meanwhile keeps on climbing without looking back. *Is he sore at me?*

He ascends with almost exaggerated care, dizzied by the museum's stone façade sweeping out in front of him. It looks to be a mile long. On either side of the exquisite central building, with its columns and cornices and corbels, are wings and additions in such various styles that it seems like someone took several of the great palaces of Europe and sandwiched them together across the horizon.

George reaches the top and turns like a king surveying his subjects from on high. He hollers down over the heads of people coming and going. "Come on, Fane! The paintings aren't getting any younger!"

Fane hesitates on the next step. His right leg hurts a little and he points at it to let George know. George nods, but Fane sees no sympathy in his face, just eyes rolling in impatience. He remembers how George hugged him after the challenging journey to the cave. Are these steps any less a challenge? Why is he being so mean? Is he mad about the money?

After a couple of minutes, he reaches the top step. George stuffs his hands into his pockets and says, "You okay?"

"Yeah. You don't have to ask that every time. I'm just a bit slower than everyone else at some things, like stairs."

"I know. Sorry to jump ahead, mate. Let's go in."

"How much does it cost?"

"Don't worry about it."

"I want to pay. I—I *need* to pay."

George grins. "Fane the big spender! Am I an orphan? Is this Daddy Warbucks before me?"

Before Fane realizes it, he's made a fist and taken a swing. George dodges and the momentum of Fane's failed roundhouse spins him around. He winces and would have fallen except George grabs him by his coat and holds him face-to-face, their chests almost touching. People coming in and out of the museum stare at them. Fane opens his mouth but cannot speak. George grabs his right wrist and forces his arm up. Fane's hand is still balled into a fist.

"If you feel that strongly about it, Adam," he says softly, his gaze fixated on Fane's hand, "then by all means pay."

"You don't understand," Fane says, but George is already walking away, leaving Fane rubbing his knuckles, trying to massage the fist away.

Our friendship is over, he thinks. What have I done? Why did I do that?

His sense of ruin makes him turn to the top step. He places the heels of his foot on the edge, hoping to slip and break his neck. He teeters but he cannot make himself fall.

"Hey, Adam."

George's voice at his back startles him. He almost does fall now, but of course George grabs him.

"What the hell is wrong? Is paying really that important to you?"

"I can't explain. It's just—"

Why can he only engage the surface of his thoughts, a surface cold and hard like glass? Why can't he shatter that glass and get to the true meaning?

"I think I understand," George says, though Fane can't imagine how. "How about this: I'll buy your ticket, and you buy mine."

"What good is that? We might as well be buying our own ticket."

"This way it's a gift."

Fane nods and they enter the museum. In the lobby he tries to apologize. "I'm sorry. For what I did."

George punches him in the shoulder. The instant pain shocks him and numbs his whole arm. Even his coat sleeve doesn't blunt the force.

"Next time, hit me like that. Don't throw a roundhouse. That's for comic books."

They get in line for a ticket, Fane rubbing his arm the entire time. They buy each other their ticket and walk across the Great Hall. Sixty or seventy people mill about and Fane wonders how they can walk at all. He's paralyzed by the sheer gigantism of this room. Towering archways soar fifty feet over his head in all directions.

"Sure is big," George says.

"I think this is what it would be like in 'Kubla Kahn.'"

"What's that?"

"A poem I read to you. 'In Xanadu did Kubla Kahn a stately—'"

"I remember it now. I guess it is like that."

Fane shakes his head, smiling, drifting in wonder. "This place is like *every* poem ever written."

Walking with his neck craned at the ceiling, he runs into a woman who tells him to watch where he's going. He's still stuttering his apology when George tugs him by the coat and leads him into an exhibit hall to the right. The art here is not what Fane expected. Glassware and porcelain of such finery gleam like jewels.

"It's like an ancient treasure room," he says. George nods approvingly.

He leans over an exhibit of sparkling blown glass with patterns of reds and blues and subtle streaks of green. He tilts his head. If he were a creature made of glass, he knows he'd have streaks of green in him.

"Sure is quiet in here."

George is right. It's *deathly* still in the room, despite the dozens of people inspecting the displays. He looks over at George and finds his friend returning a quizzical, almost nervous stare.

"What is it, mate?"

"I feel like shouting."

George's blue eyes widen and glisten. "I dare you."

Do I dare disturb the Universe?

Fane opens his mouth, making George's eyes widen still more in anticipation.

The moment passes.

George shakes his head and walks away.

"Wait."

"Later, Fane. I'm going to see what's over here."

He starts to follow George but decides he better not. The room is darker without George's presence. But how can Fane explain that? To him the deep blue of George's eyes make all the blue china plates in the glass display to his left seem pale. Fane realizes he's not seen even a thousandth of the museum's wonders, yet he already knows the greatest art is friendship, the greatest artwork a true friend. More than a friend, a—a—

It is impossible to say just what I mean, he thinks.

Fane leaves the room and moves into another gallery, finds himself alone in a rotunda lit by soft yellow light. Compared to the sparkle and luster behind him, this room seems as dim as a movie theater. It houses a collection of statues and mounted busts, and he moves among them thinking of Medusa, stopping to read brass plaques that identify scientists and statesmen. The names are not familiar to him.

Then he sees George.

He knows it's not, of course, but as he comes closer the bust only becomes more and more like his friend. He reads the nameplate: *Lord Byron.* Fane touches the bust, despite the many signs forbidding it. "So we'll go no more a-roving," he says, his voice low, almost prayerful, as he caresses the stony forehead. He loses himself staring at Byron's face.

He was like me, he thinks.

But where is Shelley? He looks to the left and right, expecting the bust to be adjacent. Shelley's not there. Such a wonderful friendship they had. He and George could be like they were, if only they wrote poetry.

"There you are," George says, coming to stand beside Fane.

"This is Lord Byron."

"Pleased to meet you," George says with a nod.

"You're acquainted already. I've read you several of his poems."

"Which ones?"

Fane lists some titles. George whistles and taps the statue on the top of the head. "Sounds like this guy practically invented poetry. Let's look at something else."

George heads off, but Fane doesn't move. A moment later George returns. "You're still not done staring?"

"No," Fane says, swallowing against a hardness in his throat.

"What's so important about him?"

"He understood how I...feel."

George cocks his head. "What do you mean, how you feel?"

"He liked—I mean, he had a clubfoot."

"A what?"

"There was something wrong with his leg, too."

George claps him on the back. "See, Fane? A bum leg won't stop you from being famous. A hundred years from now, I bet you'll have a bust too. Look at the size of your head. That's guaranteed for marble, mate."

Fane laughs. "But I don't write."

"Then be famous doing something else. Be a famous lover—that's bound to be more fun than putting words on paper."

"Byron was famous for that, too."

"You don't say? If he was alive, I bet Byron wouldn't be hanging out in a museum. He'd be wanting to see that street full of girls."

Fane lowers his voice. "That and other things."

"What other things?"

"Well, I mean...I mean that Byron also liked..."

As Fane trails off, George goes bug-eyed. He starts laughing, a giggly, manic laugh, too loud to be polite. In fact, it draws a museum guard into the room.

"*Boys*—behave yourselves."

George starts walking fast with Fane hurrying after. But he bears down a little too hard on his weak leg and a flare of pain makes him stop. He doubles over to catch his breath and slow his heartbeat. Darkness paints the periphery of his vision.

George laughed at Byron, he thinks. He laughed at what he was.

At what I am.

He sees George heading down the long hallway, and the way his body staggers suggests he's still cracking up. Fane turns and walks in the opposite direction, not carrying where he ends up. He goes through rooms and through time. He passes between continents. He finds himself in a room full of portraits of stern, ashen faces.

They're like me too, he thinks. They don't smile for the same reason I never smile. Only fools smile. The old and the wise press their lips together.

He's still standing in that room, swaying on his feet, when George eventually finds him.

"Mate, I hate to say it, but I'm bored. This feels too much like school. You get your fill of it yet? If so, let's go outside. Anywhere is better."

"George?"

"Yeah?"

"Do I seem...sad?"

"*What?*"

George reaches out for him and Fane flinches away.

"Nothing. Forget I said anything."

"You're in New York City, Adam. How can you be sad?"

"If you feel different from everyone, you can be sad anywhere."

"How do you feel different, mate?"

Fane turns away. *Different.* The worst word in the English language, especially when paired with yourself: *I'm different.*

The people in the paintings, especially the men, appear to nod to him.

"Adam?"

Fane walks and George follows.

"What's going on, mate? What's wrong?"

"I didn't mean to ruin the art for you," Fane says.

"You're not ruining the art for me. I didn't mean it about being bored. I want to stay if you do. You can teach me about stuff, like you do with poetry."

"I don't know anything."

Fane leans forward, almost charging ahead, hobbling as fast as his right leg permits. They cross into another exhibit hall. A little girl, about four, comes running into his path and he knocks her down. "Young man!" the girl's father says, and Fane hears George helping the girl up and making excuses, his words harder to discern as Fane forges ahead.

"He's upset and not thinking, sir. I'm sorry."

Fane's leg throbs as he hobbles forward, the muscles and tendons like boa constrictors attacking the narrow bone.

"Adam, wait up!"

George's running footfalls get closer. A security guard says, "You again! No running in the Museum."

George reaches him. Fane looks at everything except George's face. This is a place of ancient artifacts in brown stone, ornaments colored by fading dyes, filthy linen wrappings. Mummies.

The same security guard approaches them. "It seems like you boys are more about playing games than learning anything. What are you two doing? Playing tag?"

"We're sorry," George says. "My friend here is just upset."

"What about?"

"I don't know."

"We'll take care of him, or else *I'm* going to be upset too. I won't give you another warning."

The guard leaves, and George hits Fane in the arm, almost in the same spot he struck before and with equal force. But this time the blow is different. It feels—vengeful. Fane glares at George through reddening eyes.

"What's wrong with you, Adam? You better be sick, because I don't like getting yelled at by angry dads and policemen."

Fane tries to move away but George grabs his arm.

"Not going to talk? Is that the plan?" George laughs without humor, a hard and contemptuous sound. "Fane, I swear to God if words were teeth I'd be your dentist."

"I'm sorry."

"Just be normal, okay?"

He nods. George is really glowering at him, and it shrinks him to submission. But the glare softens after a minute; he scans the room for the first time, taking everything in.

"Ancient Egypt," he says. "My parents want to go there, but we'll probably do Europe first. This summer, maybe."

"*This* summer?" Fane's voice sounds small to his own ears.

"I think that's the plan."

"The *whole* summer?"

"How should I know?"

"But what about—"

Fane turns in a circle, but it's the world that seems to be spinning like a top, spinning out of control. The mummies lie in their tattered wrappings beneath glass cases. Ruin surrounds him, permeates him. He feels mummified and as dry and dusty as their linen. His friendship with George is over. There'll be no summer spent together. There'll be no shared room in the fall. What has he done? How has he ruined something so wonderful so fast? Stopping, dizzy, he slumps against a display and looks up to find a stone pedestal and a broken statue. The statue is just a pair of feet and legs that end at the thighs. Laughing ruefully, a poem comes immediately to mind and he spits out the words, feeling prophetic:

> *I met a traveler from an antique land*
> *Who said: 'Two vast and trunkless legs of stone*
> *Stand in the desert. Near them on the sand,*
> *Half sunk, a shattered visage lies, whose frown*

And wrinkled lip and sneer of cold command
Tell that its sculptor well those passions read
Which yet survive, stamped on these lifeless things,
The hand that mocked them and the heart that fed.
And on the pedestal these words appear:
` My name is Ozymandias, King of Kings:
Look on my works, ye mighty, and despair!'
Nothing beside remains. Round the decay
Of that colossal wreck, boundless and bare,
The lone and level sands stretch...

George stares at him, his mouth ajar, upper lip drawn back to reveal his teeth. "Come on. Let's get out of here."

"*Far away,*" Fane finishes.

They take another taxi back to the hotel. Fane leans his head against the glass and stares at the sky without talking. George says nothing as well. They get out, and Fane stands at the curb, not paying attention to anything until the cabbie yells at him. Then he discovers he's expected to pay. Trembling, he takes out his wallet and almost throws it at the driver in despair. As the taxi pulls away, Fane finds George holding out their room key. Then Fane realizes he's not done paying.

"Think you can get up to the room okay? I'll go with you if you want."

Fane takes the key. "Where are you going?"

"This is New York, Adam. Lots to do, and I'm not feeling sad like you are. You go on up, get some rest. Maybe you'll get happy."

"I feel happy when I'm with you."

George shows only the slightest hesitation before replying. "Sorry, Fane. I got a street full of girls to find."

So Fane returns to the room alone and falls across his bed. Even with the daylight coming in, the walls seem darker than before. He cries at first, lying on his side with his back to the door. He hasn't even removed his coat. The coat and the crying make him feel very hot, almost feverish. But the tears don't last long. After just a few minutes he's suddenly dry-eyed and empty, stripped out, a stone. Rising, he notices the discarded clothes next to George's bed. And he knows what he wants. He's never felt greater clarity. Right there are George's pajama bottoms and underwear, his socks and the t-shirt he's slept in. Is it so wrong, he asks himself, to touch them? Swallowing, bending forward and down, he at first contents himself to let his fingertips graze the cotton. This contentment endures for several caresses until, like a fire that must be fed, he snatches the underwear to his chest and then to his face. A faint odor electrifies him, brings another, stronger surge of tears. If George enters now, he can neither hide nor explain himself.

But George does not enter now.

He pulls the shorts from his face, shocked to realize he's soaked them with his tears. As if George might return any moment expecting to put them on, Fane waves the shorts in the air and then puts them up against the radiator. Several minutes later the underwear seems no less damp, and despite his anxiety Fane begins to think of his tears in magical, mythical terms. He imagines the story of a boy who cried with such sorrow the cloth used to collect his tears stays eternally damp.

He falls asleep clutching the underwear and wakes disoriented in a dark room. Turning on the light without thinking, he discovers George in the other bed, asleep on his back and shirtless, the hem of the sheet parallel with his navel. George's lithe torso has a soft luster about it. His muscles are clear in their definition, and his body possesses the angles and curves of a maturity that distinguishes him from other boys. When Fane looks at them he sees what he sees in the mirror—straight, uninteresting lines.

Would George's skin feel warm or cool to the touch? Did the muscles feel firm or would they yield and dimple at the barest pressure of his fingertips? Fane quietly swings his legs over the side of the bed until he's sitting up and facing George. He waits. The sound of his heartbeat proves both enormous and welcome. His pulse does not panic him as he thought it might; rather it seems to master time and make him deliberate, slow and sure. He reaches forward and touches George's stomach with the back of his fingers. The touch lasts two seconds at most before he fairly dashes back to his bed to wait for any sign of George's stirring.

George opens his eyes. One hand touches the place where Fane caressed. His voice is quiet as he rolls onto his side to look at Fane. "For the first time, I was really mad at you."

"You've been mad at me before."

"Frustrated sometimes, but not mad. What's wrong with you, Fane?"

"I don't know what you—"

"I mean all that business about being sad."

"I didn't say I was sad, George. I asked if I looked sad."

"Same thing with you, Fane."

He shrugs at the carpet.

George rolls onto his back. Neither of them speak for half a minute. Then George says, "What else is wrong with you?"

Fane's head hangs even lower.

"*Nothing.*"

"Never had a mate who treated my underwear like a teddy bear."

Fane hears the raggedness of his own breath before he actually feels the sudden difficulty of breathing. He pitches off the bed, aspirating, doubling over as he staggers toward the toilet. The bathroom tile is slick against his socks and his right leg goes out from under him. He only just avoids striking his head on the bowl and lies there sobbing and wheezing as George rushes in.

"*Mate—Adam—I'm sorry. I'm so sorry—*"

George stands over him, but Fane senses him as a shadow. That's all their friendship is now, a dark blotch, a fringe thing, driven away by the curse of his longing. Fane makes a fist and hits himself in the gut. George yells at him to stop. Fane kicks. He bashes his fist into the floor, hitting the way George showed him to hit, until the knuckles threaten to break. George bends down and grabs his wrist.

"*I'll go get a doctor. Just hang on, Adam. I'll get help.*"

Fane shakes his head. His breathing evens out. He gulps air and wipes tears from his eyes. So much of him is hurt. None of it compares to the agony in his brain.

George sighs very loudly. "Thank God, Adam. You okay?"

"I'm not okay." His voice barely qualifies as a whisper. "I'm weird."

"No, you're not. I was just teasing. I didn't mean anything by it. I'm not mad anymore. I was never *really* mad."

Fane listens to George talk. The words hardly reach him. He thinks, I'm not just weird, I'm damned. There's a flash in his mind like an exploding sun and then darkness, calming, concealing, lifting; it's the universe and in the universe floats people like him, people too burdened to fly on their own. Darkness makes everyone equal. Is the darkness death? If so, then let it come. *Come right this instant and we'll go no more a-roving.*

"I'll prove it to you, George."

"Prove what, mate?"

"That I'm weird."

Fane looks at George's feet, up his handsome legs to his white underwear, and follows further, along the contours of his stomach and chest and shoulders, until he meets George's eyes. They open wide, a reflection of his lips. A reflection of Fane's lips too, as Fane reaches up with both hands and touches what and where he wants.

"I love you," Fane says.

D*oppelganger.*
A funny word. As the child is settled into his lap, Fane tries to remember the first time he heard it. Many decades ago, back at Fowler. The boy in his lap clutches a thin hardback book. A boy and his book. How lovely. How hideous.

Fane senses the child's discomfort. The boy is perhaps four, and looks like a mirror image of himself at that age. The large skull makes the child's hair seem thin, like strands of overstretched thread. A faint odor of shampoo emanates from the child's scalp. The scent draws Fane's gaze to the top of the boy's head.

Is this me? Am I somehow sitting on my own lap?

The boy feels weightless, but his body generates intense heat that makes Fane swoon. For a moment he's certain he'll fall out of his chair, but then a large and impressively strong hand clutches his wrist.

"Dad, are you okay?"

Now a man stands over him, his face familiar, though Fane cannot place it. He has an infatuating appearance, like that of scarred beauty. His face isn't scarred, not physically, not by steel. The blade of time has touched his face, but it alone did not engrave the weary despair Fane finds in the man's otherwise youthful features. As the man's grip lingers on his wrist, Fane looks down at those clutching fingers, and a name bursts across his consciousness.

George.

Yes, this is George. George has been in the cave, and he has grown to manhood in the cave, and somehow the cave has preserved him at a certain age. It is fitting, Fane thinks, that he himself should age into the shriveled creature he is now, while George has lingered in time to become the present guardian of Fane's body. For what else can those fingers on his wrist mean? What else can the man's concern imply?

"George," he says, but the word comes out wrong, just a gargled syllable and a puff of dry air. In response, the boy laughs and kicks his little legs and rocks back and forth on Fane's lap as if he's been tickled.

"Grandpa, read me, read me," the boy squeals as he turns to wave the book in Fane's face.

"Shhh, Luke," George says, and acts like he's going to take the boy from Fane's lap. Fane finds sudden strength and fluidity in his stiff body and seizes the boy around his waist, determined to keep him for himself.

The child screams.

"Dad, don't!" George says, prying at Fane's arm. "It's okay, Luke. Grandpa's just giving you a hug."

The boy's cries calm to a sniffle and he squirms to face Fane again. A tremor passes between their bodies. Who originates it? Perhaps there's no proper distinction to be made, for as he gazes down at the boy's wide eyes Fane feels even more certain he's engaging with his double. *Doppelganger.* What ill omen is this? He thinks of the poet Shelley in Italy, walking on a terrace when he encountered a phantom of himself that answered all of his questions by pointing out at the Mediterranean Sea. Or so Mary Shelley claimed. Fane can suddenly envision the scene as if he'd eavesdropped upon it, yet he does not know where he is now or how he got here, or any detail of his life except for George and the cave.

Might this *be* the cave? It seems George once said something to him about staying in the cave, working hard to build a city for them both down there—a place to escape to when the world came to an end. Fane looks up at the man, so obviously cautious and ill-at-ease, his left hand lingering on the boy's shoulder as if ready to pull him away at a moment's notice. *George.* The man is George, George as he should have been decades ago, just entering the prime of his health and beauty. Yes, this is the cave and the cave has kept him young. Now certain of it, Fane casts a sweeping gaze around the room, judging its size, smiling with growing understanding and joy. This *is* their secret chamber. George has built for them a city in the cave, and the hidden chamber, this very room, is its heart.

And this boy is their child.

"Read me, Grandpa," the boy demands again, quite past his previous fear. Fane raises his left hand to stroke the boy's face, causing the child to giggle. He looks at George for approval and finds it. George appears relieved and very happy.

"Read me, Grandpa!" The boy jabs the book against Fane's chest.

"Shhh, Luke."

Fane grunts and lets the book be placed into his hand. With his other arm still hooked around the child's waist, he cannot manipulate the pages. But he does not need to, since the boy quickly starts turning the pages on his own, mussing through them like some cartoonish speed-reader. Fane squints only a little. Infirmities have racked up across his body, but his eyesight remains largely untroubled. His gaze detects in the blur of pages the familiar pattern of stanzas rather than paragraphs, and an ancient excitement jolts him.

"Poetry," he says, though again the word comes out husky and thick, closer to *poultry*. His other arm releases the boy and strives to stop the pages from turning. He does stop it, and the boy looks up at him as if balanced between confusion and fear, clarity and hope. His little mouth opens.

"*This* one, this one!"

George laughs. "He's so much like you, Dad. Or like Amber, I guess." Fane stares at him. Amber? A meaningless name.

When Fane does not move or begin reading, the boy twists and turns impatiently, as if stuck in the saddle of a horse that won't move. George touches him again and tells him to be still. Fane notices a drop of confidence in George's expression.

"I'm not sure Grandpa's up for reading right now, Luke. How about I read it?"

"And Grandpa listen?"

"That's right. I'll read and you and Grandpa will listen."

George tries to take the book, finds Fane unyielding, and cranes his body around so he can see the open page. Fane has already read the first line, knows already that he's read this poem many, many times in a past that is otherwise opaque to him. He opens his mouth to form the syllables as George reads, and for a moment feels a marvelous fusion between them, as if George's voice comes from Fane's own mouth.

> *Snow falling and night falling, fast, oh fast,*
> *In a field I looked into going past,*
> *And the ground almost covered smooth in snow,*
> *But a few weeds and stubble showing last.*

George stops reading out loud, though Fane notices his eyes continue reading, lips pressing more tightly together as they go, as if something is wrong with the poem. But what could that be? Here is a poem of pure loneliness— the best kind of verse, the reason poetry exists at all. George surely knows this. When they were young, George often interrupted Fane's readings with exasperated sighs or hoots, but Fane always suspected this was George's way of hiding the effect the poems had on him. George shows it nakedly now though, and Fane knows that despite his advanced age—How old *is* he?—and George's obvious youth, they are going to be closer than they ever were before, here in this cave of light, with this boy for them to raise and love.

"Let's find a happier poem," George says.

No, no, no. Fane lifts his hand and tries to tell George he's making a mistake. Much of his life has been spent finding poems of isolation and neglect precisely because they reflected how he felt. Such poems confirmed the world was as lonely and dark as his experience told him. But now is different. They must continue to seek out those old, wearisome poems, so they can look up from the page and reaffirm the new, happy state of their lives together.

Fane's arms squeeze the boy.

"Grandpa hurting!" The boy's legs kick, and Fane wraps his arms about him even tighter. Here's the love between George and himself made real and holy. The boy is reification and deification in one stroke. As the boy's struggles continue, Fane tries to whisper to him. The child's head strikes Fane's nose and Fane feels liquid fire coming from both nostrils. The heat off the boy's body is itself like a furnace. *The burnt child loves the flame.* Who said that? Byron? Wilde? Himself?

"Dad, stop it! Let go of him!"

George's hands have incredible strength, yet Fane holds tight. George turns to the door and shouts for help. Almost at once two men rush through. Fane has seen them before. They were students of his. But how long has it been since he taught anything? Images and memories stream through his mind. Dizzied, he lets go of the boy, who's screaming, "Grandpa scary! Grandpa hurt!" Even this shrill voice fades. Fane finds himself walking a college campus with a cane, following someone—George?—only to be taunted by crowds of students. 75-130-b.1. 75-130-b.1. Oh God, they know, he's thinking, they all know what I've done to—to—where is Gordon?

Fane's vision returns to the hospital room, where the man he thought was George is trying to comfort the boy with soft words and little bounces. Is this perhaps not George after all? Fane squints as if trying to pierce a veil. Is this Gordon, his youthful and handsome son touched by a little age? How old is he? Thirty? There are some lines about his eyes, though they do not detract from him. His brown hair has a few flecks of gray. It's awful to think of Gordon aging. It's more awful to think he's not George and that George is—

No, no, no, no.

"Daddy, no more Grandpa. Grandpa is scary."

"He didn't mean to scare you. I promise, Luke."

The boy turns his head and looks Fane in the eye. "Grandpa," he says, and his voice is suddenly much more mature. Fane raises a hand—

—and when he lowers it everyone is gone except the boy, and the boy is older, around twelve or thirteen years of age. He's sitting on Fane's bed, head bent toward a book he reads from in a low, assured voice.

This is...Luke, he thinks. I know him. My grandson.

He tests his lips, making them flex and stretch. After several attempts, he manages to say the boy's name.

The boy stops reading, and shifts his body to look at him. *Doppelganger.* The boy *is so* identical to how Fane looked at that age that he can hardly believe it. Oh, but his leg. Please don't let his leg be like mine, Fane thinks.

"Did I wake you, Grandpa?"

"I don't know if I was listening or dreaming." Fane swallows, making a clicking noise in his arid throat.

"Would you like me to read you a poem?"

Fane nods, reaching forward to squeeze Luke's hand. Luke squeezes back. Fane says, "You were afraid of me."

Luke laughs. "I was? When?"

"I think it was...years ago."

"I don't remember."

"Well, you were small."

Smiling, Fane turns his face to the wall. He's in an institution. He's been in and out of hospitals and nursing facilities for years. These facts do not quite rise to the level of *memories,* but he understands the reality of his situation. All that matters is he is not in prison.

Where he belongs.

There's a cup of water on the stand beside his bed. Left over from the last pills he swallowed. The pills are given by a man named Dr. Reynolds. Dr. Reynolds is a researcher specializing in dementia with a special interest in pharmaceuticals that might recover memories. Fane remembers all of this, though he cannot remember when he first arrived at this place or how long he's been here.

"Grandpa?"

"Luke. You know, I was just thinking that I'm living a poem right now."

"Which one, Grandpa?'

Does he still have inside him the voice he used to recite poetry for students? Time to find out. With perfect memory, he says: "Here I am, an old man in a dry month, being read to by a boy."

The words electrify Luke. "T.S. Eliot!"

"You know Eliot? At your age?"

The boy responds by flipping through the pages until he almost reaches the end of the book. "Mom doesn't like him."

"Mom?"

"You don't remember her?"

Fane shakes his head. He remembers a face, distant but coming closer, clarifying. They were...associates. Professors? Suddenly the face becomes very clear and so does the relationship. It's not Luke's mother, however, but his wife. The knowledge that he's been married and lived life as a married man leaves him thunderstruck. Why did he wed? What in the world attracted her to him? What desire passed between them? These questions have no answers, but for once Fane senses the absence of answers is not a problem of memory.

"Gordon. I have a son named Gordon."

"That's Dad," the boy says.

"You're my grandson. Your name is Luke."

"Yes!"

"And if I remember right, you *really* like poetry."

"Grandpa, I *love* poetry. Dad says I'm a lot like you. And Mom. Your memory is really good today!"

"What types of poetry?"

The boy turns shy. Such a sudden change might be inexplicable to most, but Fane understands. Reaching for the water, he takes a sip and forces down a swallow. He says, "I like sad poetry."

"I do, too."

"Are you sad?"

Luke shrugs. "Sometimes."

"Do you have a friend named George?"

"What, Grandpa?"

"I'm sorry. I don't know why I said that. I meant to ask if you have a favorite poet?"

"I like Shelley, but I don't understand most of what he writes."

"You're too young for Shelley. Start with Byron—he's easy and foolish and funny. Perfect for boys."

"Okay, Grandpa, I'll read some Byron."

Silence settles over the room, as if nothing remains to be said. Fane's thoughts start to stray. He grits his teeth. He's here with his grandson. The past is past. I will stay in the present, he thinks. Despite his determination, his mind feels like a leaky vessel. Faces of the dead appear to him. His parents. George. *George's parents*, who probably died with a suspicion of him in their hearts. But they are all dead. Gordon is alive. Luke is alive. He must embrace the present and try to stay in it as it moves into an uncertain future.

His arms are dappled with liver spots and the skin looks so dry and dead. His legs are covered. God knows how atrophied his right leg must be now, the foot more monkey's paw than human appendage.

"Luke, how old am I?"

"I don't know."

"Make a guess."

"Maybe eighty?" He sounds apologetic, as if the guess might be offensive.

"How old is your father?"

"I think he's thirty-five."

Fane let out a long exhale and slumps back against the mattress. "You don't know your father's age? Well, fret not. When Gordon was your age, I doubt he knew how old I was either."

"I don't want to talk about Dad."

Fane gives this sentiment little pondering. Sons not wanting to discuss their fathers feels like a long Fane family tradition.

The door opens and two men enter. One is a doctor. Ryan? Rick? He can't quite recall. The other is George: George as he should have been, George preserved, George—

George is dead, goddamnit. That's Gordon, he tells himself. My son.

"Hey, Luke. How's your Grandpa today?"

"Good," Luke says. But as Gordon comes over and puts a hand on Luke's shoulder, the boy visibly flinches.

"Dad, are you having a good day?"

Fane ignores him, fixated on the doctor as he picks up a tablet computer and consults it. The doctor smiles.

"I'll say he's having a good day. Look at this."

He shows the tablet to Gordon, whose eyebrows lift. "Wow."

"What is it?" Fane says.

"It seems you're *very* aware of your surroundings today, Adam. That's great news."

"How do you know that?"

The doctor gestures with the tablet. "The computer here is for recording purposes. I'm looking at the transcript of the talk you just had with Luke. Nearly the longest talk you've had with anyone in a year. And so lucid. I don't know whether to thank—"

"How dare you record a private conversation between me and my grandson?"

"Dad, he has my permission."

"Oh? How is that yours to give?"

He sees Gordon smile. "You really are so much like your old self today."

Fane crosses his arms at the chest and glances at Luke, who still seems shriveled up, trying to make himself small.

"He was reading poetry," Fane says.

"Yes, we found early on that your memory responds best to poetry. Not surprising considering your former profession. So we've made poetry a part of your therapy, along with the new drugs. I think the combination is working."

"I think we really owe it all to Luke," Gordon says, clapping the boy on his shoulder. Again Fane sees him shrink down. It reminds him of how Gordon used to act.

Gordon. This man is Gordon. This is his son.

George's voice says, *No, it's me, mate.*

Yes, George: George as he would have looked later on in life, still handsome, grown, perfect in body and soul, with just a little grey in his curly hair. Fane frowns. Might there also be a gray hair or two on his chest? He can remember the morning he first discovered them on himself. The tidings of death always show first on the head and chest.

"George," he says.

"The mystery man again," the doctor says, his voice jovial. He sweeps his hand across the tablet and taps it several times. "Perhaps today will be the day we finally learn who George is. Can you remember him better now, Adam?"

Fane shakes his head very fast.

"Won't you try? It's important."

"He *doesn't* want to talk about George," Luke says. "Quit trying to make him."

Fane watches the doctor disguise the irritation in his expression before turning around. "Luke, would you wait outside while your dad and I talk with your grandpa? I promise it won't be long."

"Whatever," Luke says, prompting a small rebuke from his father. He comes over and hugs Fane before he goes, and Fane hugs him back. Some force in his arms doesn't want to surrender the boy, but Luke breaks the embrace and leaves.

Gordon and the doctor now stand at his bedside. "Adam, *please* try to think about George and tell us about him."

"No."

"Dad, it's important for the therapy."

Fane wonders if the cold terror sweeping through his body shows at all in his face.

"Was he your brother, Adam?"

"No, Dad was an only child."

"Some families, when they lose a child very young, just shut up about it, act like the child never existed. That was especially true back when your father was a boy. I'm just trying every avenue."

Fane sighs. "I'll tell you who George was."

They both lean toward him.

"He was an imaginary friend."

Frustration explodes in the doctor's expression. He looks at Gordon, who puts a hand on his shoulder. "Dr. Reynolds, would it be okay if I talked to Dad alone for awhile?"

"Certainly." He put the tablet down on the table. Fane gestures toward it and the doctor snatches it up again and takes it with him.

Now they're alone.

He watches Gordon pace, staring at anything but his father. He feels like he's watching a very handsome actor about to perform a soliloquy from *Hamlet*. Or perhaps somehow Gordon *is* Hamlet, and Fane is the ghost, invisible but eternally present as he watches his son's mounting conflict.

Gordon sits on the edge of the bed and laughs ruefully. "How much can a guy fuck up?" He rubs his nose and lifts his head to look at Fane. "I'm sorry, Dad. I'm sorry I wasn't there for you when you collapsed on campus. I was too busy making the worst decision of my life that day. I guess you don't remember what happened."

"No."

"Wish I could say the same. Do you remember my dog, Dad? The two of you didn't get along, I guess. I found him on the street and took him back to the house to wash him. And I found a bar of soap and shampoo in the refrigerator. At the time, I just thought it was weird. I should have realized it meant something more. You were starting to suffer, and I wasn't there. I'm sorry I didn't come home more. It's just—"

Gordon rises and stands at Fane's bedside. Fane reaches out and touches him on the hip. Gordon flinches. He looks down with his mouth ajar, his eyes narrowing and then widening. Fane remembers the last time he saw eyes like this, identical in their cloudy confusion. It was long ago, in New York, in a hotel bathroom, in a moment when he disturbed the Universe.

"George," he says, and though he shakes his head in sorrow, he's smiling.

PART 3:

LUKE

CHAPTER EIGHT

He saw John-Mark at a bar in Anaheim on the third and final night of a tedious business trip. Gordon didn't believe it was him at first. They were sitting less than thirty feet from each other, but the crowd kept him from getting a clear view, no matter how he craned his neck.

Gordon sat at a table with three of Epson Pharmaceutical's top managers, vaguely annoyed he couldn't make out what the men were saying. During the last year, he'd had trouble distinguishing close conversations over the buzz of background noise in a crowded room. It was like he'd gone deaf in certain settings. He didn't understand it; he wasn't otherwise hard of hearing. Did his dad have these symptoms? Whenever the question occurred to him, he buried it and forced his thoughts to anything else.

He glanced at the managers, who weren't looking at him, and for once felt glad he couldn't hear them. He'd been a sales executive with Epson for the last seven years, and done okay at it considering he cared nothing about the drug industry. He'd also gotten over the novelty of business trips. The managers, Andrew, Tony, and Marlin, were in their late fifties but still acted like frat boys released on Spring Break. Even though Gordon couldn't make out the specifics of their conversation, he knew they were talking about getting pussy. They were already drunk and happier than they had any right to be considering the mediocre results of the trip.

They'd been there about twenty minutes, and Gordon braced himself for what was coming, so he wouldn't flinch or freak out. After his second Scotch on the rocks, Marlin, Gordon's direct boss—and the one who talked about pussy the most—had scooted his chair closer to the table and lowered his hands. Seated to Gordon's right, he leaned forward, as if fascinated to hear what the other two managers were saying. Beneath the table, his left hand began to pet Gordon's kneecap.

Gordon flinched despite his best efforts, but he stilled it as best he could and just looked away to his left. It was then, just for a moment, that his gaze found a gap in the crowd, and he noticed the other table with four men sitting at it, one of them tall, with a profile that showed a crooked nose. Gordon knew at once how the nose had been disfigured.

Can't be, he thought, but as he squinted, he felt a mix of dread and hope, something...complicated.

He wasn't the first guy Gordon had identified as John-Mark on this particular trip. Last year, he'd learned from one of the few college teammates he still had contact with that John-Mark lived and worked in Anaheim as a high school coach—basketball or track, Gordon couldn't remember. He'd smiled a little wistfully at the news, remembering how John-Mark used to talk about becoming a coach; he'd really hated Westervelt's strenuous practices and used to say how easy he'd take it on his players, who'd perform well because they loved him. Discovering John-Mark had made good on his dream got Gordon remembering how he always figured he'd be a coach too. He even remembered a night in their dorm room where they'd imagined their teams going at it in the state championship game. He shook his head, slowly returning to the present, slowly rediscovering the possessive caress of Marlin's fingertips.

At least John-Mark had made his goal in life. Easy to do when you don't spend eighteen months in jail.

Suddenly Andrew tapped him on the arm. Gordon looked over and found the managers with amused expressions.

"You deaf?"

Gordon smiled. "Sorry, just thinking about something."

"We are too," Tony said, lifting his empty glass and jiggling it. "Guess our waitress stepped out back to suck a dick. Go get us some drinks, buddy."

Gordon responded with the slightest nod. No one offered him any cash. Marlin's hand withdrew only when Gordon kicked his chair back to rise. Standing, he was one of the tallest people in the room and he made a slow turn to the left so he could stare better at the man who looked like John-Mark. *Was* it him? The bar was murky. He probably needed contacts, though he didn't want to admit it. He squinted again. That is John-Mark, he thought. Jesus Christ, it has to be.

Knowing he couldn't just stand there staring forever, Gordon moved toward the bar. There he lingered on the outskirts of the pressing crowd, pivoted again, as if casually impatient and bored. He couldn't see the other table from here. Probably not him anyway.

They hadn't seen each other in fifteen years, not since the trial, but Gordon knew what he looked like. After more than a decade trying to push his former teammate and friend from his thoughts, he'd finally relented when told John-Mark was coaching. Gordon found a photo online. It was from the athletics' page of a high school website. John-Mark was smiling—he had a toothy smile—and seeing it made Gordon swallow as he thought about how many of them he'd kicked out that fateful day so long ago. He looked at John-Mark's crooked nose and remembered a time when it was straight.

He'd been unable to look at the picture for long at first, but then he found himself pulling up the page at work, fixating on it while he should have been scrambling over client accounts. As old memories came back, recollections of good and easier times, Gordon dug further. He found John-Mark's profile on a social networking site; it was set to private but it had a new picture that showed John-Mark at the beach, smiling, with two little twin boys hugging his legs. This second photo must have been more current, because his hairline had receded a bit more. The same toothy smile was there though, and he looked happy. The boys looked like miniature versions of their father before—

Gordon stopped himself from finishing the thought: *before the accident.* But in his heart and mind, the fight *was* an accident, like he'd somehow stumbled on a rock and inadvertently beaten John-Mark to a pulp in the middle of Westervelt's quad. In so many ways, it *had* been a slip. One punch. Just one punch was all he intended. Then he slipped. Then the dam broke. Mixed metaphors, he thought. Amber would have a fit.

The crowd at the bar thinned out a bit. He moved closer. Hesitated. The question had been on his mind since he'd learned he was going with the managers to Anaheim: what would be the *point* of contacting him? His friendship with John-Mark was an old corpse. No need to go poking it with a stick.

But maybe he could smooth things over at least. If they really were here together in the same bar, wasn't that some sort of sign? He could at least walk over to John-Mark and say he was sorry for—for *everything.* They'd both suffered: John-Mark had endured several surgeries and rehabilitations; Gordon had done a year and a half in jail on second degree assault charges. Neither of them played basketball for Westervelt again.

A grim, cold weight settled on Gordon's chest as he considered the damage the fight had done to each of them. How could his being sorry fix all of that? The wall between them was complete, and Gordon sighed in resignation. It was cheesy as hell, he knew, but he had a daydream of giving John-Mark a hug and getting hugged back. Not reconciliation, just an acknowledgement of everything that had happened between them, the good and the bad.

Maybe John-Mark wouldn't even feel remorse though. Maybe he'd say he was still glad Shiloh got put down.

Gordon gritted his teeth and shuffled forward. The two bartenders ignored him, focusing their attention on a cluster of women to his right. Gordon didn't mind—all male bartenders were the same—but he remembered being back at Westervelt when the local bartenders used to fall over themselves to wait on him, knowing damn well he was underage. Increasingly, such moments seemed his peak in life.

His cell phone vibrated in his pocket, tickling the top of his thigh. He almost jumped in surprise. Gordon took it out and looked at the screen. Amber had sent him a video message: she and Luke waved to him; Amber wore a red towel around her head like a wig, her face drawn and white. He was glad he couldn't hear either voice in the recording. Hers would be tired and strained. How would Luke sound?

Gordon shut his eyes a moment, seeing his son's face more clearly in the dark behind his eyelids. Luke was twelve, and more like his grandfather than his father. The resemblance went beyond the physical. Watching him develop, seeing the similarities appear day by day, Gordon couldn't help but be fascinated. Watching Luke, he sometimes felt he was seeing his own father grow up in front of him—shy, more comfortable in books, somewhat sad.

I'm his sadness, he thought.

Someone shoved his back. He turned, half expecting to find John-Mark there. It was just some fat douche, eyes wide with impatience. The man pointed over Gordon's shoulder. Gordon saw the bartender waiting for him.

"Sorry," he said.

He ordered drinks, knowing just what the three managers liked. Marlin, Andrew and Tony dressed alike and drank alike and had the same expensive taste in clothes and liquor. They were not good-looking men and back at the office they boasted of bringing Gordon along on their trips just to bait women to the table. "Gord hooks them, we reel them in," Marlin would say.

Marlin. In the office he was actually a decent guy, though some of his comments made him a walking lawsuit waiting to happen for sexual harassment. Still not even the women cared because—well, it was *Marlin*. They'd gone on many business trips together without incident. But this one had been different. On the first night, with a little liquid courage, he'd make shy, furtive touches, the sort of thing that could pass for friendly gestures—like a clap on Gordon's back where the hand lingered a hair too long. The second night, these advances were taken below the table. Hidden, Marlin's caresses had become more blatant and proprietary, and Gordon had sat there like a pimp's bitch, too anxious in his confusion to do anything. Tonight was no different. And Marlin was his boss. And with Amber's illness, Gordon *needed* his job more than ever, so he'd just have to endure it. With the odd, uncertain feeling that he'd already endured it many times before.

He was jostled as he turned, and brought the drinks back sloppy. The managers shook their heads at him like he was an amusing but otherwise worthless asshole. "Gord, Gord," Tony said, then the three went back to their private conversation.

Gordon looked over and found the path to John-Mark's table clear. He took a long, hard look, almost willing the man to turn and meet his gaze.

That's him, he thought. Goddamn, that really is John-Mark.

John-Mark was laughing. Gordon couldn't hear it, but at the same time he *could*, like some form of lip-reading almost. He laughed the way Gordon remembered John-Mark laughing: he'd always lean forward and to his left when he was cracking up, exactly like the guy at the table did. Gordon started to smile at a hundred different memories. Before the grin could form though, Marlin's fingers found the top of Gordon's thigh. The smile became an awkward cough.

Otherwise, his body remained very still. Instead of turning towards Marlin and the rest, Gordon stared intensely at John-Mark a moment longer, then dropped his gaze to the floor.

If I just walk over there, he thought, what's the worst that can happen? Maybe he takes a swing at me. Maybe he actually asks me to sit down. If he did, what would I do?

Suddenly his right hand shot under the table, pinched Marlin's chubby wrist between his long fingers and forced it away. As Gordon shot up, the managers looked at him in astonishment. He made two strides towards John-Mark's table. John-Mark still hadn't looked over. Then he seemed about to and...Gordon pivoted, his pulse exploding, and plowed his way through the milling people to the men's bathroom. He was panting, and he knew it was weird to be breathless in the men's bathroom, as if being here was the fulfillment of some fantasy. The urinals were taken. One guy looked over his shoulder at him. Sweating, Gordon saw an open stall, scrambled for it and shut the door.

Sitting on the toilet, he raked his fingers through his hair. Something bad was going to happen. The thought occurred with such solemnity it was laughable. A shitload of bad things had *already* happened. His father's long, agonizing decay. Amber's cancer. The awful compulsion he felt for Luke, which felt like...some jigsaw puzzle whose crucial pieces were buried someplace inside of himself. At that moment though, Gordon felt it was all rehearsal for a much worse darkness waiting like an eager shroud. He had to be strong. He had to be a husband, a father. He had to be insurance against the fall of night.

His own need for light became literal. He pulled the cell phone from his pocket and summoned the video message. He held it close to his face as he watched and listened.

"Hi Gordon, didn't want to interrupt any of your meetings, so when you get this just think of it as a goodnight kiss from the most important people in your life. We love you, don't we, Luke?"

The unmistakable hesitancy before Luke said, *"I love you, Dad,"* made Gordon close his eyes and rest his forehead against the top of the phone. Worst of all was how Luke otherwise just sat there as Amber went on talking. His son looked like some ventriloquist's dummy his wife had neglected to operate.

"Can't wait to see you tomorrow! I hope you're having a great trip and have a good night, honey. I miss you so much."

She finished by bringing the camera lens to her lips. He smiled at that. Then he replied with a text message—*Hope you're sleeping. Hope your dreams are wonderful.*

God, it was so easy to be in love from a distance. Virtual love never seemed to have an argument, maybe because it had no context. Just now, Gordon felt the same toward Amber as he had on the day, leaving her classroom, when he simply knew he was in love with her. It was easy to forget that he'd *wanted* to go on this inane trip to get out of the house, to be away from her and that lingering sense of death, the pain in her bones he was certain she blamed on him. He knew they'd have another fight soon, within the next twenty-four hours probably. The cancer had worn her down; they'd both discovered their capacity for cruelty. Before he left for Anaheim, she'd said, "I wish I'd known what was in store for me before wasting those eighteen months. I'd have done something useful with them instead." She meant of course the time she'd spent waiting for him to get out of jail. She could always reference his jail time to cut him to the core.

Weirdly, though, he remembered his incarceration as the period when Amber loved him the most. Maybe it was an early example of the power of distance in a relationship. If the fight hadn't happened, maybe their romance would've only lasted a few months more. Then Gordon would have met some other girl, Amber would have accepted a job at a larger university, and their separate lives would be better.

Instead the fight with John-Mark revealed both of their secrets.

He was sentenced and jailed. There was no leniency, regardless of it being a first offense. Eyewitness testimony, pictures of John-Mark's battered body and the appearance of a somewhat reassembled John-Mark did not evoke sentiments of forgiveness, even factoring in Shiloh's death. Gordon was shocked by the jail sentence. The jury were all local citizens, the same people who stopped him on the street to high five him about sinking a clutch free throw. He was one of *them*, a local boy who'd made good. Plus his father was sick. His father had *collapsed*. Wouldn't anyone take that into consideration?

Amber, of course, had been floored to learn who Gordon's father was, but she had far more significant distractions. Westervelt's administration, with the same ruthlessness as Gordon's judge, fired Amber for her code violation. In hindsight, Gordon wondered if the devotion she'd shown to him in prison was just her way of pushing all other thoughts to the background. He was probably the only person she knew whose situation was worse than her own. Or maybe he represented some kind of stability for her, something that was locked away and wouldn't—*couldn't*—escape her.

Whatever her reasons, she'd been a godsend to him. Her visits helped him rebuild a shattered ego. As he'd stand before her in an orange jumpsuit, his head so heavy he could barely lift it, she was a rock. She was even helping his dad in his health crisis. Gordon could only repay that by loving her and marrying her. Now to hear her call it all a waste of her life...

His phone vibrated. A text message from Marlin—

You okay, Gord? I want you to stop by my room later to get your thoughts on the Masely sales figures.

Gordon moaned and slipped the phone back into his pocket. Then he clasped his hands and dropped his forehead to them. He was verging on prayer when he heard the bathroom door open in a surge of noise and the sound of John-Mark laughing with another guy as they came in to piss. Gordon listened to them bullshitting at the urinal. John-Mark's voice hadn't changed at all. Gordon shook his head at another rush of memories. Now, he thought. Step out now, wash your hands, look at him like you're floored to see him and say, "Oh, my God. DUDE." He saw the astonishment, saw the embrace, saw the forgiveness. They'd step outside the bar and catch up. He'd say—*You were right about Amber, dude. Fucking bitch. Man, you were so right.*

Then his life would be okay. Its path would be righted. Maybe John-Mark could get him on as an assistant coach or something. He'd be back in the world of basketball, back in the world he loved.

Gordon trembled. He thought of Amber and Luke. Hell of a thing, when what you love is poisoning you; even worse, when you're poisoning the things you love. *Their* lives would be better off without him.

The urinals flushed. A brief jet of water followed from the sink, then the door opened and John-Mark was gone. Gone. All opportunity, all hope. Gordon stared at his feet.

Now his cell phone vibrated. He knew it was Marlin; the vibrations even felt like Marlin's fat fingers drumming on the top of his right thigh. Gordon began to hyperventilate. He got up, left the stall and hurried to the sink, to splash cold water on his face. He remembered going to Amber's duplex so long ago, and soaking his shirt because it stank. The day he found Shiloh. Suddenly he thought he might cry, and he brought more water to his face. He knew he wouldn't be crying over the dog. Shiloh's death had come to represent a hundred different mistakes he'd made, a hundred different failures.

Gordon looked at his face in the mirror. There'd been a time when he could look in the mirror and know he was handsome. Now he couldn't be sure. Women still flirted with him, but they were seldom the young ones, the early twenty-somethings. Truth was, he didn't mind it when the managers boasted about using him as bait. He liked the opportunity to hit on younger women, and he could do it without betraying his marriage. And he hadn't betrayed it, not ever.

But he knew there were actions that went way beyond betrayal.

The door opened. This time it was Marlin standing there, looking pensive. Gordon pressed his lips to a thin line and nodded to him.

"You okay, Gord?"

"Yeah."

He dried his hands and stepped towards the door. Marlin flashed a smile and clapped one hand between Gordon's shoulder blades, telling him to go get some drinks.

The night, after all, was young.

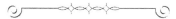

It was around nine in the morning when he got home, and he found Amber asleep on the sofa. She wore the same red towel round her head as in the video message, the rest of her body engulfed in a plush blue robe. Gordon stopped at the edge of the living room and stared, anxious over the slight rise and fall of her chest. Her breathing was almost too slight to show through the heavy cloth.

At last, contented she was alive and sleeping, Gordon came over and with the back of his fingers brushed her forehead, her cheek. He meant to go no further, and surprised himself by kneeling beside the sofa, laying his head against her chest. His mind was blank beyond the simple thought—I love her. He nuzzled Amber, seeking her body beneath the heavy robe. He understood now what the expression *fragile as a bird* meant. She seemed like some mixture of feathers and hollow bones. He realized how tight he held her and eased his embrace, afraid damage might already be done. She gave a slight sigh and opened her eyes. Cocked her head and blinked at him. "I missed you," she said.

He felt for her hand and grabbed it before it could grab him.

"Luke make it to school okay?"

She nodded.

He started to smile just as she added, "He had the nightmare again. I was so knocked out from the meds I didn't even hear him. I woke up to find him cuddled up to me, and then he told me about it."

Gordon settled back on his knees. After a moment, he said, "I think the doctors are right about it being from trauma. He knows you're really sick."

"But we've done everything to keep him from—"

"He's not blind."

Her expression became cold. "You're saying I *look* like I'm dying?"

He shook his head. "No, just that you're...ill. Everything that means...he can't cope with it, so his mind turns it into a nightmare."

"About the end of the world?"

"You *are* his world, Amber."

She nodded and squeezed his hand, her expression warm again. "So are *you*."

Gordon responded with a small, shy smile that made her cock her head.

"Don't you believe it?" she said.

He shrugged and looked her over. Though it was nearing ten, he doubted she'd had breakfast. The chemo had ruined her appetite.

"Stay right where you are," he said. "I'll cook for us."

"I don't think I can eat."

"Something simple. We'll try half a banana and toast."

She managed to laugh. "If you're actually offering to cook, I'm going to put you through more grief than that. Who cares if I can't eat it? I just want to *see* it."

He stood. "Half a banana, toast—and a bowl of Raisin Bran."

"Fancy," she said with a weak smile and lay back down. He kissed her forehead and went to work in the kitchen. As he sliced the banana, swaying on his feet, he realized just how tired he was. He'd spent the night dodging Marlin. The managers had not slept at all—except in the car, where Gordon was tasked with driving them all back from Anaheim. He'd been on the road for close to three hours.

As he grabbed two cereal bowls, Amber hobbled into the kitchen. She used a cane, which she tried never to let Luke see.

"That cereal smells good."

"Cooked it myself."

They smiled at each other, but the muscles in Gordon's neck tightened, and he felt a shooting pain in the back of his head. Amber's reliance on the cane was becoming more obvious. Her large red towel had lost its tuck, so that one end hung down over the left side of her face to drape her shoulder and breast. Sitting, she might seem exotic to him, like a swami. Standing there gaunt and leaning on a cane, she looked like his father wearing some cheap Halloween costume turban.

"Sit down, Amber. Or go back to the couch. Let me bring everything to you."

But she didn't sit down. "Do you still find me attractive?"

"Of course I do!"

He hurried his pace and checked the toaster. The bread hadn't browned yet. Cheap ass piece of shit.

"I'm sorry I asked that. I just wanted to know."

"I'll make love to you right now if you'd like. But I won't be at my best. I probably won't smell my best, either.—What the *fuck* is up with this toaster?"

"It's not plugged in," she said.

She was right. He grabbed the cord prongs and jammed them into the wall socket. As an orange glow rose from the toaster's inner dark, he stood there listening to himself breathe.

She came over. "When I was a little girl," she said, "I was fascinated by my grandmother's toaster. It was just really old and sort of dangerous looking. In a way, it looked more like an old space heater—the ones with bars that get blazing orange from the heat. I'd get real close to it and look down. It was like gazing into a furnace. Sometimes when no one was around, I'd turn the toaster on just to watch it heat up—and the way the air would rise up out of it in hot crinkles."

"You didn't put bread in it?"

She smiled. "Weird, isn't it?"

He shrugged.

She put her free hand between his shoulder blades and rubbed; his back arched, and he found himself drawing away. He couldn't slip free without turning around to look at her. The expression on her face was not one of patient understanding.

"Are you back to not wanting to be touched?"

"I'm just sensitive to it right now. Because I'm tired."

"Are you sensitive to it when you're away on business?"

"I'm not cheating on you. I would never."

He took the full bowls to the table and returned for the toast. Amber did not move or look at him. He pulled out a chair for her. When she didn't acknowledge it, he sighed and sat down and picked up a spoon.

"I'm sorry, Gordon. It's just that you're my husband. I *want* to touch you."

"You know how I am sometimes. I can't explain it."

She hobbled over to the table and eased herself into the chair next to him. "Can't or won't?"

"Don't bring up therapy again."

"But it might—"

"The last one I went to wanted to dwell on my jail time. Like he thought I got raped in there. It was creepy sitting there as he tried to make me admit to something that didn't happen."

He brought a spoonful of cereal into his mouth and ate it. Something was weird about it but he didn't have time to think; he just wanted to eat fast. Amber, however, was squinting at him.

"What?"

"You haven't poured us any milk yet."

As he realized she was right—he was eating the cereal dry—she started to rise. "Don't get up," he said, quickly rising himself, to move toward the refrigerator. "Let me serve you."

"I can get the milk."

"No," he said, "you need to rest. You need—"

Amber swung the cane at him. It struck him in the leg without much force, but enough to make him turn and gape at her. She dropped the cane and started crying.

"I'm sorry I did that. I'm so sorry. It's just—I *feel*—"

"It's okay," he said. He picked up the cane and pressed it on her until she took it. Then he returned to his chair, his head lowered as he listened to her sob.

"You're a good man. Don't think I don't know that. I just think if you got some help, if you found out *why* you have these periods when you can't stand to be touched..."

"Well, it wasn't from being in jail."

"I know. Even before Shiloh died...something was bothering you even then."

"I don't know what it would be."

"It just kills me to think maybe you hate me somehow, or have some sort of buried resentment."

"I swear I don't. You're the best thing that ever happened to me. If anything, I hate myself for all the harm I've caused you. Your job—"

"*Hey*," she said, force returning to her voice, "I've always said that being found out was a good thing. I wouldn't have discovered how much I like book publishing if I hadn't been fired from Westervelt. Chalk one up to Pangloss."

"What?"

She laughed. "I'm living in the best of all possible worlds, Gordon. Because I'm with you."

Gordon narrowed his eyes. He hated her when she was like this, all concil-iatory and *pure*, as if she expected him to have amnesia about the nasty things she'd said before he took off to Anaheim. His thoughts were a lump in his throat, and he alternated between wanting to choke on them and wanting *her* to choke on them.

"I just want to be sure it's not *me*, Gordon," she said, and he swallowed all of that back. "It's like you're disgusted by how I look, can't stand to even think of—"

"Here," he said, jutting out his arm. He unbuttoned the right cuff of his dress-shirt and rolled the sleeve all the way to his elbow. His skin's firmness and its underlying muscle tone had not changed much since college. There was one gray hair on his arm that he obsessively pulled whenever he noticed it. Right now it had not grown back.

"What?"

"I want you to touch me. As much as you like, as long as you like. You'll see I'm not disgusted by you. I could never be."

After a moment, she shook her head. "I can see it on your face even now, Gordon. It's like you're steeling yourself for it to happen. I miss the feel of you, sweeping my hands up and down your back. I miss kissing your stomach in the morning, licking you, the texture and taste of you. You were always so alive—you still are. Everything about you is like this battery of health. And knowing what I've become, I—I'm just feeling insecure."

Gordon nodded, doing his best to hide how sad her words made him. He'd liked her touch—and still liked it, when his body behaved—just as he'd en-joyed touching her, and kissing. He could still remember the long wait before they got together, and how his fantasies of being with her seemed so impos-sible to make happen. Then they had sex and all of them *did* happen. In that first summer of their relationship they'd enjoyed each other's bodies more than many couples did in a lifetime. They'd been like two suns blazing against each other. Now, in their separate ways, both seemed to be winking out of existence.

"Let's just eat, okay? We'll both be thinking a lot more clearly after break-fast."

He watched her mess with the loose end of her towel first, securing it back on her head. Then she ate the toast.

"Delicious," she said.

He got the milk and filled their bowls, then sat to eat. On the third mouthful of cereal, he felt her fingertips on his forearm. He stopped a moment, determined to smile.

"You just look too good not to take you up on your offer, babe."

"I'm trying to do better," he said. "In every way."

"Was it a good trip?"

"No."

"Want to talk about it?"

He shook his head. "I've just been thinking, about how we'll be when this is all over—when you're well again and better than ever and maybe we don't need as much money to cover all the medical stuff..."

"Yeah?"

"I'd like to become a basketball coach. Maybe go back to school and get a teaching degree. I'm not sure if I could get hired. My record—"

"You've done your time. The law's forgiven you. Forgive yourself."

"I think I'd like to coach high school basketball." He smiled as soon as the words were out. He felt powerful saying them.

She squeezed his arm. Her touch felt good. He warmed and smiled with the realization. Son of a bitch, it felt good—like her touch used to feel.

"That's wonderful, Gordon. You should start as soon as you can. Don't wait for me. Don't wait for *anything*."

"I figure if I can coach you back to health, I can get a team to the state championship game in two years, easy."

"I believe you can do anything," she said.

He nodded.

"What's wrong, Gordon?"

He let go of her hand and scratched the side of his face, pondering. "I saw John-Mark," he said. He was surprised at how casual the words sounded, considering the tightness in his chest. He studied the expression on her face and found it a mix of perplexed and troubled.

"My God. Where?"

"The guys wanted to go into this bar. It wasn't a good bar. Guess they felt like slumming. He happened to be there too."

"You're sure it was him?"

"Positive. He hasn't changed much. His face is...well, it looks okay."

Her cereal was going untouched. So was his. He motioned at it, smiled, and made an exaggerated chomping motion. She obeyed his directive for a moment. Then she looked at him and said, "Did you talk to him?"

"When I suggested I look him up before, you laughed at me."

"I know," she said in a quiet tone. "Didn't I apologize for that? We were mad at each other that night. I'm trying not to say things I know I shouldn't. Shit, I barely have time to say the things I *need* to."

"That's not true. You've got decades to live. We're going to make sure of that, remember?"

She nodded.

"It was awful the way things ended."

"Do you mean our friendship, or Shiloh?"

"Gordon—"

"Do you think I'm crazy, still being hurt over a dog? To have fucked up my life over it?"

"No," she said and he smiled, knowing full well she was lying. The truth had come out over many arguments. He remembered the long stretches when they never fought, when they were both caught up in other goals. Her career as a manuscript editor; the string of jobs he took trying to get his life back together; his father's deterioration and his attempt to be, for once, a good son. Their determination to have a child. Luke's birth had felt like the reset Gordon kept groping for in the shadows of his mind. It was a sign of fate returning him to the proper track. Until Luke turned ten, Gordon felt they were all a healthy, normal family. Then—

Well.

Amber's breast cancer was discovered a month after Luke's tenth birthday. She and Gordon were determined to hide the news from their son—detected early, the cancer could be fought with minimal side effects, the doctors told them. That diagnosis had turned out to be optimistic. Six months later, Luke started to see his mother was ill, and they had to let him know. The boy's nightmares began soon after. Amber of course saw his horrific dreams as Luke's subconscious way of dealing with the situation. Gordon had known better.

The compulsions he felt had begun around the same time as Amber's sickness. He often thought of it as his own cancer, a tumor in his mind. When the need sprang up inside of him, he felt like he was acting out some play scripted within the marrow of his bones. He couldn't understand it, this sick insanity he was manifesting toward his son. He tried to control it. But inevitably he would rise in the dead of night, and go to stand outside Luke's bedroom door. Then he would feel the darkness inside him become so great, he had to force himself into the bathroom, shut the door. Then he'd turn on the ceiling light, open his eyes wide, and force himself to stare at the bulb until he was dizzy and nauseated and blind. Sometimes this was enough to blunt the *need* inside him, and give Luke a night's reprieve. But increasingly Gordon found himself opening that bedroom door anyway.

"Are you serious about going back to school? Becoming a teacher?"

Gordon stirred out of his thoughts. He knew he must look grim.

"Sure," he said.

"So let's get on the computer right now, start looking at some colleges."

"Right now?"

"I just don't want you to lose the moment, you know? If you saw the way your eyes lit up there..."

"Wait—lose the moment? You think I'm just tossing out ideas?"

"You've had some other ideas—really good ones—that never got a follow-up."

"Because you got sick."

"Gordon, please, let's just do this."

He laughed and felt the heat on his face. "I'm pretty focused in my life, Amber. Always have been. When I want something, I just go for it."

She sat back. The wrapped towel slid a bit to the left. "That's not focus, Gordon, that's impulsiveness. And that hasn't always been your *best* trait."

There it was: another fight. Gordon found himself eager, almost vicious in his lust for it. He no longer felt tired. Amber seemed just as ready, just as needy. The fights punctuated their tender moments but had never outnumbered them—until recently. About three months ago. He'd come home from seeing his father, and she'd made some little remark like, "How was Doc Reader tonight?" He'd never gotten mad at her for using that term before. He was the one who told her about it, and she'd never used it in an unkind way. But that night, it did sound unkind, even nasty, and they'd exploded at each other.

Maybe they both needed the fights to prove they were still alive. They both seemed to be walking on eggshells all the time, and you can only take that for so long, Gordon thought, before you just want to stomp all that *fragility* into dust. Amber always seemed electrified by the fights, jolted with a welcome energy. And yes, sometimes they'd even fuck afterwards—and fuck hard, Gordon holding her arms down by the wrists so she couldn't touch him.

He was thinking of the possibility of sex as this morning's fight dragged on into the afternoon, a series of simmering spats that weren't unlike *quickies* in their urgency. He wondered which particular shouting match was going to lead to them going at it. But as the hours passed, he realized that it wasn't going to happen today, and that only made the situation that much more bitter. Luke would be home from school around four. At two, Amber collapsed back on the sofa, curled up in her huge robe, while Gordon set his phone to wake him at 3:30 and headed upstairs to lie down.

He woke feeling so hammered by fatigue he stumbled getting out of bed, his confusion so thick and tangible, it took him a second to realize he wasn't in his own room. He swallowed against his bitterness. Fuck this house, he thought. This house is the reason we're all damned. Why wasn't this his room? It had *been* his, after all; he'd grown up in this room. The walls used to be papered over with local press clippings about him. Some girlfriend had collected them into a collage, he vaguely remembered. Now this was Luke's room, and Gordon and Amber slept in the one that used to belong to his parents. Why had he agreed to this arrangement? It was Amber's fault. It was her suggestion. With his father now permanently in professional care, Gordon had basically inherited the house. Amber said it was practical to move in and make it theirs. Sure it was close to Westervelt, which she professed to hate. But it was also mortgage-free living, a bonus they both needed.

The house was haunting him. He knew it. No wonder he couldn't get his life in order when he had to live here, in a town where everyone knew he'd lost everything on a fuckup. How could he think about the future under the roof where his mom died?

Stacy. That was the name of the girl who'd cut out all the clippings for him. He hadn't thought of her in a long time, but suddenly he remembered her face; it was a part of this room. His mother was a part of it too. The tears he'd shed longing for them both—sadness and desire were the essence of this room. How many times had he jerked off within these walls, fantasizing about Stacy or some other girl? And then the actual sex. So much sex. Sex was an echo in this room. This was no room for a little boy, no room for his *son*. The walls knew too much. The walls were possessed. Every room in this goddamned house was possessed with something horrible, something that took control of him, made him come into this room in the black of night. Now it had made him fall asleep here in the middle of the day.

He turned to look down on the sheets which were a little damp from his sweat. He sniffed his arms, and found the scent of his son there, a gentle mixture of Downey fabric softener and cotton t-shirts. He trembled. I must never come in here again, he thought. But he knew he would. Already his mind was imagining tonight.

Gordon made Luke's bed, gathered a change of clothes and went downstairs to the bathroom. His mother's huge copper soaking tub was still there. Amber and Luke both loved it—particularly Luke, who when little would pretend it was a submarine with a hull breech.

Gordon shut the door, stripped and stood contemplating the dry tub. Was he really going to run himself a bath? There wasn't time. Luke would be home in half an hour, and Gordon had to be ready. Amber needed her rest.

He didn't run water. Suddenly he didn't even want a shower, though he knew he stank. He knelt by the tub and put his hand into its depths. The copper warmed to his touch—maybe the only thing in the house that did. He thought of Shiloh. He could almost see the dog as he was that day, stinking and hungry, panting away at his new surroundings. Gordon remembered not having the right shampoo, ransacking the counter drawers for anything to use; the memory made him smile. His mom's perfumes and shampoos and soaps were all gone now. Still, they'd outlasted Shiloh.

He balled his hand and pounded on the side of the tub, making a sound like a dull, warped gong. Let them go, he thought. Let go of John-Mark, let go of Shiloh, let go of Dad and restart your life. It's not too late. Let go. Let go. He struck the tub on each *let go*. The sound reminded him of something out of the Eastern meditation music Amber started listening to after she got sick. All he lacked was a low, droning chant.

From outside the house came the whine of school bus airbrakes. *Luke.* Getting up, Gordon hurried to dress and left the bathroom just as the front door opened. Luke dropped his backpack when he saw his dad and just stood there.

"Well, come here and hug me."

The boy showed the same initial hesitancy as in last night's video message. He walked over and they hugged, Gordon dropping to his knees to better embrace his son. Luke was skinny but not fragile, but he felt so delicate against Gordon's large hands. He rubbed the boy's back and then ruffled his hair.

"Did you have a good day at school?"

The boy shrugged.

"You got a mouth?"

"It was good," Luke said.

"Your mom's probably asleep in the living room, so I want you to be very quiet, okay?"

"I'm always quiet," Luke said, looking down.

"What's wrong? Is someone making fun of you in school?"

He shook his head. Gordon found himself unable to speak.

"Will we visit Grandpa soon?"

"Soon," Gordon said. He was proud but curious about Luke's fascination with his grandfather. When he was little, his grandpa scared him and he went years only seeing him on major holidays, whining about it the entire time. Something had changed. Some realization of similarity, of sympathy—Gordon had no idea. Nor would he question the boy, who now liked to read poetry to his grandfather. He took it as an article of faith that these poems would make his grandpa better. There seemed to be some truth to it.

"Go read," Gordon said, giving his son the lightest kiss on the cheek. "I'm going to order us pizza for dinner."

When Luke left, Gordon returned to the bathroom and filled the tub with water a little hotter than he could stand. He forced himself into it, wincing and sweating. The water took the pain from his muscles and lulled him towards sleep and an unwanted dream: it was last weekend, about three in the morning, the time when Amber's medication put her in her heaviest sleep, and he was going into Luke's bedroom.

The bed was different in the dream, resituated so that all the outside light came through the window and struck it with the clarity of a spotlight. Gordon looked at himself sleeping. It *was* himself, somehow, and not his son on the bed. As he stood there, his cock was hard, and he thought he could satisfy his demon by just masturbating in the doorway. He tried it a moment. Then he went in, devious in his steps. He knew which spots on the floor squeaked and which didn't. He uncovered the boy's legs first. They weren't long yet, and had just a little hair. There was no hint of their future development, but they were fine all the same. He waited a moment to make sure the boy didn't stir. Then he took out his penis, and dipped his knee until he could press it to the boy's leg. He held it there, doing nothing else, for a minute. He said a word, faint and nonsensical given the circumstances. *Gorge. Gorge.*

He started to cry. The arousal was unfathomable to him. Thank God he was molesting himself and not Luke. A tear fell upon the boy's body and Gordon froze, certain his younger self would wake. When he didn't, the tears themselves ended, replaced by a desire so insistent that he felt it like a need for fire against a bitter cold. Becoming reckless, his hands pushed the boy's shirt up. His arms were down at his sides, but the hands themselves sort of crossed over his groin. Gordon picked up each hand by the wrist and set it aside. How was he not waking himself up? He exhaled and waited, watching the revealed torso maintain its casual rise and fall. The fingertips of his right hand rested on the boy's navel. I'm only touching myself, he thought. I have a right to touch my own body. His fingernails skimmed down to the waistband, which he lifted. As he did, he bent toward the opening and peered into the little pouch of darkness. To his astonishment, there was a mirror there, hidden away like a trap. He saw his father's white, desperate face in the reflection.

Gordon woke with such a start that water splashed onto the floor. The water before him had a little white clumpy film floating in it. Gasping, he kicked himself up, almost slipped and then tumbled bodily over the side. From the floor he reached blindly for the drain stopper. He found it and the water roared away.

There was a light tap on the door, and he heard Amber say his name.

"I'm okay," he said.

To his bafflement and horror, the door opened. He thought he'd locked it. His wife was there staring at her soaking husband in an awkward position on the floor. As she limped her way to him, he hurried to get up.

"Honey, what is it?"

"Nothing," he said, attempting to laugh. "I don't take baths a lot. I thought how much it might help. I fell asleep—I had a dream."

He winced inside: this was too much and he must find something to tell her when she asked. She did ask. "It was about you and me, when all of this is over."

"When all of this is over," she repeated, sounding amused. "That's a little vague."

"I mean when you're better. When we're doing great."

She held him and he allowed it, standing there dripping rigid against her. She reached up and began to unwind the towel around her head. "Don't," he said, but it was too late. It fell away, revealing her baldness, and she brought the towel to his skin and began to dry him. She patted his chest and back. "You must be Dorian Gray," she said. He vaguely understood the reference and let it pass. She dried his arms and then pressed her towel-covered hand into his groin. When she pulled away there was a thin last line of semen stretching between the towel and the slit of his penis, as silvery and fine as spider gossamer in the early morning.

"Must have been quite the dream. I hope it comes true for both of us soon," she said, and kissed him.

CHAPTER NINE

Ever since last summer, after coming back from his stay with George, Fane had kept a road atlas with the locations of both their houses circled on it. He'd lie awake at night and take out the map from under his mattress and put his finger on the circle that represented George's house. There was a smaller circle to the right, like an orbiting moon, where Fane estimated the cave to be. He had no real way of knowing. But when he looked at the circled places, he could make himself travel to them somehow, in his dreams. And he'd think: Once I can drive, I can go to George anytime I want.

Now he *can* drive, but feels poisoned by the freedom. When he looks at the atlas he finds every space filled with a cold, unwelcoming darkness, blackest of all over George's house.

Why didn't he stop himself?

This question has filled up the hollow weeks since the return from New York, making him regret his moment on the floor when his eyes watered not from sorrow but exultation. He had disturbed the Universe and the Universe *liked* it, and light burst across the cosmos. Fane had not counted it would be as brief as it was bright. Now it is summer again, the coldest he has ever known regardless of the thermostat's reading. He reads in bed during the day, his mind absorbing none of the words as he dwells on recent memories: George's silence, George's disdain. George even shoved him aside once. It was like that every day at Fowler following New York, up until the last day, when all the boys departed with their families. He and George stood beside each other, and Fane thought *at last* amends were to be made. He waited for George to say, "Mates?" But it never came. George's parents arrived first, he got into their car and left.

That was the moment of true, intense hurt—the moment he realized George was out of his life forever, and the coming summer would be a personal winter. George would not be inviting him over during the summer. In fact, he'd overheard George confirming to Dooley that his parents were going to Europe.

He can only assume George is with them.

Despite this, Fane dreams of going to George's house, stepping onto the porch and peering through the windows. Then he'll knock on the door. Then, when he's satisfied it's empty, when he *knows* George is gone, he will go down to the pond and sit awhile, watching ghosts catch fish.

In late June, he lies to his parents, telling them George invited him over for a weekend visit. His own audacity shocks him, and he is upset over the reason why they eventually grant permission: *because they trust George.* His mother loved everything about George after finally meeting him. His father even seemed to hold his son in higher esteem at having somehow secured such a boy as his best friend. It was almost like he wanted to clap his son on the back and say, "I never knew you could achieve so much."

Only his mother frets a little about the distance of the drive, especially since her son is not experienced behind the wheel. "I just never thought Adam would be driving more than five or six miles away from here, not until he went off to college. Is his car safe for such a long distance?"

"It's not so far," his father says. "It's probably a shorter drive than we take to reach Great Aunt Etty's place. Just make sure you call us as soon as you arrive, Adam, and as soon as you leave."

Fane smiles. "I'll be okay, Mom."

"Besides, George will take care of him," his father says. "That boy has a fine head on his shoulders."

Fane keeps smiling until his lips hurt.

The next day, he sets off with some money from his dad and a small suitcase packed with clothes and his poetry anthology, just to complete the illusion. He tosses the book in at the last moment like a good luck charm, though it's been nothing but a catalog of pain since New York. There were no more readings in the woods after they came back. His real charm is the black rock George gave him. It's now a totem, a tangible reminder that George once liked him and might like him again. Somehow staring into its deep blackness does not make him despair of eternal night.

We're not friends anymore, he thinks.

He's refused to *fully* entertain such thoughts until now. But the drive, as if it's straight into the sun, obliterates any shadow of doubt. George hates him. Something inside his mind breaks with the cleanness of bone. He cries so hard he can't see the road and pulls over crookedly, leaving too much of the car still in the road. A car horn blasts as a driver veers to avoid him. Fane remembers how the traffic in New York sounded as he listened to it in the early morning, his forehead pressed to the hotel room window, his penis stiff in his underwear, his tongue moving side to side, desperate not to relinquish a taste that was mysterious and miraculous to him. He remembers turning back to look at George sleeping on his side, and feeling so sure of himself and the future. Why shouldn't he after what had happened? Then Fane left the window and got into bed with George, hesitant only moment, thinking perhaps he should ask permission. But surely after the last two hours, permission had been granted, now and forever more.

How wrong he was, and how hard Fane cries now at his mistake.

At least half an hour passes before he gets himself together. When he directs the car back onto the road, the world feels strange to him, and the steering wheel seems huge and overwhelming and beyond his control. Still, he drives on, hunched forward, battling the car and the road and himself, until he reaches the turnoff to George's house. The house is easy to spot in its relative isolation, with the forest stretching behind it and no immediate neighbors. He steers up the long driveway, and then he's parked in front of it, George's house. How can he be here? What is he to *do*?

I forgot to call home, he thinks. I'll have to double back to the last gas station I saw and telephone from there.

As the impracticalities of his plan reveal themselves to him, he decides not calling is for the best. If he calls, he'll have to spend the weekend here in the car. But if I come home today, he think, there'll be just as many questions. They'll wonder what happened between—

George and me.

Fane moans as fresh tears run down his cheeks. He wipes his eyes, and looks ahead at the house. Then he goes cold.

George stands on the front porch staring down at him.

Fane gapes at him, certain he's seeing a phantom. If George is here, then his parents must be here too. That means George lied about going to Europe. Who *else* is here? Who else from *Fowler*? He grips the steering wheel with both hands, going white-knuckled. Neither he nor George move for more than a minute.

Fane takes the first step, opening the car door.

"What the hell are you doing here?"

"I don't know," Fane says.

"So you just show up at someone's house uninvited?"

Fane looks down. He has only the same answer. "I don't know."

"Go away, Fane."

George turns for the front door. "Wait," Fane says, reaching out with his right hand. "Please don't leave! I—"

"You what?"

Fane smiles stupidly. "I don't know."

George slams the door. Fane retreats to the car, certain George's father will be coming out to yell at him. He turns the key in the ignition, the engine roars to life.

And abjectly he turns the key back. Let George's father come. Let him yell. Fane knows he deserves it.

The front door opens again. It's George.

"You leaving or what?"

Fane shakes his head.

George comes down, opens the car door and pulls Fane out. He grabs Fane by the shirt and shoves him against the car. "I don't want to see you. You got that?"

The pressure George exerts increases. Fane's feet kick for traction, and suddenly something pops in his right leg. He screams with such genuine pain, even George relents, letting him fall to the ground as he backs off.

Now Fane gasps on his side, looking at the undercarriage of the car. George's shadow falls over him, and he tries to curl into a ball, certain he's about to get pummeled worse than anything Dooley or Thompson ever did to him. And Fane knows he deserves it, for loving in a way he should not love. If George demands a thrashing to end his hate, Fane welcomes it and prays it will come. It will not be worse than the pain in his leg now, an agony like ice in his kneecap.

But the beating never materializes. George just sounds weary as he begs Fane to leave.

"I don't think I can drive. My leg's really hurt."

"Your leg. All you ever talk about is your damn leg."

"I know. I'm sorry."

"No, you're not. As long as it gets you the attention you want—"

"I *want* it to be normal."

"It'd be the only thing normal about you if it was. Now get the hell out of here. I have stuff to do."

George heads back toward the house. Fane rolls over, expecting to see George's parents standing at the door. They must wonder what's going on, after all. But the door is open and no one's there. If George closes the door behind him now, he senses, it will be the last time.

"What are you doing? Maybe I can help."

George just laughs but stops on the porch and turns. "You're a strange one, Fane. Why don't you take off now? Maybe we'll catch up back at school."

"But that'll be months—"

"The summer's always too short."

"Not to me. Every day's too long when you're lonely."

George appears unmoved by this plea. Fane gets to his feet. His right leg is sore but not impossible. He looks at his car. It's time to go. It's time to face the fact that he's unwanted here. But he can't. Didn't he promise himself he'd go down to the pond and remember better times? How can he leave without doing so?

He leaves the car and starts limping around the back of the house.

"Where are you *going?*"

"Down to the pond."

"You think you can just stroll about on my property?"

Fane shrugs and lets his feet take him where they will. The reasons for his own actions elude him. Does he want to kill whatever lingering affection George might have for him? He feels like a ghost seeking a place to haunt, and when he reaches the water's edge he sees his reflection, pale and ghastly. Yes, a ghost: a ghost before his time. Should he drown himself? Is George watching? Would George rush down in panic if he sees Fane taking the plunge? His thoughts run so deep, he doesn't hear George charging at him until it's too late—until George has yelled, "Adam Fane, the merman!" as he shoves him into the pond.

Submerged beneath the brown water, for one horrific moment, he imagines all those fish George caught and threw back swarming around him, changed from trout into piranha. He thrashes for the surface. As he does, the water clears and expands. The temperature drops from cool to icy, and there is no sign of a surface anywhere.

Then a force seizes him, an undertow like two arms that snatch him through the water at a fantastic speed, taking him up and down and sideways, twisting him through nauseating corkscrews and dizzying feats of acrobatics. He shrieks his last reserve of air in a gargle.

Somehow he's still conscious in this new universe. There's someone with him, a distant figure. Closing in, Fane sees a naked man, his arms and legs flailing. He's beautiful, as handsome as George except for a deformed foot. The force that's captured Fane now stops, holds him in front of the man. They float staring into each other's eyes.

The man cries out in gargling pleas—

"Who are you? Why do you show me these horrors?"

A splash from overhead disturbs the water, and twin dark figures kick toward them. Arms wrap around the man's torso and tug him up. Other arms wrap around Fane. In the next instant he breaks the surface. The man is gone. The water's brown again.

The pond. This is the pond.

He sputters, coughing and hacking water as George pulls him to the shore. He drapes Fane there and lies beside him panting.

"You're not even good for a joke anymore. I shove you into the pond and you're supposed to get up and be mad at me. Instead you just let yourself sink. Do you want to die or something?"

Fane continues gulping air as he struggles to understand what just happened to him. Who was that man? He sits up and stares at the water. Where had he just been? It couldn't have been the pond. He touches his head. The image of the man fades against his will. Already he seems like a vague hallucination.

George clears his throat and spits. Fane turns to him.

"Your parents didn't go to Europe?"

"They sure did."

"And they let you stay here by *yourself?*"

George shrugs. "It's just two weeks."

"I can't imagine having that much freedom. My parents would never—"

"Well, your parents aren't mine."

"What if something happened to you while they're gone?"

"What could happen, Fane?"

He tries to think and can't think of a single danger. There must be hundreds. But George is invincible.

"You could have called me if you wanted some company," Fane says.

George laughs. "Must be nice to have a car and license. You can just invite yourself to any place you want."

"I'll leave right now."

"Why are you even here?"

"I just had to see you."

"Congratulations."

Fane draws his left leg up to his chest. His right leg won't bend at all. Putting his forehead against his left knee, he tries to detect any possible sign of forgiveness from George. It doesn't come.

"You hate me, don't you?"

He's crying before he even finishes the question. George moves away from him as if the tears might be scalding. Fane's body shakes. All his fantasies of reconciliation go up in flames.

"Adam—"

"I can't stand it that you hate me."

"Adam, I do hate you. Sometimes. Not all the time."

"Because of what happened in New York?"

"Don't talk about it. Don't ever bring that up."

Fane sniffles. "If I don't, will we be friends again?"

"I don't know. You shouldn't have come here. If we could have put the whole summer between us, maybe it'd be back to normal in the fall."

"But you wouldn't want to room with me next year."

George blanches. "Not a chance, Fane. Don't want to walk in every night and see you hugging my underwear to your chest."

George gets to his feet and Fane looks up at him through a new glaze of tears. Despite all that's been said, he can't help admiring how George's wet t-shirt and shorts cling to his body, revealing contoured muscles.

George must notice, because he looks down at himself and shakes his head. "You make things so hard, Adam. That's the worst part of all this. There's a world full of girls out there, and I already know that *none* of them will ever look at me the way you do. Maybe none of them will even feel for me like you do. I don't understand it, but I did love you as a friend. Loved you enough to wish...to wish I could feel the same."

"In the hotel, you did."

George grimaces. "I don't know why I did that."

"You're the world to me, George. Even that's not big enough to say how I feel. You're my universe."

He sees so much in George's face. Regret, confusion, anger—surrender.

George pulls his shirt off and tosses it to the side. He just stands there and Fane stretches a hand toward him. It's not like it was in New York, when he reached out and grabbed. This time his hand comes slow like a supplicant's, like a beggar's. All of George's being is Fane's alms. His fingertips press against the tautness of George's skin and the firm underlying muscle. George's stomach constricts and he flinches, but there's a slight smile on his face. Fane has tickled him.

George kicks off his shoes. Fane opens his eyes very wide. Now the socks. Now the shorts. Can this be happening?

There's only a few seconds of visible, complete nakedness before George becomes a blur diving into the pond. Fane stands up faster than he ever has before, too excited to countenance any pain in his leg or anywhere else. As George's head breaks the surface, Fane's never felt so jealous of water.

"Coming in—mate?"

"You can't be serious."

"Why not? You're already soaked, right?"

He looks down at his wet clothes. Then he smiles and starts toward the edge.

"Are you going to jump in wearing your clothes?"

Fane stops again. "Like you said, they're already wet."

"No, Adam. It doesn't work that way. In this pond, you skinnydip."

"I can't."

George offers him a faint smile. It's maddening and makes his shirt feel like a straitjacket. Fane tears it off and then drops his pants. And then—he can hardly believe it—his underwear.

He jumps into the water. When he comes up, he says, "I'll do anything you ask."

George laughs and begins swimming powerfully toward the little dock at the end of the pond. "Enjoy the swim, Fane."

Stunned, Fane begins kicking, pleading for George to wait. George hoists himself onto the deck and walks over to his clothes, pulling his shirt on. Fane swims harder but the water conspires against him. It's like the pond doesn't want to release him.

George is fully dressed by the time Fane gets to shore and walks to his clothes knob-kneed with his arms crossing over his body. George stands there smiling and watching.

"Feel better, Adam?"

"No. You're the cruelest person in the world. Even Thompson and Dooley wouldn't have done that to me."

"It was a *joke*, Fane. I had to get even with you."

"For what?"

"Everything."

He lunges at George. For perhaps the first time in their friendship, George seems truly caught off guard physically. Fane doesn't knock George to the ground. He doesn't tackle him. He grabs George's shoulders and kisses him on the lips. Wild, careering thoughts about the end of the world go through his mind. His hands now sweep over George's back as if searching for a magic button on his body that, if pressed, will make George love him. He knows it does not exist and he sees his future in grim, realistic detail. Nothing so dramatic as the end of the world. Just him driving back home and falling into a lonely summer and then a lonelier fall, his bleak days accruing into the isolated years of an old man who wishes he died in his youth.

He breaks the kiss and steps back. George touches his lips, and his eyes brim with tears.

"I know our friendship is over," Fane says. "It was over before it started."

He starts back to the house and the driveway. George grabs his arm.

"I looked in your car before I came down. I saw the suitcase. Are you running away?"

"I don't know."

"What's in there?"

"Things that remind me of you. The poetry anthology. Do you remember the rock you gave me?"

George nods slowly, as if he'd rather not recall.

"That's in there, too."

"No clothes?"

Fane shrugs. "I'm sure there's a shirt or two."

"Part of me wouldn't mind joining you—if you were running away."

Fane stares. Is George serious? It hardly matters. Fane knows he's not running away. He'll drive home. But maybe they *can* run away in a sense. Briefly. To a special place.

"Take me to the cave again."

"What, right now?"

"Why not?"

"We're wet."

"We'll dry on the way."

"I'm busy, Adam."

"Busy doing what?"

"Getting ready—for company."

"*What* company?"

George steps back as Fane leans into him. "It's none of your business, is it?"

Now he heads for the house. Fane limps along beside him. "Is it someone from Fowler?"

"That's right."

"Who?"

"Guess away."

"Don't make me do that. Just tell me!"

They reach the driveway. George claps him briskly on the shoulder. "Good-bye—again—Adam."

"Is it Dooley? You hate Dooley."

"Why? Because *you* hate him?"

So that's why George didn't stop them. He was always friends with Dooley. That's why he just sat there and watched while they—

"Just tell me it's not Dooley!"

"Adam, please, *please* go."

"Not until you tell me!"

He falls to his knees and waits.

L uke began talking during it.

"*I had a dream, which was not all a dream.*"

Gordon's hand snapped back from his son's waist and he retreated, almost tripping in the dark room. The jolt made him blink and look around, asking himself how he got here, telling himself he didn't know where *here* was.

That was a lie.

Of course he knew.

Luke was awake, the realization of Gordon's worst fear. There'd been a dim certainty in Gordon's mind that Luke was always awake during it, but his son never opened his eyes and never spoke—an unspoken agreement between them, the boy's introduction to the art of negotiating for his own innocence.

"*The bright sun was extinguished, and the stars*"

Gordon strained over his own pulse to hear and understand Luke's words, which had devolved into a whispered chant. As he realized Luke wasn't awake, his shoulder muscles unclenched and the squeezing pain in his neck relented. He ran his fingers through his hair. That was close, he thought. That's it. I'm done. Whatever it takes, I'm never doing this again. It's like an addiction or something and I'm going to fight it.

"*And men forgot their passions in the dread of this their desolation*"

"Gordon?"

Startled, he spun toward the door. He'd closed it to the narrowest crack without shutting it, so he wouldn't have to mess with the knob or deal with the click of the jamb, which always seemed an explosive sound in the late night quiet of the house. He could not believe Amber was standing there, a thin dark figure framed by a faint yellow glow from the nightlight in the hallway. It was after one in the morning and he'd checked in on her before heading upstairs. She continued to sleep on the couch in the living room, her favorite place these last few months, her body making less and less of an indentation in the deep, yielding cushions. Had she faked being asleep? He was certain he hadn't made a sound as he climbed the stairs, his penis hard as he anticipated the uninterrupted moments to come.

This must be God giving me a chance, he thought. If Luke hadn't started talking in his sleep, Amber might have caught me.

"Hey," he said, keeping his voice low. He stepped toward her and then stopped, afraid of the slight light from the hallway. Fright had not taken all of his erection, still quite evident in his underwear, and he could not explain it if she saw.

"What's wrong, Gordon?" She limped in with an overreliance on her cane. He saw the barest outline of her head, realized the red towel she liked to keep wrapped round it like some memory of hair had fallen off. She must have really hurried to get up the steps. To catch me, he thought.

"*The palaces of crowned kings—the huts, the habitations of all things which dwell, were burnt for beacons*"

She stopped, her shaded face turned to the bed. Now feeling safe, Gordon went to her.

"Luke's talking in his sleep. I heard it and thought there might be something wrong. I thought it might be the nightmare again."

"Be quiet, Gordon. Just let me listen."

"*And men were gathered round their blazing homes to look once more into each other's face*"

"It's weird, Amber. I don't know what he's saying."

"*Shhh.*"

"Quit telling me to be quiet."

Her next words were hissed: "*Just shut up.*"

Gordon gritted his teeth. Sometimes Amber considered her PhD to be in everything, like she could stand here listening to Luke's gibberish and make a hundred insightful diagnoses.

"*A fearful hope was all the world contained*"

They listened side-by-side. Luke's speech was increasing its pace. The words sounded antiquated to Gordon's ears and impossible for his son to know, but Amber seemed able to anticipate them. She even said a few fragments in tandem with Luke, causing Gordon to study her in the dark.

"What is it?"

"Poetry."

"You're serious?"

"I remember it—vaguely."

"Doesn't sound like poetry to me."

"Because you're such an expert on it."

He shoved her—shoved her and lurched forward to catch her almost in the same motion, even as she cried out, her frail grip on the cane overwhelmed by her husband's force. She slipped from his grasping hands, hit the carpeted floor, and at once Gordon was there, apologizing, snugging his large body against her diminishing one, almost spooning with her. He rocked her in his arms. Above them, from the bed, Luke continued his strange chant.

"*The brows of men by the despairing light wore an unearthly aspect, as by flashes the fits fell upon them*"

"God, I'm sorry, Amber. I'm so, so sorry. You know I'm sorry."

"I'm sorry too."

"What do you have to be—"

Then he understood and grunted. She was sorry she'd married him. Sorry she'd risked so much for him. In a flash, he remembered their life together, the eager early mornings of waking beside her as her skin blushed with the dawn light, the scent of her body like spring rain, her taste like honey. In those mornings only the bedroom's quiet was out of place and unwanted, as all he wanted was to talk to her. Their conversations had been endless; sex was just a different form and forum for talking, their bodies bursting into Braille for the sweep of each other's fingers. Laying like they were now, unable to even see each other, the room's only sound a third voice fashioned from the two of them, Gordon wondered if he'd ever find such Braille on Amber again, the only communication left to him in the dark.

"And looked up with mad disquietude on the dull sky, the pall of a past world"

Luke's voice became harsher, the tone accusatory. He went on for a few more minutes. Gordon understood the images but not the sense of the words. The tension in Amber's body told him she understood both.

"Darkness had no need of aid from them—She was the Universe."

Luke stopped speaking. It took Gordon a moment to realize this. He heard and felt Amber sobbing. Had the poem upset her? In all the years he'd known her, Gordon could not recall Amber being so moved. It had always fascinated him. She loved poetry, she was excited about it, but her attitude was not at all like his father's. Dad had read poetry as if he sought to hurt himself. Amber treated it like a Sudoku puzzle, a fascinating game pregnant with cultural and political codes. The idea of her shedding a tear even over a horrific poem seemed impossible—except when the words were coming from her son's mouth.

Luke stirred. "Dad? Mom?" He sounded lost.

Gordon rose first and helped Amber to stand. Luke gasped like he was having a heart attack. "It's okay, Luke," he said, imagining how much two dark forms suddenly rising up must have terrified his son.

"Why were you on the floor?"

"We tripped," Amber said. "We heard you talking and came in to check on you. We didn't want to turn on the light."

"I was talking?"

"Yeah, buddy, you were."

"I was having a bad dream. A man was writing."

Amber moved closer, finding the bed with her cane. She settled down on the edge of the mattress. "What was he writing, Luke?"

"What I told him to. What I saw."

Luke began to sob. This spurred Gordon into action, but as soon as he got close, Luke shoved him away and cradled close to his mother. Gordon stood very still, wondering if Amber had noticed.

"Gordon, why don't you leave us alone for a bit? I know you're tired."

"You're the one who's—" He sighed. "Okay. Goodnight, Luke. *I love you.*"

He lingered long enough to make sure his son did not intend to respond. Then he slipped out of the room, remembering how cold he'd been to his own father in the times after Mom died, wanting to hurt with silence and not knowing what compelled him, except to say the loathing he felt was like some instinct—the way prey identify predators. Gordon started toward his bedroom and then pivoted to the stairs, placing his heels on the very edge of the top step. He descended this way, trying to coax fate. Please let me fall, he thought. Please let me slip and break my spine so my arms never work again.

But he was too athletic. He balanced by nature.

He found himself in the downstairs bathroom with the lights on, staring at his mother's copper soaking tub. As he bent over to look into it, a few tears beaded in the basin.

Luke's been awake every time. He just endures it, Gordon thought.

He got down on his knees and turned on the cold water. He thrust his head under the spigot and shivered.

He'd tried so hard to resist. He really had. He had to beat this sickness.

He'd gone to bed at ten, feeling confident in his mastery over the compulsion. It'd been two weeks since he last surrendered to it. Then he woke up a little after midnight. He woke from a dream that stubbornly defied recollection but lingered bodily in the sensation of being stroked by invisible fingers. He bit back the urge to shriek at this thing that had stalked him for so long, that came and went without reason, first making him horrified of being touched, and now demanding he touch his son. The urge was most overwhelming when it felt like a voice calling from within his own flesh and from within Luke, as if some creature with the same voice had been split in half and demanded unity.

Gordon pulled his head away from the icy water and gasped. He'd been holding his breath. Shutting off the water, he got up and groped for a towel as frigid streams streaked his torso. All he found was a washcloth which he rubbed against his chest and hair before propping himself along the counter on his elbows, shoulders sagging.

He looked at the ceiling. What was happening upstairs? Amber suspected something. She had to, and getting him out of Luke's room seemed the best way to get Luke to talk. When would the hammer fall? Was it descending even now? He cringed and whimpered. He'd been in jail once. In some ways he thought he'd never left it. More often these days he wished he hadn't.

Minutes passed with him just standing and waiting. Gordon heard no movement at all in the house. At last he could take it no more. To his surprise, he found Amber at the kitchen table, her face bathed in the blue glow from her laptop—the only light in the room.

"You'll hurt your eyes reading like that."

She looked up, expressionless for a moment. Then she started to giggle. It was horrible to hear. He swallowed. Her attention returned to the screen.

"Did Luke...say anything?"

"He doesn't remember much."

"Well, what *does* he remember? Sorry, Amber—I'm just worried."

"Oh, I know you're worried, Gordon."

His heart was beating very fast. Her tone sounded so casual in the dark. Was she taunting him?

"What are you doing?"

"Looking for the poem Luke was saying in his sleep."

"Did you find it?"

"Just now."

He stepped closer. "What is it?"

"It's called 'Darkness.'"

He repeated the title to himself. "Who wrote it?"

"Lord Byron."

"I've heard the name before."

"Of course you have," she said. "In his time, he was the most famous poet that ever lived."

"No, I mean I think you mentioned him before. I don't remember. Back in class, maybe."

She shrugged. "I never cared for Byron. There's not much complexity in his work as far as I'm concerned."

For a moment, Gordon thought the conversation was going to turn entirely to literature, as their talk often did in earlier times. He would have welcomed that.

Instead she said, "The question is, why is Luke reciting this poem in his sleep?"

"Maybe he read it."

"I'm quite certain he's read it, Gordon."

"I mean he's read it a lot. He's like Dad. They'd both read the same poem so many times they can quote it. Sometimes I look at Luke and think this is what would happen if you and my father had a child together."

"Gross."

"My dad's not *gross*."

Amber closed her computer, leaving them in darkness. "I'm going back to the sofa."

"Do you need any help?"

"No. I can fall onto the cushions without any assistance from you."

Gordon went to her anyway, and she did not resist. The kitchen chairs had no armrests and always gave her the most trouble.

"I bet the poem's in one of the anthologies Luke's always carrying around."

"He could have read it anywhere. It doesn't matter."

"Maybe it does," he said as they entered the living room. "He must have read it a bunch of times if he can say the whole thing in his sleep."

"I guess."

"Well, damnit, doesn't that bother you? I don't like the idea of him reading something so—awful."

She began her method of nestling herself into the deep sofa, letting the cane fall to the floor, while she put both her hands on the center cushion and tumbled over, leading with her left shoulder. Usually, this settled her onto her back without disturbing the cushions, though sometimes her shifting weight knocked them out of place. When that happened, Gordon would lift her body a little and readjust them. Tonight Amber gave no indication she needed his help.

Now on her back, she said, "Don't worry about it. Kids Luke's age are always attracted to Dystopian literature. Their world is constantly going to hell, so they like to read books that reflect that opinion. Byron's poem fits a need."

"You're right," Gordon said. "It doesn't mean anything."

"I didn't say that." She spoke through a prolonged yawn.

She was asleep almost at once, as if the enveloping cushions had siphoned off the last of her dwindling energy. Now she seemed very ill to him. She was very ill. Bursts of anger fueled stretches of vitality, but how much longer could that pattern continue? Gordon lingered a moment, dead on his feet but not ready to surrender to it. Was she really asleep? He'd been tricked once tonight into thinking she wouldn't wake up.

He left her, but went to the kitchen rather than climbing the stairs to their bedroom. Leaving the light off, he groped for her laptop and raised the cover, blinking as light sprang out like a jack-in-the-box, blinding him. He squinted until his eyes adjusted. The website she'd been on showed a long column of poetry. He recognized the first line, which was seared into his consciousness when Luke suddenly started talking. *Darkness.* Gordon sat down and read. A strange familiarity swept through him, a nauseating déjà vu. He thought the words must seem familiar because he'd just heard them all from Luke. But the sensation was different and far more jarring. The images the words conveyed rather than the words themselves were what seemed so eerie, so real—so *experienced.* But how could that be? Maybe a movie had been made from the poem. Pictures ran through his head like scenes from a film. But it was a film he starred in. He and Amber, John-Mark—

Gordon got up, doubling over from a hot stabbing pain in his guts, as if a fire alarm had gone off inside him. Wincing, he started to close the computer only to realize her browser had another tab showing the words *Child & Adolescent Counseling.* Gordon froze, his pain forgotten. He clicked on the tab. Amber had been researching child psychiatrists. She obviously meant to take Luke to one behind Gordon's back. He straightened and looked toward the living room. Lying bitch. She'd acted like the poem meant nothing. She knew better. She *suspected* more than she would ever let on.

God only knew what the specialist would discover.

It's for the best, he thought. I deserve to get caught. Take him, Amber. It can't happen soon enough.

But you're still a lying bitch.

The next morning, after only three hours of sleep, Gordon practically dragged himself back to the kitchen. Luke had gotten up on his own and sat eating cereal. Amber, regardless of her condition, usually made a point to be awake before Luke went to school. The last several months had seen a series of small surrenders in her willpower, from a promise to be awake and energetic before Luke himself got up, to a promise to at least make him breakfast, to a promise to at least be awake when he walked out the door to catch the bus. Gordon looked in on her, checking for the usual shallow rise and fall of her chest. She would hate him for not waking her.

He entered the kitchen. Luke turned his head toward him and his chewing visibly slowed. They looked at each other. Gordon could not hold his son's gaze. He hurried past and poured cereal for himself. When he looked up, he found Luke was still staring at him.

"I'm sorry," he said.

Gordon held tight to the bowl, which suddenly felt like a squirming wet fish. "What—what are you sorry for, champ?"

The boy's eyes shifted to the left, as if reading some internal script. "For waking you up last night. I know you'd rather sleep."

"Luke, buddy, don't apologize for that. Don't apologize for anything."

He took the bowl of dry cereal and sat down at the table across from his son. Hunched forward, he picked at a few flakes and put them into his mouth. Softening in the spit on his tongue, they had an ashy taste.

"I'm sorry," Luke said.

"I said you don't—"

He stopped, seeing something like a watery grave in the wide, dark eyes of his son. The lower lids brimmed with tears, perched precariously there like coffee sloshing about the rim of a mug filled too high. But they did not spill over the side.

"You want to tell me more about that dream you had? About the man writing?"

"No," Luke said.

"It doesn't sound like such a horrible dream."

The boy looked down at his bowl. He stirred his cereal twice with the spoon before letting both hands fall into his lap. A sob hitched his chest and Gordon got up and knelt beside him.

"I want to see Grandpa. I haven't seen Grandpa in over a month."

"Sure," Gordon said.

"I want to read to him."

"I think he'd like that. You know, Dr. Reynolds says Grandpa's making a lot of improvement."

Gordon felt pressure on his right wrist. He saw Luke gripping it. "I need to see Grandpa right now."

"You have to go to school, and I have to go to work."

"No!"

The shout was so loud, Gordon put his hand over Luke's mouth by reflex. "Your mom's trying to sleep. Grandpa will wait."

Luke stared at him, his gaze intense as Gordon took back his hand. "Dad," he said, "if you take me to school, I'll run away. I'll run all the way to where Grandpa is."

His son's tone of voice was so matter-of-fact Gordon believed it. He rubbed his eyes. After last night, after so many other nights, he *owed* Luke. What harm could it do to miss one day of school? Dad wouldn't be around forever, after all.

Better to keep Luke close anyway.

"Okay."

Luke got up. "I'll get my book."

Gordon almost laughed. "Now wait a minute—we're not leaving right this very second. Give it a few hours."

"You swear?"

"I do."

Amber also was too tired to raise an objection when she woke an hour later. Luke gave her a big hug with his left arm. He had a poetry anthology tucked under the right. Gordon had never seen it before.

"Can I see that, Luke?"

Luke surrendered the book with some reluctance. Gordon studied the cover. The title was simply *The Romantics: An Anthology*. It was stamped with the local public library's seal. He opened it and flipped through the table of contents. It didn't take long to confirm what he suspected. Smiling, Gordon returned the book.

"Grandpa is going to be really surprised when we show up in his room."

"Let's go," said Luke.

Thunder wakes Byron from a light slumber and he sits up calling for Loukas. The fifteen-year-old boy stands across the room, splashing his chest and face with water from a marble basin. He turns toward Byron but otherwise he does not move except to look up as more thunder shakes the ceiling. Byron does not know who owns the house here in Missolonghi—some Greek aristocrat agitating for independence and willing to dare the wrath of the Ottomans. Just four hours ago militia marched up and down the streets to boisterous cheers, the revolutionaries dressed smartly in uniforms financed by Byron and armed with weapons likewise purchased with his coin. Off shore, a naval fleet of seven ships refitted at Byron's expense fired celebratory cannons. Enrapt, it seemed to Byron the people thought they were already free. They looked like cave dwellers just discovering the sunshine. Then he saw young Loukas amid the marchers and they traded smiles. Byron thought: I am happy. Then in an instant, the sun went out and darkness fell, and the screaming people scrambled for cover. Someone lit a torch. Or so it seemed to Byron for a moment. In reality, the first of many encroaching storm clouds had covered the sun, followed by a peel of thunder almost drowned out by the naval volleys. The throngs in the street had not dispersed at all.

Even now the vision from Lake Leman persists in his head. He thought he had escaped it by coming to Greece.

"Loukas, it is only thunder. *Come here.*" He pats half the mattress still dimpled from the boy's weight.

Loukas does not know English. He curses, cries out, and weeps in Greek. Byron does not know Greek. As he found for a time with Teresa in Italy, foreign tongues make for better lovers, as guesswork lends all conversations an amiable ludicrousness. The fighting comes later, when comprehension allows for the translation of anger. Perhaps, he considers, if Claire had spoken only Chinese he might not have found her advances back in the summer of 1816 to be so...tedious.

Loukas trembles. The dark windows fill with bursts of white lightening and send him crouching in a corner.

Byron shakes his head at this. He knows the courage and passion of the boy when it comes to his country. This young man would charge into a redoubt of Turks with nothing but a sword in hand. Yet a storm makes him quake? Under other circumstances this pitiful sight might prove amusing, even seductive.

But not tonight.

"I need light, Loukas. I need the light of Greece. I need *you* to be my sun and burn forever. But you cannot burn forever, can you?"

The question seems to linger in the air like a physical thing departing Byron's lips. Since the night of prophecy eight years ago, he sometimes finds himself in quiet moments looking up at the sun and asking that very question:

You cannot burn forever, can you?

Swinging his legs off the bed, careful to make sure his right foot goes straight from the concealment of sheets to the security of its special boot, Byron grimaces. "Loukas, for the love of God, at least look at me."

Responding to his name, the adolescent lifts his trembling head to meet Byron's gaze and mutters something that sounds hostile. Byron flinches as he stares. Maybe it is the low light in the room, or because dread has paled the boy's olive complexion against his frame of black hair: but suddenly Loukas looks like Shelley when they first met by the waters of Lake Leman.

It rained then too.

Another flash of lightning illuminates the room. The lightning and the boy's face combine to stir a memory of one of Shiloh's better poems.

"What is this world's delight?" he begins, standing. The floorboards creak. "Lightning, that mocks the night, brief even as bright."

He hobbles toward Loukas. Tempting boy. But is Loukas a temptation? Can that be the right word now they have consummated their relationship? Once a temptation has been had, is its continued presence still temptation— or *indulgence?*

He reaches the boy and gently puts his fingers into his dark, thick tangles, wet now with sweat and water. *Virtue, how frail it is! Friendship, how rare! Love, how it sells poor bliss for proud despair!*

"Oh Shiloh. Shiloh, Shiloh," he says, still feeling Loukas' hair. "Shiloh, did you write those words to mock me? How many times must I confess the same thing to your ghost? How many times must I say you were right and I was wrong? And how many times after those confessions will I wake up from a nightmare that sends me to the window to see if the sun exists? How shall I make myself *believe* you were right? Shall I step inside a church and pray? Can a man pray a lie?"

Loukas flinches away, almost tearing his hair. He says something else in Greek. Byron translates it through the separate actions of his body: *You are insane and I fear you.* But as Byron turns away to hobble back to the window and watch the storm, he is almost tripped by the boy lunging for his feet. Loukas on his knees clutches Byron's legs and looks up in shivering submission.

"Oh God, Loukas, why have I come to Greece? You and your people seem to think me a general. Did I come here to play a soldier? Perhaps I came here to worship. I would worship you among the other gods collecting dust in the ruined temples on the hillside. You will forgive me for not being a monotheist.

In my ripe old age of thirty-six, I find polytheism and pantheons afford more comfort. Surely it is better not to put the Eggs of Faith in one basket, even one as fine as yours."

Loukas touches his forehead to Byron's right kneecap. This supplication, this reliance spurs arousal. He stiffens and feels the boy's hair again.

"Help me, Loukas. Help me find sunlight. For you the sun is easy—it will rise in a few hours. It always does for youth. But I won't see it or feel its light on my face when it does. God, may you never grow so old that the shadows in your life have names. Shelley, Allegra. At least my little Ada lives. I think you would like her, Loukas. Perhaps if she were a few years older, you might even... I've got a lock of her hair, you know. It is golden like the sun, not dark like yours and mine. Sleeping together, your heads would look like night and day. You—"

He feels his face flushing and calls for Fletcher. But his faithful servant is in another house two miles away, sent there by Byron himself to leave him alone with Loukas. The storm prevents his return. Byron shakes his head, wondering why he is even thinking about Fletcher. It must be because he is growing older. His younger self would still have Loukas in bed, not sitting around pondering his manservant. Is he so tired after one joust? Could he actually be jealous of his own daughter, imagining her to be a more satisfactory partner for the boy? Now Loukas taps Byron's calf, his gaze on the ceiling. Byron looks up as the boy scrambles away. It is as if he thinks the ceiling will collapse. A moment later, water begins to drip, though Byron detects no crack.

"It is nothing," Byron says, laughing, before discovering the boy shivering in the corner, knees drawn up to his chest. This is when he realizes Loukas is too young to be a soldier—or a lover.

Why am I here? Byron asks himself. Why does Loukas stay? What am I to him, and what do I *want* to be?

The thunder increases. Byron imagines the entire Mediterranean roiling. Sharp lightning flashes reveal the world outside and within. Loukas grinds his forehead against his arms. This trembling stirs Byron to even greater sympathy and shame; watching Loukas is so very much like seeing a young animal peering out from a burrow flooding from rainwater. In these desperate times, with fear and treachery everywhere, the whole world seems to be gazing skyward—the young sailor's mother from the door of her house, the sailor-son from the deck of his ship; the dissolute gambler from some stinking gutter; the poor from their ramshackles; the aristocrats from their stables; members of Parliament, members of Congress, members of tribal councils in all the untamed places of the Earth whose people starve and thirst, whose ears ache to hear prophetic words. Their eyes search the dark sky, and what does it matter if the sun refuses them and the cold embraces them? The darkness is only a chance for lesser stars to shine. If the faintest light in the heavens lends these people any speck of hope...

Byron straightens his back.

I know why I'm in Greece, he tells himself. I came here to die. But now I find I came here to live.

"Come to me, Loukas."

The boy stays in his place.

Byron goes to him and lifts him to his feet. The act stresses his right foot, forcing a wince. He sees the boy look to its source. They have not been entirely naked with each other. Byron has never been entirely naked with anyone. He has always found some way to hide the deformity—a wrap, some waddled cloth, the convenient sheet, even wearing the boot in bed. The time is right for revealing. If he did not come here to die but live; if he did not come here for darkness but for sunlight; if he came here seeking a different vision, a different prophecy, then can he abide any further shadows? Looking down at the boot, he considers how the foot has tormented him, its preferred path on the margins of life. But what joy is to be found in the margins? It is not for him. He is a poet, not an annotator.

Sweating a little, he limps to the bed with the boy in tow and sits on the edge of the mattress. His gaze never leaving the boy's face, Byron works off the special boot, the accommodating prison for malformed flesh and bone. After the boot drops away, Byron removes the last coverings, not unlike a soldier unwrapping gauze from a wound for his own inspection, and bending forward he grips his leg and presents the foot for viewing.

The boy's face scrunches up a moment, threatening to convulse away. This injures Byron more than he'd dare admit. What did he expect though? Does he deserve less? But in the end Loukas does not turn. He does not cry or smile. He stares steadily at the ruined appendage as if memorizing cruelty and regret so he'll know its visage later. His silence is a Greek silence, deep and contemplative even in a boy. Then he reaches out a tentative hand and strokes the top of the foot, his fingers going up and down the flippered length. Byron gasps. No one has ever touched the foot. It has brought him pain. He did not know the nerve endings there could possibly feel pleasure.

Suddenly, outside the window, the darkness ends, subsumed in glorious yellow. Byron cannot believe it. How can the sun—in the middle of the night—

And he begins to laugh.

"Thank you, Loukas. You have given me a new vision. I will be your prophet. I will be Greece's prophet."

The storm, of course, has not subsided. In an eyeblink, the outer dark returns to the window. Loukas clings to Byron's foot as if it is a strange charm against the weather. Byron lets himself be held even when a second leak in the ceiling happens, spilling faster drops of water onto the middle of the bed. He leans back and opens his mouth. It is not until he's swallowed deeply that he realizes the water's taste is awful, as if there might be something very wrong with it.

*N*ot until you tell me.

Fane hears his own words in another man's voice and becomes dizzy. He closes his eyes and rubs them and when they open again he's old and on a reclining bed. His back aches and his throat is terribly dry. He senses he's been talking a long time.

The man in the adjacent hair looks meditative and thoughtful with his attention on the tablet computer in his hands. Fane knows the man but has trouble placing his name until he notices the badge on his shirt. *Dr. Gary Reynolds.* Below that are the words *Geriatric Psychiatrist.*

"Adam?"

"Yes."

"You're having a very good memory day. Do you think you can continue?"

Fane studies Dr. Reynolds. He's a younger man, perhaps fifty with hair just a bit more salt than pepper. That device of his is recording everything Fane says. I remember that, he thinks. He remembers much more. His memory is very clear now, frighteningly so.

"I don't want to go on."

"Not even a little more? We've been trying to piece it together for so long now. We'd all like to know who George is. I think I'm understanding a bit now."

"Understanding my past isn't any of your business."

Dr. Reynolds accepts the rebuke without any sign of malice. "What about Gordon? He just wants to understand his father. That's all any son wants. If you're worried about what he might think, I'm pretty confident when I say—"

"Go away."

Dr. Reynolds sighs a little but surprises Fane by getting up. "Perhaps another time."

"No. You're done. As am I."

"We'll see, Adam."

"*Doctor Fane.*"

"What?"

"*Doctor.* I'm one too."

Dr. Reynolds smiles. "I can't believe how lucid you are. This is really quite remarkable and exciting."

"Because of some drug?"

"That's right. We've been trying a new drug, in combination with—"

"Stop it. Stop the drug treatment."

The smile fades. "Adam—Dr. Fane—why would you want that? You were practically in a catatonic state before we began working with you. You didn't even know when your son was in the room."

"I'm sure it wasn't often."

"But it was! Do you know his name, Dr. Fane?"

"It's Gordon."

"And the name of your grandson?"

The answer is almost instantaneous. "Luke."

"He's a fine boy. He reads to you. You *enjoy* those readings, Dr. Fane. Quit the therapy now and you'll lose all of that. *Fast.*"

"If it means losing certain memories, I'll accept it."

"I'm sure that no matter what happened between you and George it couldn't be worth sacrificing cognition—"

"It's my decision to make," Fane says.

"We'll talk about it later. I'll leave you alone now."

Fane's gaze follows the doctor until he shuts the door behind him. His eyes water as he concentrates on the room's stillness. Dr. Reynolds is right: his memory is *very* good just now, not confused in the least. He looks to see if the tablet was left on the table, but the doctor took it with him. If he talks now, there'll be no electronic Boswell recording his words. Might the doctor be lingering on the other side of the door? As Fane makes his decision, he hopes Reynolds has stayed to eavesdrop. The poor man must consider Fane a jigsaw puzzle with a crucial few pieces missing.

Looking at the door, he says, "I told George I intended to go into the cave and die. I opened the car and took out that little, pointless suitcase and started for the woods. George yelled at me. He had a higher pitch to his yells just as his laughter was actually quite a bit higher pitched than his speaking voice. But I kept going. I told myself I was calling George's bluff. I had no clue where I was going. The only time I went to the cave, we started on a trailhead that lasted about half a mile. After that, George guided us by compass."

He pauses, wondering again about Dr. Reynolds. Is his Thisbe there to hang upon his words?

"George relented and caught up to me on the trailhead. He was really a good-hearted boy, though certainly not the hero I worshipped according to my nature. Needless to say, I was already exhausted when he found me. My leg hurt very badly, and I was chafing from the wet clothes. I even had a feverish chill. I remember that very well, plus the sensation that I was going to throw up at any moment. But when George came to me yet again, I lost every feeling except the desire to be with him. I begged him to come, said I would never bother him again if he made this one indulgence. He agreed. Partly, I think he simply couldn't go back to the house and do anything while the possibility of me being lost in the woods was on his mind. But it was more than worry that convinced him to come along. 'Why do you want to go there?' he said, and I swear the immediate answer in my head was, *To live*.

"The answer I actually gave was generic. 'I just do.' George was not complicated in his thinking. 'Just because' was a very respectable philosophy to him. So he went with me, and I have no memory of the trip. It is not a fault of age: I have never had a memory of it, and I believe that during our journey we somehow mutually ceased to exist. We were not two boys who'd formed a friendship at a school we both hated. We were not two boys who'd been in the cave before. We were not two boys who experienced each other in New York. But we were passing through time, because when we reached the cave my wet clothes were completely dry—as were my lips.

"We reached the familiar outcropping of rock. I still had the absurd suitcase in my hand. It had caused me nothing but immense pain in my leg. George started laughing. 'Are you going to take that damn thing into the cave with you? Adam Fane, the big tickle.' I put it down and opened it up, taking out the one thing in the case that might matter. 'I'm not going to sit around listening to you read poetry,' he said. Neither of us had a flashlight anyway. I told him I was going to take the anthology with me and leave it there. I said I was done with poetry. These statements were supposed to impress him. They only made George laugh."

Fane rubs his chin, his attention still on the door. He imagines Dr. Reynolds salivating on the other side, one ear pressed into the wood.

"We made the ascent to the opening and then climbed down. George said it would be the last time he'd come to the cave. He was certain next year he'd be too large to squeeze through. He probably would have been right about that. I had a much slighter frame and even I had some trouble with the passage. But then we stood side by side in the darkness. Neither of us had a flashlight, but we knew where the string was. We knew we could let it guide us safely to that chamber. I found the string and began to move.

"'You're out of your mind, Fane!' Yet still he followed. His friendship was perfect, even when he despised me. Did he love me? Was he aroused in the darkness? I had to know, and turning to where he had to be, I groped for him. His body was very solid, very firm, and I moved my hand up it, dropping the anthology to the floor. I touched him for a minute before I realized I was not touching him at all. I was feeling up part of the rock face, and George snickered at me.

"Suddenly his face appeared, terrible to behold. He had a flashlight after all and he stuck it under his chin before turning it on. I don't know where the flashlight came from. Perhaps it was already in the cave, stashed there by George in case of an emergency. I screamed and lashed out by reflex. George had taught me not to make a roundhouse swing, but to jab. His lesson was more effective than I could have imagined."

Fane swallows, staring at the door, willing it to open.

"And that's all you'll ever know about what happened."

They drive twenty miles to the Memory and Aging Center where Gordon's father had been a patient for several years. Patient, guinea pig—at some point the lines of experimental medicine blurred. Gordon could still recall the day his father had his first collapse. He'd even see his father in the Westervelt quad, limping along with his cane. *Was Dad trying to find me?* The possibility had occurred to him before, in the nights he sat in jail with his memories playing out before him. Hadn't there been just a moment when he saw his father calling to him? The attitude seemed impossible to him now, but back then, almost twenty years ago, he feared being associated with his dad. He'd even changed his last name to make sure no one knew they were father and son. If he *had* really seen Dad calling to him that day, he would have been cold to him. He would have pretended the great Professor Fane did not exist.

He parked crookedly in the Center's lot, running the front tires over the concrete bumpers. The car lurched and something in the body cracked. Gordon gripped the wheel tight and looked about in confusion. Shaking his head, he put the car into reverse. Before he could hit the gas, however, Luke unfastened his seat belt and opened the door.

"What the—"

Luke ran off without shutting the door, leaving Gordon to stare dumbly at his son's fleeing figure.

"What the fuck's wrong with him?"

Gordon finished parking and got out, closing both doors. He was not quick to follow his son inside, instead loitering around the car like a man finishing a cigarette. Last night's anxieties were distant, a curious feeling he chalked up to knowing Luke's location and company. Let the boy read poetry to his Grandpa. No harm could come from it.

To anyone.

He went inside. The Center had a comfortable lobby anchored by a single receptionist station. The woman working it, Tanya, all of twenty-three, had made a pass at Gordon five months ago. She was quite chubby and reminded him of a girl he'd slept with by mistake. It was a long time ago. Still, Tanya's play for his attention reminded him he could still be seen as desirable.

That, too, had seemed a long time ago.

"Hey, Gordon," she said, no trace of awkwardness in her tone. "I buzzed Luke through. He's really growing fast."

"Yes, he is." With an unintended sigh, Gordon signed both their names into the visitor's registry.

"Are you doing okay?"

"I am. Thanks for asking, Tanya—especially today."

God, am I about to break down in front of her?

Her look of concern was evident, but she chose not to engage further and pressed the button to let Gordon proceed. He stepped into the facility's main hallway, and here the Center lost the lobby's mask of comfort.

He was in a hospital and a research facility.

His father's room was on the fourth floor—the top floor—and Gordon headed for the elevators. Dr. Reynolds intercepted him before he reached them.

"Gordon," he said, sounding very excited.

"Hey, Gary. I was on my way up to see Dad. Luke's already there."

"I know. That's why I hurried down to meet you. We have to talk."

"Could it wait? I want to make sure Luke's getting along okay."

Dr. Reynolds looked disappointed, but nodded. "Let's go up together."

In the elevator, Gordon said, "I'm sorry I haven't been around as much. I hope you understand."

"It's been fine. In a way, it's been the best thing that could have happened."

"What do you mean?"

"We used to think the best memory triggers were friends and family. With some people, they are. But the human brain is a perplexing thing. *Consciousness* is even more complex. Most medical treatments are subjective to an extent, requiring small tweaks for each patient. But your father's case is one of extraordinary subjectivity. Your presence might actually have proven to be a hindrance."

"Not very comforting."

"I suppose not. But he's not a very comforting man. You of all people might realize that."

"He wasn't that bad a father," Gordon said.

"I didn't mean to imply otherwise. I meant only in his formidability. There's a strong will there, and a curious one too. If I thought it were even possible for him to do so, I'd say some part of him actually embraces mindlessness and resists our efforts."

Gordon stared at him. "My father was damn proud of his mind."

"Of his intellectual abilities. But the mind is more than that. There's a lot more in there. Lots of bad memories. Dark things."

"Yeah," Gordon said. "I know."

They exited the elevator and walked down a shorter hall, past several closed doors. The last one opened to his father's room. Both men stopped and listened. There seemed to be a play being staged inside. Gordon heard Luke almost shouting the lines from "Darkness." His father was speaking them too, his gruff, familiar voice stronger than it'd been in years. At first, he spoke the words behind Luke, following his lead, so that each line had an echo. His father's reading sped up, and at "*All earth was but one thought—and that was death,*" their voices merged and synched, and Gordon stumbled back as if punched in the gut. Someone—someone else—was talking too. A third voice joined his father and son's chanting. He heard it plainly from the other side of the door and looked at Dr. Reynolds for confirmation. But Dr. Reynolds had turned his attention to Gordon and seemed both surprised and alarmed, holding Gordon by the shoulders and looking into his eyes. Gordon ignored him, concentrating his attention on the three voices in the room. Who was it? Who could it be? Was a nurse in there with them?

All three voices ceased. The poem was done.

"Who was that?"

"What?"

"The third voice," Gordon said. "Who was in there with them saying the poetry?"

Dr. Reynolds raised his eyebrows. "The only other voice was yours. You started reciting along with them."

"Me?"

"Why—why don't you come and sit down. I'll get you some water."

"But Luke and Dad—"

"Let me check in on them. I'm sure they're fine. You know where my office is, right?"

Gordon nodded.

"Go have a seat. *Please.*"

"Take Luke out if he's bothering Dad. Or if you think there's something wrong."

"I will. I'll see you in a few minutes, Gordon."

A few minutes became ten, then fifteen, and then half an hour. When the door opened at last, it was a nurse and not Dr. Reynolds who entered. The nurse brought him a large glass of water with ice. Gordon took a cube into his mouth and crushed it between his jaws.

"Where's Dr. Reynolds?"

"Oh, Dr. Reynolds is fine," the nurse said.

"Not exactly what I asked. Where *is* he?"

Was the nurse nervous?

"He was talking to your father and your son. They were showing him some poetry they liked, but then he got called away to another patient. He'll be back very soon and told me you needed water. Are you feeling okay?"

"Yeah. I'm going to go see Dad now."

"Dr. Reynolds really wanted to meet you in his office. Please just wait here."

"No, I'm—"

The nurse left without closing the door behind her. If she had, Gordon would have opened it and left. But the door being left open eased him a bit. He chewed another two pieces of ice. Condensation beaded the outside of the cup. He wondered which was dewier, the glass or his forehead?

He got out his phone. Nearing noon—no wonder he felt hungry. Frowning, he decided to check his email. If Dr. Reynolds wasn't back by the time he finished, Gordon would go to Dad's room and tell Luke they had to leave.

He had no Internet connection. No signal at all.

Great.

Dr. Reynolds came in, all smiles. "Really sorry about the delay, Gordon. You still feel okay?"

"Yeah. I just realized the time. I haven't had anything to eat today, and I was up late last night."

"Do you often have problems sleeping?"

Gordon laughed. "I'm not your patient—thank God."

Dr. Reynolds' cheeks flushed, but he smiled. "My wife says I can't even have a casual conversation with anyone. I always speak like a doctor. I didn't mean to sound clinical."

"It's fine. I'd like to see Dad now. Just a quick check-in, then I really need to get going."

"Sure, sure. But before you do, it's really important that you see this."

He handed Gordon a tablet computer. Gordon saw his father's case file there. Blinking, he scrolled through several screens. Too much medical jargon met his eyes.

"Can you give me the short version? What's so important?"

"Of course—sorry, I should have taken you straight to the interesting stuff. It's funny you should say *the short version*. If your dad's file were printed, it'd be about three hundred pages long. It's been said there's a novel in everyone. In a way, I guess that's what we're trying to recover here. Unfortunately for us, the novels in our patients are closer to *Ulysses* than anything else—disjointed, obscure, hard to follow. Your dad's story, while not complete, is decidedly unique."

"I have trouble imagining that."

"I think most kids do when it comes to their parents."

"My dad was an English professor his entire life. Pretty much at the same school."

"Even adult characters had childhoods, Gordon. So, of course, did your dad. His memories are strongly centered around his adolescence."

"Okay." Gordon looked back at the screen.

Dr. Reynolds leaned forward. "It's not complete. There are memories your father seems determined not to give up. But I think we'll get them in time."

Gordon glanced up, suddenly unsettled. Nothing about Dr. Reynolds' tone of voice was threatening, yet Gordon suddenly thought of him as an interrogator. And it was Gordon, and not his father, under the harsh light.

He pushed the tablet aside and got up. "I'm going to see Dad, get Luke, and go."

"Wait—"

"I'm *done* waiting."

He left the office and returned to his father's room. Dr. Reynolds did not pursue him. Inside, Gordon found his father propped in bed with his grandson's poetry anthology open in his lap.

"Where's Luke?"

"Gordon," his father said. "Come in."

Gordon stepped nearer and repeated his question.

"Gone. Getting something from the vending machine."

Gordon grunted and wearily pulled up a chair. His father's body seemed less frail, like an echo of his improved mind.

"What are you reading?"

"A poem."

Gordon leaned forward to see it. "'Darkness.' I heard you and Luke reading it together."

"You must be mistaken."

"Dr. Reynolds and I both heard you through the door."

"So the door isn't sound-proof?"

Gordon thought this a strange question. "I guess it isn't when people are shouting. You seemed to be. You and Luke."

He watched his father's gaze fall back to the book.

Gordon sighed. His father didn't even remember reading the poem with Luke, and that was forty-five minutes ago. Guess I shouldn't expect miracles after all, he thought.

"I'm sorry I can't stay, Dad. Luke and I have to go home, but I promise to come back a lot sooner next time."

"You won't be coming back."

"*What?* Why would you say that? Of course I will."

"Sit down, Gordon. Let me talk—listen to me. My mind is very clear, and I understand why."

"The drugs have been working wonders—"

"No," he said as a strange, almost serene smile touched his lips. Gordon had never seen his father with such an expression. "That's not it at all. Medicine does not explain the cure because the illness was not medical in nature. That is to say it was not biological."

Gordon raised his eyebrows and waited for an explanation.

"I've been like a phone receiving two signals," his father said.

"Dad, you're *really* not well. I'm sorry."

"When a phone receives two signals, a certain amount of static is produced. Strange voices overlap one another. This is what I think has been happening to me, and for quite some time. The symptoms may resemble dementia, perhaps, but I am certain that is only an effect of the crossed signals—increasing, maddening static."

"Okay," Gordon said, since there was nothing to do but humor his father. "So what explains your sudden clarity?"

His father glanced down at the book again. His fingers touched the open pages. "The second caller finally hung up."

Gordon swallowed and looked at the floor, and felt sorrier for his dad than he ever had before. Had Dr. Reynolds came through the door just now, he would have grabbed him by his coat and shook him for daring to act like his father was somehow better. So what if he could speak in coherent sentences if what he said was schizophrenic nonsense?

"Gordon," his father continued, "I have committed a terrible crime."

Gordon sighed again, more exasperated. "No, Dad, you didn't. Whatever it is, it's just in your head."

"I broke a school rule. A grievous one. It's what I was trying to tell you on *that* day. You remember it, don't you?"

They stared at each other.

"I do."

"I was coming to tell you that I broke Westervelt's most important code. 75-130-b.1."

Gordon shook his head, though he had the barest sense of hearing this string of numbers and letters before.

"It is the rule forbidding teacher-student relationships. Specifically ones of a sexual nature."

Gordon fought hard to keep his expression from becoming an inappropriate, immature grin. The idea of his father having sex with *any* of his students was more bizarre than any talk of *crossed connections* and *certain amounts of static*. A sudden comic surrealism shot through him.

"Well," he said, talking slow, "it's okay, Dad. It was a long time ago. No reason to beat up on yourself. You're a guy, and Mom was dead. A lot of cute girls went to Westervelt. You must have been—"

His father closed the book with a sound like a mini-explosion.

"You were the student, Gordon."

Gordon stared at him for several seconds, not sure if he'd heard correctly. Then he knew he had.

Then he knew everything.

The feasting has begun.
Unable to move, almost numb to the many leeches now attached to his body, Byron stares at the ceiling and the little crack in the plaster that let in the rainwater a few weeks ago. How had so much water come in from such a dark little fissure?

"Loukas," he says, shocked by the feebleness of his voice. Fletcher comes to him instead, and the look on his face informs Byron the boy will not be making an appearance.

The room appears and disappears. Sometimes it becomes another room, a strange room with people he has never seen before. When it is his own room again, however, he also finds it peopled with unknown faces. Greek militia men, Greek aristocrats, the grubby and the clean. Doctors of different sorts. Despite their variations, these medical men are alike in their suggestion.

Apply more leeches.

He wonders if there might be one doctor in existence with a different solution to Byron's sudden illness, and concludes there was: Pollydolly. Dear, dead Polidori, whose favorite prescription was a slap to the face. How Byron wishes for his company now. Realizing he wishes so, he sinks deeper into the certainty he is losing his mind before his pulse.

I shall not write again, he thinks.

The thought stirs some vitality in him, some will to resist. If only the leeches could take certain of his memories for food and and leave the rest of him intact. But they are greedy. He feels them drawing the words and ideas from his body, siphoning away the reservoir of creativity at his fingertips. *This* is true death, and Byron brings his right arm to the left side of his face, feels for the leech and tries to tear it off.

"No, milord," Fletcher says, rushing from whatever corner he keeps his vigil.

"It is too much blood. Too much."

"I shall go ask Dr. Millingen, milord."

Dr. Millingen must be miles hence, for Fletcher does not return. The room's existence becomes as precarious as a candle flame in the wind. The candle goes out, the room is dark. A different candle is lit, and the second room is revealed. Who are these people around him? What is the weight in his lap? His eyes glance down to find an open book. He lifts it to see the pages and finds—and finds—

Byron sobs. The second candle is snuffed. The first candle lights again. Dr. Millingen stands over him, shaking his head, his aspect grave.

"Loukas?"

"Lord Byron speaks a name. Who is Loukas?"

Fletcher is there to whisper in Dr. Millingen's right ear. Dr. Millingen's eyes go very wide as he listens.

He cannot lift his arms. The skin of his face and torso feels unburdened. The leeches have been removed. He looks out at the window and sees darkness. It must be night.

The ghost hour is upon him.

The first ghost comes: his mother. They have nothing to say to each other, and she departs through a wall.

The second ghost is Claire. She has only laughter, which Byron hasn't the strength to return. But Claire understands. He knows she does.

Shelley comes then, tall, severe, dripping seawater.

Shiloh, he thinks. Stay with me. Stay.

Polidori comes. People he has hated and loved, desired and disdained all come.

Why this silence? Are there no words in the afterlife?

The ghosts disappear with the morning. The sunlight beams bright within the room, warming everything but Byron's body. Chills add to his misery.

Dr. Millingen is back with the leeches.

"Lord Byron's fever continues. His blood has an excess of bad humor to it—we must drain it off."

With fading eyesight, Byron looks to Fletcher, ever faithful, in attendance with water and sponge and stoicism. A weak motion of Byron's hand draws the servant closer.

"Whatever it is," Byron whispers, "the leeches will not take it from my body."

Now Fletcher weeps. He is inconsolable.

Something is said in Italian or Greek. Fletcher is taken from the room.

Everyone leaves me, thinks Byron. But I have left everyone first. Ada, Shiloh, Allegra. Ada. He has no feelings for the child at all. *Ada.* A name, just a name, absent of true meaning. How can he feel for her? It has been years. If she walked into this very room right now, he would not recognize her, his daughter.

Millingen applies the leeches and squints as he inspects their work.

"I'm dying," Byron says after several painful swallows.

Millingen, not unkindly, nods his head. *Truth at last.* Byron smiles.

"Did you know I was a prophet?"

"Now is not the time to talk. Marshal your strength, milord."

"All men can be," Byron says. He does not know how successful he is. All he can hear is his own wheezing.

"Rest, milord."

Byron struggles for one more burst of strength. He twists his clubfoot to the right as far as it can go under its own power. That faithful villain still has bile. Pain shoots through him, enlivening the senses.

"Men need only shout out, *One day I shall die!* and they will be prophets."

His respiration hitches and his heart pounds. Blood courses down his face and limbs and collects like thick syrup in bowls.

The first candle goes out.

The second candle does not light.

He is floating through the void, falling toward a world engulfed in flames. But the fires are waning. Darkness is winning. Across this vast world, Byron applies his gaze and finds but two men, and they are enemies. They fight each other to see who will be fuel for the other's pyre. The fight does not last long.

Byron watches the first man throw the corpse of the second onto a dwindling flame. The survivor sits down with a book he finds on the ground, most of its pages already charred and unburnable, but with a few leafs spared. They too must feed the fire. But before that fate, the victor, naked and starving, decides to read aloud from the unspoiled pages by the light of his enemy's burning body. His is a wonderful voice, deep and sonorous, cadenced for the world's end. Byron finds the words familiar as he drifts away in the darkness—

> *So we'll go no more a roving*
> *So late into the night,*
> *Though the heart be still as loving,*
> *And the moon be still as—*

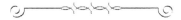

"Jesus Christ."

Gordon took one step toward his father's bed, then two back, see-sawing in panic. A surge of the creepy-crawly feelings in his thighs made him cry out and slap at his legs. He lost his balance and fell to the floor and sat there, leaning to the right, supported by both palms, his legs splayed to the side, useless and insensate as a cripple's.

His father managed to swing his own legs off the mattress. Gordon stared at them. Both were shriveled now, the healthy leg having deteriorated to match the other's deformity.

"There was a boy. He meant everything to me. He was my world in every sense of it. Then he was lost to me. Then I thought he was found again—in you."

"Sick bastard," Gordon said through an eruption of sobs. He barely registered his father's words, and wasn't sure what they meant. What he did understand was the renewed, almost explosive feeling of invisible fingers on his inner thighs. And as he slapped at his own body, he knew these awful sensations were linked to what his father was saying.

"Luke told me what you are doing to him."

He gaped up at his dad, his entire body trembling.

"No. No."

"It's my fault, Gordon. Whatever compulsion you have, it comes from what I did to you. That's why I told Dr. Reynolds. I understand he has called the police."

Gordon got to his feet, though his legs wobbled. "Where's Luke? Where is he?"

"I don't know. Safe from you. Safe from me."

There were many sounds in the hallway now. It sounded like many people rushing toward them.

The door rattled under a sharp knock.

"Gordon Fane. Are you in there?"

Gordon looked at his father, who met his stare with piteous eyes. Despite everything, despite his disgust and horror, despite his fear, Gordon softened for just a moment.

"It's okay, Gordon," his father said, whispering as he reached for his son's hands. Gordon watched as his father brought them to his own thin throat. But his father could not make Gordon's fingers open and close around his windpipe. Gordon did that himself.

They stared at each other.

"You might as well add patricide to the charges, George."

The door burst open. Guns entered the room in the outstretched hands of three police officers. Dr. Reynolds was there. So, he saw, was Amber. In the next few mad, slow seconds he wondered if she'd somehow managed to drive herself, or if the police had picked her up along the way. Would the police have done that? She looked perversely vital, her eyes filled with rage. "You fucking bastard," she said.

Then her expression changed. The guns lowered. All eyes turned to the room's only window.

Father and son's eyes were the last to turn.

The panes were dark. Screams filtered through it—distant, plentiful.

"Is it an eclipse?" Dr. Reynolds said, coming forward. Gordon watched him and the rest—even Amber—crowd around the window and press their faces to the glass. "But it's day!" someone said. "Where is the sun?" Gordon saw one of the officers who'd come to arrest him slap at the pane as if he blamed it for hiding the light.

Then he heard a sharp gasp and he alone turned his attention from the window. His father's back was arched, as if jolted by electricity. His right hand beckoned Gordon closer, and despite himself Gordon stepped over. His father's mouth was open wide, as were his eyes, which seemed fixed on something very distant. As Gordon bent nearer, he felt his father gripping his wrist. The old man was struggling to make a sound. He spoke a single word into Gordon's ear, and then his grip went slack and so did his face, and Gordon pulled back knowing his father was dead. He repeated the word to himself. Why did his father say *that*? What could it mean? Then he stifled a laugh, hand over his mouth. He felt like the victim of a joke, and as his gaze returned to the dark window and the people huddled in front of it, he realized his father had given them all the punchline.

"*Bright.*"

ACKNOWLEDGMENTS

I have many people to thank for bringing *Lord Byron's Prophecy* to the public. First and foremost, my publisher Steve Berman—without you I'm not sure where I'd be, and I'm humbled by your faith in me. Thank you, thank you, thank you. Second, my editor, Hal Duncan, whose incisive comments and dedication to this novel will forever humble and amaze me. (And folks, if you haven't read Hal Duncan's own stories, what are you waiting for?) Many thanks are also owed to Alex Jeffers, for designing the book's interior, and to Matthew Bright for his outstanding cover art. And what would I do without that special group of friends who make up my writer's group? Ed Bryant, Carter Wilson, Linda Anderson and Dirk Anderson critiqued the original manuscript over the course of 18 months, providing valuable advice in shaping the story (and while I'm at it, let me just add that if you haven't read the works of Ed Bryant and Carter Wilson, you should pick them up after you get done reading Hal). Additionally, I'd like to thank my parents and my brother Brian and sister-in-law Lena for their love and support.

ABOUT THE AUTHOR

Originally from Kentucky, SEAN EADS is a reference librarian living in Denver, CO. His first novel, *The Survivors*, was a finalist for the 2013 Lambda Literary Award. He has a Masters degree in literature from the University of Kentucky, where he read an awful lot of Byron. His favorite writers include Bradbury, Hemingway and Cormac McCarthy. You can find him online at seaneads.net.

CPSIA information can be obtained
at www.ICGtesting.com
Printed in the USA
FSOW01n1654230915
11452FS